P9-DNU-718

# Love to Love You Baby

ALSO AVAILABLE IN BEELER LARGE PRINT BY

KASEY MICHAELS

---

*CAN'T TAKE MY EYES OFF OF YOU*

# LOVE TO LOVE YOU BABY

KASEY MICHAELS

BEELER LARGE PRINT
Hampton Falls, New Hampshire, 2002

**Library of Congress Cataloging-in-Publication Data**

Michaels, Kasey
　　Love to love you baby / Kasey Michaels
　　　　p.　　cm.
　　ISBN 1-57490-391-8　(alk. paper)

Library of Congress Cataloging-in-Publication Data was not
available at the time of publication.

Libraries should call (800) 818-7574 and we will fax or mail the
CIP Data upon request.

Published in Large Print by arrangement with
Kensington Publishing Corp.

BEELER LARGE PRINT
is published by
Thomas T. Beeler, *Publisher*
Post Office Box 659
Hampton Falls, New Hampshire 03844

Typeset in 16 point Times New Roman type.
Sewn and bound on acid-free paper by
Sheridan Books in Chelsea, Michigan

*For Elizabeth "Queenie" Brosious*

*You've got to be very careful if you don't know where you are going because you might not get there.*

—*Yogi Berra*

# Chapter One

*There is one word in America that says it all and that one word is, "You never know."*

—Joaquin Andujar, pitcher

"*Brrrrnnng-brrrrrnnng.*"

"Damn it."

"*Brrrrrnnng-brrrrrnnng.*"

Jack Trehan swore again, reached out blindly in the dark, snagged the phone on his second try. The first had knocked over the already tipsy lamp his Aunt Sadie had lent him out of the goodness of her heart. And Aunt Sadie *had* no heart.

His eyes still closed, Jack aimed the handset in the vicinity of his ear and mouth and grumbled, "Nobody's home. At the sound of the tone, why don't you go take a flying—"

"Jack? Jack, sweetie, is that you?"

Jack's eyes opened all at once, sort of the way they would if someone had just crept into his darkened bedroom and dumped a bucket of icy Gatorade over his head. He transferred the phone to his "listening" ear, pushed up the pillows behind him, found the pull cord on the hula-dancer lamp with the neon pink fringed shade. Aunt Sadie also had no taste. "Cecily?"

"Oh, you remembered my voice, Jack. That's *so* insightful of you. But, then, I always said you were a very old soul, with just *gobs* of intellect and earned wisdom. Oh, wait. I think that was Daddy. You're the one I used to think was the reincarnation of Wyatt Earp. Strong, honest, but maybe just a *tad* sure of himself. Cocky, even. At least, that's how both those actors

1

played him in the movies. Kevin Costner was one of them—you know, that actor who made a movie about a mailman with webbed toes? Oh wait, that was something else, wasn't it? Maybe two something else's?"

"Two something else's, Cecily. Definitely," Jack said, grinning in spite of himself.

"Darn! Oh, well, back to Wyatt. I don't remember the other actor, even though I liked him better. I've never figured out why they made two movies, Jack, did you? I mean, okay, so maybe he *was* Wyatt Big-whoop Earp. But *two*? I really think one would have covered it, don't you?"

"Absolutely. Cecily?" Jack said—almost pleaded—his cousin's childish, high-pitched voice making his ear itch as he blinked at the dial of his alarm clock. He hadn't seen or heard from Cecily in over a year, but some people . . . well, they make an indelible impression. "Could we cut to the chase here? It's two in the morning. And it was Kurt Russell. I liked him better, too."

"Ah, thank you, Jack. I would have *racked* my brain half the night if you hadn't told me. But why are you concerned about the time? Time isn't relevant, Jack, you know that. It's artificial, just something someone made up. Some neat freak who wanted to control everyone else. Probably anal retentive, too, don't you think? And it's two-fifteen here in Bayonne. Your clock must be wrong. That isn't like you, Jack. Not that *you're* anal retentive, of course. I'd *never* say that about you. I wish they'd find another description. That one's so *icky*. Must we constantly use sex and body parts to describe things? Like male and female plugs—in electricity, you understand. I find that particularly disgusting. And

2

calling cars she, and then smugly gassing her up by sticking a *thing* into her *thing*, and—"

"God almighty, Cecily, you're killing me here," Jack interrupted, holding a hand to his pounding head. "You're back home in Bayonne, right? Same artificial time zone and everything. So can't this wait for the morning? I'll call you."

"Oh, sorry, Jack. You know how I get carried away. I'm *very* intense. Blue Rainbow tells me that all the time. I jump in with both feet, try to feel the whole experience, and sometimes lose my way. It's a great trial to me, but Blue Rainbow has promised, cross his heart, that he'll teach me how to channel my energy flow, harness it, find my karmic center. Isn't that *sweet* of him?"

"Yeah. Just darling." Jack was out of bed now, pacing on the bare hardwood floor. Blue Rainbow was a man. He'd gathered that much. With Cecily, there was always a man. But he'd be damned if he'd ask about the guy, because then Cecily would tell him, and then *he'd* have to jump with both feet—out of his second-story window and kill himself. "Cecily," he said when she ran down— or at least paused to take a breath. "Is there a reason you've called me in the middle of the night, or are we just being chatty?"

The small, chilly silence on the other end of the line told Jack that he'd insulted his cousin, which was next door to hurting her, and closer than he wanted to consider to making her cry. He hated when Cecily cried. She talked when she cried, and hiccuped, and it was pure hell to try to understand her.

"Cecily? I'm sorry, honey," he said—and he really was. The last time Cecily had launched into a crying, talking, hiccuping jag, he'd ended up owning five

3

hundred shares of stock in Creative Pyrotechnics, her boyfriend's company. That had gone bust—or boom— six months later, along with the boyfriend, and one small town's Fourth of July celebration. He'd heard later that Cecily had buried the boyfriend in a jar. A small jar.

"You're sorry? Well, that's easy enough for you to *say*, Jack," Cecily said, and he could hear the tears in her voice. "You can be really hor-*hic*-rid, Jack, do you know that? And . . . and I always thought you li-*hic*-ked me, that you were the *nice* one. That's why I called you. Because you always understand, and you always help. Just like . . . well, just like Wyatt-*hic*-Earp."

Sitting down on the edge of his bed—nearly falling down, as he'd forgotten that his bed was no more than a king-size mattress and box spring, stacked on the floor—Jack took a deep breath and tried to control himself. "Okay, Cecily, honey, okay. Let's just calm down now. Tell me what's wrong. Let me help. Honest, honey, all I want to do is help."

*Because then you'll go away and I can get some sleep.* But he didn't say that.

He waited as Cecily tried to compose herself. She hiccuped once more, blew her nose extremely close to the phone, then took in a deep breath, let it out slowly. Jack could imagine just how she looked as she did this. She looked cute. Cecily always looked cute. Big blue eyes, soft blond hair, a petite package of curves. So much on the outside. So little on the inside. Still, he loved her. You'd have to be the kind of person who kicks puppies not to love Cecily Morretti.

"Okay," she said at last, "here goes. It's *so* embarrassing. You remember how last year I was living in that commune in Oregon? Reading all those self-help

4

books? Trying to educate myself? Pull myself up by my own—is that *bootstraps*? Does anyone really wear those anymore? Oh, we wear boots, sure, but bootstraps? I don't think we—"

"Cecily. Concentrate, baby. You can do this."

"Well, no, Jack," she answered, starting to cry once more. "That's . . . that's just it. I *couldn't* do it. I thought I had it right, but then I realized I had it wrong. The books said get in touch with your inner child. But I thought that meant the child inside. I was *so* wrong, and then I was sort of *stuck*, you know. I mean, what do you do with the child inside, once she gets *out*? You do see the diff-*hic*-erence, don't you, and how difficult that could-*hic*-be."

"Sure," Jack agreed quickly. Hell, he'd agree to anything his cousin said, if she'd just not start that hiccupping again. "Inner child, child inside. Inner child, child outside. There's a difference. Got it. There. Does that help? Because I just want to help, Cecily. Anything I can do to help."

She was crying again. Tears of joy, probably. But even tears of joy came with hiccups. "Oh, thank you, Jack! I knew you could understand, and I *knew* you'd help me. You've always been so *kind*. Blue Rainbow insists that I leave with him tomorrow, and Joey's no help—*why* I came back to Bay-*hic*-onne to ask for *his* help I'll never be able to tell you. My brother is a waste, Jack—a *total* waste!"

"Still trying to break into the local wise guys, is he?" Jack asked, but Cecily was on a roll and didn't answer. She just kept talking.

Now Cecily's words were tumbling over themselves as her mind (always a dangerous thing) seemed to go into third gear. "And how does one find one's karmic

5

center in Bayonne? I mean, really, Jack—*New Jersey?* So I was at my wit's end. But you're going to help. There's time, if Blue Rainbow can just find the keys to our rental. Oh, wait. Here they are, in my pock-*hic*-et. Isn't that always the last place you look? But this is wonderful! We can get there, get back to Jersey in time, and be on our way on the morning flight from Newark. You still get up real early, don't you? You probably do. Oh . . . I can't thank you *enough*, Jack. I just ca-*hic*-n't."

"Then don't try," Jack said, feeling pretty smug. He didn't know what he'd said, but obviously he'd given her the right answers. Not that he was going to push his luck and do something dumb, like ask where in blazes she and Blue Rainbow were going. *Get there, get back?* Go where, get back to where? Bayonne? No, not Bayonne. Newark. The airport was in Newark. The woman made no sense. Still, if he asked, she'd probably tell him they were taking a hot air balloon to Jupiter, and he didn't want to know that. He really didn't. "Why don't you call me when you get back?"

"It could be months. *Years*," Cecily told him, but the smile was back in her voice—which meant she was once more sounding like Betty Boop on helium. "And you're all right with that? Are you *really* sure you want to do this?"

Do what? What had he just agreed to do? Had he actually agreed to do *anything?* He hadn't the faintest idea what she was talking about. Still, ignorance was bliss, and with Cecily, very often ignorance was downright necessary to one's sanity. "Honey, if it makes you happy, I'm just fine with . . . whatever," Jack told her, already collapsing toward the pile of pillows, more than ready to go back to sleep.

He aimed the phone at the cardboard box he'd been

6

using as a nightstand, saying through a yawn, "Just glad I could help."

Keely McBride rolled over, punched her pillow, flopped her head down once more, moaning in mingled mental agony and frustration. She couldn't sleep. She might never sleep again. Ever.

How did insomniacs do it? Why hadn't they all just said the heck with this baloney, killed themselves, and gotten it over with? What did people *do* all night long, when they couldn't sleep? Count sheep? Ridiculous. Besides, it didn't work. Keely knew, because she'd tried it.

The portable television set in her bedroom hadn't helped either, even though she'd kept it on until two in the morning, watching infomercials, then a "Gilligan's Island" rerun that had never been one of her favorites. Nothing. Not even one heavy, drooping eyelid.

In fact, if she got any *more* wide awake, she could stop wasting time and go re-shingle the roof or something.

She was just too nervous to sleep, too scared. She had one shot, just one, and it was coming with one Sadie Trehan and the next sunrise. How was she supposed to sleep? Giving up on what had been a bad idea from the moment she'd crawled into bed some six hours earlier, Keely tossed back the covers and headed toward the bathroom to take a shower.

It wasn't as if the running water would wake anyone else in the house, because there wasn't anyone else in the house. She was alone. All alone. Aunt Mary didn't have any living houseplants, let alone a tabby cat or nervous lapdog to keep her niece company while the older woman was off honeymooning in Greece. You'd think one's only aunt would have more consideration, damn it, because Keely could do with a purring cat or a yapping dog. She'd settle for a hamster and its squeaky wheel—anything to break the silence, anything she could talk to, complain to. Bitch to.

Keely had a lot of bitching to do.

For starters, she was in Allentown—*back* in Allentown—because her fledgling interior design business in Manhattan had gone belly-up only fifteen months after she'd first opened the doors.

How Keely hated to fail, especially when her one and only lover had so smugly declared "You'll never make it without me" when she'd left his bed, his employ, and set out to buck the odds that 70 percent of all new businesses fail in the first two years.

God, how she hated statistics, being a statistic. Almost as much as she'd hated Gregory Fontaine— which she didn't anymore, because to hate somebody you'd actually have had to have *liked* him at some point—and she'd figured out that there had been nothing likable about Gregory Fontaine.

He was handsome, sure. And successful. And he'd hired her straight out of college, the ink on her diploma still wet (and her only work reference from Aunt Mary, who anybody with even a pea for a brain would know had to have given a glowing recommendation, even if Keely had been the worst interior designer since the first jerk had hung a moose head on his den wall).

Ah, yes, Gregory Fontaine. He'd been suave and debonair and dined in all the right restaurants and knew the right people and could quote lines from every Neil Simon play. He also bit his toenails. Keely liked to remember that Gregory Fontaine bit his toenails. It was *so* vindicating.

Keely stood under the stinging spray, her head bowed so that her honey blond hair turned darkly golden. She poured shampoo into her hand and worked up a thick, creamy lather in her hair, trying to wash away any bad thoughts.

It didn't work. It never did. She never felt more awake, aware, or alive just because she'd washed her hair. She certainly had never had an orgasm courtesy of some new nature-smelling shampoo.

There was so much of life she'd missed out on. Spraying room deodorizer had never turned her living room into a flower garden. Toothpaste had never put a blinking, diamondlike starburst in her smile. No genie had ever popped out of her all-purpose cleanser bottle and danced her around her sparkling-clean kitchen. And as for her sex life? Hell, nobody had "validated her tires" since she'd waved Gregory Fontaine ta-ta eighteen months ago.

Her life was one huge downward spiral, that's what it was. Business, gone. Manhattan apartment, gone. Future, gone. Love life? Hell, it hadn't been that good, but that, too, was gone. Way gone.

Here she was, back in Allentown, back to her roots, back to the beginning, to the same bedroom at Aunt Mary's she'd slept in while growing up, dreaming of getting "out." She had not passed Go, and she sure hadn't collected any money. If it weren't for Aunt Mary, she'd pretty much be on the streets, or selling furniture in some shopping mall department store for nine bucks an hour and every third Saturday off.

"So, okay," Keely told herself—and maybe the towel rack, or the toilet, or anything that might be listening—"maybe I have had one piece of good luck. Aunt Mary's in Greece, billing and cooing until late August, and I'm

9

running the shop. I'm even getting fifty percent of any commissions. This is not bad. This is not nirvana, granted, but this is not bad. So lighten up, McBride. Brush your not-quite-diamond-white teeth, figure out what you're going to wear, and get ready to dazzle your new big customer in . . ." she walked back into the bedroom, wrapped in a towel, ". . . precisely seven hours. Oh God, what do I do for the next seven hours?"

At six-thirty, Jack was already up, shaved and showered, dressed, and heading to the kitchen for his first cup of coffee. It was June, the sun was shining, the weather was already warm, and he should have been in even sunnier California, getting ready for tonight's game between the Athletics and the Yankees.

Instead, he was here, in Whitehall, a stone's throw from the larger city of Allentown, and he had nothing to do, nowhere to go . . . and precious little to sit down on, considering that his furniture consisted of the mattress and box spring, a couple of lamps, a flat screen television set, and one lumpy chair.

Jack had mastered the coffeemaker his Aunt Sadie had lent him—hey, anything Joe DiMaggio could do, Jack Trehan could do, damn it—and his morning coffee was hot and waiting for him. He stood, leaning against the kitchen counter, and looked around the room. Big. Modern. Empty.

The whole house was empty, and smelled new, which it sort of was. There was an echo, thanks to the hardwood floors and the cathedral ceilings. There was sunlight pouring through huge, floor-to-ceiling windows.

There was no privacy, little comfort, and Jack was still kicking himself for allowing his agent, Mortimer

"More and More" Moore talk him into buying the ridiculous mansion. A great tax write-off, Mort had told him at the time.

Yeah, well, maybe. And he could use the tax write-off, he supposed.

In truth, the house was already a year old, even if it was still empty. Jack had thought the place would remain empty until he retired from baseball. Instead, it had remained empty for only that one year, until he'd been forced out of the game.

Big damn difference, and now Jack looked at the house as if it were some sort of punishment he had to endure. Being home again, back in Pennsylvania, back in the Lehigh Valley. What a comedown.

He should have stayed in Manhattan, where he owned his own condo on the forty-seventh floor of one of the classiest addresses in the city. And he could have, too. Except that being in Manhattan reminded him that he wanted to be in the Bronx, at the ball field, working on his curve ball.

So he'd locked up the condo and run home, run to the house Mort had talked him into buying, even run to his Aunt Sadie, who lived above the four-car garage . . . five snug rooms she jokingly called "the dower house."

Aunt Sadie had furniture. She had pots and pans. She had more than two towels.

She also had a guest room, but Jack would rather sleep on a park bench than in Sadie Trehan's guest room, which was furnished in early kitsch. Hell, the Hawaiian hula-skirt girl lamp had been about the most *normal* thing in the entire room.

"Yeah, well," Jack said, pushing himself away from the counter, "today, Jack old boy, is the first day of the

11

rest of your life—whatever that means—so you'd better get on with it."

Getting on with it meant meeting with the interior decorator Sadie had hired, and hoping the guy wasn't a fan of Sadie's decor. Getting on with it meant trying to figure out how he was going to fill his days, his nights, his weeks and years, now that he'd lost his first and only love, baseball.

Getting on with it, since he was feeling pretty down and small steps were probably all he could take at the moment, meant going to the front door and praying Sadie had kept her word and ordered the morning paper for him.

The Yankees were on a West Coast road trip, and Jack knew last night's game stats probably hadn't made the newspaper, so he grabbed the remote off the bar separating the kitchen and den, aimed it at the television. Nothing like a little morning ESPN to make him feel like going out in the backyard and wailing like a lost soul.

Auto racing. No scores, no stats. ESPN was running a frigging rerun of a frigging auto race. Jack hit the remote once more, shutting off the set. "Life just keeps getting better and better," he grumbled, once more heading for the front door.

The phone on the bar rang, stopping him, reminding him that he'd heard the phone ring in the middle of the night, stupidly answered it, and found Cecily on the other end.

This time he'd be smarter. This time he'd check the Caller ID before he picked up.

"Mort," Jack muttered out loud, then raised his eyes toward the ceiling, debating whether or not to answer. Last time Mort had called, it had been to try to talk him into doing a mouthwash ad for Japanese television. According to Mort, Jack had to strike now, while he was still relatively "hot," before he became "yesterday's news."

Mort was a real brick. Supportive. A friend in need and a friend in deed.

Yeah. Right.

Jack pushed the button, lifted the cordless phone to his ear. "Morning, Mort," he said, once more heading for the door. "What is it today? Hemorrhoid cream for the Netherlands? Erectile dysfunction medications for—oh, hell, I wouldn't do one of those for *anybody*."

Mort's booming voice had Jack easing the phone away from his ear. "Good one, Jack. Good one! Hey, ever wonder why Bob Dole couldn't have helped his fellow sufferers with a public service message instead of taking big bucks from a drug company? I have. Smart man, Dole. A man after my own heart. You can make bucks from anything if you just angle it right. Free for nothing is good for nothing, I say. Anyway, glad to hear you've got some of that old fight back."

"A compliment, Mort?" Jack said warily. Mort Moore had all the sensitivity of a killer shark. "What do you want?"

"Want? Me? Want something? Jack, Jack, Jack. You know all I ever want is what's best for you. I just wanted you to know I nixed that mouthwash ad. You were right on with that one. Not your thing, definitely."

"Uh-huh," Jack said, his right hand on the front door knob. "What *is* my thing, definitely?"

"Corvettes," Mort said, and Jack could almost see the wicked grin on his agent's face. "A two-day shoot in Arizona—lots of open space there, or something like that. You, the car, a beautiful girl in the seat beside you. Some drivel about the pitching ace and his new driving ace—lame, but they're working on the copy. And you get to keep the car, Jack. So? What do you think?"

Jack removed his hand from the doorknob, rubbed at his chin. "A Corvette? Beats the hell out of mouthwash, Mort. Okay, but let me think about it. I'm still not so sure about going the endorsement route. My name on a glove is fine, but I wonder if it's really *honest* to start putting my face and name out there, outside of sports."

"Strike while the iron is hot, Jack," Mort reminded him. "Not every ex-Yankee has a Mr. Coffee in his future. Now listen up—I'm heading South this morning. Gotta check out this kid from Florida State who's thinking of coming out early for the NFL draft. Big, big boy. Hits the line like a ton of bricks, scares the crap out of the offense, but won't take a step in any direction without his mama being there to watch out for him. So I'm going down to charm the mama, size up the kid. I wouldn't want to see anybody take advantage of him, you know?"

"You're a real prince, Mort," Jack told him, shaking his head. "Your percentage of the kid's contract means nothing to you, right?"

"And don't forget the signing bonus," the agent told him, chuckling. "Okay, that's it from here, Jack. I'll be in touch in a few days, sooner if I hear from the ad agency. Don't get in any trouble while I'm gone."

"Trouble? When did I ever get in—oh, forget it," Jack muttered, hearing the dial tone in his ear. "Trouble," he repeated, reaching for the doorknob yet again. "Mort's thinking about the wrong Trehan. I'm not Tim. I'm Jack, the good twin." He turned the knob, pulled open the front door, bent down to pick up the newspaper. "I never get in trouble. I just get injured and retired at twenty-eight, along with an empty house and an agent who's letting me know I'm soon going to be yesterday's—*holy shit!*"

Jack looked down at the huge wicker wash basket sitting at the base of the three steps leading to his front door. Looked at the pink plastic bits and pieces of luggage stuffed into it. Looked at the plastic seat or whatever it was wedged in the center of the basket. Looked at the *thing* inside the plastic seat.

Nah. Couldn't be. He was hallucinating.

Jack closed his eyes, opened them again. Looked again. The thing in the seat looked back at him. Grinned at him, showing pink gums and one small tooth. Kicked at the blanket over its feet.

Oh God. Oh God, oh God, *oh God.*

His first instinct was to run back into the house and slam the door. Lock it. But that wouldn't work.

He gave a moment's thought to the neighbors, but since his house was located on three acres and his nearest neighbor was at least two blocks away, there wasn't much fear that anybody would see him standing outside, looking down at a baby in a basket.

A baby in a basket?

Whose baby?

*His* baby?

Jack repeatedly slapped his arms against his sides and looked around, trying to appear nonchalant.

*His* baby? Could that be possible? He'd never been a playboy, never really slept around with all the women who just about threw themselves at major league baseball players.

But he hadn't been exactly celibate, either.

*His* baby?

Possible. Anything was possible, right? Oh God.

He tossed the newspaper and phone behind him, into

15

the foyer, flapped his arms some more, swallowed hard, did a small, nervous dance on the top step.

Oh God, oh God, oh God.

"Knock it off, knock it off," he told himself. "Get a grip here, Trehan. This could be anybody's baby. Doesn't have to be *your* baby. But, just to be safe, go down the steps, pick it up, get it inside before anybody sees you."

That all sounded good, except that Jack's feet hadn't been listening, so that he was still standing on the top step, and the baby was still sitting right there, out in the open, *grinning* up at him.

"Sadie," Jack breathed at last. That was it; he'd call Sadie. His aunt would know what to do.

"No, no, not Sadie," he corrected himself quickly, picturing his aunt and what she'd say. "Not until you know what the hell's going on."

That much decided, Jack finally went down the steps, bent over the basket. The baby reached up both arms, tried to grab at his nose as he lifted the heavy basket, carried it inside the house.

Kicking the door closed with one foot, he stood in the empty foyer, looking toward the empty living room. Where to put the basket? Like it mattered where he put it. What mattered was that it was *there*.

Jack carried the basket through the house, into the kitchen, finally depositing it on the tile floor, his head bent low over the basket because the baby had somehow gotten one hand into his mouth and was digging tiny fingernails into his gums behind his front teeth. He had to pry the little fingers away, one by one. The kid could probably bend iron, with a grip like that.

Running his tongue around his mouth, wondering if he now needed a tetanus shot—or if the kid did—Jack finally noticed a business-size white envelope tucked into the basket.

Ah, the obligatory note left with the baby in the basket. The note that would explain everything—just like in the movies. "Man, I hate when that happens," Jack grumbled, only slightly hysterical as he gingerly picked up the envelope.

Written on the envelope were the first three nails in his coffin: *To Darling Jack*. He recognized the handwriting at once. Nobody but his cousin Cecily dotted her *i*'s with little hearts, crossed her *t*'s with small bows.

The note inside was short and not very informative, as Cecily wrote just as she spoke, in circles and as the spirit hit her:

*Darling Jack,*

*Thank you so much for agreeing to take little Magenta Moon for me. You always were such a darling, as opposed to Joey, who's such a jerk. She's about six months old, I think, but hasn't had her shots because I didn't get around to it—Blue Rainbow tells me you should know this. He also said this letter must tell you that I give you all rights to take care of her. So you have all rights, okay? There's also some official-looking papers stuffed in her diaper bag, in case you need them. Blue Rainbow once thought he wanted to be a lawyer, but that didn't work. Something about his rap sheet, whatever that is? Oh, she's probably going to be hungry soon. There's some bottles for her in one of the bags. Well, gotta run. Just think, Jack—Katmandu!*

*Love,*
*Cecily (Moon Flower) Morretti*

"Jesus H. Christ." Jack sat down on the floor, still holding the note, and looked at Magenta Moon. *The inner child, the child inside.* It all made sense now. Too late, it all made sense. Well, Cecily kind of sense, anyway.

"You never could get anything right, could you, Cecily?" he asked as Magenta Moon began to cry; then he lowered his head into his hands. Given his druthers, he'd rather be in Tokyo . . . gargling.

# Chapter Two

*When you come to a fork*
*in the road, take it.*

—Yogi Berra

NOT QUITE EIGHT THIRTY. DAMN.

Keely tried to take her time as she drove along the narrow macadam road leading uphill in an area of Whitehall formerly known as Egypt. Actually, it was still known as Egypt to the natives, just as other parts of the township were referred to as Stiles, Cementon, West Catasauqua, Mickleys, and Fullerton. That was a lot of names for one township, and the changeover, mostly done to suit the U.S. Post Office, had ended with six "Main Streets," all in different areas of Whitehall.

Keely was driving along Egypt's version of Main Street now, or she had been, until the signposts inexplicably changed to Main Boulevard, then to Old Main Road, and then to no signs at all. A person could get very lost trying to find Sadie Trehan's almost-a-mansion.

That was why Keely had made a dry run the day

before, and it was why she was early now, because she had actually remembered the route. She was partly proud of herself, partly wondering if it was worse to be thirty minutes early or thirty minutes late.

She had two choices: Stop at the doughnut shop at the next corner and show up with either powdered sugar or strawberry jelly on her blouse, or turn right at that same corner and head up the hill to Sadie Trehan's house, arriving before the appointed hour of nine A.M.

The doughnut lost and Keely turned right, carefully navigating in Aunt Mary's classy black Mercedes with the teardrop headlights. Since all that Keely had ever navigated was her now departed Mustang and, lately, the New York subway system, she had to keep fighting down the feeling that she was piloting a very large boat.

"But a boat that makes one hell of an impression on the customers," Keely reminded herself aloud as she took a left into the sweep of driveway that wended uphill, through about an acre of trees, then circled in front of Sadie Trehan's house. "Of course, not as much of an impression as one's own interior decorator *talking* to herself. So shut up, Keely, and watch the road."

The car definitely did look good, sitting in the driveway of the huge tan brick house after she'd wriggled the key out of the ignition. Keely got out, stood glancing at the house, trying to decide if it had been meant to be modern while trying to look old, or meant to look old while trying to appear modern.

The windows were huge, including one enormous oriel window in front of what had to be a two-story foyer, a crystal teardrop chandelier roughly the size of the Mercedes visible through the glass. There were at least five separate roof lines, jutting here, jutting there, indicating cathedral ceilings, probably a lot of skylights.

The front door was dark brown; the gutters were real copper.

According to Sadie Trehan, the house consisted of approximately twelve thousand square feet on two main living levels, and the fifteen rooms were all completely empty, ready to be decorated.

Megabucks here. Megabucks. And 50 percent of 10 percent of megabucks was . . . megabucks.

Not that the house didn't appeal to Keely artistically. Not that she wasn't itching to get inside, talk to Sadie Trehan, get some idea of what the owner might be looking for in the way of colors, of furniture, carpets, drapes. The interior decorator in Keely was excited, hoped to be creatively challenged.

Yeah. Sure. All that good stuff.

*Megabucks, megabucks, megabucks. Good-bye MasterCard bill,* hasta la vista *Visa, bury that old Discover Card balance. Megabucks, megabucks, megabucks.*

"Stop it," Keely scolded herself as she climbed the three shallow steps to a pleasantly wide front entry. "Concentrate on the job, for crying out loud. Topiary in pots. That would look good, flanking either side of the double doors. And maybe some geraniums, for color. And a *doormat.* God, the woman doesn't even have a doormat? What's fifty percent of ten percent of a doormat running these days?"

She pushed the doorbell, then stepped back a pace, straightened her shoulders, ran both hands down the front of her very stylish, if three-year-old navy suit. She looked good, she looked professional, and if she had to agree to hang miniature, glow-in-the-dark plastic pickles from the foyer chandelier to make Sadie Trehan a happy camper, she'd do it, because

20

there was no way in hell she was going to blow this job.

One of the front doors opened a crack and a male head was exposed. The head had dark blond hair with a curious, lighter blond streak a little above the left temple. The hair was thick, and sort of shaggy. The eyes were a quite wonderful cobalt blue. The nose was straight. The cheeks were tan. And the mouth was open.

"Whaddya want?"

It was a question. It was an accusation. And the man, although drop-dead gorgeous, didn't look exactly sane.

Keely couldn't help herself; she stepped back yet another pace, pressing her hands to her chest. "Me? What do I want? Um . . . nothing, I guess. I thought Sadie Trehan lived here. My mistake." She waved her hands at him. "Just . . . just go back to whatever it was you were doing. Well, gotta go. Sorry."

She turned to retrace her steps to the Mercedes, wondering if she'd narrowly escaped a serial killer or just a guy who really, really didn't like mornings.

"Wait!"

Keely stopped, made a face. She'd always been too damn obedient. Probably a side effect of those three years in the Girl Scouts. Aunt Mary had always said that was a mistake, and had cost her a small fortune paying for cookies into the bargain.

Keely turned around, slowly, to see that the man had stepped out onto the porch. He wasn't just an angry head anymore. Now he was an angry head with a long, lean body attached to it. And he was wet, or at least his left shoulder and the front of his shirt were wet. There were small white *lumps* in the wet. And he smelled bad. He really smelled bad.

"I . . . I really have to go," Keely said, backing toward

21

the car. "I have an appointment, and I'm going to be late."

The man was at the bottom of the steps now, walking toward her, one finger pointed at her face. "I know who you are. You're the interior decorator, right? Sadie hired you."

"You . . ." Keely cleared her throat. She'd been so hoping she'd gotten the wrong address. "You *know* Ms. Trehan?"

Nodding his head, the man said, "Yeah. Sadie's my aunt, and she hired you to get me some furniture. But I thought you were a man."

"Really," Keely said, reminding herself that she was a woman who had walked down Forty-second Street to take the bus to Allentown from the bowels of the New York Port Authority. She didn't scare easy. If this guy wanted to talk, she'd talk. "Why a man? Do you think only a man can decorate a man's house? Do you always make assumptions?"

The man's tanned and handsome face split in a grin that sent slashing creases into his cheeks. "Me? Make assumptions? A minute ago, lady, and I'll bet I'm not wrong, you were thinking I was about to pull you inside the house and practice my Anatomy One-oh-one course on you."

This conversation—could anyone call this a conversation?—was getting more bizarre by the minute. "You're a doctor?"

"Ah, another assumption. No, I'm not a doctor. And, although I like guessing games as much as the next guy, I don't have time to stand around, watching you try to figure me out, remember where you might have seen my face before today. My ego's riding low enough as it is."

Keely tipped her head to one side, trying to digest all

he'd said. "Your ego? Why? Am I supposed to recognize you or something?"

"Or something." He pushed a hand through his hair, pulled it away, and cursed at the clump of something white and squishy he'd come away with. "Never mind. Just to set you straight, Sadie Trehan is my aunt, and she lives over the garages out back. I'm the owner of the house, Jack Trehan. Jack Trehan? Still doesn't ring any bells for you, does it? Mort's right—how soon they forget. Man, I'm sure having one hell of a morning. Look, maybe we can do this another time, okay? I'm . . . I'm sort of busy right now."

"Plastering the ceiling?" Keely asked. "What *is* that all over you?"

Jack Trehan wiped his hand on his khaki slacks. "Trust me, you don't want to know. But like I said, we'll do this another time. Maybe in a month or two, something like that."

"A month or—no!" Keely took a quick breath, tried to calm herself. If this guy owned the house, then *he* was her client. Her only client. Furnishing a place of this size would give her enough money to get out of Dodge and she was bound and determined to get out of Dodge and back to Manhattan. "Surely, Mr. Trehan, you don't want to live here another month without any furniture? Your aunt told me the house was empty. I mean, are you really living in an *empty* house?"

Jack Trehan pulled a face. "It isn't as empty as it was about an hour ago," he said, then shook his head. Then he looked at Keely, looked at her closely. "You really want this job?"

Keely lifted her eyes heavenward for a moment, then swallowed down hard. "Yes, Mr. Trehan. I *really* do want this job."

23

He looked at her for long moments. "What do you know about babies?"

Babies? Keely nearly swallowed her tongue. She'd been asked a lot of questions by clients. Her background, where she'd gotten her degree, names of other clients who could be used as references . . . even if she was opposed to decorating around small video cameras hidden in one stockbroker's bedroom. She'd declined that job, then kicked herself for her ethics, considering she'd been two months behind in her rent at the time.

But never, never, had she been asked what she knew about babies.

"Babies?" she repeated after a moment. "What do I *know* about them?"

"Yes, Ms. McBride," Jack said, looking back over his shoulder, toward the open doorway. "Babies. What do you know about them?"

Keely wet her lips. "Well . . . they come in two sexes, pink and blue . . ."

"Okay, forget it," Jack told her, waving her off. "It was a bad idea anyway. Come back in a month, Ms. McBride, maybe two. Maybe never."

"Wait!"

Obviously Jack Trehan hadn't had obedience drummed into him by the Boy Scouts or anyone else in authority, because he didn't wait. He just kept going, heading back inside the house.

Keely caught the door just before it closed and barreled inside with him. "Why do you want to know if I know anything about babies? If I said I did, would it make some difference somehow?"

She stopped talking as Jack turned around and grabbed her by her upper arms, holding her in place. She wanted to look around, had caught a glimpse of a

24

vast emptiness, but she had a feeling now was not the time to start waxing poetic over chintz and valances. "You're hurting me," she said instead.

Jack dropped his hands. "Sorry. I just didn't want you to . . . well, never mind. We can talk here."

"Here being the foyer," Keely said, looking up at the chandelier. "Nice light. Pity you can't sit on it. Where *do* you sit, Mr. Trehan?"

"The answer to that ought to be obvious, Ms. McBride," Jack said, a crooked smile making him look suddenly boyish and not half so scary. "Now answer my question, please. What do you know about babies?"

Keely got the sudden impression that her answer would determine whether she'd be furnishing this house (and making megabucks) or sitting on her own rump, twiddling her thumbs while waiting for some suburban wife with more money than taste to show up asking her to find a footstool in mauve satin for her poodle, Fluffy.

"I know enough," she answered at last. "I've got a Girl Scout badge in child care." Actually, she'd earned only two badges, one for swimming and another for making some dumb basket out of Popsicle sticks. She really hadn't been a very good Girl Scout. But there was no reason for Jack Trehan to know that. "Why?"

Before he could answer, both their heads turned at the sound of aloud wail coming from somewhere deep in the house. "Damn it!" Jack exploded, turning to trot toward the sound.

Keely followed, her eyes flashing left and right as she passed along the wide hallway, looking at the white walled, empty rooms to either side. She actually stopped when she saw the area definitely designed to serve as a formal dining room, marveling at the snow-white pillars, the raised parquet floor, the entire wall of windows looking out over the grounds. What she could do with a space like this!

Another wail brought her back to her senses, and she continued on her way, entering the enormous kitchen in time to see Jack Trehan on his knees in front of a huge wicker wash basket, saying, "Aw, come on. Don't cry, M and M. Please don't cry."

Her mouth closed, her tongue poking at the inside of her left check, Keely tiptoed closer, then peered over Jack's shoulder to see the red-faced, really unhappy infant propped in a seat that was stuck inside the basket. Now she knew why his shirt was wet and lumpy, and why he smelled so bad. The baby was just as soggy, and smelled twice as bad. "Just when you think you've seen everything . . ." she said, shaking her head. "Yours?"

Jack's head jerked around as he looked up at her, his blue eyes flashing dangerously. "*No*, not *mine*. And stop smirking, because this isn't funny."

"Yes, it is," Keely contradicted. "I mean, trust me . . . this is funny. She's got great lungs, doesn't she? I'm assuming it's a girl. Pink blanket. Where's her mommy?"

"Out of missile range, unfortunately," Jack grumbled, trying to insert a pacifier in a rosebud mouth that was open wide enough to play garage to a Mack truck. "Damn it! I held her, fed her. What's her problem?"

Keely's experience with children wasn't extensive. It wasn't even close to extensive. She'd been orphaned young, an only child, and raised by her Aunt Mary, who hadn't married until two weeks ago, at the age of fifty-seven. She'd baby-sat a time or two, years ago, but never for an infant.

"Maybe . . ." she said, dredging her brain for an answer. "Maybe she's . . . *wet?*"

26

"Yeah, well, I tried to find a bib or something, but I couldn't, and she kept trying to eat the paper towels."

"No, not that kind of wet. I can see that her little dress is wet—and why would anybody dress an infant in dark purple? I meant her *other* end."

"Her other—? Oh." Jack, still holding the pacifier, sat back on his haunches, looked like he might be getting ready to make a break for it, head for the hills. "Oh, well, isn't *that* great?" He looked up at Keely. "How bad do you want this job, Ms. McBride?"

Keely already had a feeling this question was coming, and she was prepared to lie her head clean off if that was what it took. "Let me see if I have this right, okay? Are you saying, Mr. Trehan, that you're going to judge me on my child care techniques, rather than on my résumé?"

His closemouthed grin and raised eyebrows answered her question even before he added, "Yup. That's what I'm saying." He stood up, stepped away from the basket. "This is my cousin's baby, Magenta Moon . . . I've been calling her M and M, which is pretty bad, but nothing's as bad as Magenta Moon. She just arrived about an hour ago. I'm . . . I'm going to be taking care of her for a while—am taking care of her."

Keely winced as M and M began howling once more. "Taking care of her, are you? You could have fooled me."

Jack's tanned cheeks turned a remarkable brick red, an angry red, as if he was considering joining M and M in a tantrum duet. "You know what, Ms. McBride? You're a wiseass, and I don't think I like you. So forget about it. I withdraw the offer. I'm just going to go call some . . . some *service* or something."

"No! Don't do that," Keely said, quickly bending

down to unstrap M and M from her seat, then pick her up before she could regain her sanity, before she could remember that she was, by and large, deathly afraid of babies. "Look, see . . . I'm taking care of her," she said, bouncing up and down with the infant, holding M and M at arm's length. "Aren't I, baby?" she asked, exactly one second before M and M smiled, burped, then upchucked all over Keely's suit and legs. Even her shoes.

Keely gaped at Jack Trehan, horrified. "Look what she did!"

"Yeah, I see it. Great aim, huh?" He grinned. "A guy could get to like this kid. Welcome to my world, Ms. McBride. Clean her up—and yourself—and you're hired for the duration."

Keely sat M and M back in her seat and began looking around for some paper towels, finding a roll next to the sink. "Define duration, Mr. Trehan," she urged, wetting a wad consisting of about six feet of towels under the tap.

"Until the house is furnished, and until I can find someone else to take care of M and M. I'm sure I can find somebody, but for now, Ms. McBride—you're it."

"Oh happy day," Keely muttered under her breath, swiping at the front of her suit with the wet towels. "Oh, yuk! I got some under my fingernails. Yukka, yukka, *yuk!*"

"Yeah, that pretty much says it. Have fun, Ms. McBride. I'm off to take a shower. I'll bet you want one, too, but I live here, so I get to go first. Life's like that, not fair at all," Jack said, then turned on his heels and left the room.

"Jack Trehan? Jack*ass* is more like it," Keely muttered under her breath as she watched him go, knowing he wouldn't be any help if he stayed, and then looked down at M and M, who was crying again. "If you think that's going to make my heart break for you, you're *way* wrong, kiddo," she warned the child. She spread her arms as she approached the basket. "This is—was—my best suit."

M and M stopped crying, looked up at Keely. Smiled.

"And don't be cute," Keely warned, wagging a finger at the child. "Being cute won't help you one bit, little girl, not when you smell so bad. Trust me, I'm not a soft touch when it comes to cute."

M and M grabbed at her bare toes, caught one foot, and aimed it toward her mouth as she watched Keely with her huge blue eyes.

"Okay, so I'll admit it. *That's* cute. I sort of like that. But it's not adorable, so don't get a big head, all right, because you have a long way to go before I forget about the suit. This is just a job, and you're nothing more to me than a means to an end," Keely said, sighing as she knelt on the floor, looked at M and M, and tried to decide which *end* to clean up first.

Jack stood under the pulsating spray from the shower— all six jets, randomly placed on three tiled walls—and swore until he'd run out of cuss words. That took at least three minutes. A man didn't ride a bus in the minor leagues for a year and spend the next seven seasons traveling the country with professional baseball players and not grow his vocabulary. Jack could swear in English, in Spanish, and, thanks to the new reliever, Sarno Akita, a fair bit of Japanese.

The cussing, unfortunately, didn't help.

How could Cecily have done this to him?

No, scratch that. Of course Cecily could have done this to him. She was Cecily. She was the child who'd

29

never grown up, Bayonne's answer to Peter Pan, but with an unlimited trust fund left to her by her daddy, king of Bayonne's dry cleaners.

She'd been married at seventeen, to a polo player from Brazil, divorced at eighteen, in drug rehab at nineteen, and a hopeful noviate at a carmelite nunnery at twenty. At twenty-two she'd financed her lover's internet company—selling Jersey tomatoes by mail, a plan that never had a chance of getting off the ground— and, the last Jack had heard from her (after the Creative Pyrotechnics fiasco), she'd been "finding herself" in that commune.

Now she was Moon Flower, on her way to Tibet with Blue Rainbow, leaving behind Magenta Moon, the inner child who had become the child outside—the child being yet another little experiment in life that just hadn't turned out the way she'd hoped. And it probably all made sense to her.

Jack wondered if strychnine didn't taste too bad, or if he should just go up to the roof and jump off.

He slammed his hand against the knob controlling the shower and banged open the glass door, heading for the rack that held his two towels. Both were still damp. "Damn! First thing on that dame's list—towels."

Mention of "that dame" started Jack thinking about what he'd just done. He'd hired an interior decorator—a smart mouthed interior decorator—to play nanny to Cecily's kid. This was probably not a smart move, but he'd been desperate, beyond desperate.

Well, it would only be for a day or two. He'd figure out something else, somewhere else to put the kid. Sadie would be no help; she'd never had kids of her own, slept until almost noon every day, and would probably only like M and M if she had a key in her back and could be

30

wound up to play "Edelweis." Other than that, Sadie would expect the kid to sit in a corner and shut up until it was time to play again.

Cecily had mentioned her brother, Joey. If Jack knew nothing more about Cecily than that she'd gone to Joey for help, it would have disqualified her for anything that required more thought than breathing.

Because Joey was a flake. Joey was an idiot. Joey thought he should be in the Mafia, thought he was in the Mafia, or at least acted like he was, dressed and spoke as if he was. He even wanted everyone to call him Joey "Two Eyes" Morretti. Probably so the idiot could remember how many he had.

*See what happens when you die and leave your kids five-million-dollar trust funds? Better his aunt and uncle had spent it all on tango lessons, and maybe their very own platinum card at QVC.*

Jack laughed silently at the thought, remembering that Aunt Flo and Uncle Guido had been pretty powerless to control their two offspring from aboveground. If they'd missed heaven and gone to hell, their punishment must be watching daily videos of Cecily and Joey on the loose with their hard-earned martinizing money.

So Joey was out. Jack couldn't send M and M to Uncle Two Eyes and still be able to look at himself in the mirror.

Sadie was out. Definitely out—usually hovering about five miles into the ozone.

Tim? Jack hesitated as he pulled on his slacks. What about Tim?

"Yeah, what about Tim," Jack said, walking over to the mirror to look at his bare chest, at the surgical scars along his left elbow, riding low on his shoulder. "Tim's

31

still at the big dance, Jack," he reminded himself bitterly, hating himself for feeling sorry for himself, almost as much as he hated himself for feeling jealous of his twin.

Baseball. It had been both of their lives, for as long as he could remember. Oh, there'd been football and basketball in high school, but it was baseball that consumed them both. From the time they'd been five or six, it had been Jack throwing the ball, Tim catching; Jack throwing the ball, Tim hitting. Hour after hour, day after day, year after year. Their dad had built a pitcher's mound in the backyard, constructed a batting cage out of iron pipes and chicken wire. He'd even drilled a hole in a baseball, suspended it from a chain in the garage ceiling, then put up an old rug for them to hit into in the off-season.

Baseball, baseball, baseball.

It had been their lives.

It was still Tim's life, his brother now in his eighth season as catcher for the Phillies, leading the club in both doubles and triples and probably heading for yet another Golden Glove award.

But it wasn't Jack's life. Not anymore. Not since the last rotator cuff surgery last winter, and one hellishly lousy spring training camp, culminating in his retirement before the Yankees could cut him loose. He'd cried during his press conference on ESPN, damn near bawled like a baby, then crawled into his condo and hid. Now he was hiding in Whitehall, of all places, still licking his wounds while his twin was second in the over-all voting so far for the All-Star game.

Tell Tim he'd stupidly inherited Cecily's baby for God knows how long? Oh no. Not hardly.

"Which leaves the smart mouth downstairs," Jack told his reflection before turning away, heading for the walk-in closet and a clean shirt. "What's her name again? Kathy? Karen? No . . . Keely. That's it. What the hell kind of name is Keely?"

Jack pulled the tan shirt over his head, his head popping free as he realized that he knew nothing about this woman. He'd left M and M downstairs with a stranger who had been handpicked by Aunt Sadie, queen of the silly fairies.

And he said Cecily was nuts? What did that make him?

Desperate. Definitely desperate.

He looked at the clock sitting on the box beside his stacked mattress and box spring. Nine-thirty. Shouldn't it be at least noon? Or maybe September? Because this had been the longest two hours in his life.

But it was only nine-thirty, and he couldn't hide up here all day. He had to go back downstairs, see the woman, see the baby. Figure out what to do with the woman, do with the baby.

He'd rather be facing Mark McGwire in an interleague game, in the bottom of the ninth, with the score tied and the bases loaded.

Jack loped down the back stairs that led directly into the kitchen, stopping dead when he saw the baby in the sink, the woman holding the sink's power spray over the baby's head. "What in *hell* are you doing? Trying to *drown* the kid?"

Keely, clearly startled by Jack's bellow, turned quickly, losing her grip on the wet, slippery infant— who then sort of slowly *slid* down lower into the sink. "Oh God! Oh God, look what you made me do!" she yelled, grabbing at M and M with both hands, pulling her upright again. "She's so damn *slippery*."

M and M was wailing again, her blond hair stuck to

33

her head, her long eyelashes all spiky and clumped as she opened and closed her eyes and water dripped off her nose.

"Is she all right?" Jack asked, reluctantly approaching the sink.

"Yes, she's all right . . . I suppose. She's yelling, isn't she?" Keely responded, holding M and M's upper arm with one hand, using her free hand to blot the baby's face with paper towels. "And she was liking it, too, until you showed up." She threw the damp paper towels on the counter and lifted Keely out of the sink, a hand under each arm. M and M's arms and legs were wiggling, her smooth buttocks riding above chubby legs marked with at least four fat creases. "Here," Keely said, shoving those buttocks at Jack, "hold her until I get more towels."

"Hold her?" Jack backed up rapidly. "Are you frigging *nuts?* You just said she was slippery."

Keely held on as M and M laughed, and wriggled, and reached for Keely's hair. "Well then, if you won't hold her, *you* get the paper towels. And may I add, it's a poor kitchen that has no proper dish towels. Old Mother Hubbard had a full pantry, compared to you. One mug, one can of coffee grounds, half a loaf of bread, and some Chinese take-out that died in the year of the dog. It's pitiful, that's what it is."

He ignored her complaints, concentrating on his new job as paper towel-getter. He could do that. He'd won two Cy Young awards—he could fetch paper towels. He quickly slipped past Keely—literally, as the floor was wet—and snagged the roll from the countertop. "Now what?"

"Dry her off," Keely said, rolling her eyes. "And hurry up—this kid should be on a diet."

34

Dry her off. Jack hesitated, holding a length of paper toweling he'd stripped from the roll. Dry her off. How could he dry her off? He approached from behind, one end of the paper toweling in his hand, and began wrapping it around M and M's bare bottom, her wriggling legs.

Once, twice, three times around, until M and M was in a cocoon of paper towels and Keely finally said, "That ought to do it, thanks. Now you can hold her and she won't slip."

"She's still dripping wet," Jack pointed out, ripping off another section of toweling and draping it over M and M's wet head. The infant giggled, shook her head, and the towel fell to the floor. "And she's not cooperating, damn it."

"Don't swear in front of the child," Keely bit out, shoving M and M at him, so that he was forced to take her. She then took a deep breath, stood up straight, smoothed down the front of her once crisp white blouse. "I've got to find something for this kid to wear. There has to be something in one of those bags in the wash basket."

"What was wrong with what she had on?" Jack asked, carefully sitting down on the floor, figuring that M and M would have less distance to fall if he lost his grip on her.

"Are you kidding? She was all wet . . . and *stinky*. What didn't come out the top end when she spit up on me made its way out the bottom end right after you deserted me. I couldn't do anything else but give her a bath."

Jack shifted his eyes right, then left. He'd noticed a new smell when he'd entered the kitchen, not a pleasant smell, and now he looked at a small pile of discarded clothing on the floor and saw what looked like a disposable diaper—a *full* disposable diaper—perched

35

right on top of the mound. Then he looked across the room at the sink.

"Let me get this straight," he said after a moment. "M and M sh—, er, did something in her pants, and your answer to that was to stick her backside in my kitchen sink? My *sink?* I might want to put *dishes* in that sink, woman!"

Keely had pulled two large, tightly packed pink plastic zipper bags out of the wash basket and was rummaging through them, selecting small garments. "Oh, shut up," she said, otherwise ignoring him as she pulled a disposable diaper out of a box of them and placed it with the clothing. "Diaper, shirt, dress, socks. That ought to do it. Oh God, look how *small* this stuff is. Just like a doll's. So cute!"

"Having fun, Ms. McBride?" Jack asked, trying to hold on to M and M as the damp paper towels began to come apart and the baby tried to reach up, destroy what was left of his bottom lip and gums. "That's good. Because I'm not. Trust me in this. I'm *not.* I don't like babies. Not even cute babies."

"She is cute, isn't she?" Keely said, spreading the pink blanket on the floor, then gingerly lifting M and M out of Jack's arms and laying her down on the blanket. "And pretty much like one of the dolls I used to play with, except she moves more, of course. I think I can dress her. I remember how." Then she picked up the disposable diaper, turned it one way, then another, and frowned. "Okay, maybe not all at once. But I'll figure it out."

"Good. You do that," Jack said, easing himself to his feet. "I'm going to go catch last night's ball scores on ESPN."

"Figures," Keely said, but she was talking to M and M, not Jack. "Make the baby, zip up the pants, and go

36

watch ESPN. Remember this, sweetheart: men. They're all alike."

"She . . . is . . . *not* . . . my . . . baby." Jack pronounced each word slowly, distinctly. "She is my cousin's baby. And what the hell *should* I be doing?"

Keely redid the tapes on the disposable diaper, then sat back, admiring her work. "There, that ought to hold her." She pushed a lock of honey blond hair out of her eyes and looked up at Jack. "What *should* you be doing? Well, if I could make a suggestion, Mr. Trehan, I'd say you should be figuring out how to strap that little seat in the backseat of your car, so we can go shopping."

He eyed her warily. "Shopping for what?"

Keely rolled her eyes. "For M and M, of course. I mean, you can wait for new furniture, but M and M can't. Or were you planning to have her sleep in her seat? And have you decided which is to be her bedroom? I should know, take a few measurements, and then we can be on our way. We can stop at my aunt's shop—I can change clothes, because we live above the shop—then pick up the van, and be able to bring everything home with us. I *have* decorated a nursery before, you understand. I was thinking about a cherry wood crib with a canopy top—with a white eyelet canopy—and a matching dressing table, and a rocking chair, of course, and—"

Jack bent down, grabbed the car seat, and headed for the door, practicing his Japanese.

# Chapter Three

*I'm not going to buy my kids
an encyclopedia. Let them
walk to school like I did.*

—Yogi Berra

IN THE END, THEY TOOK AUNT MARY'S MERCEDES, AS Jack's sports car was only a two-door, and if he'd hit his head one more time trying to get the baby seat strapped in, M and M was going to learn words no child ought to know.

"Nice car," Jack said as they rolled down Main Street, Jack at the wheel, heading for MacArthur Road, the main artery of the township, and the road leading straight into Allentown. "The interior decorating business must be a good one. Which reminds me—how much are you costing me, Ms. McBride?"

"Not nearly enough," Keely said, squeezing the white plastic garbage bag that sat on her lap, the bag holding her ruined jacket. She shifted on the seat, looked back at M and M. "Well, would you look at that—she's asleep." She turned around once more, feeling, if not competent, then at least lucky. "She really is a cute baby."

"Aren't all babies cute?" Jack asked, peeking into the rearview mirror.

"I guess so, to their parents," Keely said consideringly. "But my friend Sheila? Her kid looked like Woody Allen when he was born, I swear he did, although he's gotten past that phase, thank God. Sheila lives in Wisconsin, and sent me a video of little Justin right after he was born. Pitiful. Just pitiful. But M and

38

M is cute as a button. That wispy blond hair—it curled when it was wet, did you know that? I'm betting she'll have gorgeous ringlets soon and then hate her curls later, the way I hate mine. And those *huge* blue eyes, and those black lashes? You're going to have to beat the boys away with a stick when she grows up."

"I'm not going to be anywhere around when M and M grows up," Jack reminded her, easing into the passing lane as they drove toward Allentown.

"Oh, yeah, that's right. She's not your kid. I keep forgetting that. Must be the blond hair you've both got."

"*You've* got blond hair, Ms. McBride," Jack pointed out. "And I'm telling you, M and M is my cousin's kid. She—oh, hell, who'd believe me? Let's just say Cecily is out of town for a while, and I'm taking care of the kid. Correction: *You're* taking care of the kid."

Keely was silent for a few moments, then finally nodded. "Okay, and I'm sorry for teasing you. I know she's not yours. I found the letter from your cousin when I was cleaning up the kitchen. Shouldn't you be reporting her to the police? I mean, it sounds to me like she's *abandoning* M and M, not just dropping her off for a couple of days, unless Katmandu is in Pennsylvania, and we both know it's not. And who's Joey? The father?"

"Joey is Cecily's brother," Jack said.

Keely noticed a tightening of the muscles around Jack's mouth. "Not your favorite person, right? Oh—turn right up ahead, on Tilghman. The shop is between Twenty-first and Twenty-second, on the left. There's parking behind the shop. You really should get over to the right now, and not wait until the last minute."

Jack stepped on the gas, passing a line of four cars, then quickly cut into the right lane in order to make the turn.

"Well, that was fun," Keely said, opening her eyes

once more. "I guess I should have kept my mouth shut. But at least now I know that if I want you to do something, all I have to do is not tell you to do it."

He shot her a grin that put very sexy slashes in his cheeks. "At last, a woman who understands me, because I definitely do like women who keep their mouths shut."

"Yeah, I'll bet, and their brains on hold," Keely muttered. "I thought I recognized the type. So, are you going to tell me about this Joey person, or am I supposed to wait until you volunteer information? Just so I know the ground rules, okay?"

The interior of the car was frigid for the next three blocks, and not because of the air-conditioning. Finally Jack said, "Joey is Cecily's brother, just like I told you. Joey and Cecily are from Bayonne—that's in New Jersey."

"I know where Bayonne is," Keely interrupted. "I just didn't know anyone really lived there. Oops, sorry. I didn't mean to stop the flow. Go on."

Jack sighed, eased the car to a stop at a red light at Nineteenth Street. "Joey thinks he should belong to the mob."

"The mob?" Keely's jaw dropped. "You mean *the Mob?* And Cecily wanted to leave M and M with him?"

"Relax, Ms. McBride. Joey doesn't belong to the mob. He's seen all the *Godfather* films, but that's about as far as it goes. I don't like him because he's an idiot, not because I'm afraid he's going to put an icepick in my throat."

"Oh," Keely said, relaxing slightly as they turned left, then right, into the alley behind her aunt's shop, which was located in a converted brick house. "Well, that's okay then. I'm glad Cecily left M and M with you." She opened the car door, then looked back at the baby. "Still asleep. Why don't you wait here? I won't be long. I just have to change clothes and get the keys to the van."

40

"And pack a suitcase," Jack added, effectively halting Keely as she was about to gently close the door, so as not to wake M and M.

"Say what?" she asked, sticking her head back inside the car. "What do you mean, pack a suitcase?"

"And if you have a sleeping bag, you might want to bring that, too, at least until you buy me some more beds. Or did you think I was going to be alone in the house with the kid while you worked nine to five?"

"I . . . I . . ." Keely looked into the backseat, at the sleeping baby, then at Jack. "I . . ."

"Right. My sentiments exactly, Ms. McBride. Now get it in gear, okay? Who knows how long she'll sleep?"

"I hate you," Keely said, finding her voice at last, fortunately not until she was climbing the stairs to the living quarters she shared with her aunt. "Hate, hate, *hate* you, Jack Trehan," she repeated as she quickly changed into a denim skirt and white summer sweater, then dove into her closet, emerged with a large suitcase, threw it on the bed, unzipped it.

"Hate, loathe, and *detest* you, Jack Trehan," she continued as she opened drawers, flung clothing in the general direction of the suitcase, then loaded toiletries into another zippered bag, topped off deodorant and toothpaste with a hair dryer and her small bag of makeup.

"The things you won't do for money," Keely growled at her reflection in the mirror above the sink. "Shame on you."

Throwing the toiletries into the suitcase, she zipped it closed, grabbed her quilt and pillow from the bed, and headed for the stairs once more, the quilt dragging on the floor. She stopped only when she saw the message light blinking on her aunt's answering machine.

41

There could be messages downstairs, on the answering machine in the shop, but Keely knew she didn't have time to check. Aunt Mary had completed most of her projects before the wedding, so there wasn't all that much unfinished business for Keely to handle—which had been another reason she'd been doing back flips ever since she got the call from Sadie Trehan. If there were messages downstairs, they could wait. But she would take the time—and let Jack Trehan just twiddle his thumbs a while longer—while she checked to see if Aunt Mary had called.

Dropping the quilt and pillow, Keely pressed the message button, already smiling as she anticipated hearing her Aunt Mary's voice. She'd been phoning almost daily to report on the glories of Greece and holy wedlock.

"Hi, Keely, sorry to have missed you. Listen, I know it's been a long time, darling, but I—"

Keely smacked at the STOP button, frantic to block out Gregory Fontaine's voice. What did he want? Not that she cared. She most certainly didn't *care*. She bit her lip, drummed her fingers against her cheek as she entertained scenarios. He wanted her back. He loved her. He couldn't live without her. He still couldn't locate the nifty measuring tape she copped as her "severance pay" and wondered if she knew where it was.

"Oh, hell," she said, hitting the PLAY button once more. "Might as well get it over with."

"—thought you ought to hear this from me. I've just rented your space. You know I'd considered enlarging the business, and you have to admit that you really lucked out, picking up the place on Sixty-seventh at that price. And I know Leibowitz said he'd hold it for you another six months, but that was only if you kept paying the rent, which you haven't—you're a full three weeks

42

late with the rent for June, Keely. So . . . well, so I took over the lease. Fontaine's is now on both the East and West sides of Manhattan . . . and you're welcome back. Anytime. You could run the branch for me, right out of your old shop—well, my new shop. I mean that, Keely. We can work things out, I know it. Look, gotta go. Shavonna wants to show me her new design for a project we're doing out on the Island. So take care, be good, and don't hate me, Keely. I do love you, pumpkin, but business is business, right?"

Keely stood glaring at the answering machine as the END OF MESSAGES electronic voice was engaged. She fought the urge to rip the machine from the table, fling it against the wall. "You *miserable* . . . three weeks? Gregory Fontaine, you are one rotten sonofabitch! Three lousy weeks!"

"Got a problem . . . pumpkin?"

Keely whirled around quickly, her feet tangling in the discarded quilt so that she went down, rather hard, landing on her hands and knees. "You!" she accused, looking up at Jack Trehan. "What are . . . how dare . . . where's M and M?"

"Sound asleep in the backseat. Don't worry, I locked the car but left the engine running, to keep the air conditioner on."

"Oh . . . okay," Keely said, getting to her feet. "I suppose that's—wait a minute. You locked the car? Where are the keys?"

"Oh, please. Do you really think I'd—"

"Show . . . me . . . the . . . keys."

Jack slipped a hand into his slacks pocket. Slipped his other hand into his other pocket. Frowned. Looked sheepish. "Um . . ." He lifted his empty hands out of his pockets, waved them at her. "This is your fault, you

43

know. If you'd moved your butt a little instead of listening to your messages and doing God only knows what else, then I wouldn't have had to—"

"You jackass!" Keely nearly tripped over the quilt again as she lunged for her aunt's desk, pulled open the center drawer. There were the keys to the van. There was the second set of keys to the Mercedes. She pulled them both out and headed for the stairs. "Grab that stuff, genius, and follow me."

How could his cousin have trusted him with her baby? You couldn't trust this guy with a stuffed teddy bear, yet alone a small, helpless infant. Not that she was much better, granted, but then, it didn't take much to be better than Jack Trehan.

She barreled down the stairs, Jack hard on her heels. "I was kidding, damn it," he called after her. "Look, look—here are the keys. I wouldn't lock the keys in the car. Do you think I'm an idiot?"

Keely stopped at the bottom of the stairs, glared up at him. "Never ask the obvious," she gritted out, then banged out of the house, leaving Jack to manage his own way through the door with her suitcase and bedding.

She ran over to the car and peeked inside the rear window, to see M and M still fast asleep, although her mouth was doing some puckering motions around the pink pacifier still stuck between her lips. "She's all right," Keely said, all but collapsing against the side of the car in relief as Jack joined her, pushing the button on the key ring that opened the trunk.

"Of course she's all right," he said, shaking his head. "What did you think she was going to do? Get out, go waltzing down to the corner pub for a brew?"

Keely didn't bother answering, but just shot a cold, hard stare at this . . . this *man,* and headed for the van.

44

She hated men. She definitely hated men. Gregory Fontaine, Jack Trehan, all men. And she had every right! They were pond scum, every last one of them.

"Follow me, okay?" she told him. "We'll go back down Tilghman to Eighth, hang a left, hang a right at Washington, and then a left at Seventh, which puts us back onto MacArthur Road, heading for the store I have in mind. You got that?"

"Ms. McBride, I grew up here," Jack told her, opening the door to the Mercedes. "I know Seventh is one way at Tilghman so that we have to cut down Eighth and over to Washington, where it's not one way. I know Seventh turns into MacArthur Road once it hits Whitehall. I even know how to get to the malls. And if you'd stop treating me as if I were brain dead, I'll highly appreciate it."

"If you stopped *acting* as if you were brain dead, I'd appreciate it," she told him, breaking a nail as she yanked open the door to the van. "Damn it! Now look what you made me do!"

"I did that? From over here? Has anyone ever told you, Ms. McBride, that you may not be a well woman?"

"I already knew that. I've got to be crazy," she shouted back at him. "I'm working for *you*, remember?" And then, suddenly realizing that his response, his most logical response, would be "Yeah, but not for long!" she quickly got into the van and backed out into the alley, on her way to making her first considerable inroads on Jack Trehan's bank account—and beginning the replenishing of her own.

Jack would rather be back in Double-A, stuck on the side of a country road as a new tire was put on the team bus so that they could continue their five-hour drive to East Nowhere and play another ball game in front of fans who had shown up mostly to watch the hog and chicken races scheduled for the end of the fifth inning.

He'd rather be anywhere but where he was, which was stuck smack in the middle of baby land. "What are you doing?" he asked Keely as she headed toward a line of shopping carts.

"I'm getting a shopping cart, what does it look like I'm doing?"

"For a crib? Do you think it will fit?" he snapped back, watching as she settled the still sleeping M and M in some kind of seat built into the cart. He took a moment to admire her long legs below the hem of the denim skirt, then shook his head. Was he out of his frigging mind? The woman was poison!

Keely turned the cart and headed through the automatic doors, into the store, which was about the size of two football fields.

"This store is just for baby stuff?" Jack asked, looking around in amazement. "The kid could only weigh fifteen or so pounds. She can't walk, can't talk, only has one tooth—how much could she need?"

Keely, obviously, wasn't listening. "I firmly believe in having a plan in places like this," she told him, aiming the cart to the right. "We start at the beginning and work our way through, row by row. Here—what's this?"

Jack saw one of the salesclerks smiling at him as if to say, "Oh, what a good daddy, going shopping with the baby," and quickly turned away, picking up the box Keely had indicated. "I don't know. It says something here about—no, they've got to be kidding. Who'd do that?"

Keely grabbed the box and turned it around, looking at the pictures on the back. "Oh, isn't that cute? You can make plaster of Paris molds of M and M's little feet and hands. Look, they even include a mounting board, so

46

you can display everything on a shelf. Let's get it."

"Let's not," Jack said, taking the box from Keely and replacing it on the shelf. "I'll just have the kid bronzed. It's easier."

Keely rolled her eyes at him, then grabbed the box again, dropped it into the cart. "You're just not going to allow yourself to enjoy this, are you?"

"What was your first clue?" Jack responded tightly, watching as she picked up yet another box. "Do you have to look at everything? At this rate, we'll be here for hours."

"Possibly days," Keely agreed, throwing a *Baby Memories, A Time Capsule* album into the cart. "Okay, next row."

"Next row, next row," Jack grumbled under his breath, but the clerk was looking at him again, so he followed after Keely.

He looked up at the sign marking the aisle. "Child Safety? What's this about?"

Keely handed him a small package filled with plastic plugs to be inserted in wall outlets. "There's lots more," she said, a rather dangerous "I want it, I want it all" gleam in her big brown eyes as she scanned the shelves. "Locks for cabinets, something to put on doorknobs so little hands can't open them. Oh, look at this! I just love gadgets. Don't you love gadgets? This is a keeper for M and M's pacifier, to keep it clean. It even hooks onto stuff, like her stroller or diaper bag. See, it says so right here. Oh—and I've got to get this," she said, tossing the pacifier keeper into the cart while already picking up another packet.

Jack saw the bits of terry cloth inside the plastic packet and read the description over Keely's shoulder. "Knee pads? Why? Is M and M going to take up rollerblading tomorrow, and nobody told me?"

47

"These are for when she starts crawling, to protect those soft little knees."

Jack pulled at his nose, considering this. "Crawling? She's going to start crawling? When?"

"I haven't the faintest idea. I'm an interior decorator, not Mr. Spock."

"Um . . . I know I'm only relying on my memory, but I think that would be *Doctor* Spock. Mr. Spock was the "Star Trek" guy, the one with the ears."

"Whatever," Keely told him without interest, tossing the package into the cart, and then several more packages, none of which he wanted explained. They'd gone two aisles and the cart was already filling up. "But we ought to be ready, don't you think? Katmandu is pretty far away, so who knows when your cousin will come back."

"I'm trying not to think at all, Ms. McBride," Jack told her honestly. Keely didn't know Cecily the way he did, although that damn note had probably given her a lot of clues as to his cousin's lifelong flightiness. Jack was still busy attempting to forget the time, when they were all kids, that Cecily had told them all to go hide, then lost interest in the game and went inside to bed without finding anyone. Dipstick Joey had stayed hidden until the streetlights had gone on, then run home, sobbing.

They rounded another aisle, and Jack stopped, reached for a box on the shelf, just trying to do his part. "Do you need one of these?" he asked helpfully, looking at an artist's rendition of a bottle with what looked like a funnel stuck to the top. "What is this? A horn?"

Keely took the box from him and put it back on the shelf. "We don't need that, okay? Come on. Next aisle."

"But you haven't bought anything in this aisle. I'm not coming back once we're past it," he called after her, picking up the box once more, reading the blurb on the front. He replaced the box, looked at others lining the shelves, all of them different, yet all of them designed for the same purpose. *Breast pump.* He closed his eyes, tried to imagine what the funnel part did, what the rest of the contraption did.

"God, that must *hurt*," he said, shivering, and then chased after Keely once more.

The cart was definitely filling up. Night light. Tinted window shade for the car. Small rearview mirror to attach beneath the car's mirror, the better to see baby in the backseat. First aid and safety videos for the VCR. A thermometer that went in the ear. Another one that went . . . he dropped that back into the cart, once more trying to put a mental block up between himself and reality. A machine for baby's nursery that played different sounds—heartbeat, babbling brook, bird song, white noise. A plastic "guard" that snapped over the controls on the television. Okay, he liked that one.

Keely called him away from a display of at least fifteen different kinds of pacifiers, to show him her latest treasure. "Look. A television monitor for M and M's nursery. We can hear her, we can see her, and later it turns into a small TV, just for her. Isn't that remarkable?"

Jack peered at the price. "Remarkable," he agreed, wincing.

The box went into the cart, and they were off again, this time stopping at a row filled with different bottles. "These are the same brand M and M already has," Keely said, loading a half dozen into the cart, along with a box of plastic "inserts," whatever the hell they were. Then she picked up some accessories, showing him a pack of really disgusting, orangish, round nipples, and explaining, "It says these are the closest thing to mother. What do you think?"

"You're doing this on purpose, aren't you? Pay back for something you think I've done," Jack accused, feeling his cheeks growing hot, his hands growing cold. "Just buy the damn stuff and let's get out of here."

She bought. Bottle brushes, nipple brushes, more pacifiers, toothpaste, and a toothbrush—for one small tooth. A rubber gum massager. Shampoo, powder, lotion. A medical kit. Spoons and dishes. Two cases of the same brand of formula Keely had found in M and M's wash basket.

Bibs. Jack bought the bibs. A dozen of them.

Next to go into the cart was a small microwave for the nursery, to heat bottles in the middle of the night without having to go downstairs. What *would* they think up next?

A moment later, Jack found out. What they'd thought up next was a magic can for wrapping and disposing of dirty diapers, then hiding them out of sight. The cutaway picture of the inside of the pail showed a line of diapers, each wrapped in its own plastic cocoon— sort of like a lumpy strand of pearls, or a white boa constrictor that had somehow swallowed a whole litter of small animals. He wanted to buy two, just to be able to play with one of them, but Keely rolled her eyes and he gave up the idea, heading back to the front of the store to get another cart.

First to go into the new cart was a humidifier in the shape of a duck. He didn't even question it.

Then a bathtub. A seat to go inside the bathtub. Bath toys. A net bag to hold the bath toys. A strangely shaped kneeling seat to put next to the tub, for the washer to lean on while scrubbing the washee.

Towels, washcloths. He insisted on lots of towels.

"This is interesting," Keely said, having actually walked down two more aisles without tossing anything else into the carts. "It says to push this button to try it out."

Jack watched as Keely turned the box holding a brown plush teddy bear and pushed an exposed button on the back of the box. He expected to hear a lullaby. What he heard, when Keely pushed the box in his face, was the sound of a heart beating—from the inside.

"Sounds of the womb," Keely said. "I was wondering if they'd put in sounds of someone's stomach gurgling. Yeah, well, the bear's cute," she said as the box hit the cart. "I could do the entire room in a teddy bear motif, you know, because the white eyelet may be pretty, but it's rather delicate. Yes, I think I'll try to go with the bears."

"Do that. Follow them straight into their den. They might like it if you bring along some mustard and ketchup."

"Funny," Keely told him, and pushed the cart around the corner to the next aisle.

Baby wipes. Baby wipes warmer. Both were tossed into the cart, but Keely was only "warming up," for now they'd gotten to the big stuff.

"She has one of these," Jack pointed out as Keely walked down a wide aisle lined on both sides with at least two dozen varieties of car seats. Jack looked at one seat that he was pretty sure could withstand a launch in the space shuttle. "They're kidding here, right? *Designer label* car seats?"

Keely backtracked, looked at the seat Jack had indicated. "Pull out one of the sheets from that plastic holder," she told him. "We just turn it in at the checkout and they'll get us one. Because we should have two, you know. One for your car, one for mine."

"She doesn't need two seats, damn it," Jack said, folding his arms over his chest, fully prepared to fight this one to the death. He wasn't a poor man, but Keely McBride was quickly running up a tab that could rival the national debt.

Keely jammed one fist on her hip. "Okay—scenario: I have to go somewhere—while M and M is napping, so don't make your eyes all wide like that—and suddenly you need to take her somewhere. She's choking, or she's out of diapers, or you get some wild urge for Chicken McNuggets. *I've* got the car seat, the *only* car seat. Now what, genius?"

Jack pulled the tag.

After that, everything became sort of a blur.

Two baby carriers, one that would sort of wrap M and M to Keely's chest, and a second one, made to be worn on Jack's back, that would probably be suitable for assaulting Everest.

Crib, crib mattress, chest of drawers, changing table. Sheets, blankets, bumper pads, dust ruffle, mobile, matching lamp, wallpaper border, curtains, and pillows. A stroller made with one huge wheel in front, two in back, so that M and M could go along on his morning jog—like *that* was ever going to happen. Sherpa seat pad for the stroller, cup holder for the stroller-pusher. Rain hood for the stroller, mosquito netting for the stroller.

High chair. Low chair. Bouncing chair. Gliding chair. Hang in a doorway jiggle up and down chair. Swing. Playpen. Portable crib.

All color-coordinated. And with accessories to match.

Hamper. Teething rings. Pads. More pads, just bigger. White satin hangers. A toy box. A talking butterfly. One-time-use cameras to record M and M's growth for the memory book. Picture frames to hold more pictures.

A huge bottle of odor remover that Jack would have considered cheap at twice the price.

Three how-to-raise-the-baby books, including one from Dr. Spock. Compact discs of classical music and lullabies. Brush and comb. A gallon jug of "just for baby" drinking water that Jack considered outrageous at half the price.

New diaper bags because they matched the teddy bear motif of everything else. Puffy wall hangings, including one teddy bear dressed in a baseball uniform that Jack insisted upon buying. "You sexist or something? M and M can't like baseball?" he'd asked when Keely protested. The baseball bear stayed, as did a soft baseball Jack found—pink—with places to write M and M's "starting weight, home field, and opening day." Keely thought that was "adorable."

Jack wanted to smack her.

M and M, who had slept through the entire shopping orgy, began to stir as they pushed the two overloaded carts to the checkout. She opened her huge blue eyes, looked around, and her bottom lip began to quiver. A moment later she was in full throat, howling to bring down the roof.

"What's the matter with her?" Jack asked, looking at Keely. Keely was looking at him, the same question in her eyes.

Keely shrugged. "Do you think she's hungry again?"

"How the hell would *I* know?" Jack shot back at her. "You're in charge, remember? I thought you said you knew about babies."

"Yeah? Well, guess what. I *lied*," Keely all but shouted, to be heard above M and M's wails. "Did you bring a bottle with you?"

Jack smacked a hand against his forehead. "*No-o-o-o,*
53

I didn't bring a bottle with me. That's your job, lady."

"Oh. Right." Keely reached into her huge purse, withdrawing an insulated cylinder with a zip top. "I forgot. This was in with her things." She unzipped the cylinder and pulled out a full bottle of formula. "Here you go, baby," she said, sticking the nipple in M and M's mouth.

"You're first supposed to squeeze all the air out of the plastic bag inside," someone behind them said, and both Keely and Jack turned around—and M and M started to wail again because the bottle had been yanked out of her mouth.

"I'm supposed to—what?" Keely asked as Jack looked down at a little girl who couldn't be more than seven or eight years old. Great. Seven or eight years old, and *she* knew more than McBride. It figured. He wondered if the kid could be paid by the hour.

"Here, I'll show you," the little girl said, taking the bottle from Keely, squeezing the liner, and then expertly inserting the nipple into M and M's widely opened mouth. "We had twins last month, so Mom lets me help," the child explained. "There. Do you think you can handle it now?"

"Smart-ass kid," Keely grumbled after thanking the child and watching her skip away to rejoin her mother. "Everyone's an expert these days."

"You're not," Jack pointed out sourly. "Do you think we can get out of here now? M and M isn't the only one who's hungry."

"And that's my problem *how?* I won't cook for you."

"I won't ask you to."

"You'd better not."

"I'd rather be reduced to going out back to graze."

"You mean you don't already do that? I would have thought a horse's a—"

"Jack Trehan! Oh, my God, Sally, look—it's Jack Trehan!"

Keely frowned, not finishing a sentence that would probably have gotten her fired on the spot, and both of them turned to look at the man now approaching them, his right hand held out in greeting.

"I'm right, aren't I? You are Jack Trehan? Pitcher, Yankees, two Cy Youngs? Man, what a tough break, having your arm go on you like that. Well, the Yankee's loss is our gain. I'm Bill Hunsberger, by the way. Played ball myself, but nothing like you, that's for sure. Welcome home, Jack, and thanks for all the great games."

"You're welcome," Jack said, shaking the man's hand. "It's good to be home." He was dying to look at Keely, dying to see her standing there, bug-eyed, her mouth hanging open. Maybe she didn't recognize him, but the rest of the world did, damn it!

"Sally?" the man called over his shoulder, still not relinquishing Jack's hand. "Sally, you're always so slow. Come on over here, for God's sake. I was right, it is Jack Trehan. Give me that shopping list, why don't you, and stop standing there acting like I'm doing something wrong." He turned back to Jack. "You wouldn't mind signing Sally's shopping list, would you? For my kid, Sean. He's only two months old, but someday he's going to treasure that autograph."

Sally approached, an infant hanging in a sling around her belly, her arms full of disposable diapers, a purse and diaper bag hanging over her left shoulder. Pack mules carried less, but Bill's hands were empty as he impatiently waved his wife over to them.

"Don't you want to help her?" Keely asked as Sally struggled to hold the pack of diapers between her knees as she rummaged in her purse for pen and paper.

55

"Naw, she can handle it," Bill said, still looking at Jack.

"Men," Keely growled, motioning for Jack to hold the bottle while she went to help Sally. "You're all idiots."

"What's the matter with the wife, Jack?" Bill Hunsberger asked, jerking a thumb over his shoulder toward Keely, who was helping Sally hold her packages. "Mine's the same way. Baby blues, that's what the doc calls it. Pain in the ass is what I call it. Like women haven't been having babies for years."

"For a long time," Jack agreed, but quietly, because he had a feeling that if Keely heard him, he'd pay for it later. "And she's not my wife. This isn't even my baby." Why he felt compelled to share that information with a stranger he didn't know, but he thought it was important.

And not that it mattered, because Bill wasn't listening. "How's your brother, Jack? Tim the Tiger's arm is okay, right? Like, this bum arm stuff isn't a twin thing, is it? He's still okay? I mean, he's hitting the hell out of the ball right now, isn't he?"

"Yeah. Hitting the hell out of the ball," Jack said, his teeth clenched as he scribbled his name on the scrap of paper Sally handed him. "Well, it's been great, Bill, but we have to go now, get the little woman home and all of that. Keely? You ready to check out?"

"You might want to burp her now," Sally Hunsberger said rather meekly, pointing at M and M.

"Your turn, *Slugger*. Mr. Ego. Mr. What Do You Mean You Don't Know Me, But I'm Not Going To Tell You Who I am—like I'd really *care*," Keely said as she took hold of the other cart, aimed it toward the checkout counter. "Oh, and for what it's worth, I'm a Mets fan. I *hate* the Yankees."

"Oh, yeah, *pumpkin?* Well, guess what—you're fired!"

She wheeled back to face him. "Oh, good. Now I get to go home and you get M and M all to yourself. Have fun. She seems to load her pants right after she has a bottle."

Jack opened his mouth to tell her to go to hell, then rethought the sentiment as the words "load her pants" struck home with him. "Don't push me, lady," he warned tightly.

"And don't you call me 'pumpkin,' " Keely responded, her jaw similarly clenched.

"Deal," Jack gritted out, hating himself. That remark probably had been a low blow. He could see it in the pain that had sparked in Keely's eyes. But, damn, she could piss off Miss Manners!

"Deal," Keely repeated. "But it's still your turn to get upchucked on. I'm going to go unload the carts."

Jack looked at Keely, looked down at M and M, who was still sucking on the-most-like-mother nipple. "God," he moaned quietly, thinking back to his conversation with Cecily. "I should have just said no."

"I know the feeling," Sally Hunsberger said, walking past him. "Damn, do I ever know the feeling."

# Chapter Four

*I've seen the future and it's much
like the present only longer.*

—Dan Quisenberry, pitcher

KEELY SAT ON THE FLOOR IN THE MIDDLE OF THE ROOM picked for M and M's nursery and wondered where to begin. Who said money didn't buy you a lot anymore?

Three-thousand-plus dollars ($3782.57, to be exact) still bought you same-day delivery and free setup, it turned out. And then there was 10 percent of almost four thousand dollars, and 50 percent of that.

Not bad for a half-day's work. Not hot damn, we're in the money—but not terrible, either.

In fact, things were going pretty well. Kind of well. Sort of well. Okay, so things weren't entirely awful. It was a start.

M and M was a darling baby. That was for openers. She drank when you gave her a bottle, burped when you patted her on the back, filled her diaper, then went to sleep. This also was not a bad thing, especially since Keely had yet to crack open any of the child-care books, and she was pretty sure there was a lot more to this taking-care-of-baby stuff than she'd encountered so far.

M and M was taking another nap, downstairs, in the seat safely stuck inside the wash basket, because Keely needed to go through the dozens of huge plastic bags now sitting on the bedroom floor with her, to try to make some sort of order out of the chaos.

She reached into the first bag as she looked around the room, liking the placement of the pecan wood crib, the matching dresser and changing table. Good traffic flow, allowing a clear path to the connecting bathroom. Good light, considering the room was on the east side of the house, to catch the morning sun. Nice color scheme, the green and beige muted plaid, the soft brown teddy bears that danced along the material.

The walls needed more than their existing basic coat of stark white paint, but that could wait. The wallpaper border and stuffed, puffy wall hangings could wait. More important now was finding some sort of order, planning some kind of system, some inkling of a schedule, for M and M, for herself.

Keely looked at the package she'd removed from the first bag. "Stupid thing, but it sure rattled Cousin Jack's chain," she said, looking at the step-by-step drawings of just how to take a plaster of Paris mold of M and M's foot for posterity. She stood up, carried the box to the huge walk-in closet, stuffed it on the shelf above the hanger-bar, then promptly forgot it.

Then she really went to work, placing the diaper pail next to the changing table, loading drawers with pads and sheets she'd wash as soon as she could find the time, carrying all the bath accessories into the bathroom, finding them all homes.

Keely was a neat person. Not a neat freak, not exactly, but she did believe in putting everything in its place and keeping it there. Tabletops were for inspired choices of flowers, knickknacks, decorative accent pieces that each made their own statement about the owner's taste and lifestyle. Closets were one of her near fetishes, and she could nearly drool over closet organizers, specially built-in shelving, color-coordinated shoe boxes.

Which is why, after about an hour, Keely was feeling pretty frustrated. She'd designed nurseries before, but that had been furniture and drapes—not the day-to-day, actually-*living*-with-a-baby type stuff.

There was no way to organize a baby, just no way. The powder and lotion containers, the jar of Vaseline, the baby wipes—all of it just sat there in the open, not adding a single bit of aesthetics to the decor. The huge pack of disposable diapers certainly could be stored in the closet, but she'd always have to remember to restock the drawer beneath the changing table, or else run the risk of having M and M bare-bottomed on the table and the nearest diaper twenty feet away.

"Babies are *messy*. They *sprawl*, like a two-thousand-pound gorilla, taking up space everywhere and anywhere," Keely concluded, hands on her hips as she looked around the room. The plastic bags were gone, most everything was put away, the crib was made up with all the new color-coordinated bedding, but the room still looked stuck together rather than put together. "And I'm beat," she added, running a hand through her hair, pushing errant blond curls behind her ears. "Time for a little break, a glass of something cold, and a nice, soft chair."

That's when Keely realized that one morning, almost four thousand dollars, and another two hours of work had added up to partially settling M and M—but did nothing to furnish the rest of the house.

Other than M and M's bedroom, the upstairs rooms were all empty, except for the master suite, which was . . . well, it was just pitiful, that's what it was. The man might as well be living under a bridge.

Downstairs, there was only one old chair in the huge den, a chair that should have been given a decent burial long ago. One sixties-era pole lamp, and one humongous television set that would take all her skill to decorate around so that it didn't look like the den was really a drive-in theater and the most logical furnishings would be a '57 Chevy, a speaker pole, and an open box of condoms.

She walked past the empty dining room, into the near-empty kitchen, gratified to see that M and M was still asleep. If there wasn't any furniture, at least there might be some food in the house that she'd overlooked earlier.

Keely had her head stuck inside the refrigerator, trying to figure out what she could make with ketchup, mustard, the last three Cecily-prepared bottles of formula, and what she hoped wasn't a very old egg, when Jack spoke from mere inches behind her. "Heads up," he said quietly. "Sadie's on her way over to check us out."

Keely didn't mean to take him literally, but he'd startled her, so that the back of her head definitely did come up, then sharply collided with the refrigerator door. "Damn it, Trehan!" she exploded, rubbing at her head.

At which point M and M woke up. Began to wail.

"Now look what you've done!" Keely pointed at M and M, whose face was rapidly turning fiery red. "You woke the baby."

"*I* woke the baby?" Jack said, both eyebrows raised in a way that made Keely want to smash the egg into his annoying face. "How? Did I slam the door when I came in? No. Did I stomp my feet? No. Did I yell? No-o-o-o, that wasn't me, was it? Me? I was baby-sitting, much against my will, while you played house upstairs for two hours. Then I take one small break, to go see my aunt and tell her what's going on, and I come back, tiptoeing in the door, tiptoeing across the floor, *whispering*—and you go ballistic."

‑God, he was smug. The man was just . . . *smug*. Keely decided she really hated smug in a man, even if his eyes were the most beautiful cobalt blue. *Especially* because his eyes were that beautiful cobalt blue. Doubly especially because, damn him, he was right.

So Keely took refuge in indignation, rightful or not, and stayed on the attack. "You left the baby alone again? How could you do that?" she asked, opening the car seat strap and lifting M and M into her arms. "What kind of *cretin* would leave a child alone? First in the car, and now again here. If you don't want the responsibility, Trehan, call your cousin Joey. He couldn't do any worse than you are."

Jack threw up his hands. "Five minutes. I was only gone for five minutes. Ten, tops. Christ, she was sleeping—she was *snoring*."

Keely shot him another dirty look, then opened the refrigerator, pulling out a bottle. "Here," she said, handing it to Jack. "Squeeze the air out, like the kid said. I'll change her diaper here on the floor. Then I'm calling the store and having them deliver another changing table and diaper pail, for somewhere downstairs. I don't know why I didn't think of it earlier."

"I told you we needed two diaper pails, if you'll recall. However, that being said, I have a question for you." Jack held the bottle out in front of him. "Refresh my memory, Ms. McBride. Where in our contract does it say I take orders from you?"

M and M had settled down in Keely's arms and was now contentedly pulling Keely's hair, trying to stuff a few locks into her mouth. "Forgive me, Mr. Big Baseball Star used to everybody bowing down in front of him," Keely shot back, glaring at Jack. "*Please* squeeze the air out of the liner like the kid said. There, is that better?"

"I don't like you, Ms. McBride," Jack said with some feeling. "I mean, I really, *really* don't like you."

"Ah, did you hear that, baby?" Keely said, trying to disengage M and M's chubby fingers from her hair. It had been a long day, one way and another, what with her new and unexpected job, Gregory Fontaine's news, and all the rest of it. Keely's temper suddenly outstripped her common sense and the memory of her checkbook balance. "Daddy doesn't love Mommy anymore. But he still *needs* her, and it's driving him crazy. Isn't that nice?"

"That's it! I mean, that . . . is . . . *it*. You're fired, Ms. McBride, and this time it sticks. I'll mail you a check for services rendered, but you're gone. Three strikes—hell, about six—and now you're out of here. My Aunt Sadie can watch M and M until I figure out what else to do, but I'll be damned if I'll have you in this house another minute. Got that?"

"Yoohoo! Here I am. Where's the alien baby?"

Keely, who had belatedly realized that she hadn't eaten all day and her low sugar had made her suicidal—why else would she have mouthed off to her only chance to reline her pockets?—turned to look at the woman who'd just entered the kitchen through the back door.

Jack had turned as well, and now spoke to his aunt. "Not an alien baby, Sadie. Cecily's baby."

"Same thing," Sadie Trehan said airily, shrugging her shoulders as she walked across the room, approaching Keely and M and M. "Oh, look at that. Isn't she *sweet*? Just like a little doll. Looks nothing like my late and unlamented brother-in-law, thank God, and rest his dry cleaning soul. Nothing like Florence, either, which is also a blessing, considering Flo and I were identical twins. I still think Florence tricked him, and both her kids belonged to the milkman. Who are you?" she asked Keely.

Good question. Keely wasn't sure anymore. She hadn't been sure since she'd first seen Jack Trehan's head popping out through the doorway early this morning. Everything after that had been a rather surreal experience; spit-up, paper towels, slippery infant, slipperier Gregory Fontaine—the bastard—her employer turning out to be a famous baseball player.

But Sadie Trehan put the topper on all of it. Short, pudgy in a way that looked good on her, Sadie was one of those apple-cheeked women who could be forty or eighty, because they never really aged. Her hair was a curly silver-white halo, her eyes huge and blue, her teeth the too-perfect white and straight of full dentures.

That was all okay. Just fine. But when you took all of Sadie Trehan and added in her navy blue Mickey Mouse shirt, her bright green-and-yellow-plaid Bermuda shorts (and dimpled knees), and her pink, fluffy kitty-cat slippers? Well, it was getting more than a little strange here at Happy Trehan Acres, that's what.

"I . . . I'm Keely McBride, Ms. Trehan. We spoke on the phone last week, when you hired me," Keely managed at last, pushing M and M into Jack's unwilling arms. "And your nephew just fired me, so I'll be going now, straight back to sanity, if I have any luck at all. Nice to meet you."

"John James Trehan, what did you do?" Sadie asked, grabbing at Keely's arm as she made to head for the nearest exit. "I thought you said she did a wonderful job this morning, taking care of the baby, furnishing a nursery. I also thought you finally were getting over your sulk and your bad temper. So you can't play baseball anymore? So what? That doesn't mean you can go around like some growling bear, biting everyone's head off. There is a child here who needs your help. There is a house here so empty I can hear my own voice echo, which isn't pleasant. Can't you see that there are things more important than a game?"

Keely watched, amazed, as Sadie Trehan turned big Jack Trehan into an itty-bitty little boy, a shame-faced child who still wanted to punch something but knew he'd be punished if he tried it. "I'm sorry, Aunt Sadie," he said, walking over to Keely, handing M and M back to her. "And I guess I do owe you some kind of apology. I really do need you around for M and M, you know, at least for a few days, until I can figure out something else to do," he admitted. "It's not your fault you've got a smart mouth and a lousy attitude."

"Gee, thanks," Keely said, rolling her eyes. "Remind me to ask you to write a letter of recommendation for my prospective clients once this is over. Now, if you'll excuse me, I think I'll take M and M upstairs to change her. And after that we need to find some food around here, or we'll literally be biting each other's heads off."

She got as far as the doorway when she stopped, sighed, shrugged her shoulders. Man, it was the pits having a polite upbringing, being saddled with a conscience.

"Okay," she said, heading back into the room, "here it is. You said you were sorry, so I'm going to say it, too. I'm sorry. I've been a first-class bitch. I need this job, Trehan. Worse, I need this job so badly I'll pretty much jump through any hoop I have to jump through to keep it, which is really, really torquing me, you know? I didn't go to school to be a baby-sitter. I had my own shop, in Manhattan, but it went belly-up. The guy you heard on my answering machine was my old boss, and my once lover—big, *big* mistake there—telling me he's taken over the lease on my shop and offering me the chance to work for him again, the bastard. So this hasn't been one of my better days, you know?"

"No, I didn't know. That's a tough one," Jack interrupted. "I'm sorry I teased you about that pumpkin thing. Really."

"Yeah, well, I'm sorry I didn't punch Gregory Fontaine in the chops before I left Manhattan, too, but that's the way it goes, and that part of my life is over, soon to be forgotten. So here's how it is now: I've come back home to Allentown, my tail between my legs, to

65

help my aunt at her shop while she cruises the Greek Isles or whatever, on her honeymoon. I'm in debt up to my ears, I'm lucky to have a roof over my head, and I know it, but I get fifty percent of her commission on any jobs I get while she's gone. Take care of M and M, walk your dog, clean your pool—you name it and I'll do it, just to keep this job. I'll hate myself, and you, but I'll damn well do it. I'm just trying to tell you that I wasn't cut out to be Little Miss Domestic Tranquility and I think I'll bake cookies from scratch today—not even when things were going well, okay?"

"Tail, ears, head, sunshine, no cookies. Got it. But fifty percent of what? I probably should have asked. I mean, I've already seen the damage you can do in one morning. By the time this place is furnished, I could be cashing in my pension to pay you."

"I doubt that. Cy Young? I'll bet your contract had more zeros in it than I can count—and I'm counting on at least one of those zeros being mine. Now, where was I? Oh, yeah. You were a gift from heaven, Trehan, and my salvation, and then you handed me this kid as a condition to my employment. I know nothing about babies that I haven't learned either from the movies, TV shows, or commercials. Nothing! But that doesn't mean I don't need your money, or that you don't need my help. You don't like me? Fine. I'm not all that cracked up about you, either. The way I see it, you're too damned used to getting your own way, being treated like the big shot, the sports hero. Well, whoop-de-doo. I'm all impressed. *Not.* I just want to do my job, *all* of my job, and take as much of your money as I can get, so that *I* can get out of Allentown and back to where I belong. You can understand that, can't you? I mean, you weren't the only one sent back to the minor leagues,

66

damn it, and you're not the only one with an ax to grind. Oh, and if you don't stop calling this poor abandoned child M and M I think I'm going to have to hurt you. Are we clear here now?"

"Clear as crystal. And don't swear around the baby."

"Oh, Jack. Jack, Jack, Jack," Sadie said, her grin as wide as the one on Mickey Mouse's cartoon face. "Keep her, boy. You'll never find so much honesty in one package again."

"Put a sock in it, Sadie." Jack shot his aunt a look that only made her smile wider, then grabbed his car keys from the counter, heading for the door. His hand on the doorknob, he looked back at Keely. "Take care of M and—the kid, okay? I'll be back when I get back."

"Well, wasn't that unpleasant?" Sadie asked as the door slammed. "I'd offer to help you, dear, but I know absolutely nothing about infants and have steadfastly refused to learn for sixty years. I don't want to jeopardize my record. Besides, my ceramics class starts in twenty minutes, and I still have to pick up Mitzi. I'll be late if I don't leave now. Jack said something about pumpkins. Do you like pumpkins? That's a coincidence, isn't it? We're starting on our holiday decorations, and today it's pumpkins for Halloween. Mine are going to be pink. I mean, why do it if you're only going to do the obvious, right? How *boring*. And I adore pink."

"Pink pumpkins?" Keely said as Sadie paused to take a breath. "Why, I guess . . . I suppose . . ."

"Never mind. I'll make you one. It's the least I can do. I don't remember the last time I saw Jack so completely incensed. He's been miles down in the dumps ever since he retired, and it's nice to see a little fire in his eyes again. Even Timothy couldn't get him to do anything except sit and sulk, feel sorry for himself,

67

and make nasty remarks. I'm surprised he and Timothy didn't end in a fist fight; I mean it. But now he's *alive* again, I can see it, although if you'll take an old lady's advice, you might want to tone it down a little now that you've made your point, just so he doesn't fire you again. You'll be good for him, I know it. You and this little thing both. Oh, and I wonder: Aren't you supposed to *warm* the milk for a baby? Never mind. I'm sure I don't really want to know. Well, gotta go!"

Keely opened her mouth, held out her hand, one finger raised, about to call Sadie Trehan back, then thought better of it. Some things are just better left alone.

"Warm the formula? That does seem to make sense, but how do I do it? Wait a minute—the microwave we bought. How could I have forgotten that? Man, am I ever in over my head. Come on, baby," she said, heading for the stairs that led from the kitchen to the rear of the upstairs hall.

She stopped at the top landing and looked out the window in time to see a small red convertible literally peeling down the drive, Sadie at the wheel. "Guess it's a good thing I didn't try to stop her, huh? What a strange, silly woman. By and large, sweetheart, you've got some pretty weird relatives. Yeah, well, we change you, we dust a little powder on your tush. We'll read the directions on the new bottles we just bought, and then we'll see what Mr. Spock says we do after that. I'm a college graduate, after all. I can read directions. Now, is that a plan or what?"

At the last moment, Jack had veered away from the garages, deciding what he needed was a long walk. A drive might end in road rage, he was so primed to *pop*.

Cripes, what a morning! Baby on his doorstep, smart mouth in his kitchen, Sadie on the loose. He hadn't even gotten to see the ball scores on ESPN.

Not that the sky would fall if he missed finding out how the Yankees had done last night. Nobody from the Yankees had called to see how *he* was doing, right?

Nobody wrote. Nobody called. Nobody gave a damn.

He was yesterday's news, the pitcher who could have gone to the Hall of Fame, the "used-to-be" who was only good now for after-dinner speeches at youth sports banquets and showing up for old-timers' games, his beer gut hanging over his belt.

And all while Tim went on and on. Catching. Slugging. Heading for the first-string All-Star team next month. Girls hanging all over him, ESPN calling for interviews. Getting the best table in restaurants, being recognized on the streets. Hanging out with the guys, swapping stories, pulling practical jokes on the bullpen catcher.

Not having to grow up, damn it!

That thought stopped him, just as he was about to give a kick to a stone that had somehow ended up on his well-manicured lawn. Grow up? Wasn't he a grown-up? Didn't he *want* to be a grown-up?

A game. Sadie had called his profession a game. Which it was, for the fans. For those who operated between the white lines, it was a whole hell of a lot more than just a game.

Scrabble was a game. Tiddledywinks was a game.

Baseball? Hell, baseball was a way of life!

Jack pulled up a patch of grass and sat himself down, leaning his back against a tree trunk as he considered a few things.

Baseball had never been a game to him; even though

it was called a game, what went on was called *playing* the game. He closed his eyes, remembering a quote from Pete Rose: "I'd walk through hell in a gasoline suit to play baseball."

Jack was pretty sure where Pete was coming from with that statement, that cry from the heart.

He knew that for him there was nothing else; he hadn't ever wanted to know anything else. He lived for the sights, the sounds, the smells. The look on the batter's face when he swung from the heels and connected with nothing but air, as Jack's curve whizzed by him, made a *pop* in the catcher's mitt. The three no-hitters, the all but perfect game. His lucky socks. That long walk to the mound, the sometimes even longer walk back to the dugout.

The guys. The fans. The attention.

All of that, all of that. But it was the *game* that he missed the most. The science of it, the mechanics, the strategies, the feel of the ball in his hand, the explosion of its release. The guys, the stats, the hot-foots they pulled during a laugher, when there was nothing to do in the dugout but have fun because the score was already sixteen to nothing. The sound of his spikes as he walked across the locker-room floor, damn it! He loved it. He loved it all.

He missed it all so much.

"God," Jack muttered, scrubbing at his face, trying to rub the memories out of his brain. "I lose the game, I've got an empty house, Cecily's kid, a bigmouthed pain in my ass out to empty my bank account and drive me nuts, and a whole bunch of *nothing* to look forward to. Add a tax audit, and my day would be complete."

He stood up, grabbed his car keys out of his pocket as he headed for the garage. "I've got to cut this out. I hate pity parties, and I sure don't like being the guest of honor. Sadie's right. I'm a mess, pathetic even. Something's gotta give here, and soon."

Keely turned the shopping cart to her right at the end of the row, heading for the next aisle. She'd missed shopping in a huge market, where she could buy anything from paper towels to filet mignon, all in one easy trip. Manhattan was full of delis, and small, specialty shops. Putting a meal together could mean stops at four different small stores, and the prices were enough to break your heart

She turned into the aisle reserved for canned vegetables, sauces, nine million varieties of pasta, and quickly grabbed at the baby's hand as she steered too close to a stack of canned corn. "You have more tentacles than an octopus, little girl," Keely said, still pushing the cart with one hand . . . right up until the moment the cart collided with one heading in the opposite direction.

"Oh! Sorry about that," she apologized quickly, instinctively checking to see if the baby was all right, although she was neatly strapped in to a baby seat built into the cart. "I wasn't watching where I was going."

"No kidding, Sherlock."

Keely looked up, straight into the gorgeous, maddening, sexy, and at the same time condemning blue eyes of one Jack Trehan. "*You*. What are you doing here?"

"Running jokes about women drivers through my head?" Jack suggested, then added, "I'm starving, that's why I'm here. Man cannot live by McDonald's quarter-pounders alone. I know, I've tried. Why are you here? And who's paying for that?" he asked, gesturing toward the heavily loaded cart.

Keely looked at the contents of the cart. "The Midol and shampoo are mine. I'll submit a bill to you for the rest of it. Do you like chicken? I thought we'd have chicken for dinner. Or hadn't you figured out yet that if I'm living at the house, I have to eat? I figure I can compromise a little, can cook for you, too, while I'm at it."

She gestured toward a white bag in the cart. "Want a doughnut? I've already eaten three, but there are two left. Or did you have lunch somewhere else?"

He looked at her out of the corner of his eye. "You cook?" He said it in the same tone he might have used to ask, "You make bombs in your basement?"

"Yes, I cook," Keely told him. "Oh, and I bought a couple of throwaway pans for the chicken and some baked potatoes, but I will have to do some heavy-duty shopping for pots, pans, dishes. I don't like paper plates, either. And I have to ask you—how long have you been living in that house? Living like . . . like . . . well, it couldn't have been for long, could it?"

"Less than a week," Jack told her, swinging his cart around so that they could walk, side-by-side, down the wide aisle. "I had the place built last year, and Sadie moved in over the garages, but I'd never planned on really *living* there. At least not for another ten years or so. I have a condo in Manhattan."

Keely pulled down two long, thin boxes of #11 pasta. "Ah, the obligatory condo in Manhattan. Overlooking the park, I'm sure. Lucky, solvent you. I had a third-floor walk-up in Brooklyn, with no air-conditioning in the summer and very little heat in the winter. I miss it like I'd miss a hair shirt."

"Traveling with the team, it just made sense to have my home base in New York," Jack told her as he dumped five cans of chili into his cart—dropping them next to two bottles of salsa and an economy size bag of corn tortillas. Obviously the man was a connoisseur of fine junk food, and with a cast-iron stomach. The only other items in his cart were a *TV Guide*, a pack of beef jerky, and a jar of hot sausages.

"See you're eating from all the basic food groups— spices, fat, preservatives. Breath mints and antacids might be a good choice, when we get to that aisle. So you didn't come back here, even to visit? Even in the off-season?"

"Tim—that's my brother—has a house here, and I usually bunk with him when I'm in town. The house is a tax write-off, that's all, and a way to give Sadie a place of her own. Or at least it was."

"I like your aunt Sadie. She's making me a pink pumpkin in ceramics class." They turned the corner, heading for the next aisle, the baby oohing and aahing at the lights above her head. "You know," Keely said after a moment, "I think we're having a conversation here, our first real conversation since we met this morning. It's rather nice, not throwing darts at each other all the time, especially since we're living together now. Are you as surprised as I am?"

He stopped his cart, and she had to look back at him.

"What? Now what did I say that's put your knickers in a twist?" she asked, just as willing to fight as to converse; the guy really did rub her the wrong way. Rich. Idle. Sucking up air and watching his stocks grow, and pushing all the real work onto everyone else. All while feeling sorry for himself, like his life was over. He ought to try being out of work *and* broke, and see how much he liked that! "Well? What's wrong now?"

"Nothing," he said after a moment. "I just . . . that

73

is . . . well, we will be living together for a while, like you just said, but that's because of M and M, not for any other reason. I just don't want you getting any ideas."

"Getting any—*what*! Oh, brother," Keely spat, shaking her head. "Go away, Jack Trehan. Get out of here now, while your head still fits through the doorway and you can stagger out to the parking lot. Getting any ideas? Yeah. Right. Like that's going to happen. Come on, kid, I think I'm in the mood for some expensive candy and ice cream shopping."

"Hey, look—don't get all . . . oh, the hell with it," she heard Jack say as she pushed the cart down the aisle.

She didn't look back.

# Chapter Five

*. . . but the saddest words of all to a*
*pitcher are three: "Take him out."*
—Christy Matthewson, pitcher

AUNT MARY'S CHARGE CARDS AND LINE OF CREDIT wouldn't cool down enough to touch for some time, or at least until Jack Trehan wrote one whopping big check, but Keely had made some very satisfying purchases in the past two days.

With M and M on her hip—she just called her "the baby" now, unable and unwilling to stick with the horrible M and M label—she had gone on a search-and-purchase mission through Macy's, Strawbridges, Sears, and even Wal-Mart, on a buying spree the likes of which probably hadn't been seen in Whitehall in a long time.

They now had pots and pans, dozens of them. Even a double boiler, which Keely had always secretly wanted, yet never purchased for herself. She'd picked up lovely plates at Pier One, then used the colors from the fruit-covered dishes—blues and greens and rusty reds, mustardy yellows—to accessorize the rest of the kitchen.

Now a wooden block of quite excellent knives sat on the counter, along with a white toaster, a blender, a Cuisinart that should have been plated with gold, it was that expensive, and a KitchenAid stand-up mixer with a motor powerful enough to mix concrete.

A huge wrought iron rack above the center island held the new assortment of copper-bottomed pans (installation by McBride, mistress of the portable drill and molly bolts). A glass-topped table with metal underpinnings and four matching chairs sat beneath a Tiffany style lamp that repeated the grapes and fruit motif that also was carried through to the glass fruit nesting in a clear, fluted glass bowl on the tabletop.

Bits and pieces were still missing, like the potted plants she planned to put in the corner near the French doors leading to the patio, but those could wait. This was a time for essentials. And, yes, Keely had decided, glass fruit on the kitchen table *was* an essential.

So she'd started with the kitchen, moving quickly to the bathrooms, where the neutral-beige fixtures made it easy for her to pick whatever color scheme struck her, and follow it through with curtains, towels, soap dishes, and thick, plush area rugs. She'd done up the powder room in blues and purples, the main bath in grass greens and bright yellows, and the master bath in black and white. Her own guest bath was done in peach and green, and the rest were left for another day.

The incompleteness of the job frustrated her, almost as much as having to stop dead every few minutes and see how the baby was, see how dinner was coming along, throw towels in the washing machine, or try to figure out where Jack Trehan was, because the man just wasn't ever home.

Not that she cared. Not as long as he was on time for meals.

But, hey, could he show just a little interest here? No, she supposed not. If he could step out of the shower and reach for a dry towel, what did he care if she'd hunted through the entire mall for just the right texture, just the right size? If he could sit down and feed his face with oven-roasted chicken and twice-baked potatoes, what did he care if she'd had to scrub those potatoes while holding a cranky baby who only shut up when she was being held?

That was another thing: She was taking a self-help crash course in the care and feeding of babies, and it wasn't easy. She'd watched the videos, read the books, and M and M was a good baby. But that didn't mean Keely wasn't still nervous, or that she wanted to spend all day talking to a baby who could only smile back at her. She felt like a neglected wife, a stressed-out, overworked mother, and she wasn't even married.

The man was oblivious, that's what he was. He walked around in a daze, watched the boob tube for hours on end, and then disappeared without a trace, going who only knew where, only showing up again in time to eat, shower, or watch more television. To him, Keely didn't exist. M and M didn't exist.

And another thing—the phone never rang. Shouldn't the phone ring at least once in a while? Didn't the guy have any friends? Then again, why should he? He wasn't exactly the friendly sort, now was he?

Still, Keely couldn't say she wasn't having the time of her life. The man made few rules: take care of the kid, furnish the house. No budget, no limits, no "Could you have the room painted to match my eyes?" He was about as hands-off an employer as a gal could wish for, and Keely nightly added up what she spent, multiplied it by ten percent, then divided by two. Still not megabucks, but she was getting there . . . and she'd only just begun. There was still an echo in the house.

But now she wanted, needed, his help. She couldn't furnish fifteen rooms without *some* sort of input from the client, and trying to figure out his taste based on one old chair, one TV, and a lamp with a hula girl on it— well, that just didn't work.

So he'd have to come with her on her next shopping trip, he'd just have to. The trick was in trying to figure out a way to make him understand that.

"You need a couch," she said Wednesday night at dinner, plopping a bowl of garlic mashed potatoes down on the tabletop, then sitting down across from him. A very domestic scene, if anyone was peeking in the windows; but then, looks were often deceiving.

"I need a lot of things," he answered, reaching for the bowl. "Buy them."

"Yes, I agree. Buy them. But *what* them? What do you like? French Provincial seems wrong, but I don't see you as wanting lots of chrome and wildly modern stuff either. Then there's the problem of delivery. I can't order special fabrics or shop where the furniture isn't available for quick delivery, which greatly limits my choices. I hate that."

Jack held up both hands, waving her to silence. "I don't get it. Where is any of this *my* problem?"

Keely momentarily imagined loading her spoon with mashed potatoes, then catapulting it across the table, smack into his face. "Oh, I don't know," she said, gritting her teeth. "Maybe it's your problem because you're the one who has to *live* with my choices. For instance, do you like the black-and-white motif in your bathroom?"

"That's a motif?" Jack asked, raising his eyebrows. "Well, damn, I've got a motif. Who would have thunk it. I thought I had towels."

"And rugs, and accessories, and—oh, never mind. Yes, you have towels. Thanks to me, you have towels. Now you need a couch. Chairs, lamps, carpets, drapes. Art for the tables, the walls. Are you saying you want me to pick everything? You want to leave the choices *entirely* up to me? I could think that faux leopard skin would look great on the dining room walls, you know."

Jack pinched his fingers at the bridge of his nose. "Look, Keely, I know this doesn't make much sense to you, but I just don't care, okay?"

"You would if I bought the most fashionable, uncomfortable furniture I could find," she interrupted.

"Would I? I'm living with one chair now and I'm making it. M and M has more furniture than I do. Who cares?"

"Who cares? I'm sleeping on the floor for the past two nights, and the man says who cares?"

"So buy a bed. Buy six beds. There's six bedrooms, right? Just get it done, okay?"

Keely sat back, shaking her head. "I don't get it. Is this depression? Are you really this upset about not being able to play baseball anymore? Should you be seeing somebody?"

"Oh, nice, nice," Jack said, slamming his fork on the

tabletop. "What comes next? Are you going to try to *analyze* me now, Keely? And I'm not depressed, damn it!"

"Could have fooled me," Keely said under her breath, earning herself a wicked look that probably should have warned her to keep her mouth shut, if Keely responded well to warnings.

"I'm thinking about renting the house out, that's all," Jack admitted, picking up his fork again, stabbing it into a piece of pork chop. "I just need furniture until I figure out what to do with M and M, where I'm going to put her until Cecily comes back, and then I'm probably going to rent the place, furnished if you do your job, unfurnished if you don't. I don't belong here."

Keely had pretty much stopped listening after he'd mentioned M and M. "Where to put her? What do you mean, where to *put* her? She's staying here, with you."

"That's impossible," Jack said shortly. "I might . . . well, I might be going to Japan."

"Japan?" Keely squeezed her eyes shut, knowing she was repeating what he said, knowing she was showing an interest she shouldn't be showing, knowing she was going to keep pushing until she got herself into big trouble. "What the hell is in Japan?"

"Baseball," Jack said, biting out the word as if it had landed, bitter, on his tongue. "I could only pitch every four or five days, and only in relief, but I still have enough of an arm left to give me a couple more seasons. Not in our majors, but over there, I'd be fine. Maybe I'd even get my arm back. It could happen."

Keely sat back in her chair, looked at him levelly. "You're nuts," she said frankly. "I mean it, Trehan. You're nuts. You'd chance ruining your arm completely, maybe maiming yourself, for a couple more seasons of baseball—in *Japan?* And what about the baby? You'd just leave, go off without the baby? How could you do that?"

Jack pushed back his chair, stood up. "We're not having this conversation," he told her, throwing down his napkin. "And the pork chops are tough," he ended before slamming out of the kitchen, just like an angry husband . . . while Keely sat there, just like a frustrated, insulted wife.

And they weren't even married.

Jack knew what was wrong with this house. There weren't enough doors, that's what was wrong. The rooms on the main living level all just sort of flowed together into one big room with some divider walls tossed in to push the furniture against. Screw the couches, he wanted doors. Doors that closed, locking out aunts and babies and a woman who always seemed to be where he didn't want her to be, tape measure in hand, ways to sink his bank balance at the ready.

He picked up the telephone in the den and walked into the powder room, shutting the door behind him. He felt like an idiot. Big Baseball Star (has-been baseball star) Hides In Bathroom. Film at eleven.

Yeah, well. He punched in the numbers on his brother's cell phone.

"Paradise Hotel, open all night. Bedwarming a specialty."

"Oh yeah? Well, book me two rooms overlooking the park, okay?" Jack said, shaking his head.

"Oh, hi, Jack," Tim Trehan said. "Sorry about that. I was expecting somebody else."

"Yeah, I'll bet you were. What's her name, if you even remembered to get her name."

"I remember, I remember. Give me a minute. Trixie?

No, that was Cincinnati. Okay, I got it now. If this is Chicago, then it must be Suzanne. See? And you thought I was the love 'em and leave 'em type."

"You are," Jack said, leaning against the sink, wondering if Tim could hear the echo in the tiled room across the new, wireless world. "Nice game yesterday; I saw it on cable. You're still taking too big a lead off second, though, you know, hot shot. Somebody's gonna burn your ass one of these days. Nothing looks dumber on the highlight clips than some clueless boob caught leaning the wrong way off second."

"Yeah, well, you never made it as far as second, brother mine," Tim shot back, laughing. "Good thing you could throw the ball, because you sure as hell never could hit it worth a damn. So, what's up?"

"Nothing. I'm watching grass grow. You should try it, it's very relaxing."

"I'll pass, thanks. And I mean it, what's up? You sound kind of . . . hollow."

Okay, so Tim could hear the echo. "All right, I do have a favor to ask."

"Ah, a favor. If it has anything to do with me peeing into a cup and impersonating you at a paternity hearing, forget it. Besides, I think we have the same DNA."

It was an old joke between them, but still Jack smiled. As identical twins, they'd traded places for school tests, dentist appointments, and even a date or two. "No, it's nothing like that, I promise. But I could use your help."

"Spill it," Tim said, and Jack could hear him moving around the hotel room, probably getting ready to head to Wrigley Field for the four o'clock game.

"Mort has a scout coming here Friday morning," Jack said, then waited for Tim's response.

"Scout? What kind of scout? Indian scout? Talent

81

scout? Mort's got you auditioning to play a part in a movie? You were great as Mr. Dental Floss to my Mr. Six-year Molar in Mrs. Harrison's class, but I don't think you're really ready for the big time, bro. But, hey, that's just me. What do I know? You go for it."

"Baseball scout," Jack said, then went on quickly, explaining himself, trying to sell himself. "I retired, sure, but the Yanks were ready to cut me loose, my contract's up next month, and they don't care if I play again, as long as it isn't here. So Mort arranged for a scout to come see me, a scout for a Japanese ball club. I don't want to do mouthwash ads, I want to pitch. And I can still pitch, Tim. Not a full game anymore, not at the major-league level, here in the States, but my name would be enough to fill seats in Japan for a couple of years."

There was silence, complete and utter, on the other end of the phone.

"Tim? Tim, you still there? Look, don't give me opinions, okay, just help me out. I can't leave the game yet, Tim. I'm not ready. The tryout has to be secret, because I don't want the press anywhere near this. You're back from your road trip late tonight, and you can drive up from Philly tomorrow morning, meet me at the high school ball field, and catch for me. Just like the old days, Tim. I pitch, you catch. It'll just look like the two of us, working out. Nobody'd know the difference. Tim? Say something, Tim."

"You're nuts," Tim answered at last.

Jack was beginning to sense a trend here. That made two—Keely, and now Tim. They both thought he was nuts. Mort didn't think he was nuts, but then, Mort got 10 percent of every penny Jack made, so maybe his couldn't be called an objective opinion.

"Okay, Tim, I'm nuts. Now close your eyes for a second and think about this. There's a knock on your door in the next five minutes, and the coach comes in to tell you you're being unconditionally released if you don't volunarily retire. You're through and, in his opinion, there isn't a franchise in the country willing to pick up your contract. And, damn, he's right—there isn't. What would you do, Tim? Take it on the chin, be a man, go home and find a hobby for the next fifty years? Maybe whittling. Would you like whittling, Tim?"

"Jack . . . Jack, Jack, Jack," Tim said, and Jack could see his brother in his mind's eye, pacing the floor, shaking his head. "You don't want to go out that way. Pitiful, some sad, pathetic shadow of your former self, hanging on past your prime . . ."

"My prime? I was just hitting my stride, Tim, and you know it. If it hadn't been for my rotator cuff, I'd still be out there, taking my—"

"Jack," Tim interrupted firmly, "you're probably going to the Hall of Fame. Sure, you only pitched in the majors for seven years. Sandy Koufax didn't do much more, and he got there. Okay, maybe not on the first shot for you, but you'll get there. You've got two Cy Youngs, three World Series rings. You want to risk all that to play mediocre ball with a mediocre arm? People remember best what they see last. Do you want them to remember you in Yankee pinstripes, or bowing to the batter before you lob him a fat one that goes over the fence?"

Jack sat down, on the only seat available to him. "I can't hack it, Tim. I'm trying—God, I'm trying—but I just can't hack it. I've got to give it another shot, at least *try* to get back in the game."

There was another small silence, and then Tim said, "Okay, bro. You talking the field at Whitehall High? I can be there by nine. Friday morning, right? Is that good enough?"

Jack felt his body collapsing with relief. "Thanks, Tim. I knew I could count on you."

"Yeah? Well, you can. Because I'm catching that ball you're throwing, remember that. And if I say you don't have it anymore, then you damn well don't have it anymore. Are you ready to hear that—from me, from your brother?"

"No, I'm not ready to hear that," Jack answered honestly. "But I'd believe you. See you tomorrow morning. And thanks."

Jack hit the disconnect button and let himself out of the bathroom, wondering where Keely, the Wonder Woman Decorator, was lurking now, ready to jump out at him asking if he liked cherry or blond woods.

Nothing. She wasn't in the living room, measuring for drapes. She wasn't in the den, making the evil eye at a perfectly fine television set. She wasn't in the kitchen, although something sure smelled good—he was pretty sure the smell came from something in a pot on the counter. Stew? He walked over, lifted the lid so that steam escaped into the air. Yeah, stew. He liked stew. Not that he'd tell her that.

He looked up at the clock Keely had hung above the sink, mentally figuring out how much time he had between now and dinner, then deciding to go out to the garage and throw a little. He'd gotten a tire, hung it from a rope inside the garage, and backed it up with a strong net. Standing outside the open door, on a mound of dirt he'd hauled onto the driveway, he'd created a crude but workable setup for working out his arm, the inside of the tire making a strict strike zone. It was how he had learned, all those years ago, and it was how he chose to work now.

He reached up to his right shoulder, rubbing at it: Okay, so he was sore, a little worse than just sore. Who wouldn't be sore? He hadn't pitched in two months. And maybe he was pushing a little hard; three workouts a day. But, then, he had the rest of his life to rest, if this didn't work out . . . and three kinds of liniment in his medicine chest.

He was just heading for the back door when he heard it, stopped. M and M. Crying. The sound came to him down the back staircase. He waited a second, then headed toward the door once more, hesitating with his hand on the doorknob. The kid was still crying, and getting louder.

Where was Keely? Why wasn't she picking the kid up? She had that kid on her hip so often, anyone would think the two of them were attached, for crying out loud.

M and M's wails grew louder, angrier.

"Aw, hell," Jack said, letting go of the doorknob, heading for the stairs.

This wasn't a part of his plans, any of his plans. He needed M and M around like he needed another rotator-cuff surgery. Damn Cecily. Damn Keely for not living up to her end of the bargain. Damn him for getting himself into this mess in the first place. He should have called Joey, better yet, Child Welfare, within minutes of finding M and M on his doorstep.

That's what any sane man would have done.

Jack walked down the hallway, peering into each room he passed, looking for Keely. It was as if the woman had disappeared into the ether.

The door to M and M's room was open, and her wails

85

filled the upstairs hallway. Jack sighed, squared his shoulders, and walked in, to see M and M sitting in the middle of the crib mattress, flowered jammies riding high on her chubby legs, blond curls stuck to her head by a combination of perspiration, tears, and probably snot. Her cheeks were red, her huge blue eyes looking like drenched violets. Drenched violets? Where the hell had *that* come from?

Jack shook his head and approached the crib. "Hey, kiddo, what's up?" he asked.

M and M shut up, looked at him. Her bottom lip trembled, her entire body shuddered. And then she raised her arms to him as yet another tear rolled down her chubby cheek.

"Oh, no," Jack said, backing up a step. "Not in this lifetime. I had a year of you for a couple of hours the other day, and that was more than enough, okay?"

M and M shuddered again, whimpered. She drew in a deep breath, let it out in a hiccuping half sigh, half sob.

"Not working, kiddo. I'm not feeling the least bit guilty. I took you in, got you this great crib. But nobody said I was going to play daddy, you got that.? No daddy. No, no daddy."

"Da," M and M said, waving her arms. "Da-da-da!"

Jack's eyes opened wider. "Who taught you that?"

"Da-da-da-da-*da!*"

"I am *not* your—Jack looked around behind him, saw that he was still alone in the room with M and M. "Oh, hell," he said, surrendering. Did he have any choice? If he walked away, she'd just go off again, so he might as well pick her up.

He looked at the crib railing, wondering how to lower it, because it looked as if it could be lowered. And it probably could, he decided about a minute later, by someone with a degree in mechanical engineering. That wasn't him.

He reached over the bars, gingerly grabbed M and M beneath her arms, and hefted her out of the crib. M and M immediately shoved two wet, sticky hands into his face, one grabbing onto his ear, one unerringly closing around his bottom lip.

"Da-da-da-da-da!"

Da-da—that is, Jack—in a move made purely in self-defense, carried M and M over to the changing table, laid her down, pried her fingers loose. He grabbed a small terry-cloth square from the shelf under the table and began wiping M and M down as she looked up at him, dark eyelashes kissing with moisture, her rosebud mouth still open, still singing the same "Da-da" song.

"There? Better now?" he asked, not realizing that his voice had gone rather soft, gentle. "Now, do you want to tell me what's wrong? Hmmm?" he said, careful to hold on to her little wrists. "Come on, tell Jack what's wrong. Did that big bad Keely leave you here all alone? Bad Keely. Bad, bad Keely."

M and M's bottom lip did its thing again, and Jack quickly smiled once he realized he'd been frowning. Grinning ear to ear, even as he wondered why he was doing it, he repeated, "Bad, bad Keely."

M and M cooed, or gurgled, or whatever it was she did. Whatever it was, it was darn cute.

"Yeah, that's it," he said, encouraged. Keeping his tone light, his smile in place as he leaned over the baby, he went on, "Keely bad. Jack good, but Keely b-a-a-d-d. Not bad-looking, grant you . . . but she's got a *mouth* on her . . . and an *attitude* . . ."

M and M cooed.

"Oh, you know that, do you? Well, I guess you

87

should, being with her all the time. Poor kid. But she's a real pain, isn't she? She fell as flat on her face as I did on mine, and now she's swaggering around here, acting like she'll be back on her feet in no time. Shopping, cooking, decorating, taking care of you, and making it all look so damn—er, so darn easy. Letting me know she's pulling herself back up by her own bootstraps, while I'm just sulking. Bootstraps! Cecily used that word, as I remember, which should tell us something, right? But that's what she thinks, you know. I can tell. Grinding my face in it, that's what she's doing."

M and M frowned, blinked.

"What? You think I'm overreacting?" Jack asked the baby. "I'm not, you know. She made it plain that first day. She's resourceful, and I'm a self-pitying idiot. Yeah, well, as long as she's being good to you, huh, sweetheart? And you are a sweetheart, aren't you? When you're dry, and don't smell bad. And you've got the fattest belly . . ."

Jack lifted the hem of the pajama top, exposing that firm, fat belly, then gave in to an impulse he'd never understand. He bent his head, pressed his lips to M and M's belly and blew . . . blew air bubbles against that soft skin.

And M and M giggled.

She really giggled!

Jack lifted his head, smiled at the baby. "You liked that?" he asked, feeling pretty proud of himself. Five minutes ago, the kid had been yelling to bring the house down, and now she was giggling. Who said this taking care of babies stuff was so damn hard? Anything Keely McBride could do, he could do better, or at least just as well.

He bent his head again, blew more air bubbles . . . and M and M giggled again.

He let go of her hands as she began kicking her feet, and her fingers quickly gripped his ears, her tiny nails digging into him as he bent, blew more bubbles.

M and M giggled.

Jack laughed.

And Keely, standing just inside the doorway, watched for a few moments, blinking quickly so that her eyes would stop their sudden stinging, then turned, pulled her terry robe closer around her body, and went off to get dressed after her shower.

Ten minutes later, Keely made her way back down the hallway, careful to loudly hum a tune, so that Jack would know she was coming.

She turned the corner into the baby's room, to see Jack standing next to the changing table, his shaggy dark blond hair sticking up stiffly in a couple of spots, one hand on the baby's bare belly, and a where-the-hell-have-*you*-been glare on his face.

He even said it: "Where the hell have *you* been? I've been stuck with a screaming kid for an hour now."

"An hour?" Keely repeated, raising an eyebrow. "Oh, I doubt that, considering I only stepped into the shower a half hour ago, and Mary Margaret was sound asleep at the time. I know, because I checked."

"Yeah, well maybe it just *felt* like an hour. I've got a lot to do, you know, and I don't have time to be baby-sitting M and—*what* did you call her?"

"Mary Margaret," Keely said, feeling just a little bit silly. "Or Margaret Mary. That would work, too, right? I just can't keep on calling this adorable child M and M. I told you that."

"Mary Margaret Morretti. Sounds like every teacher's pet at the local parochial school."

"You like Magenta Moon Morretti better?"

Jack looked down at the baby. "I wouldn't do that to a dog," he said, then picked up Mary Margaret and walked toward Keely. "Here, your turn. I'm outta here."

Keely quickly followed after him—she wouldn't quite call it "dogging his heels," but the term fit pretty well. "Got places to go, people to see, huh? Busy, busy, busy. Doing *what?* Taking a class in Japanese? Composing a letter to Cecily, telling her you turned this sweet little baby over to some child welfare agency because you have this burning need to go overseas and make an ass out of yourself? How can you be so . . . so selfish!"

Jack had gotten as far as the top landing of the back stairs before he stopped, raised his spread hands to shoulder height, and turned around, fire in his eyes. "Shut. Up."

Keely took a single step backward, made a big production out of pulling Mary Margaret closer to her. "Ooooh, now we're scared," she said, using the sarcasm her Aunt Mary had warned her would someday end with needing her jaw wired shut for six weeks, if not worse. But she didn't care. *Somebody* had to consider Mary Margaret's best interests, and it looked like she'd been elected, or drafted, or something.

Jack raised his hands further, slammed them against either side of his head. "I'm *paying* you? I've got to be out of my tiny mind!"

"Yeah, well, you are out of your tiny mind, Trehan," Keely went on, squeezing Mary Margaret so tightly that the child began to whimper, struggle in her arms. "I didn't ask for this kid either, you know, but I've got her, and you've got her, and I'll be *damned* if I'm going to let you walk away from her. She's not just a

90

responsibility, or an inconvenience. She's a *baby*. She needs her family."

"We're *not* her family. Her family is certifiable, but we're still not her family, even if I am thinking about committing myself, because *you're driving me nuts*. M and—Mary Margaret is not my problem. I don't even like kids."

Keely kept her mouth closed for about ten seconds while Jack stood there, glaring at her. "Saw you," she said then, lifting her chin.

"Saw me? Saw me what? You saw me? What in hell is that supposed to mean?"

"It means, Mr. *Jerk* Trehan, that I saw you with Mary Margaret. Blowing bubbles on her belly." She sort of stretched her compressed lips, smacked them together a time or two, making a sort of popping sound, then said it again: "Yup." *Smack, smack, pop, pop.* "Yes, indeedy. Saw you."

She watched, smiling, as Jack Trehan turned on his heels—not before his cheeks had flushed an angry, guilty red—and slammed down the steps.

Keely then turned to head back down the hall, to change Mary Margaret's diaper, get her dressed after her nap. "Japan my trim and shapely patootie! He's going to stay right here with you, sweetheart, and you're going to stay right here with him. Because that's the way it's supposed to be, if only he'd stop feeling sorry for himself long enough to figure out that one door doesn't close unless another one opens, as my Aunt Mary used to say. You'll get him yet, kiddo, I promise," she told the baby, kissing Mary Margaret's forehead.

She laid the cooing infant on the changing table and began unsnapping her pajamas. "We'll get you dressed, you can have a bottle, and then we're going to go buy us a couch, and that's just for starters. You like going bye-bye in the car, don't you, sweetheart? But first, let's practice some more, all right. Here we go. Da. Da. *Da-da-da.*"

# Chapter Six

*A lot of things run through your head*
*when you're going in to relieve in a tight spot.*
*One of them was, "Should I spike myself?"*
                                        —Lefty Gomez, pitcher

MARY MARGARET, ALWAYS THE LADY, GAVE OUT with a genteel burp, then smiled at Keely.

"Yes, that was lovely," Keely complimented her, one eye on the kitchen clock. "All done now? Good. Because now we go find Da-da, okay? He's going shopping with us this afternoon, whether he knows it or not."

Keely stood up, carried the plate holding the last of her tuna fish salad sandwich to the sink, and looked out the window, hoping to see Jack's car still parked on the edge of the drive that wound around to the garages that sat lower on the hillside, out of sight of the house. Why the man didn't park *in* the garage eluded her, but maybe he had a reason—a stupid, male reason, but a reason.

"Good. He's still lurking around here somewhere, doing his pity poor little me impersonation. I've got the car seat in the car, the stroller in the trunk, and a shopping list as long as an orangutan's arm. I drive the car, he pilots the van, and we won't come home without a mattress for Aunt Keely. How does that sound? Now, we'll just go get your sun bonnet and we'll be on our

92

way to—oh, nuts." Keely turned away from the window, wishing she hadn't seen Sadie Trehan wave to her as she headed up the path from her apartment over the distant garages.

"Okay, kiddo, look busy," Keely said, grabbing up the sun bonnet covered in tiny pink rosebuds, then reaching for her car keys. "Busy, busy, busy, just ready to head out the door, right? Places to go, people to see, no time to chat, so sorry."

"Yoohoo! Kee-ly!" she heard through the open kitchen window, then turned, smile in place, ready to get rid of Jack's aunt as fast as she could. Not that she didn't like the woman. She barely knew her. But she had *plans.*

The back door opened and Sadie Trehan stepped inside. "Ah, there you are. And with the baby, too. Wonderful. Stay there, I'll be right back."

Keely had already opened her mouth to say she had just been on the verge of leaving to run some highly important errands, but she shut her mouth again rather than speak to an empty, open doorway.

She looked around the room, spotted Mary Margaret's empty bottle on the table, and picked it up, carried that to the sink as well. That took about ten seconds. Still, with Mary Margaret on her hip, she went over to the refrigerator and yanked open the freezer door while mentally debating defrosting some veal for cutlets, or hoping she and Jack wouldn't have killed each other before she could talk him into grabbing some takeout at the local KFC. This "a woman's work is never done" crap was beginning to get on her nerves.

Reaching inside with her free hand, Keely tried locating the package of veal. What her hand landed on was a plastic bag filled with ice. One bag, two bags.

Three. The refrigerator was the kind that came with a service bar built into the freezer door, the kind that shot out ice water or crushed or cubed ice on command. There was no reason, no need, to store ice in plastic bags. "Now, why in the world would—?"

"All right, I'm back. And we've got company," Sadie trilled, so Keely put back the bag of ice—not really cubes, but a misshapen *lump* of ice that probably had once been cubes, then melted and refrozen—and turned around.

"Hello," she said, blinking, trying not to stare. "Who's this, Sadie?"

*What's* this would have been a better question.

What—who it was, was a female, that much was obvious. But from what solar system? Tiny, no more than five feet high, and probably weighing less than a hundred pounds (Keely hated her already), the girl nevertheless seemed to fill the kitchen. With color. She wore lime green Seventies-retro bell bottoms that hung low enough to expose the slim silver ring through her navel. Her striped crop top of lime green, hot pink, and putrid purple was reproduced in the matching streaks in her long, straight blond hair. Her eyelids were purple, her cheeks hot pink, and her lips—good God almighty, her lips were green.

She had another silver ring through her left eye brow and at least six silver hoops marching up her left ear, half as many on her right earlobe. And when Keely at last found her voice and said hello, the multicolored creature gave herself a small shake, spread her arms wide, and said, "Right back at ya, Keel," then wagged her tongue at Keely, exposing a small silver ball stuck in the center of that pink, wiggly . . . oh, yuk!

"This is Petra, Keely," Sadie said rather proudly,

putting one arm around the girl's shoulders. "Mitzi's stepdaughter, here for the summer. She's studying art in Philadelphia. Isn't that nice?"

Petra was already moving toward Keely, who had instinctively wrapped both arms tightly around Mary Margaret, in case whatever Petra had might be catching. "So this is the little squirt? She's outrageous! Those big eyes, those curls. I mean, can you even deal? I can't even *deal!*"

"Deal with what?" Keely asked, stepping back a pace.

"With how outrageous she is, how *cute.*" Petra put out her hands, waggled her heavily ringed fingers invitingly. "Can I hold her?"

Keely felt her mind going blank, as if she were some small animal being mesmerized by an exotic snake. "No-o-o-o, I don't think so . . ." she began, just as Mary Margaret cooed and reached out her arms to the Technicolor Teen.

"Well, would you look at that," Sadie Trehan said. "It's just like Mitzi told me. Petra, you certainly do have a way with children. Instant rapport, don't you think, Keely? Go on, let Petra hold her."

Mary Margaret was squirming in her arms, so that Keely didn't really have much choice. She handed the baby to Petra. After all, it wasn't like the kid could get far before Keely tackled her.

Keely looked at Sadie, the woman's Hawaiian print pedal pushers and "Bite Me" T-shirt having very little power to shock now that Petra was in the room. "Well, this has been . . . grand, really, but I'm afraid you caught us just as we were leaving."

"Leaving for where, dear?" Sadie asked, lifting the lid on the cookie jar Keely hadn't been able to resist—a round, squat creation that looked an awful lot like

Cartman from "South Park." "Oh, you're going to the supermarket?" she asked, lowering the lid once more on the empty jar. "Jack says you're a pretty good cook, so I had hopes. Do you bake, dear?"

Keely watched as Petra stuck out her tongue, exposing the silver ball, and Mary Margaret reached for it, giggling. How bad could exposing a child this young to a walking, talking Piercing Pagoda be? "Huh?" she said belatedly, realizing that Sadie had been talking to her.

"Bake," Sadie repeated. "Do you bake? Cookies, cakes? Pies?"

"Cookies," Keely answered absently, walking over to retrieve Mary Margaret before any serious contamination could set in. The baby turned her head, ignoring Keely, and began playing with Petra's rainbow hair. Abandoned—Keely had been abandoned by a fickle little turncoat in a sun bonnet. She put down her arms, pretending Mary Margaret's defection hadn't hurt, and turned back to Sadie. "Not that I've had time . . ."

"Ah, but you will now, dear," Sadie said; crowed, actually. "Keely McBride, meet your new baby-sitter, Petra Polinski. It's all settled. You need more time to get the echo out of this place, and Petra needs some spending money now that George—that's Mitzi's husband—cut off her allowance because of some silly parking tickets she got while at school. A solution that suits everyone. I already asked Jack, and he said it was fine with him. So? Am I a genius or what?"

Keely leaned one hip against the counter. How had this happened? Rejected by Mary Margaret. Replaced by an air-headed kid with a hole in her navel and several dozen in her head, most of them between her ears. All without warning.

96

It hurt. Damn, it hurt.

"Oh, God," she mumbled under her breath. And then she got mad. With one last look at Petra Polinski, who was now seated in a chair, bouncing a delighted Mary Margaret on her lap, Keely headed for the door, intent on killing Jack Trehan—and no jury in the country would convict her!

It wasn't the roar of the crowd Jack missed, it was the damn tire. Missed the hole, missed the rim, missed the whole damn thing. Hell, he was lucky to have hit the net.

Rubbing at his shoulder, he bent to pick up another ball, then straightened, found the rubber with his toe, and glared down the tire. He put his right hand behind his back and rotated the ball between his fingers, deciding on a pitch.

He lifted his Yankee cap with a push from his mitt, wiping his forearm on his brow, blotting away beads of perspiration that had come half from physical exertion, half from the damn anxiety that he couldn't seem to beat down. He felt his T-shirt sticking to his back and thought seriously about calling the practice session short so he could go turn the garden hose on himself.

But, no. Tim and the scout were coming tomorrow morning. He had to keep working.

So what would he try now? Not heat, definitely. He didn't have enough heat in his arm right now to warm a leftover taco. He'd worked the curve ball in his morning workout and didn't want to chance aggravating his old elbow injury by throwing more curves now.

But those were his two best pitches. The fast ball, the sinking curve. Those were the pitches that had got him to the majors, had kept him in the majors.

So what was left? If you couldn't blow the batter down with heat, you had to learn how to dazzle him with bullshit. Without speed, there was still finesse, variety, and luck. And wasn't it Hall of Fame hurler Lefty Gomez who'd said he'd rather be lucky than good? Then again, Jack remembered, Gomez had also been quoted as saying he'd got a great new invention, a revolving bowl for tired goldfish.

Hey, everything a pitcher said couldn't be profound, right?

Jack positioned his fingers, deciding on a slider. Still glaring at the center of the tire, as if it were really the catcher's mitt, he went into his motion, stopping at the height of it, ready to fling his leg forward, come through with the ball.

"Yo! You—Babe Frigging Ruth! You just hold it right there!"

Jack stumbled forward, his concentration broken, nearly landing on his face on the driveway.

"Holy, jumping—what in *hell* is the matter with you, lady?" he shouted, glaring at Keely.

She had called to him from about twenty feet away and now was advancing on him with all the determination of a pissed-off elephant looking for a village to stomp into splinters. "Me? What's the matter with *me*? Did I just throw my innocent cousin straight into the jaws of a pierced, dyed, and lobotomized *flake?* I don't think so!"

Jack pulled off his glove, tucked it under his arm as he walked off the makeshift mound. "You know, I've thought this about you. You're just the sort of intense, overachieving, sure-of-herself kind of person who snaps sooner or later. What are you talking about?"

"I have *not* snapped—but don't you tempt me,

98

because I'd snap all over you. Petra Polinski—that's what I'm talking about. How could you? God, Trehan, she has to glow in the dark! Worse, if you stuck a flashlight to one ear, you could use the beam coming out the other ear like a lighthouse lamp. And you expect me to turn Mary Margaret over to her, just because I get on your nerves, hit you with the truth, and the truth hurts? In a pig's eye, Jack Trehan. In a pig's eye!"

He stood his ground, amazed at how attractive Keely McBride was when incensed. Her huge brown eyes had turned almost black with rage, and her honey-blond hair was coming free from its pins, so that fairly tight, corkscrew curls kissed her flushed cheeks, her slim neck. All as she walked toward him on her long legs, her body moving straight up to her hips with each step, giving him a mind picture that would probably get him killed if she could see it. Not that she didn't already look like murder was on her mind.

"I don't know what you're talking about," he said, backing up onto the mound a little, raising himself higher, even though she only came to about chin level anyway. "Oh. Wait. This is about Sadie's pal Mitzi's stepkid, right?"

"Ah," Keely purred—the purr of a lioness pleased with just how the gazelle's leg tasted, "so you *do* remember. Who said there's only one male brain, and all of you have to share it? Guess you got it today, huh, sport? But you couldn't have had it when you saw Petra Polinski."

"Saw her? I didn't see her. Why would I have to see her? Sadie said she was a good kid, and that's enough for me. Besides, I thought you wanted to get this job done before Christmas. Dragging M and—Mary Margaret with you all over town can't be making your job easier." He spread his hands, palms up. "So now you have help. I think it's brilliant, personally."

Keely looked at him, her eyelids slitted, her jaw working even as she kept her lips closely shut.

"What?" he asked, starting to feel guilty, God only knew why. "What's the problem? I'm not firing you. You still get to take me to the cleaners. And the kid can only be here days, because she's taking some evening classes somewhere, so you're still as indispensable as I hate you being."

Taking a deep breath, Keely blew heated air out her nostrils. Jack tried not to put up his arms, ready to defend himself. First an elephant, then a lioness, and now a bull ready to charge. Probably bad comparisons, considering she was only about five foot six, couldn't weigh more than a hundred and twenty pounds, dripping wet and rolled in mud.

But he couldn't help himself. The usual comparisons, when thinking about pretty women, were that they were graceful doves, or sleek kittens, or cuddly, fuzzy little something-or-others. Keely McBride was none of those. She might look the part, but Jack wasn't stupid. She had all the soft, cuddly instincts of a hyena. And a mouth and disposition to match.

"Come . . . with . . . me," she said at last, then turned on her heel and started back across the grass, heading up the hill, toward the house. It wasn't a request, it was an order.

Jack put down his mitt and followed her, intrigued in spite of himself. Because something had sure set Keely off, and he kind of wanted to see what it was. If it was Mitzi's stepdaughter, he'd give the girl a raise, even before she started the job.

He had to break into a trot to catch up with Keely,

although he didn't do that right away, rather enjoying watching her hips sway as she climbed the hill. Hey, a guy took his pleasures where he could get them!

"So exactly what's the matter with Mitzi's stepdaughter?" he asked when he fell into step with Keely about a hundred feet from the house. "I didn't quite get what you were saying back there."

"That's because there aren't enough words to describe her," Keely bit out. "You'll see soon enough."

She moved ahead of him, skirting the in-ground pool, and hit the flagstone patio first, pushing open the door to the kitchen, then standing back, motioning for him to enter ahead of her.

"You're weird," he told her as he pushed the ball cap farther back on his head and stepped into the kitchen. "I mean, you're really out there."

"Hey, thanks," came a voice from his left, behind the open door: "You're kind of out there yourself. Especially if you like sweat, right? Because you sorta reek, you know?"

Jack's head swiveled on his neck at the sound of a young, ridiculously cheerful female voice. "Pardon me?" he asked, right before his eyeballs froze at the sight in front of him.

It was a circus clown, it was a character stepping off a psychedelic Volkswagen bus, it was a public service ad for "Do you know where your children are?" It was . . . it was . . . it was *holding M and M!* "Sadie!"

His Aunt Sadie wandered in from the den, holding a cellophane bag of oatmeal cookies, the kind with white icing slathered on them and left to harden. "Yes, dear? I was watching my soap. You know, on your huge screen, those bedroom scenes seem to take on a whole new perspective. Is there a problem?"

101

Glaring at Sadie, he stuck his left arm out, pointing toward Petra Polinski. "*This* is your idea of a solution? Hey, Charles Manson might get out on bail one of these days. Maybe we should wait for him to take care of M and M."

"Don't be facetious, dude," Petra said, putting Mary Margaret into her jumper seat and walking over to stand in front of him. "I'm going through a phase, okay, and this one is about over anyway. Lighten up. I won't hurt the kid. I'm certified in CPR, know the Heimlich Maneuver, the whole ball of wax. That was another phase, but I am *so* over that one. Thought I wanted to be a doctor. Granted, Daddy liked that phase better, but hey, I'm an artist now. An artist has to try new things, right? So why don't you stop wigging out, like the little lady behind you is doing, and give me a chance?"

"How old are you?" Jack asked, stalling for time, as all brave hunters do until they can find a stick. Because he had to get Petra Polinski out of here before M and M was emotionally scarred for life.

Petra rolled her eyes. "Like, I knew I should bring a résumé? Jeez Louise. Okay, here goes: I'm seventeen."

"No, you're not," Jack said. "You can't be, because Sadie said you were a junior in college. I distinctly remember her saying that."

"Well, duh," Petra said, dropping her jaw. "You never heard of child geniuses? Because you're looking at one, you know. I've been in college since I was twelve. I just don't seem to ever graduate."

Jack blinked several times, rapidly, then turned back toward his aunt. "Sadie?"

"She's fine, Jack. Mitzi promised me. And this is just a phase. Last year she was tutoring other students in physics. Petra's just a free spirit, investigating life. Besides, I think she's colorful."

Jack didn't know how to answer and was happy to be saved by Keely, who pushed him to one side as she approached the teenager. "Okay, *genius*. What do you do if Mary Margaret's choking?" she asked, leaning forward from the waist, her every muscle tensed.

Petra rolled her eyes. "Well, if she were a grown-up, I'd use the standard method, but that would break her little ribs. So I'd lay her down, find the same spot on her upper belly, then give her a couple of quick *pushes*, like this," she ended, demonstrating with her hands. "And, it's like totally rad, I mean it, when that little piece of whatever comes popping right out of the doll's mouth. We practiced on dolls."

"A-ha!" Keely crowed, as if Petra had just admitted she'd done it in the library, with the wrench. "So you've never actually *performed* the maneuver on a real baby."

Petra inspected her short, stubby, green-painted fingernails. An American flag was painted on her left pinky. "Yeah, right, girl. Like *you* have?"

Jack coughed to cover a laugh and went over to the cabinets, pulling out a glass he stuck under the dispenser in the refrigerator door, then emptied the glass in a few deep swallows. Then he reached inside the freezer, grabbed one of his ice bags, and held it to his shoulder as he leaned against the countertop to watch. This could be fun.

"What do you do if the house is on fire?" Keely persisted, and Jack remembered the titles on the stack of VCR tapes he'd found in the den, knowing one was on child safety.

"Oh, cool, we're going to have a real quiz?" Petra asked, settling herself in one of the kitchen chairs. "Okay. I grab the kid, the portable phone, and my bottle

103

of nail polish—in that order—and get out of the house. Call nine-one-one and break out the marshmallows. Next question?"

Jack could see Keely's eyes beginning to glisten, as if—and who would have thunk it—she might burst into tears at any moment. He put down the ice bag, pushed himself away from the kitchen counter, and walked over to Keely, grabbed her by one elbow. "Okay, she passes the test, right? You've got yourself some help. Now, what do you say you go measure something while I shower, and then the two of us can go buy a couch. Does that work for you?"

Keely's bottom lip began to tremble, but she bit down on it with her top teeth, nodding her agreement.

"Fine. Great," Jack said, wondering what had hit him, why he'd suddenly turned into Mr. Nice Guy, especially when he couldn't stand the woman. And, hey, she knew M and M was just a job, just like decorating the house was just a job. She shouldn't have let herself get so involved. M and M was a temporary problem, not a permanent fixture in either of their lives.

Right?

They took the van. There was no reason not to take the van, considering they didn't need a back seat for Mary Margaret's car seat, because Mary Margaret—better known as the Traitor—was busy with her new best friend, Psychedelic Petra.

Keely sat in the passenger seat, arms folded across her chest, still blinking more than usual because if she didn't, she might just burst into tears.

Which was stupid. Beyond stupid.

She'd known Mary Margaret for four days. Four very short, endlessly long days.

"You all right?"

Keely turned her head slightly, to look at Jack's profile. "Of course I'm all right. Why wouldn't I be all right? What are you implying? That I'm not all right? That I'm . . . that I'm brokenhearted or something because Mary Margaret prefers that walking, talking painter's palette to me?" She looked forward once more, chin tilted. "Don't be ridiculous."

"Well, I guess that's settled," Jack replied, and Keely considered unscrewing the large round knob on the floor shift and feeding it to him. "You know, I didn't think of it at the time, but it probably wouldn't be a good thing if you got too attached to M and—Candy. Sorry, but she's just not big enough yet to haul around a mouthful like Mary Margaret, and Candy just sort of fits. Anyway, this is temporary, for both of us. All three of us. None of us should get attached to her, because she has to go back."

"Oh, for God's sake! Go back? What is she now—a piece of merchandise? Nice color, pretty good fit, but I think I really wanted something else. Go back. Babies don't *go back.*"

"This one does. Or are you telling me you read that note from my cousin and still think I'm the father?"

Keely dropped her chin to her chest. "No, I don't think you're the father." She lifted her eyes, looked out through the windshield, seeing nothing but the empty spaces of rural Whitehall Township. The empty space that would be in her heart when Mary Margaret's mother climbed down from her mountain and came to claim her child. Not that she'd probably be there to see that—because she would be long gone by that time anyway.

"Damn kid," she said at last, and her voice cracked, her eyes stung, and she quickly turned her head, looking blindly out the side window.

105

She didn't see trees, she didn't see grass, or houses or telephone poles. She saw Mary Margaret smiling up at her, reaching her arms up to her when she walked into a room. She could almost feel those chubby arms around her neck, smell the baby's sweet smell after a bath.

Keely realized suddenly that Jack had pulled onto the shoulder of the road, cut the engine.

"You really like her, don't you?"

"She's all right," Keely said, giving in, letting him see her wipe at her wet eyes. "Oh, this is stupid!"

"I don't know," Jack said, his voice light, as if he was smiling—not that she'd turn and look at him. "It's kind of nice to know that Attila the Hun has a soft side."

"I am *not* Attila the—" Keely said, at last turning to look at her employer-cum-pain-in-the-rump. "Oh, hell, maybe I am. Gregory said bossy is my worst failing. Right after trying to organize the world."

Jack's left eyebrow rose slightly. "Really? I would have put Big-Mouth-Know-It-All first on my list. But, hey, whatever works."

Keely saw his smile (which probably saved his life, or at least four of his 206 bones), and sat back against the seat, closing her eyes. "I try *so* hard."

"Yeah, I'll give you that one," Jack agreed, reaching over, patting her hand. "Why do you suppose that is? Maybe your mother was frightened by an underachiever?"

Keely barely remembered her own mother, but she wasn't going to tell Jack that. No siblings, no cousins; only her Aunt Mary, who never applauded when she did right, but surely knew how to make Keely feel like worm sweat whenever she did wrong—so Keely had worked very hard at never being wrong. She and her aunt had become friends once Keely was grown, but they'd had a lot of tough years.

106

"I like being in control," was all Keely said, looking at him. She could have said, "I hate for anyone to know I don't know everything, that I sometimes feel so out of my depth that three lifesavers wouldn't keep me from drowning," but she didn't. "What's so wrong with that?"

"Nothing, if you're leading troops into battle, I suppose, but do you have to be so damn efficient about it?"

Keely felt hurt, and when she felt hurt, she went on the attack. "I guess that would bother you, wouldn't it, Trehan? I mean, you don't even sleep efficiently. Your bed is a mess every morning."

"Yes, and you make it every morning, while I'm still in the shower, or downstairs drinking coffee made from freshly ground beans. Four days and I feel part pampered, part . . . I don't know. Scolded?"

"Scolded? Because I make your bed?"

"No. Because you seem to think I wouldn't make my bed."

"Would you?"

He shrugged. "Possibly. But that's not the real point. The point is, you came in here—"

"At your request," she pointed out, once more eyeing the round black ball on the gear shift.

"Okay, at my request. I was desperate. You didn't know a thing about babies, but did that stop you? Hell, no. Within hours, you'd furnished the nursery. Within a couple more hours, you'd watched six child care videos and read three books on the care and feeding of babies. You've gotten the kitchen up and running, you cook, you're still able to start furnishing the house, and you put that damn pot rack up without even asking for my help."

107

Keely shook her head. "Is *that* what's eating you? You're mad about the pot rack? That's ridiculous. Besides, I'd first have to *find* you in order to ask your help. Of course, now I know where you are. You're down at the garages, making an idiot of yourself."

"In the interests of détente, I'm going to ignore that," Jack told her, his jaw rather tight. "But I would like to remind you that what I do with my life is my business."

"Yes, and how I handle mine is mine," Keely shot back at him.

"That's what I thought, too, Keely," Jack told her after a few moments. "Right up until the moment you stood in the kitchen, your heart breaking, while Candy cooed at Petra. You're getting attached to the kid, Keely, and that's not good. You have to remember that this is only a job, and you'll be gone in a couple of weeks. Hell, Candy may be gone sooner than that, if Cecily comes back. So don't . . . get . . . attached."

"You mean, the way you aren't getting attached?" Keely asked, suddenly understanding why Jack kept so much distance between himself and Mary Mar—Candy. "You're crazy about her, too, aren't you?"

"No, I am *not* crazy about her," Jack answered, turning the key in the ignition, looking over his shoulder, then pulling the van back onto the roadway. "I'm going to Japan soon, remember? There's a lot of things I want in this life, but a kid—any kid—sure as hell isn't one of them. Now, how about you give me some directions, so I know where I'm going today?"

Keely narrowed her eyelids, glared at him. "I wouldn't dare think to tell you where to go. That would be bossy."

"Yeah, and probably nothing you'd want to say out loud near Candy," Jack said, his eyes on the road. "I get

108

your drift. However, I think we can make an exception in this case, considering I really don't know where we're going. I won't hold it against you, honest. My list is already long enough, believe me."

"Just head down MacArthur Road and I'll tell you where to turn." She reached down to the floor, picked up her looseleaf notebook, and began paging through it. "Now, remember, we have to buy out of stock, at least for the most part, because ordering will take six to nine weeks. We carry what we can and bend arms to get early delivery on everything else."

Jack took his eyes off the road for a moment, to look over at the notebook. "I may be wrong, but I think the invasion at Normandy was put together with less paperwork. What are you—we—buying today?"

"Mattress and box spring for the guest room, my room, for starters. I'd like the den furnished, your bedroom, at least the guest bedroom I'm in right now. I'd like a large, round table in the foyer, underneath the chandelier, and we really need to get rid of the echo in the living room, so if we can find a few carpets, that would help. However, we're only getting the basics today, things we—you—just can't live without much longer. I definitely want to order most of the furniture, the better furniture, from Aunt Mary's usual suppliers. Oh, by the way, I've taken the liberty of hiring a cleaning service. They show up tomorrow." She closed the notebook, looked at him. "Unless you think that's too efficient?"

"No, I suppose not. I couldn't ask you to clean the house, right?"

"Not in this lifetime, unless you cloned me, and I'm already pretty sure I know your answer to that one," Keely said, relaxing a little. Then she went for broke. "I also called an old acquaintance from high school, remembering that she planned to become a nurse, and got the name of the best pediatrician in town. Mary Margaret has an appointment with him next Tuesday at ten o'clock."

Keely felt the van slow as Jack took his foot off the gas. "Why? She's not sick, is she?"

"No," Keely said, enjoying his reaction. Wasn't getting attached? Ha! "It's just that your cousin's note mentioned that Mary Margaret hasn't had her shots yet, and every book I read gives a list of shots she needs. She's *way* behind. Besides, she's supposed to have something called 'well baby' checkups. There's only one little thing I haven't mentioned—you've got the note from Cecily, saying you're in charge of Mary Margaret, so I think you'll have to go along, at least for the first appointment. Unless you're already in Japan," she ended, not all that kindly.

Jack gave the steering wheel a soft hit with his fist. "Damn Cecily. Now I'm going to the doctor with the kid?" He looked at Keely. "Are you sure I have to go along? What if the doctor wants to give her one of those shots you're talking about?"

"Turn right at the next light," Keely said, grinning at him. "And what's the matter? Does the big, bad baseball star faint when he sees a needle?"

Jack slammed the palm of his hand upward on the turn signal, then cut into the right lane, muttering something that actually sounded Japanese.

Keely didn't think it was anything *nice*. She wriggled slightly on the uncomfortable seat and shut her mouth.

# Chapter Seven

*You can observe a lot just by watching.*

— Yogi Berra

THIS WASN'T A FURNITURE STORE, IT WAS A WAREHOUSE masquerading as a furniture store. Couches, chairs, tables were all piled nearly to the ceiling, and small forklifts ran up and down the long aisles, beeping, blinking blue lights attached to poles stuck on them. Jack was nearly run down twice before they'd made their way through the warehouse to the large showroom in the rear of the building.

One look at the showroom and Jack wanted to be back in the warehouse, be anywhere else. Men didn't belong in places like this. Car showrooms; that's where men belonged. He could talk pistons and speed. He didn't know chintz from cheesecake—and had no desire to learn.

Keely, however, obviously was smack-dab in her element. She had also learned absolutely nothing from his gentle hints that maybe she should try to ease up a little on her take-charge personality. Attila the Hun goes shopping; that was Keely McBride.

"We'll look first, thank you," she told a hopeful salesman who broke away from a gaggle of similarly desperate-looking men to approach them the moment they were through the showroom doors. "If we find anything that suits, we'll be back. In the meantime, we'd like to be left alone."

"I'll take that," Jack said, plucking the business card the salesman was holding out to Keely, who had already

111

aimed herself at the first row of displays. "You might want to use this free time to have a cup of black coffee, take a self-defense class—anything you can think of to prepare you in case she does find something she likes."

"Yes . . . er, thank you," the salesman said, then pointed at Jack. "Say, aren't you—?"

"Probably," Jack said, smiling. "We'll see you in a bit, okay?"

Keely was halfway down the first aisle before Jack caught up to her, walking as she scribbled in her notebook. He didn't know why, and sure didn't want to stop, investigate his feelings, get in touch with his inner idiot, but he was actually getting a kick out of watching her do her thing.

"Find anything yet?" he asked, then pointed to a dark green leather couch. "That's not bad. And they've got it set up with matching chairs, a couple of tables, some lamps. Looks good. We can just buy it all and get out of here."

She stopped dead, turned, and looked at him. "Buy by the room? Oh, wonderful. My client is one of *those.*"

"Meaning?" Jack said, his back straightening, his enjoyment in her forgotten. It was if she'd just lumped him in with all the other knuckle-dragging animals in the wild kingdom, and pretty low on the food chain at that.

"Meaning, anybody can buy by the room, allow someone else to dictate what goes with what. Anyone without a lick of imagination, that is. You don't need me, all you need is someone to tell you what you like."

"Aren't you telling me what I like?" he asked, looking at her closely before he stepped back a pace. "Oh, no. Forget it. I hired *you.* I am *not* going to get dragged into this decorating stuff. I'm just here to drive the van. Buy the green couch, damn it, and let's get done here."

"Sit on it, Trehan."

"Hey, do you use that same mouth around my baby cousin?"

Keely rolled her eyes. "No, I mean—sit on it. Sit on the couch. You like it, you buy it. It's a good size and will fit nicely in that large room. But not all this other stuff. You didn't hire me just to point and click. I design rooms, I don't do cookie-cutter decorating."

Jack remembered his minor-league coach with more fondness, and that guy hadn't only ordered him around, he'd spit tobacco juice on his shoes while he was doing it. Still, Jack walked over and sat down. Spread his arms on the back of the cushions, crossed his legs. "This thing is hard as a rock," he said, amazed, because it had looked good enough.

"And it's not real leather, and you'd be replacing it in three years. Now, can we get on with this? And as I told you, this is only a stopgap measure, buying a few necessities. Most of your furniture will be much more . . . upscale."

"Upscale. Is that a synonym for expensive? Because I have a feeling it is."

Keely tipped her head, looked at him. "Okay, short course in furnishing a space. You do it right the first time, you don't have to do it again. The best woods, the most well-constructed couches, chairs, which can eventually be reupholstered, not replaced. Good costs money, but so does not-so-good, and you'll be replacing not-so-good too often. We can get mattresses and frames here, some carpets for low-traffic areas, basic furniture for your den, buy the basics for a few of the bedrooms, because this store has some fairly decent

113

bedroom furniture. Surprisingly, there's also a couch back there that would be perfect in your living room. But that's it for today, except that today I'll also learn more about what you like as you point out what you like. You like leather couches, fine. I make suggestions as to which is your best buy, the best style and color, but you have the final yes or no on everything. That's how I work. So get up. Come on—up, up, up."

Obediently, he got to his feet, once more following after Keely . . . considering ways to kill her, stash the body where no one would ever find it.

"Try that one," she said, halfway down the next aisle, and she pointed to a sort of beige leather couch that looked to be made up of several different pieces stuck together, even curved at one end.

He sank into the cushions. He could smell the leather, leather so soft it was nearly a sin to run his hands over it. "Not bad," he said, shrugging, then looked at the price tag. That was one thing Keely didn't seem to do— look at price tags. "Holy—is that for this whole arrangement? The chairs, the lamps, those flowers?"

"It's for the couch," Keely told him, sitting down on the matching chair and reaching for the price tag. "We'll talk. Don't ever believe the price tag. But remember, we have to shop where everything is already in stock. This not only limits our choices but affects the price."

He leaned over as she was ready to stand up, holding her down by placing a hand on her arm. "I think we need to clear something up here first, okay? I'm rich. You know it, I know it. But I wasn't always rich, and I won't always be rich if I don't look at price tags. My mother would have had a nervous breakdown if she saw that price tag. Hell, she'd never have seen it, because we had the same damn brown-and-green plaid couch in the living room for twenty years. Am I making myself clear here?"

"Well, it's about time," Keely said, sitting back in the chair. "Oh, this *is* comfortable, isn't it? Anyway, I've been waiting for you to give me *some* input, Jack. Starting with a budget would be nice. How much were you planning to spend?"

He took back his hand, shoved it into his hair. "I don't have the faintest damned idea."

"Fifteen rooms, Jack, starting from the bare walls and working our way from kitchen dish towels to doormats, and everything in between. I admit I've never had a job this big, but I've given it some thought. Here, what do you think of this?" She opened her notebook, wrote down a figure, and turned the book so that he could see it.

Jack blinked, swallowed. "Does that include tax?" he asked after a moment. He'd made twelve million dollars last year alone, and still he had trouble spending money he certainly could afford to spend. "No, never mind. Don't answer that. It's a reasonable figure, I suppose. I guess I'm just reacting to some childhood flashbacks that had a lot to do with eating everything on my plate because food didn't grow on trees." He smiled at a sudden memory. "Tim once pointed out to Mom that lots of food grows on trees. Dad wouldn't let him play ball for a week, for sassing Mom."

Keely laughed. "Your brother sounds a lot like me, somehow incapable of knowing when to keep our mouths shut. But I think you have to thank your parents for teaching you the value of money. We're always reading about sports stars who spend their millions in minutes and end up bankrupt."

"Yeah, well, that's not going to happen here," Jack

115

said, getting to his feet, which wasn't all that easy, considering how deeply he'd settled into the soft couch. "Now let's go spend some money, but not on this couch. It's a man-eater."

He helped Keely to her feet, and the heat of her hand in his did something dumb, something totally stupid and unexpected, to his insides. He looked at her, she looked at him, and then she thanked him, headed out of the room display and into the aisle.

"Okay, Goldilocks," she said, and her voice sounded a little wobbly—which he rather liked. "We've found too hard, we've found too soft. Now we look for just right. Because so far we've gotten a whole lot of no place."

"Yeah, we sure have," Jack said, lying through his teeth because they had gotten someplace today. He'd learned that Keely McBride had a tongue of pure brass, but she used it to protect herself, not score points off others. He'd learned that he wasn't the only one who'd taken a single look at Candy and started having gooey feelings. And he'd learned that touching Keely was probably harmful to his mental health.

And it only got worse—or better—when they got to the aisle displaying about sixty different mattresses. Keely did the usual sort of poking at them, sitting on them, but from the way she lingered, frowned, he could tell that this was one area where she wasn't all that darn sure of herself.

"Wouldn't it be better if you lie down on them, really tried them out?" he suggested, picking one mattress and box spring set that seemed to have a huge, quilted pillow sewn on top and then sprawling on it. "See? You sleep on beds, you don't sit on them. This one's pretty good. Come here," he said, patting the expanse beside him. "Try it out."

116

Keely smoothed her honey-blond hair, drawn back in a tight French twist, as usual, and shook her head. "I don't think so. If you like it, that's good enough. We'll need two queen size and two singles, for the corner guest room. I might get more inventive in the other bedrooms, use couches, day beds, that sort of thing, but they can wait. All right, come on, get up. We still have lots to do."

"Nope," Jack said, biting back a grin. He liked the way Keely looked when flustered. Her cheeks got pink, she blinked too much, and she kept poking at her hair, so that some of the curls broke free, got sort of fuzzy around her face and neck. "Not until you lie down here, test it yourself." Now he did grin. "I mean, I've come to trust your judgment, Keely. So . . . judge."

She threw her notebook down on one of the other mattresses and approached the one Jack was lying on, glaring down at him. "This is ridiculous."

"True, but do it anyway, Keely. Humor me."

She sat down on the side of the bed, her back stiff, then jackknifed until her legs were raised high enough to clear the mattress, then stretched them out straight in front of her.

"Better, but it's not sit on the bed, Keely, it's *lie* on the bed."

She lay down, crossed her hands in front of her, looked up at the ceiling. "It's okay," she said shortly. "A little soft, but okay."

Jack rolled onto his side, propped up his head with his bent arm, and looked down into Keely's face. "You like it firmer?" he asked, unable to stop himself.

The next thing he knew, he was lying on his back, and Keely was standing beside the mattress, her notebook once more in her hands. "If play time's over, Trehan, I'd like to continue?"

117

"Me, too, but we can't always have what we want, can we, Miss McBride?" he said, grinning as she stomped off down the aisle. What was wrong with him? He didn't even like the woman, let alone desire her. Did he?

One hour and sixteen long aisles of furniture later, Keely was ready for the salesman. Whether or not he was ready for her Jack couldn't be sure, because the man approached rather slowly, as if wondering if he first shouldn't arm himself with a whip and a chair.

"Here's the deal," Keely said without preamble, once she'd introduced herself and found out their salesman's name was Curtis. "We buy, Curtis, we buy a lot, and we get a twenty-five-percent discount on everything we buy. Jack, show him your credit cards."

"Oh, no, no," Curtis said, waving away the suggestion even as Jack—deciding blind obedience would get him home fastest—reached for his wallet. "There's no need, Mr. Trehan. Your credit is good with us. No limit. I've already spoken to my manager. He'd like an autograph for his son, though, if that's all right with you?"

"How nice," Keely said, but her smile didn't reach her eyes. Curtis had barely looked at her business card before stuffing it into his shirt pocket, and now he was just about swooning over Jack. It was entirely possible, Jack decided, that good old Curtis harbored a death wish. "And the twenty-five percent?" Keely continued. "And immediate delivery at no extra charge?"

"Well, I don't know about that," Curtis said, easing a finger into his shirt collar, looking uncomfortable. "I mean, we've dealt with your company before, but only with the owner, and only with a fifteen-percent discount. I don't think—"

"Good-bye, Curtis, have a nice day," Keely said, reaching into his shirt pocket and retrieving her card. "Come on, Jack. We're wasting our time here."

Jack, who had been sitting in a nearby chair, watching Keely operate, got to his feet, shrugged at Curtis, and began following Keely toward the showroom door. God, but he loved watching her as she walked away. He only wondered if he enjoyed the view that much, or if he knew he'd be safer if she just kept on walking, straight out of his life.

"Good tactic, if it works," he told Keely as he caught up to her. "I didn't know you were a gambling woman."

"I'm not," Keely admitted, slipping her hand through his arm. "Do you mind? I'm shaking so badly, I think I might fall down. Don't walk too fast; give him time to chase down his manager."

She wasn't kidding, he could feel her trembling. "Hey, I can afford the difference. I don't need a full twenty-five-percent discount. I'm really not a tightwad, you know."

"I know that, and I plan to get as much money out of you as I can, but principle is principle. Twenty-five percent is not out of the question, not when we're buying as much as we're buying. Granted, I make more if you get less of a discount from Curtis, but Curtis has to learn that *he* makes no money if we walk, and *I* have to live with myself. You're my client, my customer. I wouldn't allow you to be taken to the cleaners, even if you were Bill Gates, okay?"

Jack felt this insane urge to stop, haul Keely into his arms, and plant a huge kiss on her. He fought down that urge. "So this is strictly business, right? You'd be this upset—shaking, actually—over any client?"

She didn't answer him, which was probably a good

thing, but only said, "Can you please stop and tie your sneaker? I can't look back, in case Curtis is following us, but you could take a peek while you pretend to retie your sneaker."

"I'm wearing loafers," Jack pointed out, "but I suppose I could fake it."

"No, never mind. Either he follows us or he doesn't. But, oh," she said, sighing, "I really did love that headboard. And you liked the leather couch. And there's that one vase . . ."

"We could go back," Jack suggested, feeling the last strings tying him to his mother's frugal apron strings breaking loose with a small *boing*.

"No, we can't. Come on. You can buy me a hamburger."

"Wait!" Curtis called out just as Jack had opened the door to the van, stepping back so that Keely could climb into the passenger seat. "Ms. McBride, Mr. Trehan—please, wait!"

Jack watched the worry line between Keely's eyebrows smooth out as a smile touched her lips. "Did you hear something, *Mr. Trehan?*"

"Possibly," he answered her, delighting in her grin. "Maybe it was the wind? Sounds of traffic from the highway?"

"Yes, that's probably it."

"So how far do we take this? Do I acknowledge old Curtis, or do I get in the van, start the engine?"

"I have this lovely mental picture," Keely told him, "of the van heading out of the parking lot, Curtis running behind, yelling 'Thirty percent, thirty percent.' "

"You're new to this gambling stuff, so don't get greedy. Know when to hold 'em, Keely, and know when to fold 'em," Jack warned, then motioned for her to get back out of the van as Curtis, nearly breathless, skidded to a halt at the front of the van—possibly ready to throw himself in front of the wheels, if necessary.

"Twenty . . . twenty percent," Curtis gasped out. "That's as much as I could get. And free delivery and setup tomorrow."

Keely turned to Jack, looking hopeful. "What do you think?"

He couldn't help himself. He grinned at her. "I think we have a winner."

And then it began. Jack walked the aisles with Keely and Curtis, the same aisles he'd walked for the past hour, and saw things he'd never seen before.

She plucked a couch from one spot, a chair from another. Combined both with a table from yet a third collection. "Those two lamps, the flower arrangement from that table over there—but not the table—the potted plant at the end of the aisle. No, no, Curtis, don't stop to take down style numbers, just slap some sold stickers on everything. And do try to keep up; I want to be home in time for the baby's bath."

"Where are you putting all this stuff?" Jack asked in a whisper as Curtis put a bright red SOLD sticker on yet another piece of furniture, this one a round area rug that looked like something out of the *Arabian Nights.*

"Round table, round carpet, both for the foyer," Keely answered reasonably. "It's wool, it's imported, and it's fairly good, although definitely not the same quality you'd find in many upscale condos in Manhattan. But we're not in Manhattan, and I think a suburban family home should be well-furnished, but also comfortable, livable. From everything you told me earlier, if I were to put a twenty-thousand-dollar carpet in your foyer, you'd never walk on it."

Jack eyed the round carpet once more. "Twenty thousand? So how much is this one?"

"Fifteen hundred. Minus twenty percent. There, now don't you feel like a real bargain hunter?"

"Twenty thousand, huh?" he repeated, looking at the carpet yet again. "Keely, you're finally starting to make me feel good about hiring you. I said do what you want, just get it done. I'm a baseball player from a small town. I bought my condo furnished, and only my manager saw it before the sale went through. I had no damn idea what this stuff costs. Anybody else would have taken me to the cleaners."

"Yeah," Keely said, still walking, still pointing at items for Curtis to tag, "and don't think the thought hasn't crossed my mind. And, to tell you the truth, if it weren't for Mary Margaret, I might have done just that."

"Candy? What does Candy have to do with it?"

"I don't know," Keely said, stopping, turning to face him. "But it sounds good when I say it, I feel good when I say it, and if I stop to figure out why, I just might hate myself in the morning. Let's just say I'm enjoying myself, and learning about myself at the same time. Someday, in fact, I'm going to make a very good mother."

This time, when Keely moved on, Curtis at her heels, Jack stayed where he was.

Keely peeked in at Mary Margaret, smiling when she saw the baby had barely moved since she'd put her down for the night and left Jack in charge while she ran through Macy's at top speed, buying bedding for her— that is, the guest room.

He'd protested at first, saying something about

122

having to do something down at the garages—yeah, like she couldn't figure out what the "something" was. But when she came home it was to see him try to hide one of the ice-filled bags beside his chair, so maybe he needed to rest his arm more than he'd needed to practice, or work out, or whatever pitchers called it.

"Arm feeling a little better?" she'd asked as she'd come out of the kitchen, walked into the den, saw that the baby monitor was sitting on the old fiberglass TV tray set up beside the chair. Had Jack been watching Mary Margaret sleep? "I hope you didn't hurt it too much, helping me get the mattress up the stairs. You won't have to lift a finger tomorrow, but I really did want to sleep on at least half of a real bed tonight."

"It wasn't any problem, and who said my arm hurts?" he'd shot back, and Keely left the room again, without trying to imagine the new furniture in it.

She should wash the mattress pad and sheets before putting them on the bed, and would have if she weren't so exhausted. Spending money was tiring, even if it was somebody else's money.

Tomorrow the bed frames would come, along with all the furniture, rugs, lamps, and other accessories that would have to do until she had a chance to visit local antiques and speciality shops.

But the basics were pretty well done for the den and three of the bedrooms. She had the living room and dining room, study, exercise room, master suite sitting room, the glassed-in porch on the east side of the house, three bedrooms, and the upstairs living room to go; still, it wasn't too bad for one day's work.

Once the sheets were on the mattress—leaving the bedspread for tomorrow and the box spring and bed frame, or else it would just drag on the floor—Keely pulled a freshly washed nightshirt and a pair of cotton underpants from the neat piles on the floor, and headed into the bathroom.

She showered quickly, sparing only a moment to wonder, yet again, what it would be like to take a shower in Jack's bathroom. All those water jets! If she had a shower like that, she'd probably live in it. Still, the guest room bath was light years away from the ancient plumbing in her Brooklyn apartment, the apartment that had meant she'd taken a step up the success ladder and now couldn't miss less.

She couldn't miss Manhattan less, she realized as she toweled herself off and then pulled her nightshirt over her head. She was too busy to think about her old life, and couldn't even work up a head of steam over Gregory's takeover of her lease on the shop. As for Gregory himself? What *had* she been thinking when she fell into bed with that pompous ass?

All her life, she'd wanted to leave Allentown, move up to some big city like New York. All her life she'd wanted to prove herself, needed to prove herself. And she'd failed. She'd lost her business, her apartment, all her money. She'd come home a failure.

So why didn't she feel like a failure anymore? She felt good, the best she'd felt in a long, long time. Maybe ever.

She felt *needed.* Her Aunt Mary had needed her to take over the business for a while. Mary Margaret needed her. Jack Trehan—Lord knew he needed somebody!

Keely hugged herself, headed for the hallway, taking the time to check on the baby once more before calling it a night.

She stepped out of her room and turned left, without

124

looking where she was going—and bumped smack in to Jack.

He held out his arms, steadying her, saying, "I just came upstairs to find you. Candy's moving around in there. I can see her on the monitor."

Keely mentally pulled down the hem of her navy blue nightshirt, although she didn't actually reach for the material; that would only draw attention to the fact that it stopped a good six inches above her knees. "Babies do move around, Jack," she told him, trying not to sigh as he let go of her arms, trying not to believe she'd miss his touch.

"I know," he told her, stabbing the fingers of one hand into his hair, so that she noticed, once again, that intriguing lighter blond streak above his left temple. "But I was watching one of those videos while you were gone, and babies can get their heads stuck in corners, under those bumper pad things you have in the crib, or even poke their heads through the bars, choke. I mean, it's a real concern. That's what it was called on the video—a real concern."

He was so sweet. Look at him, all worried—concerned.

"Jack, Mary Margaret is six months old, according to your cousin. She's old enough and strong enough not to get tangled in the bumper pads if they're put on correctly, and the crib we bought meets all the newest safety standards. I checked, the moment I watched the video."

He pressed his palms to his temples. "God, I had no idea how *hard* this is," he said, shaking his head. "There's so much to think about, so much to worry about. The kid's so little, so helpless. I don't know how Candy survived, living with Cecily for six months."

"Personally, I prefer not to think about that," Keely said honestly. "I just keep hoping she won't come back."

Jack's eyes widened. "Won't come back? She *has* to come back. I can't raise Candy. I don't *want* to raise Candy."

"Because you're going to go pitch in Japan," Keely said, all her warm, fuzzy feelings for Jack evaporating in an instant. "You know, Trehan, you're a lot like your cousin. She goes to Tibet, you go to Japan, and Mary Margaret goes—where, Jack? To her uncle, who you tell me is as bad as his sister? Or maybe to some sort of foster care until she's eighteen. Yeah, well, not your table, right, Jack? Not your problem."

She went to turn, walk away, but he grabbed her by the shoulders, held her in place. "Do you *ever* shut up?" he asked, glaring at her. "I didn't ask for this, I didn't ask for any of it. What the hell am I supposed to do?"

Keely looked at him for long moments. "I don't know," she said honestly. "I just know that that baby in there deserves better than either you or your cousin seem willing to deliver. I'm here now, not because you hired me to be here, but because *somebody* has to care about that sweet child. I may not have started off that way, but that's how I've ended up, and you can't fire me because you need me too badly and Petra has evening classes and Aunt Sadie is too old and too happy with her own life to do your dirty work for you. Tell me, Jack, when do you stop passing the buck and figure out that *you're* in charge of Mary Margaret?"

His fingers squeezed a little tighter. "Do you have any idea how much I'd like to throw you out of here?"

"I've a very good idea of how much you want to be rid of me. You've pretty much gotten it down to a daily

126

explanation, sometimes an hourly one. So don't just hint, Trehan, tell me to go. Come on, tell me to leave."

"I can't," he said, stepping away from her. Keely nearly fell down, her knees all but buckling beneath her. He spoke as if she weren't still there, able to hear him. "I've got Tim coming tomorrow morning for the tryout, I've got that commercial in Arizona next week . . ."

*Try out?* Whoa! Keely needed to back up a bit. She didn't have enough knowledge, or interest, to be a commentator on ESPN, but she was a fan, and she understood the term. Japan wasn't a done deal, as she had believed. He had to try out; just like a rookie, just like a guy nobody wanted anymore. That was why he was down at the garages. He was practicing, not keeping in shape, the ink already drying on a contract with the Tokyo Tigers or some such team.

How humiliating for him! Two-time Cy Young Yankee ace, and now he had been shot down to the point where he had to *try out* for a team halfway across the world?

He'd lost his career, he'd ended up back where he started—housed better, more solvent, but still back where he'd started. He had this huge house but no furniture. His brother was still in the majors, which had to stick in Jack's craw, no matter how much he might love his brother. And now, just to top things off, he had Mary Margaret . . . and her.

Keely was surprised the guy hadn't decided to go down to the garages and suck on his car's tailpipe.

She put out one hand, touched his arm. "Jack . . . I'm sorry," she said, really meaning it. "I've got a big mouth. I shouldn't have gotten so mad at you when you told me about this Japan business. I thought you were just looking for another fat contract and the hell with the

127

kid, with anything else. But that's not it, is it? You really don't know what to do with yourself, now that you're out of baseball."

He bristled immediately. "*I* decide when I'm out of baseball. I came back from the first rotator cuff surgery. I can come back from this one. I was too quick to retire."

His protests sounded so much like her own, as she'd tried to hang on to a failing business, a dream gone sour. "The Yankees didn't think so, though, did they? The doctors didn't think so. Don't you think the Yankees would have held on to you if they thought you could pitch again?"

He half turned away from her, then turned back, glared at her. "Oh, this is good. She decorates, she cooks, she takes care of babies. And now she's an orthopedist, a team owner, and even a shrink, and all for ten percent of the price of a couple of couches. How did I get so lucky? Well, thank you very much, Miss McBride, and good night."

"Jack, wait!" Keely called out, then headed down the hallway after him, forgetting her bare legs, forgetting that, except for one small baby, she and Jack were a man and a woman alone in a huge house. She grabbed on to his arm once more, his right arm, and then quickly let go, remembering how he'd iced that arm earlier. He stopped. He waited.

And she couldn't think of a single thing to say to him.

"Oh, Jack, I'm really so sorry," she said at last, putting her arms around him. "Life isn't fair, is it?"

She pressed her cheek against his chest, trying to comfort him because she knew how it felt when your dreams lay smashed at your feet. It hurt. It hurt a lot.

She felt his arms go around her even as he lowered

128

his head to rest against hers. "This isn't smart, Keely," he said after a few moments. "I think you ought to go to bed now."

She nodded against his chest, stood back when he removed his arms from her, and looked up into his face. "Good luck tomorrow, Jack. And I mean that. I really mean that."

Then she turned and ran back down the hall.

# Chapter Eight

*I felt like shouting out that I had made a ball curve.*
— Candy Cummings, pitcher

KEELY WASN'T ALL THAT CRACKED UP ABOUT GETTING up with the sun, especially after spending a pretty much sleepless night, trying to rework that scene with Jack to where she didn't come off looking like a brainless nincompoop. Worse: a brainless nincompoop on the make.

But Mary Margaret's room was on the east side of the house, and when the sun came up, Mary Margaret got up with it, her bottom damp, her belly empty, and her lungs in great working order.

The windows in Jack's house might be architectural gems, and the house might be isolated enough from its neighbors to ensure privacy, and surrounded by lovely views, but the time had come to think of window dressings.

With Mary Margaret dressed, fed, and sitting in the jump seat that fastened around the top of the door frame—rather like bungee jumping for the infant set—Keely sat at the kitchen table, surrounded by a half-dozen sample books containing varieties of drapery material, blinds, and shades she'd dragged inside from the van.

She'd already decided on window coverings for the downstairs rooms and was mulling over room-darkening shades for Mary Margaret's bedroom when Petra Polinski showed up. Keely had left the back door unlocked after she'd returned from the van, which, to Petra, was obviously an invitation to walk right in.

"Hey, blondie, how fares the world this morning?" Petra asked, heading for the coffeepot. "Or, in layman's terms, what's up?"

"You are, which is surprising. I thought teenagers slept until noon during the summer." Keely said this while looking at Petra, who had poured her coffee, taken a sip, and was now squatting down in front of a delighted Mary Margaret.

Babies really must like color. That had to be the attraction. And today Petra was red. Fire engine red shorts, red sneakers, red halter top . . . red streaks in her blond hair. It was like looking at a life-size STOP sign.

Petra picked up a rattle, handed it to Mary Margaret, and came back over to the table, poking at the edge of one of the thick sample books. "Drapes, huh? You want my help?"

Keely ran her gaze up and down Petra one more time. "Um . . . thanks. But I don't think so."

"Sure you do." Petra sat down, opened one of the books, began turning over sample after sample of drapery material. "Oh, now this is nice," she said, stopping at one of the pages, smoothing her hand over the sample. "Good mix of fabric and design, heavy without being overwhelming. And it's an eighteenth-century pattern, a real classic, which would probably

130

look great in the dining room. Ivory sheers, drapes that drag on the floor, a swag, definitely. You are going formal in there, aren't you? I mean, with the Ionic columns and that gorgeous oriel window, you'd have to keep the dramatic tone."

Keely sat back in her chair, eyeing Petra warily. "Let me take a wild shot at this. Another phase?"

Petra nodded, ripping off a piece of note paper and marking the page with it before moving on. "I designed and decorated my own doll house when I was seven. My grandfather built it—big sucker, three stories. I discovered I'm partial to Regency and Georgian designs—some Victorian, but not too much—although I have a great admiration for Frank Lloyd Wright. But there's just more *soul* in Sheraton, Chippendale, Inigo Jones, don't you think? Wow, cool! You already have this page marked. For the living room, right? We must be on some cosmic wave link, huh? Bet that scares the bejeebers out of you."

Keely sat forward on her chair, an elbow propped on the table, dropped her chin into her hand. "*How* old are you? You did say sixteen or seventeen, didn't you?"

"And never been kissed," Petra replied, grinning. "Yeah, right." She went back to the sample book, eying each page with a critical eye. "So? Are you going to go watch?"

Keely was still trying to reconcile herself to the idea that Petra was just as advertised: a budding genius. Well, she was definitely a budding *something*. "Watch? Watch what?"

Petra closed the book, stood, rolled her eyes. "Jack, of course. Sadie told Mitzi, and Mitzi told me. Tim Trehan Jack's brother, and catcher for the Phillies—is coming up here to help Jack with his tryout with some baseball scout. They're meeting over at the high school at nine o'clock. Jeez, don't they tell you anything?"

Keely shifted in her chair. "I knew that," she said, hoping she didn't sound defensive. "I was invited, of course," she lied, "but I have this huge furniture delivery scheduled for ten this morning, so I can't go."

Mary Margaret became bored with her jump seat and began to whimper, so Petra quickly picked her up and slapped her against her hip as if she'd been lugging babies around for years. "Bummer. Do you want me to handle it?"

Keely smiled. Such a sweet girl, if naive. "Thank you, but no. I have to tell the delivery people where everything belongs."

Petra walked over to the table, leaned toward Keely. "Do you *want* to go? Sadie told Mitzi that you've got the hots for Jack. Hey, I'd go for him myself, but he is sort of ancient, you know. So you probably do want to go, right?"

Pushing back her chair, Keely stood, walked over to pour herself another cup of coffee. Her hands were shaking, and she spilled some on the counter. As she reached for a paper towel, she said, "I am Jack's employee, Petra. I do *not* have the hots for him."

"Yeah, sure, and Britney Spears sings live. Give it a rest, Keely, I see what's going on. You and Jack, living here together with only Candy as chaperone? I'm telling you, girl, Sadie and Mitzi have this whole torrid romance thing going on about you two. Not that it's bad. They're old; they need something to keep the blood pumping."

"Do your teachers list 'incorrigible' on your report cards?" Keely asked, feeling the blood rush to her cheeks.

"Not since kindergarten. After I built a replica of the Lincoln Memorial out of toothpicks and cotton balls in first grade, they just called me gifted and pretended I wasn't the one who rubbed bubble gum in Jenny Arburto's hair. They're all just upset that I hate math, even if I am good at it. Child prodigies are supposed to be real math junkies, you know. Me? I'm more eclectic. It might be on purpose, some latent immaturity I haven't licked, but I'm not sure. That's why I'm dropping my art courses and picking up psych next semester. Brains and Daddy's money—they'll take you anywhere you want to go."

Petra opened Keely's notebook and began paging through the renderings she'd made of each room. "These are good," she said, "very complete. Everything nice and neat, detailed. Not too difficult to decipher. The Xs mark what you've already bought, right? You've shown just where each piece of furniture goes. Labeled, indexed, drawn to scale. I can do this, tell the delivery people where to put everything. Why don't you go watch lover boy work out?"

"No . . . I couldn't," Keely said, looking up at the clock. Eight thirty. "I mean, he didn't really invite me—"

"Yeah, I knew that. *Big* lie. A real whopper, Keel. Don't have to be a prodigy to know that one."

"Thanks. It's so nice to know I'm transparent," Keely said, shaking her head. "But anyway, I doubt he really wants an audience . . ."

But Petra wasn't listening. She thrust Mary Margaret at Keely, saying, "I think she pooped. Better change her before you go. Candy-babe and I took a walk yesterday, with that big wheeled stroller. It works just great on grass."

"I—I should take Mary Margaret with me?"

133

Petra shrugged. "I would. Simple logic: He can't throw a ball at you if you're holding the kid, right?"

"Right," Keely said, squaring her shoulders. "And I would like Mary Margaret to meet her cousin Tim. She should do that, shouldn't she?"

Petra grinned, showing bright white teeth beneath her blood red lips—an improvement over yesterday's green lipstick, but not by much. "Hey, whatever excuse works, that's my motto."

Jack had been up, showered, and out of the house before dawn. He'd packed the trunk of his car with his mitt, a pitching rubber in case the high school removed theirs from the mound between games, and a bag of balls. He had his mitt and spikes in a leather bag, a supply of rosin, and a lump in his stomach the size of Cleveland.

He'd eaten breakfast in a local diner and regretted the meal almost immediately. Almost as much as he regretted the three cups of coffee he'd downed as he waited for the sun to rise so he could drive over to the ball field.

His mind was a mess. How could he think through his mechanics when all he saw when he closed his eyes was Keely, standing in the hallway—all loose blond curls and legs that went on forever—looking at him with pity in her eyes?

Pity. He sat in the front seat of his sports car, leaned his head back, and sighed. He'd seen a lot of different emotions in lots of beautiful female eyes, but he'd be damned if he'd ever seen pity.

Was he pitiful? Damn, no! Pitiful was the *last* thing he was. He was Jack Trehan, ace right-hander for the New York Yankees, that's what he was.

*Was.*

He reached his left hand across his body, rubbed at his right shoulder. There was an ache in his shoulder, an ache that never quite went away since he'd started his workouts again, but he wasn't the only hurler who had to pitch through pain. Pain was part of the game.

Leaving your curve ball hanging high and fat, looking like a big, juicy grapefruit coming in over the plate, wasn't.

Oh, this was good. What a pep talk he was giving himself! He ought to hire himself out as a motivational speaker. Why didn't he just go home, forget about the whole thing?

Jack swore under his breath, opened the car door, and stepped outside. The sun was up, the sky was blue, and a soft breeze blew across the empty parking lot. He could hear a lawn mower somewhere, in the direction of the football field, but he was pretty much alone. The baseball diamond was to the rear of the campus, so nobody would be able to recognize him from the road.

He opened the trunk of his car and pulled out his spikes, leaned against the rear bumper as he changed shoes, then gathered up his gear and headed across the grass to the field. He dropped his gear next to the bench on the first base line, then went through his warm-up stretches.

It had all started here, for him and Tim. They'd been playing for years, but this was their field of dreams, the place where all the college scouts, even a few major league scouts, had come to see the Trehan twins play. The perfect battery, brother pitching to brother.

Except for spring training and a couple of inter-league games for which they were on opposing teams, they hadn't played together since college.

But it had all started here. If it ended here, maybe that would make that final good-bye just a little bit all right.

Jack checked the mound, seeing the rubber already in place, then kicked at the dirt a little, doing the pitcher's version of housekeeping, setting up the mound the way he liked it best. He even got down on his hands and knees, smoothing the clay mound, tossing a few stones into the infield. Stalling for time. Finally, he was done. He stood up, looked in toward the backstop, and saw his brother standing there, in full gear, his mitt under his arm, his mask tipped back on his head.

Did he once look like that, so at ease in his own skin? He and Tim were very alike in their builds, although Tim's legs were more developed after years of squatting in the catcher's crouch. But, other than that, looking at Tim was rather like looking into a mirror.

"Yo, bro, great day for a little pitch and catch," Tim Trehan said, walking toward the mound.

"You're early," Jack said, brushing the clay and sand off his hands, then shaking Tim's. "Thanks for coming."

Tim grinned, his face tanned, crinkles forming around his eyes. "Hey, it was the least I could do. What's a game yesterday, a long flight, a drive up here and back to Philly, and a two-nighter tonight between brothers?"

"Okay, rub it in. I'll owe you one," Jack said as the two of them stood there, with nothing to do but avoid the subject of Jack's arm. "Hey," he said after a moment, "do you remember that game with Northampton, our senior year? That big lefty—what was his name? I tried to pitch him tight, and he fouled it straight back into your throat, right below your mask. You went down like a rock."

"Gee, good memories," Tim said, his grin lopsided, not all that amused. "Now can we talk about how he hit your next pitch right past Doyle at third, bringing in the winning run?"

136

"I don't remember that part," Jack said, although he did. He'd been so scared when Tim hit the dirt, just lay there. His mind sure hadn't been on the next pitch.

"We were good, though," Tim said, sighing. He turned in a slow circle, looking at the field. "Man, this place brings back memories. We just about lived on this campus, from kindergarten until graduation. Hey, do you remember the time I climbed that tree at recess? Mrs. Liddy screamed at me and I fell out, broke my kneecap."

Jack bent and picked up his glove. "I remember. About a month later, I rode my bike into a tree and broke my right kneecap. Yours was the left. Mom thought we'd planned it."

"Yeah, like we planned all the other stuff. You threw your first touchdown on that field over there, and another one later that night, as I recall, with one Susie 'Hot Lips' Williams."

Jack laughed at the memory. "I lied about that. I didn't get past the twenty yard line with Susie."

"Oh, yeah? Well then, I guess it's time I confess I didn't score quite as well with Mindy Frett a couple of weeks later as I told you I did."

"You *lied?*" Jack said, goggling at his brother.

"Oh, don't look so surprised. You know how it was with us. One of us did it first and the other followed right after, doing pretty much the same damn thing. You said you scored with Susie. What else was I to say? Although I should have known, shouldn't I?"

"Yeah, well, just be glad you aren't following in my footsteps this time around," Jack said, cutting off any further reminiscences. "What say we warm up before the scout gets here?"

"Good idea," Tim said, turning as he pulled down his mask. Then he stopped. "Uh-oh, blonde at nine o'clock.

137

Never mind, she's got a kid with her. Yeah, well, I have to be at the stadium at two anyway—"

Jack looked over toward third and saw Keely standing there, Candy in the stroller she was pushing in front of her. "Damn," he bit out, looking away before she decided to wave at him. "What's she doing here?"

Tim lifted his mask yet again. "You know her?"

Jack slapped his mitt against his thigh, trying to figure out how much he could say to Tim and how much his brother would then figure out on his own. "She's my interior decorator, Keely McBride. If I'm going to live here, I've got to have some furniture in that barn of mine."

"Interesting. And that's her kid?"

"No, Candy's not hers. She's Cecily's, and I'm baby-sitting. Look, it's a long story and the scout will be here any minute. I need to warm up."

"Baby-sitting. Uh-huh," Tim said, looking over at Keely, looking back at Jack. "Oh, I've got to hear this one, bro. Promise me."

Jack nodded as Tim walked back to the plate, then crouched behind it. "Nice and easy, Jack," he called out, slamming his fist into the oversize mitt. "Just loosen up with a few tosses before you try anything else."

Jack rolled his shoulders, pretended he didn't feel Keely's eyes on him, and stepped onto the rubber. And then he forgot her. He forgot everything except the ball in his hand and the glove in his brother's.

Tim always loved to chatter. The guy had a mouth on him that never quit, and he was in rare form this morning. As Jack threw, Tim kept up a running stream of inane, one-way dialogue:

"Okay, ace, that's enough lolli-popping. Burn one in here."

138

"Yo! A cutter! That one brushed him back. Hey, batter-batter-batter. Watch out for the chin music."

"High and tight, Jack, high and tight. Damn—that one would have landed in the alley. Try it again.

"Paint the black, Jack, paint the black. Yes! Outside corner . . . and strike two!"

Jack was working up a sweat, but it felt good. He was back on the mound, his brother behind the plate. He had the rosin bag in his hand, the next pitch in his mind. That last curve had behaved just the way it should, breaking right over the plate. God, how he loved the curve ball!

It was good. It really felt good, great, to be on the mound again.

After about forty pitches, what didn't feel good was his arm. It was dead, just hanging there, and his pitches were beginning to just hang there, too, fat and ready for the imaginary batter to hit.

He caught the ball Tim threw back to him, then took off his ball cap, blotted sweat from his forehead as his brother came out to the hill to talk to him.

"How's the arm?"

"It hurts like a bitch," Jack admitted, although he said so quietly, because the scout had arrived about ten minutes earlier and was standing behind the backstop, radar gun in his hand. "Did he say the speed on that last pitch?"

"Eighty-seven," Tim told him, nodding. "Not bad, Jack, but if that's the best you've got, I think you're in trouble. And try to bring 'em down a hair. You're too high."

Knowing he'd routinely pitched ninety-three miles per hour last season, Jack screwed the cap back down on his head, fighting off the urge to rub at his right shoulder. "Let's mix it up a little."

"Are you sure? He's seen enough. You're looking a little pale, bro."

"I'm sure," Jack replied, tight-lipped. "Let's go."

A half hour later, Jack and the scout stood on the first base line. The scout talked; Jack listened.

Then Jack talked, shook the scout's hand, and walked away.

"So? What happened?" Tim asked, carrying his shin guards and chest protector, his mask still tipped back on his head.

"He wants me," Jack said as Keely, pushing Candy in front of her, headed toward them. She stopped some distance away, close enough to hear, not close enough to be introduced.

"He wants—? Well, damn, Jack, that's great! Great," Tim said, almost succeeding in hiding the disbelief in his voice. "So, what did you tell him?"

"I told him I'd think about it," Jack said, looking at Keely, who was looking at the clay at her feet. "Then he told me that while I think about it, and I'd better not think too long, I should remember that they were buying a name, and that's all they were buying." He took a deep breath, let it out slowly. "So I told him to go to hell, we shook hands, I gave him directions back to the airport, and that was it."

Keely's head jerked up, and Jack could see tears in her eyes, tears she blinked away, quickly leaning down to pick up Candy, fish a pacifier out of her skirt pocket, and busy herself fussing with the child.

Jack walked over to the bench and picked up his bag, Tim following.

"You have an ice bag in there?" Tim asked. "You really should ice that arm down before it gets any worse."

Jack reached into the bag, pulled out a one-time-use bag, activated it by squeezing it, and held it to his shoulder. "Was I that bad, Tim?"

"Hell, no," his brother told him, picking up Jack's bag, handing it to him. "Your slider was okay, and you can still clip those corners when you're on, but your fast ball's gone, Jack. It's just gone, and your curve hangs way too high."

"Yeah, I know," Jack said, looking over at Keely once more. "God, how I love the curve ball. I remember the first time Dad said I was old enough, let me throw one. It was like magic, Tim. Magic . . ."

"Are you going to be all right?"

Jack snapped himself back to the reality that this was it; it was over, all over. "Sure, Tim, I'll be fine. I knew it, you know. I just didn't want to admit it, couldn't admit it." He looked around the ball field, sighed. "I started here, I ended here." He forced a smile. "Damn shame there isn't a poet around, to immortalize this tender moment in verse, right?"

"As long as he doesn't start it off with 'Here lies Jack . . .' " Tim backed up three paces, motioned for Jack to follow him. "Come on. I want to meet your interior decorator, and then you can tell me why you've got Cecily's kid. Hell, you can tell me why Cecily's got a kid."


"I like your brother," Keely said as Mary Margaret slept in her infant seat and she and jack finished up the leftover beef stew. She made great stew and knew it but had never quite mastered how not to make enough to feed a small army.

"*Uuummmpf,* " Jack answered, taking another bite of buttered bread.

141

Keely tried to decide if this was an improvement over the dead silence that had fallen right after Jack had introduced Tim to her, then grabbed his bag from his brother, turned on his heel, and left them standing there.

It was now five o'clock and this was the first she'd seen him since then, and considering the way he was making sure his mouth stayed full of food, clearly he still wasn't ready to talk.

So okay. So she'd talk for him.

"Yes, I really like him. We had an early lunch together, you know, before he had to leave for Philly. That's why I served dinner early, because I had an early lunch." She mentally kicked herself, ordered herself to stop blabbering. "He told me all about Cecily and her brother, Joey, and even a few stories about the two of you when you were kids."

Jack took another bite of stew. If he kept his head bent any closer to the plate in his effort to avoid her eyes, he could just dive in and forget about having to use a fork.

"So then he asked if I liked kinky sex, and I said, sure, love it . . . so I've asked Petra to baby-sit and I'm driving down to Philly tonight, to meet him after the game."

Beef stew, Keely learned as she wiped down the fruit centerpiece, the glass tabletop, and a small bit of wall, had remarkable sticking tendencies once propelled, *spit* actually, by a man who then glared at her as he choked, coughed, then slammed down his fork and stomped out of the kitchen.

Well, what was a girl supposed to do? Tiptoe around, keep her mouth shut, pretend she didn't know that Jack Trehan had probably just lived through one of the most miserable days of his life? Some other girl, maybe. But not her.

142

She'd come back to the house after lunch with Tim, hoping to see Jack's car down at the garages, but he hadn't come home.

She'd walked around the house with Petra, delighting in the new furniture, adjusting a lamp shade or two, planning where she'd like to see an arrangement of pictures, thought about the placement of a mirror, mentally hired painters.

She'd let Petra put Mary Margaret down for her nap and finished picking out drapes and blinds and the necessary hardware, then faxed a "rush" order to her supplier via her laptop computer.

And she'd looked out the window. A lot. But Jack hadn't come home.

By three-thirty, she'd settled herself on the new couch in the den and begun sorting through the VCR tapes that had been piled beside Jack's chair, a chair that was now mercifully banished to the garages.

The tapes had all been neatly hand labeled, and she'd inserted one into the VCR. The label said WORLD SERIES. GAME SIX.

She'd fast-forwarded through most of it, always watching for moments Jack appeared on the tape. He had been on the mound that day, and he'd gone six and two-thirds innings, then left with the score five-to-two, in favor of the Yankees. "As the crowd gives Trehan a standing ovation," the commentator said, "we remind you that this may be the last time any of us sees the great right-handed ace in a Yankee uniform. Jack Trehan undergoes a second rotator-cuff surgery next week."

"Yes, Bill, that's right," another commentator said as Keely watched Jack come back out of the dugout, tip his hat to the cheering hometown crowd, "and that reminds me of something Don Drysdale, another great, said years ago. I've got it right here. Drysdale said, 'A torn rotator cuff is a cancer for a pitcher, and if a pitcher gets a badly torn one, he has to face the facts, it's all over baby.' For Jack Trehan's sake, let's hope it's not all over baby."

Keely had cried then, watching Jack as he took that bow, more serious than smiling, watching as he disappeared down the dugout steps one last time.

She'd ejected the tape and done her best to ignore the one labeled ESPN, FAREWELL NEWS CONFERENCE as she stacked all of the tapes inside the new end table.

Jack must have spent the time since his retirement sitting in this den, watching those same tapes, over and over again. Why didn't he just poke a sharp stick in his eye? It couldn't hurt any worse than that.

Keely wrung out the cloth one last time, then hung it over the built-in rack beneath the sink.

Why wouldn't she let him alone? He deserved time to mourn his lost career, didn't he? She'd spent the first week back under Aunt Mary's roof sitting around in her rattiest pajamas, eating butter brickle ice cream from the container and feeling grease collect in her hair. Everybody deserved time to mourn a lost dream.

The thing was, she'd still be sitting on her Aunt Mary's couch if she'd been left alone, if Aunt Mary hadn't told her that she had two choices—shape up or ship out—because as of Monday morning, she was charging her niece rent.

Nobody was telling Jack Trehan anything. He had enough money to sit on his duff for the rest of his life, replaying the VCR tapes, holding his own pity party. Not that this was her problem. She had a house to decorate, a career in Manhattan to resurrect. But Mary

Margaret deserved more. Japan might be out of the picture now, but Jack still had to figure out that *he* was in charge of his cousin's welfare.

Certainly not Cecily, not after she'd heard about Jack's flaky, irresponsible cousin from Tim. And definitely not Joey Morretti, who had to have all the brainpower of a doorstop. It didn't matter if Cecily finally came home; she couldn't be allowed to regain custody of Mary Margaret, control over Mary Margaret's future.

Keely saw that. Now she had to make Jack see it . . . and all while making sure she did *not* let her heart become involved, not with Mary Margaret and most definitely not with Jack.

Jack packed up his equipment as the sun began to set, having cleaned his glove and spikes after dinner, then stuffed the bag on a shelf in the garage.

Maybe one day he'd dig out his mitt, have it sealed inside a cube of plastic or something dumb like that. Then he could put it on a shelf in his den, along with the trophies, plaques, his uniform, a few balls, and whatever else he kept now in his condo, and stand around, beer can in hand, talking about the good old days with a bunch of pals who'd stopped in to watch a game on the tube.

But not just yet.

Still, he felt all right. It was amazing, more than shocking, but he really did feel all right. He'd given it his best shot and it hadn't worked.

So okay. So it was over. Hey, he'd had a good run. A great run.

He was going to be all right.

Right after he called Mort.

145

Jack pulled the cell phone from the front seat of his car and punched in the code that dialed his agent's cell phone.

"What?" Mort yelled into the phone a few moments later. To Mort, cell phones were tin cans with long, invisible strings on them, and to be heard, he knew he needed to shout.

"Mort, it's me, Jack."

"I'm not talking to you, kid," Mort Mortimer said, then proceeded to make a liar out of himself. "You turned it down? You don't turn stuff down, boy. I turn offers down, and then I let them swing in the breeze a little, so they come back with a better number. Then we say yes. And the only reason I'm talking to you now is because they already came back. Five million for two years. Chicken feed, I grant you, but better than I'd hoped. Plus a signing bonus, and another one if you help them get to their version of the series. They yelled, they screamed, they moaned and groaned, but I kept squeezing until I got 'em. Your contract with the Yanks is done as of July one anyway, so there's no problem there. Now all we need to do is see the contracts and it's Sayonara, Uncle Sam; hello, Tokyo."

"I don't want it," Jack told his agent as he slammed the door of his car and began climbing the sloping hill toward the back of the house. The sun was lighting up the entire rear of the house, glinting off the water in the pool. A great big chunk of the world would give its right arm to live in this house. Hell, he *had* given his right arm to live in this house.

An unexpected calm enveloped him, and he actually felt a new spring in his step. His arm still hurt like a bitch, but it would feel better tomorrow, and feel even better the day after that.

"Jack? Jack?" Jack took the phone away from his ear; Mort was really in full throat now. "Jack? I didn't hear you. I mean, I couldn't have heard you, could I? Jack! You can't turn this down. Nobody turns down five million dollars! Damn it, Jack—talk to me!"

"See you in Arizona next week, Mort. Fax me the particulars. Oh, and the Corvette? I want a red one." Jack flipped the phone shut and kept walking.

# Chapter Nine

*I knew when my career was over.*
*In 1965 my baseball card*
*came out with no picture.*

—Bob Uecker

IN THE END, SELF-PRESERVATION WON OUT OVER Keely's near compulsion to chase down Jack Trehan, sit him down—tie him down, if necessary—and tell him she understood how he felt. She understood, she sympathized, but now he had to stop thinking about his lost career and start thinking about the future. About Mary Margaret.

So she gave him the weekend. Jack didn't know he'd been given the weekend, but Keely felt pretty good about her magnanimous gesture. It never occurred to her that she was in no position to *give* him anything, or that she had no right to poke her nose into his business. She would have been amazed if anyone told her that she might be bossy, interfering. She was just the sort of person who, when she felt she was right, just assumed that the rest of the world also knew she was right. Or, as her Aunt Mary had been heard to say, not always with a smile, "Keely would have made a great dictator."

So, operating in this marvelous generosity of spirit, Keely made great meals, kept herself busy with Mary Margaret, and stayed out of the den all day Sunday while Jack channel-surfed, probably lowering his I.Q. by several points as he watched ESPN, then six different baseball games, then ESPN again, from early morning until nearly midnight.

Monday morning, however, all bets were off, so she handed Mary Margaret over to Petra and hunted down Jack, who was swimming laps in the pool.

And nearly lost her nerve, her resolve, and possibly even—only temporarily—the ability to remember her own name.

He'd just climbed out of the pool, the sun shining on his wet, glistening skin, on the soft golden hair that lightly covered his arms and legs, his flat, muscular chest. Wide shoulders, narrow hips, the long, lean, muscular frame of the ballplayer. His dark blond hair looked even darker as it lay wet and plastered to his well-shaped head, set off the pretty damn magnificent planes of his face, his absolutely perfect nose and brow and chin. Even his bare feet were sexy, damn him.

He didn't see her, just raised his hands to push his fingers through his hair, ruffle it. Which was worse on her equilibrium? His hair slicked back or damply curling around his face? Then he turned, bent from the waist to retrieve his towel, and Keely got her first clear view of Jack Trehan's butt in a bathing suit.

A law. There ought to be a law against Jack Trehan's butt in a bathing suit.

Still, she had come out here to talk to the man, and that was just what she was going to do. Hand him some home truths, wake him up to his responsibilities. All

148

that good stuff. But maybe she'd sort of *ease* herself into it . . .

"Hi," she said, inwardly wincing. That was too bright, too cheerful. And if her voice got any higher, she could call dogs with it. "That is, good morning, Jack. How . . . how's the water?"

He rubbed his head with the towel, then draped it over his shoulders. "Wet. Is something the matter? You look sort of flushed."

"What? Me? No, no," Keely said, backing up a pace as Jack came closer. Close enough to smell the chlorine on his skin, count the small spattering of freckles on his chest.

"You want to talk to me, right?" he asked, stepping even closer, so that she took yet another step backwards. "You've been a good girl all weekend, but you're just *dying* to talk to me, aren't you? Offer me your condolences, tell me how sorry you are that my ball career is over, that from now on all I've got left is the rest of my life, with nothing to fill it. Even better, you've got a way to fill it for me, don't you, Keely? I can fill it with Candy, raising Candy."

He tipped his head to one side as he looked at her. "How am I doing so far?"

Keely wet her lips, averted her eyes. "Well . . . actually . . . I mean . . ." She closed her mouth, counted to three. "Hey," she said, beginning again, this time with only her anger to guide her, "what's wrong with that? You've got the time, you've got the money— you've got this house. Why not keep Mary Mar— Candy?"

He raised his eyebrows, his grin bordering on wicked. "I told you Mary Margaret was too big a name for her right now. You've got to give her time to grow into it.

149

But we'll talk about that later. For now, we'll talk about how I'm supposed to take care of her, okay? I mean, are you applying for another job here, Keely? And if you are, which job would that be? Nanny? *Live-in* nanny?"

"This has nothing to do with me!" Keely protested, wishing she could believe her own denial. "I'm going back to Manhattan, remember?" Then she winced, because it wasn't exactly politic to mention her own hopeful comeback, right after he'd just lost his last chance at one of his own. "Oh, Jack," she said, reaching out a hand, touching his damp yet warm arm. "I'm sorry. I shouldn't have . . . I mean, that was low."

Jack shook his head, grinned. "You think you can do it, don't you? You really think you can go back. You didn't make it the first time. What makes you think it'll be easier this time around?"

"Nothing," Keely admitted quietly. This conversation wasn't taking her anywhere she wanted to go. Still, it was better if he believed she wanted nothing more than to head back to Manhattan. It was safer for her to believe she wanted nothing more than to head back to Manhattan, even if her biggest reason for doing so still remained making one rat fink Gregory I-told-you-so Fontaine eat his words.

She'd like to think her motive was more noble, or that she still felt this burning desire to "make it there" in the Big Apple, be a career woman, show her Aunt Mary she had what it took to succeed. None of these were noble reasons, but they were all Keely had right now. That, and a nearly overwhelming desire to push down the spiky wet curls sticking up on Jack's head. She'd give half her commission on this job to be able to feel free to make such an intimate gesture.

"But you've got to try, don't you?" Jack said as Keely

150

lost herself in the jumbled mess her powers of reason had become since the first time she'd stepped inside Jack Trehan's life.

"Yes," she said, grabbing at the straw he'd handed her. "I've got to try, Jack. You, more than anyone else, know I've got to try."

Something passed over Jack's face, some sort of . . . cloud, and Keely watched as he took off the towel, threw it on the tile beside the pool. "Yeah. Guess that's all you can do, seeing as you don't want to do anything else. I don't blame you." Then he turned, dove back into the pool, leaving Keely to try to figure out just what the hell had happened . . . or not happened.

Keely propped the telephone between her ear and shoulder, sorting through an accumulation of mail as the phone rang in her aunt's Athens hotel. Bill, bill, bill, circular, bill, bill, letter from Gregory, bill, bill—*letter from Gregory?*

She reached for the antique brass letter opener her aunt kept on her desk just as Mary McBride Forrester came on the line. "Hello? Hello? Whoever you are, do you speak English?"

"Hi, Aunt Mary," Keely said, putting down the opener, but then turning the envelope over and over, as if she could summon up some sort of X-ray vision and see the letter inside. "I'm returning your call."

"My six calls, you mean," her aunt shot back across the miles. "Where have you been? Is the shop all right? Did Mrs. Morgan's library table arrive safely?"

"Everything's fine, Aunt Mary. And the library table was delivered two weeks ago, remember? How's Greece?"

Keely could hear the sigh across the long-distance

151

lines as the woman took in a deep breath, then waited until her aunt was two minutes into what would probably be a five minute monologue before reaching for the letter opener again.

As her aunt talked, Keely read:

*Dearest Keely,*

*You haven't returned any of my telephone messages, and I don't blame you. I've been a pig, haven't I? Well, the time has come to make it all up to you, darling. I've just heard about the most marvelous little space in the Village. Perfect for your shop, and the rent is perfect for you.*

*The landlord tells me his tenants vacate the first of August, at which time he's doing a little remodeling—without my input, which is his loss—a little fumigating, but don't you worry about that. this is, after all, New York, where the men are men and the roaches are everywhere. I'm enclosing his card so you can contact him. I said he should expect your call.*

*Good luck, my dear girl. We're off to Paris, Shavonna and I, to shop, and won't be back for at least a month. Remember Paris, Keely? Ah . . . we'll always have Paris . . .*

*Gregory*

"Keely? Keely, are you there? Damn phones."

"Hmmm? What? Oh! Yes, I'm here, Aunt Mary," Keely said, still looking at the letter. "It . . . it all sounds so wonderful!"

"Travelers' complaint sounds *wonderful?* The poor man has swallowed so much Imodium, I doubt he'll ever again be able to—well, never mind. We're leaving

152

Athens tomorrow, Keely, for the last leg of our cruise, so you won't hear from me for a while. For God's sake, child, don't burn the place down. Just finish whatever you're working on now and put the CLOSED sign up until we're back."

"When will that be, Aunt Mary? I thought you were coming home next week."

"Keely, a person does this honeymoon stuff just once, if she's doing it right. We cruise, we sightsee, and maybe we stop off in Paris or Rome on our way home. I'm going with the flow, as I remember you calling it, for the first time in my life. It's wonderful! All right, I have to go. The sun's setting here, and the view from our balcony is breathtaking."

Keely was left holding a buzzing phone, which she put down as she sank into the desk chair. Paris. Everybody was going to Paris. And where was she going?

Nowhere. Whether she stayed here or moved back to Manhattan, from the moment she'd first held Candy, first sat across the dinner table from Jack, she'd had the sinking feeling that she was going absolutely nowhere. Which was a damn shame, now that she knew just where she wanted to go.

She stood up, crumpled the letter, and threw it into the waste can. She went upstairs to her bedroom and packed up more of her clothing to take back to Jack's house. She threw out the newspapers, hit the ERASE button on the upstairs phone line without listening to the messages from Gregory, and closed all the shades so that the sun wouldn't fade her aunt's dark blue carpets.

She dumped fairly ancient milk down the kitchen sink drain, threw out a half loaf of stale bread, and wrapped up the garbage for the next morning's pickup.

153

She hung the CLOSED sign on the front door of the shop.

And she made it all the way to the car before she stopped, went back, fished the crumpled letter and business card out of the waste can, and jammed both into her purse before heading back to Whitehall.

When she arrived, it was to find a note on the kitchen table, a note from Petra. She'd written it in Spanish, so that all Keely could make out was that Petra had gone to the *dentista,* and that Jack was acting as *cuidaniños de bebé.*

Jack was acting as sitter to the baby?

Keely instantly panicked. Where? Where was Jack? Where was the baby? She ran upstairs. No Jack. No Candy. She ran back downstairs. Ditto.

And then she stopped, shook her head, and realized that she was panicking when she should be rejoicing. Wasn't this what she wanted? Jack and Candy, bonding? Getting to know each other. Appreciate each other. Forging a connection.

Without her as part of the equation.

"Stop it!" she commanded herself, making one last pass through the downstairs rooms before heading for the garages. "Just stop it. You love the baby, and that's it. You don't even *like* Jack Tre—*Ohmigod!*"

Keely broke into a run, sliding to a stop after she'd thrown open the gate and entered the fenced-in pool area. "Jack Trehan—are you out of your tiny mind? Get her out of there!"

She watched as Jack, Candy held tight in his arms, turned around in the pool, looked up at her. "Look, Candy, Aunt Keely's home, and she's turning all red and splotchy. Isn't that cute? Smile, McBride, you're scaring the kid."

154

"Jack, I mean it. Get that baby out of there. She could drown."

"She isn't going to drown. I've got her."

"Oh, yeah? The other day you couldn't hold her and she was wrapped in paper towels. And what if you get a cramp and go under? What happens to Candy then?"

Jack sighed, began walking through the shallow end of the pool, toward the cement steps. "What do you do, Keely? Sit up nights, thinking of everything that can go wrong in any situation? I didn't go into the deep end, and besides, Candy likes the water. Don't you, sweetheart?" he ended, nuzzling Candy's neck.

The baby giggled, grabbed Jack's ear. "Da. Da-da-da-da!"

Someone was really going to have to watch Candy as she got older, was able to walk away in a grocery store or something. She had gone straight to Petra. Now she was drooling all over Jack. The kid would walk away with anybody. She'd have to be taught about strangers. Would Jack teach her about not talking to strangers?

"Come here, darling," Keely urged the baby, holding out her arms to her. "Let me dry you off."

Candy turned her head, buried her face against Jack's chest. "It would appear she isn't ready to get out. Do you have a bathing suit? Why don't you join us? We'll use the buddy system. Then, when I get that cramp and sink to the bottom, I can first toss Candy in your direction."

Keely bit her bottom lip, devastated, knowing she was being silly but still devastated. Candy had turned away from her. In truth, that was a good thing. After all, she wouldn't be here forever, probably wouldn't be here for more than a few more weeks, tops. Getting Candy attached to Jack, and Jack to her, was just what Keely wanted.

155

So why did it hurt so much?

"Keely? Come on. The pool's heated, you know, otherwise I wouldn't have brought Candy in here with me."

Keely nodded, not trusting her voice, and returned to the house, carrying her suitcase upstairs. She had thrown a bathing suit into it at the last minute, telling herself she'd swim at night, when Jack wasn't in the pool.

She really had to stop telling herself lies.

Jack lifted Candy out of the water, laughing as her diaper, hanging low underneath her one-piece sunsuit, dripped water back into the pool. The baby kicked her legs, waved her hands, and Jack lowered her once more, then lifted her, lowered her, bobbing her up and down as Candy giggled.

"Up and down, up and down. Whee, Candy! Up and down, up and down. Silly Aunt Keely. I've got you, don't I, Candy? Up and down, up and down—oh, shit!"

Jack grabbed at the back of Candy's sunsuit, pulling her out of the water, lifting her high against his chest. Water streamed off the baby's face and she sucked in her breath . . . sucked it in, sucked it in, sucked it in . . . until at last she let out with a wail that could probably be heard in isolated caves in Tibet.

"It's all right, honey, it's all right," Jack soothed frantically, wiping at her face, pushing her drenched curls back from her forehead. His heart was beating so fast and hard he could hear it in his ears. "I just lost my grip for a second there, that's all. Aw, come on, Candy, please cut it out. Aunt Doomsayer will be back any minute, and if Cousin Jack has to hear her say 'I told you so,' you probably won't see this pool again until you're sixteen."

156

Candy cried for another few minutes, then slowly stopped as Jack tickled her belly, let her shove her hand in his mouth. The kid seemed to have a real desire to see if she could pull his bottom teeth out of his head.

"Ah, swee? Dwat's bether," Jack told her, speaking around the baby's fingers until she let go. "And that's better yet, thank you. And look, Candy, it's only water." He cupped his hand, dipped it into the pool, then splashed himself in the face. "See? Only water. Now you do it."

He took Candy's hand, dipped it in the water, then pretended to be shocked, made a face, when he helped her splash him. "That's it," he said as Candy laughed, leaned half out of his arms, splashed again.

God, he loved how this kid felt in his arms. Her skin smooth and cool, her small weight made even less as her chubbiness was made buoyant by the water.

And she was smart. Damn, this kid was smart. She picked up on the splashing bit right away. Obviously she wasn't overloaded with Morretti genes and had gotten her brains from the Trehan side of the family.

Jack heard the back door open and watched as Keely walked toward the pool area, not really feeling Candy's little fingernails digging into his gums once more, as his jaw involuntarily dropped open. Where the hell had he had his head for the past week? Up his—?

He'd known Keely McBride was pretty, had already appreciated her long legs, her curly blond hair, whether she wore it loose or scraped it back and pinned it to her head, trying to look professional. He already knew he could be attracted to her, *was* attracted to her.

But Keely McBride in a bathing suit was a revelation to him. She walked with her spine straight, her chin lifted, her arms moving easily at her sides. And her

157

skin! So creamy white against the navy blue of her swimsuit. Jack's mind went on overload, along with his hormones. The swell of her breasts. The remarkable straightness of her legs. The slimness of her waist. The flare of her hips. The whole package. He sank lower in the pool, hoping it was colder down there.

"You look . . ." he began as Keely halted on the second cement step, the water coming up just past her ankles.

"Like the underbelly of a fish, I know," Keely supplied when Jack lost his train of thought. Hell, he'd just about lost his mind. "According to the experts, I'll be very happy when I'm ninety and have the best skin in the nursing home, but for now, having to slap on sunscreen because otherwise I burn badly just makes me look like I've spent most of my life in a dark cave."

"Petra put sunscreen on Candy before she left for the dentist," Jack said, feeling ridiculously eager to score points with Keely. "I—I made her do it."

Keely walked down two more steps, tipped her head, looked at him.

"Oh, okay, so Petra thought of it. I didn't have a clue. Still, you can't blame a guy for trying."

"Do you mind if I swim a couple of laps, to warm up?" Keely asked, then pushed herself forward, striking out into the center of the pool without waiting for an answer.

"Can you say rhetorical question, Candy?" Jack asked his cousin as he watched Keely slicing neatly through the water. "Because that's what Aunt Keely asks, rhetorical questions—the kind that, to her at least, don't require an answer. Like, 'Do you mind if I waltz in here, take over your life, and tell you how to live it?' That sort of question."

Candy giggled and slapped her hands on the surface of the pool.

"Yeah, I know, you like her. I like her, too. Sort of. So what'll we do about this, huh?"

Keely swam two laps before she stopped in front of Jack and Candy, reached out so that the baby squirmed away from her cousin and let Keely hold her.

"Oh! She feels so *good*," Keely said, her brown eyes wide with amazement as Candy wrapped slippery wet arms around her neck. "Are you having fun, sweetie?" she asked as Candy pressed her forehead against Keely's cheek.

Jack just stood there, waist deep in water, looking at the two of them. Both blond. Both with their hair darkened by the water, yet already forming into ringlets. Keely sank down into the pool, so that just their two heads were visible, put her arms beneath Candy's, and slowly turned in a circle, playing tugboat with Candy or something like that. His dad used to call it tugboat when he'd pull him and Tim around the local public pool.

And while their mother stood on the edge, yelling, "Frank! Hold on to them. Frank, you're going to drown those two boys!"

Jack smiled, shook his head. Memories.

"Here, let me do that," he said, and took hold of Candy's hands, half-supporting her on one bent knee as he pulled her through the water, not realizing he was saying, much as his father had said years earlier, "Putt-putt, putt-putt, *toot, toot,* here comes Candy the tugboat."

And not realizing that not all the moisture on Keely's cheeks was from the water in the pool . . .

❖❖❖

159

"Putt-putt-putt . . ." Jack singsonged under his breath as he sat in his den, a happy man.

He'd had himself a day. A good day. A damn good day.

Life didn't have to revolve around a five-man rotation. He didn't have to worry where his lucky socks were. He didn't have to spend long hours in the training room, his arm stuck in the whirlpool bath or jammed into a vat of ice.

He didn't have to study films, or sit in the dugout watching batters, devising strategies for pitching to them the next night. No more team flights, team meetings, schlepping his luggage, sleeping in hotel rooms, eating in restaurants that hadn't even heard the words *cheese steak,* yet alone known how to cook one.

Nope. He could just sit here, watch the tube, take a nap, down a whole bag of potato chips. The little woman upstairs, putting the kid to bed, the bills paid. No stress, no muss, no fuss. Just one day following the other.

God. He just might throw up.

Yeah, well, he thought, changing the channel, at least he'd given it a shot. Domestic bliss. And he'd had fun today. But was this any way to live a life? No. No way.

Maybe.

He had a responsibility to Candy. He knew that. An idiot would know that. Cecily could come back tomorrow or stay away for the next five years. Either way, Cecily was *not* going to get her hands on Candy again. She was just too damn irresponsible.

While he was responsible. Right?

Wrong. He was unemployed. Rich, granted, but unemployed—unemployable. Single. And playing tugboat was a far cry from actually raising a kid.

But there was Keely, wasn't there?

160

She liked Candy. Hell, she was soppy over her.

Except that Keely was going back to New York right after she finished decorating his house, her pockets filled with the money he'd pay her. She'd made that clear enough. If Keely was nothing else, she was direct, honest. He was a means to an end for her.

Jack hit the controller, mindlessly surfing the channels as he thought some more.

Okay, so Keely would leave when the house was done. Unless she had to stay long enough to get even soppier over Candy, be unable to leave her. Because Jack needed Keely, or someone like her, if he was going to convince a judge that he should have custody of his cousin.

Keely was already on the scene. She was here, she was competent, and the judge would probably be afraid to say no to her. Lord knew Jack was afraid to say no to her, not when she had a full head of steam working for her.

Besides, he liked her. Bossy, opinionated, take-charge, hates to be wrong, out to prove herself . . . vulnerable, soft-hearted, honest, smart, competent, a great cook. And beautiful. What the hell was wrong with this Gregory guy? How had he let her get away?

"Probably wasn't man enough for her," Jack said, picking up his soda can, taking a large swallow that went down the wrong pipe, so that he ended by choking, coughing, as he reached over to grab the ringing phone.

"Jack? Is that you?"

"Yeah . . . yeah . . . hold on," Jack said, covering the mouthpiece as he coughed, then cleared his throat. "Hi, Tim," he said after a moment, wiping at his eyes. "Good game yesterday. What's up?"

"Word's out, that's what's up. Johnson, from *The Daily News,* cornered me at my locker after the game,

161

wanted to know if it was true you turned down the Japanese deal because the White Sox are interested."

"Chicago? Chicago isn't interested in me. And who told them about the Japanese deal? What did you tell them?"

"The truth, that I hadn't heard anything. But Johnson said he had it from an inside source. You know the translation for that one, right? Mort."

Jack hit the MUTE button on the TV and sat back in his chair. "If there isn't any interest, make up your own. Yeah, that sounds just like Mort. I guess I have to make it plainer to him. I'm done. Not only am I done, but I'm finally feeling pretty good about being done. I've got a life to live, you know. I've got Candy here, a nice house, plenty of money—I don't need the hassle anymore, Tim. I really don't."

"So you're going domestic, Jack? Let me guess: Keely's got something to do with this, hasn't she?"

"Keely?" Jack shook his head. "No, of course not. What would she have to do with anything?"

"I *saw* her, Jack," Tim reminded him. "And it's not only great looks, she's a nice lady. Just make sure you know what you're doing. I wouldn't want you to get caught up on the rebound."

Jack stood, began to pace. "Rebound? What rebound? Did Sandra Bullock dump me and I didn't know about it? Hell, I don't know Sandra Bullock."

"I mean on the rebound from your first love— baseball—and from losing your career," Tim told him. "You're at loose ends, bro, which could make home and hearth—and baby and blonde—look pretty good to you. Just be careful, okay? Look, I've got to go now. We're catching a flight to Florida tonight, but it's only for two games. We'll be back in Philly again on Thursday for a

162

pretty good stretch at home. Maybe we can get together then? You can bring the little family down."

"It's not my little—oh, forget it. Give me a call when you get back."

Jack put down the phone, then lowered himself onto the leather couch. He had to think about this. No. No, he didn't. He didn't have to think about this, because there was nothing to think about. Rebound? Tim was nuts. And he, Jack Trehan, wasn't stupid!

Oh, yeah? So why had he been watching the House and Garden Channel, on mute, for the last ten minutes? It wasn't as if he had any big plans for stenciling a border of ducks around the top of the den walls.

He threw down the controller and just about jumped out of his seat, heading for the kitchen. "Keely!" he called out, heading up the backstairs, but not before grabbing a hunk of freshly made brownie from the pan beside the stove. "Keely? Where are you?"

She poked her head outside her door, made a face at him. "What? Is something wrong? You're going to wake Candy."

He wanted to shout at her: "Yeah, there's something wrong. You're damn right there's something wrong. How did you get me to think I wanted any of this?"

Instead he winced a little, said, "I'm sorry. I didn't realize she was asleep. Would . . . would you come downstairs for a minute? I nee—want to talk to you."

"Well," she said, still with only her head visible, "I'm not dressed . . ."

"I've seen you in your nightgown before, remember?"

"No, Jack, you don't get it. I mean, I'm not dressed. Not at all. Give me a couple of minutes, okay?"

Jack stood just outside her closed door for about one of those minutes, considering what would have happened if he'd just barged into her bedroom without knocking.

"Get a grip, Trehan," he told himself as he headed back down the stairs and got a fresh can of soda from the door of the refrigerator. He fought down the urge to hold the cold can to his temples, like some overwhelmed old lady about to faint, and headed back into the den.

He collapsed onto the couch, then quickly stood up again and sat down in one of the chairs. Better they should be chair-to-chair and not side-by-side on the couch.

"So? What's up?" Keely asked, walking into the room in her bare feet, wearing God only knew what under a short pink terry-cloth robe. *Please let her be wearing something under that robe.*

"Sit down, Keely," he said, then leaned forward in his chair, his elbows on his knees., "I think we need to understand each other here, okay?"

She sat, then looked at him out of the corners of her eyes. "Understand each other how, Jack?"

"I'm not sure," he admitted, shaking his head. "For now, let's just remember that I'm your employer, and you're my employee."

"No."

"What?"

"I'm not your employee. I'm working for you, but I'm not your employee. Not in the strictest sense. In the strictest sense, I'm working for my Aunt Mary. You've just temporarily hired my services."

"I don't *want* your serv—oh, hell!" Jack couldn't sit still, because if he sat still he had a mind-blowing front seat view of Keely's long, bare legs. He got to his feet, walked over to stand with his back to the television set.

164

"Look, Keely, we've sort of gotten ourselves into a mess here. You weren't supposed to be living here."

"But Candy—"

"Yes, yes, I know," he said, cutting her off. "There wasn't supposed to be a Candy, either. I don't know how it happened, but we really made a mess of this. I should have called Joey right away. Called somebody. I wasn't thinking straight, Keely. I admit that. I was too wrapped up in what was going on in my own life, setting up the tryout—feeling sorry for myself."

She nodded her head. "Well, when you're right, you're right, Jack," she said.

"Gee, thanks. You couldn't lie, tell me I had every right to feel sorry for myself?"

"Well, of course you had every right."

"Thanks," he said shortly, wondering where this conversation was going. So far, it was going nowhere.

Keely stood up, walked around the coffee table to stand in front of him. He could back up, but all that would do would be to crash him into the TV, and make him look as stupid as he felt at the moment. Damn Tim. Leave it to his brother to screw up his head.

"Look, Jack, let me help you out here, okay? You had a bad break, no question. And then, before you could totally come to grips with it, Candy landed on your doorstep. *I* landed on your doorstep. You needed help, I needed money, and we struck a bargain. How am I doing so far?" She lifted one hand, brushed at the corner of his mouth, sending shock waves straight through him. "Sorry. You had a bit of brownie stuck there," she said, her cheeks coloring. "Anyway, shall I continue?"

He gave her a quick wave of both hands, wordlessly giving her permission to continue. He would have said something, except he could smell some really nice

165

perfume, or maybe just soap, and he liked the way it smelled. He liked the way her hair looked, pulled back in a silly ponytail, with small little wisps curling at the nape of her neck. And why hadn't he ever noticed that she had these little golden flecks in her brown eyes?

"Jack? Are you still listening?" Keely asked, tipping her head as she looked at him. Damn, what did she see when she looked at him? Hopefully, she couldn't see what he was thinking.

"I'm listening," he told her, stepping past her, going over to the coffee table to arm himself with his can of soda. He took a long drink. "Go on."

"There isn't that much more to say. You had that tryout, you decided not to take the offer to go to Japan, and now you're finally free to come to grips with the fact that your career is over. So now, now that you've figured that out, you've also finally looked around and noticed that Candy's still here. I'm still here."

"Candy's staying here," Jack said tightly, because that was the one thing in this world he could be sure of right now. "I'm hiring a lawyer in the morning. A battalion of lawyers, if that's what it takes."

Keely's smile grabbed at his gut, twisted it. "Oh, Jack—that's wonderful. Just wonderful! I knew you'd fall in love with her if you just gave yourself half a chance."

Okay, he had his opening. Now, with Tim's warning still ringing in his ears, he stepped up, ready to take one last swing, go for the fence. "I'm happy you approve. Besides, I have a responsibility to the whole family. Candy is family, remember. But that also means I have to make some sort of permanent arrangements. Candy's had people walking in and out of her life ever since she was born, if I know my cousin, and I do. She needs

166

something more permanent. So," he ended, taking a deep breath, "I'd like to ask you something."

Keely stood very still. "Go on. Ask."

"All right. I know this wasn't part of the deal. Hell, most of this wasn't part of the deal. But sometimes, without any warning . . . well, things happen, don't they? What started out one way ends up another, right? I know you didn't come here to take care of Candy, and I probably shouldn't ask you to think of anything more permanent. But . . . well, I have to think about more permanent arrangements. So"— he took a deep breath, finished in a rush—"would you help me find a nanny for Candy?"

"Find a . . . you want me to . . . but you said *perm*—that is, you didn't want . . . ?" Keely bit her lips together, nodded. "Sure," she said brightly. Really brightly. "I'll get on it first thing tomorrow. I'd be . . . I'd be happy to help. Anything else? Because I'm sort of tired."

"No, nothing else," he said, picking up the remote control and aiming it toward the television set.

"Candy has her appointment with the pediatrician tomorrow," Keely added. "You are still going, aren't you?"

"Yeah. Sure," Jack said, surfing the channels, not seeing a damn thing. "And thanks for helping me get all of this rolling. I really appreciate your help."

"Sure, no problem. Well, good night, then," Keely said, and slowly left the room, although he could hear her break into a run when she couldn't have been more than halfway through the kitchen.

Jack swore under his breath, throwing down the remote control. Step up to the plate and take a swing? Where had that come from? Tim could have told him, anybody could have told him. He never had been able to hit worth a damn . . .

# Chapter Ten

*I hated to bat against Drysdale. After*
*he hit you he'd come around, look at*
*the bruise on your arm and say,*
*"Do you want me to sign it?"*

—Mickey Mantle

KEELY CAREFULLY FOLDED HER DENIM SKIRT, THEN
flung it in the general direction of her suitcase, where a
pile of clothing already tilted heavily to the left. The
skirt was just too much, and the entire pile tipped over,
clothing and suitcase both tumbling off the bed and onto
the floor.

"Damn it!" she said, looking at the mess she'd made.
She wiped at her damp cheeks with the back of one
hand, knowing she was behaving like an idiot. So who
cared? She certainly didn't care. She just wanted out of
here—now.

Keely pressed her hands to her head, tried to regulate
her breathing, which had been quick and shallow for so
long that she decided she just might be hyperventilating.
Oh, that would be good. Just what she needed, to have
to go back downstairs and find a paper bag to breathe
into while Jack watched.

How could she have been so *stupid?* She'd actually
thought—hoped, believed—that Jack Trehan had been
about to offer her an *arrangement.* More than an
arrangement. She thought he was going to ask her to
marry him. Not a love match—neither of them would
even think such a thing—but one of those old-
fashioned marriages of convenience, this one for the
convenience of Jack, who wanted to show a stable

environment for Candy when he went before the judge.

It would have been an insulting offer, highly insulting. He knew she wanted to go back to Manhattan—she'd certainly told him often enough. (Whom had she been reminding? Him, or herself?) But he also knew she was crazy about Candy, and she'd make her a good mother, damn it.

And what was she, anyway? Chopped liver? A marriage of convenience was one thing, but didn't the man have eyes in his head? It wasn't as if she were ninety years old, or cursed with two heads and a tail, or anything like that. He liked her legs. She already knew he liked her legs; a girl just knew that sort of thing, right?

She thought he'd liked more of her than just her legs. She thought he'd realized that the other night, when she'd so stupidly put her arms around him, and he'd looked at her as if he hadn't wanted to let her go. Had that just been born of proximity? And just what was so bad about proximity anyway?

She certainly liked more of him than just that silly, boyish smile of his. And his bluer than blue eyes. And the way he got all silly and cute when he was around Candy, then tried to pretend his soft heart hadn't been touched, captured, in Candy's two usually damp little hands.

But marry him? Where had that idea come from? What had made her think that was where his "I need a favor" was going . . . and why was she so stupidly disappointed that it never got there?

What did she think she'd gotten caught up in, anyway, some dumb movie-of-the-week? David Hasselhoff gets stuck with baby, hires Valerie Bertinelli off the street, falls in love with baby and Valerie, neglectful biological mother Calista Flockhart, in her

169

one altruistic action of her entire life, conveniently falls off cliff in Tibet after giving baby to David in her will, which was scratched on a rock as she lay dying—and the new little family lives happily ever after?

Idiocy! Pure idiocy!

Besides, she didn't really even *like* Jack Trehan. She was attracted to him, definitely, but that didn't mean she liked him. Much. Maybe a little. Oh, okay, so the guy kind of grew on you . . . so does moss, if you don't move around often enough.

What had she been thinking? She had a career waiting for her back in Manhattan. Even Gregory had finally realized that, or he wouldn't have put her on to the shop in the Village. Gregory was a lot of things, but nothing he did was because he couldn't help himself, he just had this great big heart. Gregory? A heart? Hardly.

So what did she want with a kid, or with Jack Trehan? Nothing, that's what she wanted. She'd had some temporary aberration, that's all, maybe from sniffing too many brownie fumes. She'd been playing the happy homemaker for more than a week now, decorating, cooking, smiling, and talking—even arguing—across the dinner table, taking care of the baby. It had all come together to temporarily warp her brain. She'd actually begun to enjoy herself, discover things about herself she'd never known. That she wasn't like her Aunt Mary. She did have the makings of a mother, a wife. That there was more out there than trying to be the best, never wrong and never failing.

"Well, girl," she said, going down on her knees to begin picking up her clothing, "that was profound, wasn't it? So, now that you've started analyzing yourself, let's mull this one over for a while—were you falling for the happy family stuff or were you looking for a way not to go back to Manhattan, maybe to fail again? Or, worst of all, were you actually falling for Jack Trehan?"

As luck would have it, good or bad, she wasn't sure, there was a knock on her door just then, so that she didn't have to try to answer any of those questions.

"What?" she asked, still on her knees. "It's late, Jack. Go to bed."

Obedient the man wasn't, because she heard the door opening behind her, and Jack's footsteps on the hardwood floor. She sat back on her heels, turned her head. "Go away."

"What are you doing? I heard a bump on the floor a little while ago."

"Yeah. It's next on my list—buy more carpets. That way, when I murder you for barging into my room unannounced, the *thunk* of your body hitting the floor won't wake Candy."

"Cute. You've such a way with words, Keely." Jack went down on his heels beside her, picked up a blouse, which she quickly snatched from his hand to toss it on top of a black lace bra that lay on the floor. "Going somewhere?"

"Unpacking," she lied, grabbing an armful of clothes and tossing them onto the bed as she stood up. "I told you I'd brought more clothing back from the shop with me. The suitcase slipped off the bed."

Jack grabbed at the nightshirt she'd worn a few days ago, then washed and put back in a drawer. "So this is all stuff from your aunt's place? You own two of these?" he asked as he stood up as well, stood entirely too close to her.

"Okay, okay, so I was maybe thinking about leaving. Sue me."

He still held the nightshirt, sort of waved it in front of her face. "For breach of contract, or for lying?"

Keely turned her back on him, or the nightshirt, or both. "I . . . I had a *moment.* But I'm over it. I'm not leaving. I need the money, remember?"

"How could I forget?" Jack asked, putting his hands on her shoulders, turning her to face him. "Look, Keely, I was sitting downstairs, going over our conversation, and something occurred to me. I mean, I don't think I explained myself very well. In fact"—he gave a slight cough—"somebody could almost think I had been about to say something totally different from what I said. Am I making sense here?"

"Not at all," Keely told him, ducking out from under his hands and picking up a hanger, sliding it inside one of her blouses. "Because if one was to think you might have thought you were about to say something different than what you intended to say, then one would, could, possibly think that you'd maybe *meant* to say something other than what you said. Which you didn't."

Jack tipped his head to one side, looked at her owlishly. "Are we doing some interior decorator imitation of Abbott and Costello's 'Who's On First' routine? Because I didn't understand a word of that."

"Yes—you—did," Keely told him shortly, picking up another hanger, momentarily considering how it would look if she squashed it down on Jack's head. "Not only that, but you weren't satisfied with just not saying what you almost said. Now you've come up here and almost said it again, just to remind me that you didn't say it. Tell me, did you knock down the same batter twice in the same game?"

"Only if I wasn't thrown out the first time," Jack told

her, his lopsided smile hurting her heart, her pride, and probably threatening her sanity.

"Yeah, well, you don't have to knock me down twice, Jack Trehan. I've got it. I understand perfectly. I'm here to take care of Candy and furnish this house. Anything else I may do—cook for you, take a swim in your pool, *talk* to you—is all stuff I've decided to do on my own. You never asked me to do any of it, so I shouldn't start getting ideas. Is that it? Because if it is, you can go now. Go to bed, go downstairs, go to hell. Go anywhere, Jack, because I don't want you here anymore."

When it came to getting in the last word, Keely had pretty much developed the practice into an art form. But she was destined to never remember exactly what she'd just said, because suddenly Jack's hands were on her shoulders again, and his mouth was against hers.

He didn't actually take her into his arms, so she could have moved away if she wanted, slapped his face, called him names. Something. Instead, she did nothing. She just stood there, her eyes closed, her arms sort of waving in the air, and pressed her mouth against his, trying not to sag against him as her knees melted.

"There," he said a moment later, having moved back so that his face was mere inches from hers. "That wasn't so bad, was it? We do a lot better when we're not talking to each other. Maybe Tim was only half right. Maybe we can build on that."

And then he was gone, and Keely all but staggered over to the bed to sit down, try to calm her rapidly beating heart.

The bubble-gum-chewing girl at the front desk looked up as Jack leaned on the counter, Keely beside him, holding Candy. "Ah, she's cute. So you're the parents?"

Keely opened her mouth, but Jack spoke before she could say anything. "Yes."

"Fine. She looks a lot like your wife, doesn't she? Please just sit down over there, fill out these forms, and the doctor will be with you shortly. Oh, and I need to make copies of your health insurance card."

"That's all right," Jack told her. "I'll be paying by credit card."

"Oh, but—" the girl began, so Jack smiled at her again and said, "Trust me—I can afford it, honest."

"Mr. Trehan, *nobody* can afford it these days," the girl said, then shrugged, reaching for the ringing phone.

"Why did you do that?" Keely asked as he sat down beside her, squinting at the forms on the clipboard. Not that she was complaining, although she would never tell him that. "We're not her parents."

"Look," he told her, "you know that and I know that. The doctor will know that. But do you really want to spend the next ten minutes explaining our situation to that kid over there? Because I don't."

"You've got a point," Keely agreed, holding Candy so that the baby could practice her new trick, standing up on Keely's thighs. "Did you bring the note from Cecily?"

"Yes, or did you think I left it in the car after I told you I had it with me when you asked me that same question right after we left the house?"

"I'm sorry," she said, sighing. "I guess I'm nervous. I keep thinking the doctor is going to call someone, have Candy taken away from us—from you."

Jack put down the pen he was using and rubbed a knuckle beneath Candy's chin. "That isn't going to happen. I've got an appointment with an old school pal, Jimmy Haggerty, tomorrow morning. He promised he'd take care of everything."

174

"How good a lawyer can he be if people still call him Jimmy?"

Jack laughed, shook his head. "You're crazy, you know that? Now relax. I promise, everything's going to be fine."

Four hours later, Keely was wishing she'd had Jack open a vein and write that promise in blood, because Candy was feverish, crying, and refused to allow anyone but Keely to hold her.

"You gave her the medicine?" Petra asked, sitting cross-legged on the floor, having given up making monkey faces at Candy to try to take her mind off her troubles.

"Yes, as soon as we got home. The doctor said this might happen anyway. She'll feel bad for a few hours, her little leg will be sore, but by tonight she'll be fine." Candy struggled in her arms, and Keely winced as the baby's left fist caught her square on the nose. "If we live that long." She grabbed hold of Candy's fist and kissed it. "Please, baby, don't cry. It breaks my heart."

"Your heart, my ears," Petra said, getting to her feet, brushing down her baby blue skirt with the bib top that went so well with her snow-white starched cotton blouse with the Peter Pan collar. Her hair was just blond today, no streaks, and she had it pulled up into ponytails on either side of her head. She wore no makeup, no rings through anything, and she had on white, lace-edged ankle socks with black patent Mary Jane shoes. "I'm outta here."

"Going home to dunk Oreos in milk? Or maybe to watch reruns of 'Little House on the Prairie'?" Keely asked, bouncing Candy on her hip because five minutes ago the baby seemed to like that. Now she hated it and cried even harder, her little face red, her perspiration-damp curls clinging to her head.

175

"Ha, ha. You're a riot, Keely. And you've just proven my point, so thanks. Nobody likes me normal. Candy sure doesn't. I'll tell Dad; he'll be so bummed. And then maybe I can change out of this scary costume and get on with my life."

"Wait a minute," Keely said, following after her. "You put those clothes on because you think they'd make you look *normal*?"

Petra looked down at herself, then up at Keely. "Yeah. Your point?"

"Nothing. Never mind," Keely said, and watched Petra skip across the lawn, on her way back to Oz, or wherever she was going. Then she took Candy over to the Cartman-look-alike cookie jar and began lifting and lowering the lid. "Look, Candy, Cartman's losing his head. Oops! There it goes! Now it's back. Silly Cartman. Isn't that funny?"

"Only if you haven't laughed in twenty years," Jack said, and Keely turned to see him lounging against the door frame. "Are your marbles inside that jar, Keely? Because I think you might have just lost them."

Keely snapped. "Oh, and you think you can do better?" she asked, advancing toward him, Candy still crying, struggling in her arms.

"I don't know," he said. "Let me try. Because I think you deserve a break."

Tears stung Keely's eyes as she handed Candy over to Jack, and she quickly turned away to hide them from him. She was so grateful to him, she could have wept. How did single parents do it?

"There you go, Candy," Jack was saying soothingly, rubbing the baby's back as she hiccupped, sniffled several times, but—mercifully—stopped crying.

"How'd you do that?" Keely asked, impressed, and

just a little jealous that Jack had succeeded where she had so obviously failed. "Does she have an OFF switch I missed?"

"I don't know," Jack said as Candy laid her head on his shoulder, still sniffling, hiccupping. "Must be that famous Trehan charm. Either that or you're too tense and nervous, and Candy senses it."

Keely shot him a say-what? look.

"Okay, so I've been reading. What else is there to do when you're stuck in a waiting room with fifteen screaming kids and a bunch of mothers saying what a great guy you are for coming along to the doctor's office with your wife. I wasn't about to tell them I'd bailed when the doctor said it was time for Candy's exam and shot, so I stuck my head in the first magazine I could find. Tense mothers make tense babies. I read that."

"I am *not* tense," Keely said, folding her arms in front of her, then belatedly relaxing her shoulders, realizing that she'd been holding herself stiffly for hours, possibly days . . . months . . . all her life.

"Candy thinks you are," Jack pointed out. "Maybe not the other day, in the pool, but do you think she'd go to just anyone, and not always to the one who feeds her, washes her, dresses her? You're afraid of her, and she knows it. Competent, but afraid. Capable, but afraid. A know-it-all, but afraid. I could go on," he added, continuing his singsong taunt, "but I won't."

"That's ridiculous, and it's time for her bottle. Give her to me. Wouldn't you know she'd fall asleep when she's supposed to be eating?"

"Let her sleep, the poor kid's exhausted," Jack said, easing himself into one of the chairs in the den. "I'm not doing anything, and I can watch TV just as easily with

177

her on my shoulder. Besides, that was also in the article I read—telling all about not always keeping to a strict schedule, as if the world will end if the kid sleeps through a bottle or stays up past her bedtime once in a while."

Keely's mouth twisted. "Did you bring home a couple of those inserts? You know, the ones that you can fill in, then send away for a subscription to the magazine? Hell, Trehan, maybe you'd want to write an article for the magazine. They could call it 'Smug Cousin Knows Best.' "

"Temper, temper, McBride," Jack said, smiling up at her. "Although I have to admit it, I kind of like pushing your buttons. You're *so* easy."

Keely looked at him for long moments, then gave him a quick kick in the shin. "There. Maybe we can build on *that!*" she said, using his own words against him, and left the room, grabbing up the car keys because she had to go to the grocery store and pick up Candy's first jars of actual food. And maybe a little rat fink poison for Candy's Cousin Jack.

She shouldn't go, shouldn't leave. Candy might wake, still be cranky from her shot, and Jack wouldn't be able to handle her. Not that Keely wished Candy would cry. Certainly not. But the sweetheart could think about depositing a little present in her diaper for her Cousin Jack, just to score points with her Aunt Keely.

By the time Keely had loaded three plastic bags of groceries in the trunk of her car and returned to the house, she had forgiven Jack. It was hard not to forgive Jack, which was one of the reasons she'd still been angry with him until she got to the candy section and broke down, buying him some M & M's.

She wondered when mothers had time to think. In the past twenty-four hours she'd been offered a chance at another shop in Manhattan, been attracted to Jack, been rejected by Jack, made a fool of herself, been *kissed* by Jack, and had dealt with Candy's reaction to her first baby shots. She'd washed two loads of clothes—one of Candy's, another of towels—cooked one dinner and one breakfast, argued with Jack (again), and run to the grocery store . . . and it was time for her to cook dinner once more. Who could think? Who'd have time to think? It had to have been a man who'd come up with the term Bored Housewife Syndrome, because it sure couldn't have been a woman!

If she did have time to think, she'd think about that kiss. Definitely. She'd think about her reaction to it, and the look on Jack's face when it was over. She'd think about how maybe he *had* been about to say what she'd thought he was going to say.

And she'd think about how she would have answered him if he had turned into David Hasselhoff and she into Valerie Bertinelli.

"They probably would have gone to commercial, to give her time to learn her lines," Keely muttered to herself, walking up from the garages with her head down, two plastic bags hanging over one arm, her other filled with purse, the last bag, and a big bunch of carnations she'd bought on impulse as she stood in the checkout line.

"*Keely. Psst—Keely. Over here.*"

She looked up. "Aunt Sadie?"

Sadie Trehan was half-hidden by a holly bush, the top half of her, the part that could be seen, decked out in a lime green sort of tent with bright orange bull's-eyes on it. If it was Aunt Sadie Season, and she was trying to

179

hide from the hunters, the woman was definitely out of luck.

"Come here, come here," Sadie urged as she frantically waved Keely forward. "We've got trouble."

"Trouble?" Keely's thoughts went immediately to Candy. "What do you mean?"

"I mean trouble," Aunt Sadie repeated. "With a capital T and that rhymes with *P* and that stands for Pipsqueak. Oh, all right. Joey Morretti. It stands for Joey Morretti. Hey, cut me some slack. I'm working under pressure here."

Keely unconsciously lowered her voice. "Two Eyes? The Mafia one? Cecily's brother from Bayonne?" she asked, crouching beside Sadie. "What's *he* doing here?"

"Nothing good, I can tell you that. He says he's come to get Candy. Petra was up at the house, looking for you, and she overheard Jack telling him to go to hell. It's trouble, Keely. I just know it. With a capital *T* and that rhymes with *P* and—"

"Yeah, yeah, I got it, I got it," Keely said, straightening once she realized she'd actually been hiding behind a holly bush. She squinted toward the house, as if it were an enemy bunker she was about to assault, armed only with a bunch of carnations. "I'm going in. You want to come along?"

"Me?" Sadie's eyes got wide as she stepped back a pace, pressed both hands to her chest. "Would I be out here if I thought I belonged in there? I don't think so!"

"You're afraid of him?"

Sadie patted her curls. "Of Joey? Don't be silly. I just don't want to be in the way when Jack tosses the little twirp through a window."

"Oh, boy," Keely breathed, starting for the house at a dead run, quickly skirting the pool, all but slamming

180

into the back door before she could get her hand around the handle, let herself in.

She put the bags on the table, not caring if the butter brickle ice cream melted, and tiptoed toward the den. It was empty. The whole house was quiet. Too quiet.

Where was Candy? Oh, God, where was Candy?

Keely raced for the back staircase, holding her breath until she opened the door to the nursery and saw Candy's rounded rump stuck straight up in the air as the baby slept in her crib.

"Thank God," she breathed, collapsing against the doorjamb.

"Cute little button, isn't she?"

Keely nearly jumped out of her shoes. "What? Who?" She pushed the door open the rest of the way and saw a mountain sitting in the rocking chair that had been delivered two days earlier. She crazily tried to remember if the thing was made of solid oak and could hold his weight if he started to rock. "Who are you?"

The mountain stood up, and as he was standing between the window and Keely, his large frame just about blocked all the light coming in through the window, as if there'd been a sudden total eclipse of the sun. Keely looked up, and up, calculating that the strange man was at least six feet six inches tall and probably weighed about as much as a compact car.

He had legs like tree trunks, shoulders the width of a love seat, and his huge hands hung like hams at the ends of his immense arms. And yet he wasn't fat. He was just *big*. Really, *really* big.

Bald as a cue ball. Young, no more than nineteen or twenty. He smiled, and on anyone else his teeth would have been beaver-sized. On him, they were almost little, and there was about a half-inch gap between his top front teeth.

He held out his hand, and Keely, not knowing what else to do, took it, felt her hand being swallowed up whole. "Please tell me you aren't Joey Morretti," she squeaked, as the bones in her hand sort of crossed over each other.

"No, ma'am," the giant said, his voice completely at odds with his size, for it was rather high, and quite soft. Almost gentle, even reassuring. "I'm Bruno, ma'am. Bruno Armano. But you can call me Sweetness. Everybody does, even my old Granny, rest her."

"*Oooh*-kay . . . Sweetness," Keely said carefully, happy to recover her hand, unable to refrain from cradling it against her until the blood flow returned to her fingers. What was that old saying? Just keep being nice until you can find a big rock? Yeah, and a stepladder, so she could climb up it to hit him with that rock. "So—Sweetness . . . what are you doing here?"

Sweetness pointed behind her, toward the doorway. "We really should go outside, ma'am, so as not to wake the little princess. I fed her and burped her and changed her, and she needs her sleep now, don't you think, ma'am?"

Keely stepped aside and watched Sweetness exit the room, bowing his head so that he could make it under the arch, then followed after him. This man had fed Candy? Burped and changed her?

Good God. Jack must be lying somewhere, in three or more pieces. Because he certainly wouldn't have allowed Sweetness—what kind of name was that for a mountain?—anywhere near Candy if he was still alive.

"Um . . . where's Jack?" Keely asked as brightly as possible, once she and Sweetness were standing in the hallway, several feet away from Candy's bedroom.

"Mr. Trehan?" Sweetness smiled. "I always wanted to meet a real major league baseball player. They never let me play baseball, only football. I was the center. Coach said I was the center, and both sides of the offensive line." He frowned when Keely didn't respond. "It was a joke, ma'am. But Mr. Trehan? He's downstairs somewhere, with Mr. Morretti."

Keely's head was beginning to pound. "And you came here today with Mr. Morretti because . . . ?"

Sweetness bobbed his huge bald head up and down, finishing her question for her. ". . . because he's my owner," he said rather proudly. "I'm his fighter. Heavyweight division. Mr. Morretti calls me the Beast of Bayonne. Had it sewn on the back of this really neat black satin robe he bought me and everything. But you can still call me Sweetness."

"And welcome to the Twilight Zone, ladies and germs," Keely muttered under her breath, then smiled up at the Beast of Bayonne. "Tell you what— Sweetness. You stay here, guarding Candy, because that's what you're doing, right? And I'll just go on downstairs and say hi to Jack and Two—to Mr. Morretti. Is that all right with you?"

"Sure!" Sweetness agreed happily, nothing if not the obedient sort. "Mr. Trehan already told me who you are, which is why I didn't have to coldcock you or nothin'. You just go downstairs and don't worry about the little princess. She'll be just fine, long as I'm here."

Keely fought back a whimper. "Thank you, Sweetness. I really appreciate that. The baby-sitting, the not coldcocking me, all of it. Yes, well, then . . . bye!"

She didn't break into a run until she got to the main staircase, at which time she all but flew down the stairs, then aimed herself toward the living room.

# Chapter Eleven

*It's a whole new ball game.*

—Sports saying

OH, THIS WAS GOOD. JOEY WAS GIVING HIM THE STARE. Using both his "two eyes," even keeping them looking in the same direction.

Jack figured he was supposed to be afraid, maybe even cringe. Fat chance of that. Joey Morretti couldn't stare down a Twinkie.

Poor Joey. He'd inherited his martinizing father's looks and size, which meant he was short, with a narrow, weaselly-looking face dominated by a thin, hooked nose, and his coal-black hair had already begun to fall out by the time he was nineteen. He had hair plugs now, obviously implanted by the lowest bidder, and the top of his head had the same barely reclaimed look of rows of small clumps of saw grass recently planted in a sun-bleached white sand dune down at the Jersey Shore.

Mostly, Jack knew, Joey dressed like Sonny Corleone, in the first *Godfather* movie, right down to the suspenders, sleeveless undershirts, and pleated dress slacks. Except he didn't have James Caan's broad shoulders, so his suspenders kept falling down, and he had to be careful, use the backup of a belt or else lose his pants.

Today, fortunately, he'd dressed more formally, in a shiny black gangster suit with white pinstripes, a black dress shirt, and a white silk tie. He looked, to Jack, like either a poor man's Al Capone or a poor man's Regis Philbin. Either way, the look just didn't quite work.

184

"Not working, Joey, sorry," Jack said, following along with that train of thought as he sat comfortably on his new couch in the otherwise almost empty living room. Nice couch. Keely had chosen well. "Hey, do you remember the time Tim and I de-pants'd you? Easter, wasn't it? We were about twelve, and you were nine? I think Sadie still has the pictures. I'll bet she'd have a set made up for you, if you want."

Joey blinked.

Well, that had taken all of about ten seconds. The guy had about the same powers of concentration as a hamster. Jack decided to go for two. "And then there was that time Aunt Flo and Uncle Guido went to Sicily and you and Cecily stayed with us for a couple of weeks. Good times, Joey. You only wet the bed twice. I guess maybe it's time to tell you that Tim and I poured water on the mattress, and you, while you were sleeping. Get it, Joey? You only thought you'd—"

His cousin jumped up from his seat on the kitchen chair Jack had dragged into the room for him, pointing a finger at Jack. "I could put a contract out on ya in five minutes, ya know. Five minutes!"

"Jack?"

Jack turned at the sound of Keely's voice, saw the frightened look on her face. "Just a minute, Keely," he said, then turned back to Joey. "You stay here, okay? Don't move, don't touch anything, and for God's sake don't steal anything. I'll be right back."

Walking over to Keely, he took hold of her elbow and steered her toward the hallway, then into the kitchen. "Hi," he said, once he'd pulled out a chair, motioned for her to sit down before he walked over to the counter, peeked into one of the bags. "So, what's up? Snag any bargains? Hey, look here. Isn't this ice

185

cream going to melt if you don't put it away?"

Keely hopped up from her chair, not really having settled into it, and grabbed the half gallon of butter brickle from Jack's hand. "Screw the ice cream, Trehan. There's a *gangster* in your living room!" She opened the freezer door, jammed the ice cream inside, slammed the door, then whirled to face him. "And the Beast of Bayonne is upstairs, doing his jolly Green Giant impression while supposedly guarding Candy! My God, Trehan, I go away for one lousy *hour* and this is what I come home to?"

Jack suppressed a smile. Man, she was hot; he watched to see if steam would start coming out of her ears. "You met Sweetness? Nice kid."

Keely pressed one hand to her forehead, the other to her hip, and glared at him with wide, angry eyes. "I don't believe this. I don't believe *you*. Because this isn't funny, Jack. None of this is funny. And you . . . you just let that idiot in there *threaten* you, and then you insulted him. Are you *nuts?*"

Jack walked over to her, hands half raised in case he had to ward off a blow, then took hold of her shoulders, pressed her back down into the chair. "It's Joey, Keely. He has as much chance of putting out a contract on me as he has of winning the Mr. Universe contest. He *thinks* he's connected, Keely. Big difference between playacting at being a wise guy and really being one. Hell, Joey got laughed out of the local street gang when he was fourteen. Seems he thought they all should sing and dance while they were fighting, like in *West Side Story*."

Keely bit her lips together, but then her shoulders sort of shook, and she finally grinned. "That's funny."

Jack nodded his head. "Yes, it is, even if I just made that one up. What's *not* funny is that Joey has decided to

186

take Candy back to Bayonne with him. That's why he brought the Beast of Bayonne along, as backup muscle in case I said no."

Keely leaned back in her chair. "Yes, that's what I was afraid of, the moment I found out your cousin was here. Sweetness says Joey owns him. Does he?"

"In a way," Jack informed her. "This is something new. He owns the kid's contract. Joey thinks that having his own fighter will score points for him as he tries, yet again, to pretend he's mob-connected. It's all a *game,* Keely. Joey's little mind game he can afford to play with himself—thanks to my aunt and uncle's money. Just like Cecily, except she spends her share on these crazy starts of hers. The Morretti kids, they're the joke of Bayonne. And believe me, you've got to go some in Bayonne to cop *that* title."

"A joke, maybe, but you said it wasn't funny, which must mean you think Joey can take Candy. Can he?"

Jack shrugged. "Possession *is* nine-tenths of the law, or so I've heard. But, yeah, I am concerned, which is why I've got a call in to Jimmy, but he's in court. Thing is, Keely, I'm only a cousin to Candy, when you get right down to it. Joey is Candy's uncle, and Cecily's brother. This could get sticky if we don't knock him down, fast."

"You and your lawyer, you mean?" Keely asked.

"Okay. Him, too. But for now . . . well, just come with me and follow my lead. I want Joey back on the road to Bayonne before he can think up a reason to stay here overnight."

"He'd do that?" Keely asked nervously, her hand in Jack's as he pulled her back down the hallway, toward the living room. "How?"

"I don't know. I just know he has this thing about

being a part of the family or something. Hates being rejected. Once, he pretended to have sprained his ankle tripping over Tim's leg—which Tim may or may not have put in his way. Last time it was because he had night blindness and couldn't drive after dark. He ended up bunking in with Sadie for two weeks, which is why my aunt is probably hiding under her bed right now. I'm telling you, Keely, I'm betting he has three alligator suitcases packed and in his trunk, just waiting for some way to get himself invited to stay."

"You know, it sounds like maybe if you and Tim had been nicer to him when you all were kids, Joey wouldn't be so bad," Keely said as they approached the living room.

"Really?" Jack stood to one side, inviting her to take a good look at Joey Morretti in action, then come to her own conclusions.

Joey was on his feet, stuffing one of the pair of small brass elephants Keely had bought to place on the coffee table, into his suit jacket pocket.

"Oh, okay, so he's a little . . . strange," Keely agreed as Jack grinned at her. "But don't antagonize him, all right? This is too important."

"Exactly," Jack said as he pulled Keely into the living room. "That's why I know you'll go along with this. Joey?" he said, startling his cousin, who had been reaching for the second elephant, "I'm sorry about the interruption. Let me introduce you to Keely." He took a deep breath, slid his arm around Keely's waist. "Keely McBride, allow me to introduce you to my cousin, Joseph Morretti. Joey, this is the wonderful woman I told you about, Keely McBride, my fiancée."

Jack felt Keely sort of sag beside him and held on tight to her waist. "Steady," he whispered as Joey

188

walked forward, chin lifted as he straightened his tie, obviously intent on stealing Keely from his cousin and making her his personal, and willing, love slave.

Keely smiled, speaking quietly, through clenched teeth. "You lousy, sneaking son of a—well, yes, *hello, Mr. Morretti,*" she ended brightly as Joey extended his right hand and she—with a small nudge from Jack— took it, only for an instant. "I've . . . I've heard so much about you. All of it flattering, I'm sure. Why, I believe Jack has told me you're his favorite cousin."

Jack bent down, pretended to kiss her behind her ear. "Don't overdo it, McBride. He's dense, but he's not completely stupid." Then he smiled at his cousin. "Sorry, I just can't seem to keep my hands off her. She just said yes last night, didn't you, darling?"

Keely tilted her chin and batted her eyelashes at him, and Jack knew he was in trouble. Keely confirmed this when she said, "Oh, darling, can I tell him?" Then she turned to Joey. "He *cried,* Mr. Morretti. He got down on his knees, said the most beautiful things to me . . . and then he *cried.*"

She snuggled against Jack's shoulder, gazing up at him in mock adoration. "I'll never forget it, Jack. Never."

He dug his fingers into her waist, but Keely never flinched. He should have known she wouldn't flinch. The woman was a menace. "Don't tell *all* our secrets, darling," he warned, his tone warm and syrupy. "After all, what we did after that should remain . . . private. Although," he ended, looking at Joey, "I've got to tell you, this woman has fantastic stamina."

He felt Keely's heel come down on his instep, not banging down, just sort of placed there; then the full weight of her body followed as she pretended to affectionately lean closer against him.

"We're going to look at rings tomorrow," Keely went on, as Jack was too busy trying not to wince to say anything else and Joey was just standing there, not saying anything at all. "I told Jack I didn't need a ring to know that he loves me, but he insisted. He says he's going to buy me the biggest diamond in all of Allentown. Isn't that sweet?"

At last, Joey Morretti broke his silence. "I knows dis guy, Jack, ya know, back in Bayonne? Get ya a great rock, only a little warm, if ya, ya know, takes my drift."

Keely pressed her face against Jack's chest, and with his arm still around her, he could tell that she was laughing. "Well, thank you, Joey. But I think I can handle it."

Joey shrugged, then frowned, then reached inside his jacket, all the way to his sleeve, and gave a pull— obviously to yank his suspender back onto his shoulder. "Hey, makes no never-mind to me, ya know, where ya spend yer money. But it don't change anything, ya know, Jack. This getting hitched crap, so the kid has both a mama and a daddy. That's bull. Cecily would want the kid, ya know, with me."

"She left her with me, Joey," Jack said as Keely moved slightly away from him, then took his hand in hers, squeezing it in warning.

"Yeah? Well, not forever," Joey countered. "She's comin' back, ya know, sooner or later."

"Possible, very possible," Jack agreed. "But, until then, Candy stays with me. So let it go, Joey. There's no way a judge will give you temporary custody over Keely's and my own petition. We can offer her a more stable home, a family. What can you offer her? The Bayonne Mafia Debutante's Ball, black tie and machine guns optional? Christ, Joey, *think!*"

"Jack . . ." Keely warned quietly.

"Okay, okay," Jack said, trying to keep himself from exploding. "Look, we'll talk about this later. Right now, we should think about some supper. You hungry, Joey? I'll bet Sweetness is. Keely—do we have half a cow in the freezer?"

Keely's hands were shaking as she set the kitchen table for four. "I don't believe this is happening," she said, accepting a thick stack of paper napkins from Jack, who had just reentered the kitchen. "I don't believe I'm about to break bread with the Beast of Bayonne, the Nutcase of Bayonne, and my supposed fiancé. Where's the Cheshire Cat, Jack, because I think I just fell through the looking glass. And just think, last week I thought bankruptcy was the worst thing that could ever happen to me. Oh, never mind. What did Jimmy the lawyer say?"

"Nothing I'd like to repeat in mixed company," Jack told her, then grabbed another handful of napkins from the holder on the counter. "Here, we need a bunch of these if Joey's eating with us. I once saw him redecorate my aunt's entire kitchen with just one bowl of linguine."

"Don't change the subject," Keely ordered, grabbing Jack's arm. "What did the lawyer say?"

"He said," Jack told her, sighing, "that lying to Joey Morretti was stupid but legal. Lying to a judge, however, can get a person his own orange jumpsuit."

"Oh," Keely said quietly. "I hadn't thought of that." She glared up at Jack. "And, obviously, neither did you. So now what? We drop the engagement as a bad idea, right? Jack? I said, we drop the engagement as a bad idea? Jack! *Say* something."

He lowered his head, looked so pitiful, so helpless. "I

can't let her go, Keely. Not to Cecily, not to Joey. But Jimmy says Cecily's note isn't enough. Either I fight, and somehow find Cecily, get her to sign over custody, or it's a pretty sure thing that Joey gets Candy."

Keely's stomach did a small flip. "But . . . but . . . you're a baseball star. You've got this big name, this big house—*tons* of money. Candy would never want for anything. You're the perfect choice."

"I'm also single, not the closest blood relative, have no outward means of employment, and I've already lied to Joey about you, which his lawyer will be quick to point out to the judge, proving I'm not trustworthy. And just to top it off, I've got this woman living with me, without benefit of holy wedlock, setting a bad example for little Candy. Besides, Jimmy says judges often bend over backward not to show preferential treatment to celebrities, which means I'm screwed, no matter how you look at it."

"Oh. When you put it all that way . . ." Keely pulled out a chair, sat down. "So now what?"

"Well, we *are* doing something. Jimmy's already got my verbal okay to hire a couple of private investigators to hunt down Cecily in Timbucktu, or wherever the hell she is. A good outfit, out of Philly. D&S, or something like that. But that kind of search takes time, especially since Cecily could be anywhere by now. Tibet. Australia. Paris."

"Yeah, Paris. I hear it's a popular place," Keely said, fleetingly thinking of Gregory and the fact that he and his new "assistant," Shavonna, were probably on their way there right now. Not that it mattered. Nothing mattered, except keeping Candy here, with Jack. With her?

"And I'm going to invite Joey to stay here for the next few days."

"Good God, why?"

"To keep him from his lawyer's office in Bayonne, for one thing. We keep him here, we keep him happy and busy, and while we're doing that, Candy's safe enough. It's not much, but it buys us a little time."

"Is there anything else? Did Jimmy suggest anything else?"

"Yeah, he did," Jack said, heading for the back door. "He suggested we follow through, get married. That would probably win it for me with the judge. Fat chance of that, right? Excuse me, I've got to go warn Aunt Sadie that Joey's going to be staying with us for a while. Ten to one she starts digging a moat around her apartment."

Keely, her mouth dropped open, watched him go.

Jack came downstairs early the next morning just as Keely was closing the front door, shutting it with a push of her hip because her hands were full of flowers. "What's up? Who sent those?"

"I don't know," Keely answered, carefully lowering the inexpensive glass vase onto the foyer table. "Let me see the card. Oh! Well, isn't that sweet. They're from Curtis."

"Who?" Jack asked, pulling the card from her hand. " 'Hope to hear from you again soon, Curtis.' " He looked at the vase jammed with pink roses, then at Keely. "Exactly how much money did we spend at that furniture store? And shouldn't he have sent those flowers to me?"

"You want Curtis to send you flowers?" Keely asked, touching one delicate bloom.

"Hell, no," Jack said, then turned and walked down the hallway toward the kitchen. "Just ditch that card

193

before Joey sees it. He'll think you're cheating on me."

Keely followed after him, into the kitchen, then stopped, pointed at the luggage stacked near the back door. "What's this? I could swear I saw Sweetness carry six bags upstairs last night. Surely there can't be more."

Jack leaned back against the countertop. "Those are mine. I've got a flight out of here this afternoon, right after my appointment with Jimmy. I'm heading to Arizona to film a commercial and kill my agent. I should be back in two days. Can you handle everything while I'm gone?"

"Me?" Keely asked, pressing a hand against her chest. "You're leaving *me* here to handle everything?" She dramatically threw up her hands, rolled her eyes heavenward. "If that isn't *just* like a man. I've got a baby, a psychedelic child genius sitter, the poster child for send-this-boy-to-a-shrink, and a *mountain* who ate a dozen pancakes this morning before he came up for air, burped, and asked for a dozen more. I've got furniture to buy, colors to select, three more bedrooms to furnish just in case anybody *else* shows up, and your aunt wants me to re-do her living room, in pink, to match some flamingo wallpaper she found looking through one of my sample books. And you're *leaving?* Oh, no. Oh, no-no-no. Not unless it's over my dead body!"

"Ah, isn't that sweet," Petra said, walking into the kitchen, Candy on her hip. "The lovers are having their first fight. Close your ears, Candy, you don't want to hear this."

"Shut up," Keely and Jack ordered in unison.

Petra gave a slight toss of her long hair—blond today, with black tips—and said, "Okay, I can take a hint. If you don't want my help, I won't help. Even if I do have a solution for you."

194

She turned to leave the kitchen, but Jack's "Wait!" stopped her, so that she turned around, grinned at both of them . . . at which point Keely figured out that she'd been wrong, the Cheshire Cat *was* in residence here in Wonderland.

"Okay," Petra said, handing Candy to Keely, for the child was leaning out of her arms, reaching toward Keely, "here's the deal. You take Mamasan here along to Arizona, and Sweetness and I take care of Candy. We rent the box set of the *Godfather* movies for Joey, which will keep him happy, and you two can both catch a break. And don't say you don't need a break, because if I ever saw two people who needed to go somewhere and get their heads screwed on straight, it's you two. Oh, and I'll keep handing Candy to Joey whenever she's unhappy, until he figures out he wants nothing to do with her. That's aversion therapy . . . at least kind of."

Keely had already started shaking her head before Petra was half done with her brilliant plan. "No. It's impossible. I will not leave Candy here with a man who might try to take her away, take her to Bayonne."

"Sweetness won't let him," Petra said rather smugly. "Sweetness won't do anything I don't ask him to do. We've established a rapport. That means—"

"I *know* what that means, and no," Keely persisted. "Besides, what would I want in Arizona?" *Please, Petra,* she prayed silently, *don't try to answer that one.*

"We could take Candy with us," Jack suggested, then frowned. "Maybe I'd better clear that one with Jimmy, though. He told me yesterday that he was trying to get an emergency court order keeping Candy here in Pennsylvania until the custody thing is settled."

"So? That's perfect," Petra said, looking at Keely. "We tell old Two Eyes that there's a court order saying

195

he can't take Candy out of this house, and you two don't have anything to do in Arizona except relax, unwind, maybe even—and, gee, here's a concept—*talk* to each other."

She took Candy back from Keely, headed toward the back door. "I honest to God don't know how shrinks keep from beating their patients' heads together," she mumbled. "I may have to rethink this psych business . . ."

The silence in the kitchen was so tense that Keely immediately filled it with the sound of her own voice. What she said was, "She's a child. She doesn't understand the implications. Not that we'd be doing anything except what she said, getting away for a couple of days, giving ourselves some time away from Candy, time to think."

"Yeah," Jack agreed, not looking at her. "It's not a good idea. Not that she and Sweetness couldn't take care of Candy for two days. We already know Candy likes Petra, and Sweetness told me last night that he's the oldest of twelve brothers and sisters and has been taking care of babies all his life. But no. It wouldn't work. We'd probably kill each other while we were still flying over Ohio."

"Probably," Keely agreed, busying herself unloading the dishwasher, stacking the plates on the counter. "I've never been to Arizona. I'll bet it's hot there this time of year. Being June and all."

"Yeah, real hot. And we're filming near some state park, like out in the desert, I guess."

"Hot," Keely repeated, sorting silverware into the drawer. "And you'd be working. We probably wouldn't even see each other except at night, for dinner or whatever."

"Or whatever."

"It would all be rather pointless, really."

"Right," Jack agreed. "Dumb idea."

"So we're agreed," Keely said. "It's not possible."

"Absolutely."

"It's a stupid idea."

"Definitely. Stupid idea. Okay, I have to go now or I'll be late for my meeting with Jimmy."

Jack pushed himself away from the counter, headed for the back door. He stopped, his hand on the doorknob. "They're sending a private jet, so we're a little flexible, but I really would like to get out of here around noon. Can you be packed and ready to leave by the time the car gets here for us at eleven-thirty?"

Keely kept her back turned to him. "Yeah, I can do that."

"All right, here's the doctor's phone number," Keely said, scribbling on a notepad, "and the name and number of the closest pharmacy. You've got Jack's cell phone number in case you need to reach us. For anything else, just dial nine-one-one." She ripped off the sheet and handed it to Petra, who was sitting across from her at the kitchen table.

Petra took the paper, laid it beside the others already on the tabletop. "Let's see what we've got here, okay? First, we've got a list of foods Candy can have now. Applesauce, rice cereal, and formula."

"Only two teaspoonfuls of applesauce," Keely reminded her, even though she'd written it all down. "One teaspoon yesterday, two today, a tablespoonful tomorrow, just to make sure she isn't allergic. After that, you can feed her as much as she wants, except not too much, because she needs to drink all of her formula.

197

Same with the rice cereal. Two teaspoonfuls today, a tablespoon tomorrow."

"Gee. It's like quantum physics. I hope I can handle the pressure," Petra said, rolling her eyes. "Okay, so I've got the phone numbers, I've got the instructions about her food. I've got a schedule for her bath, her naps, her playtime. Don't ever let anyone call you anal, Keely, because I already said it. But just to clear this up—does this mean we can't take Candy out for pizza and fries?"

Keely pressed her hands to her temples. "Oh, I can't do this. I can't leave. What was I thinking?"

"Oh, come on, Keely, I was just kidding. Candy will be fine. We'll all be fine. It's only for two days. And not to be mean or anything, but less than two weeks ago, you didn't even know Candy existed."

Keely blinked back tears as she looked down at Candy, who was in her jump seat, industriously trying to put her entire fist in her mouth. "I know," she said, sighing. "And yet there are moments when I think my life would be impossible without her." She looked at Petra, sighed. "It's good that I'm leaving her for a while. It's good preparation for when I'll leave her for good. I mean, it wouldn't do to have her get too attached, right?"

"Right," Petra agreed with a profound nod. "You'll be leaving both of them, Candy and Jack. Not a good idea, getting attached."

Keely wiped at her eyes. "Oh, great. This from the girl who arranged it so that I end up in Arizona with Jack for two days. I mean, you could have mentioned this *attached* stuff sooner."

"Hey," Petra said, shrugging, "I'm a genius, not 'Dear Abby.' Not that I couldn't be. Did I tell you

Sweetness and I are going to work out together? He's going to teach me how to jump rope. I never learned. Then, in exchange, I'm going to teach him how to box."

Keely's head hurt, it really did. "What do you mean, you're going to teach him how to box? Isn't he a professional fighter?"

"If you mean does he get paid for falling down, sure. Joey only puts him in fights he's already been told to lose. That's criminal, by the way."

"But Jack told me Joey isn't really involved in criminal activity," Keely said, mentally unpacking her bags. "Maybe he's finally graduated to the real thing."

"I don't think so," Petra told her, unstrapping Candy from her jump seat, picking her up. "Sweetness says that's just the way it is in this one club in Bayonne. But I think he's got potential. Who knows, I may buy out his contract, become a fight manager."

"Been saving your allowance, have you, Petra?" Keely asked, pushing away from the kitchen table, trying to put some distance between herself and Petra's latest phase.

"Mock me if you must," Petra intoned rather majestically, "but I see a great future here. Besides, it'll drive Dad nuts."

"There's always that," Keely agreed, going over to the window to watch for Jack's car. "Is it that important to you to upset your father?"

"Hey, it's what teenagers do, part of the code. I'm just trying to be a normal teenager."

Keely laughed out loud. "How many teenagers do you know who own their own boxer?"

Petra shifted Candy to her left hip. "Do I smoke or do drugs? No. Do I stay out late with guys? No. Do I skip school, get lousy grades, pierce things?"

Keely turned around, stepped closer to Petra. "That's it. That's what's been bothering me. No rings. Not in your eyebrow, on your earlobes, or through your navel. And no marks, either, no scars. Do you mean to tell me you *glued* those things on the first day I met you?"

"Even the one in my tongue, although that was a little tricky, I grant you," Petra told her. "You mean you didn't figure that out until now? Wow, Candy's going to run rings around you when she's a teenager."

"I won't be here when Candy's a teenager," Keely reminded her.

"I know. You're going to be in New York, decorating penthouses, going to all the best parties, maybe even having your own segment on CNN on Saturday mornings. Keely McBride, Big Success."

Keely was silent for a few moments, then looked at Petra. "Exactly how many psychology textbooks have you read since you entered this new phase?"

"Four. I'm a speed reader," Petra told her. "It's a pity I'm giving it up, though, because I could write a whole thesis on you. Jack, too. But I think that, right now, I'd rather explain the absolutely marvelous science behind a good right cross to Sweetness. Oh, look, here comes Jack. Are you going to tell him you're not going with him?"

Keely held out her hands and Candy giggled, leaned toward her, so that Keely could scoop her up, hold her close against her cheek. "Is Aunt Keely doing the right thing, Candy?" she asked the baby, who was busily pulling at her French twist, reaching for the pins that held Keely's curls in check.

She loved the way Candy filled her arms, warmed her heart. She loved the way the baby made her feel wanted, needed. But was that enough? Enough for her, enough

200

for Jack? Could they let their love and concern for Candy push them into something that would eventually, if not immediately, make all three of them unhappy?

Keely didn't know. What she did know was that suddenly Jack was standing in the kitchen, looking at her as she held Candy—with this *look* in his eyes—and suddenly her stomach had gotten lodged halfway up her throat.

"Da! Da-da-da-da!" Candy crowed as Jack entered the house, squirming in Keely's arms, trying to get to him. He crossed the kitchen in just a few steps and took the baby in his arms, kissed the top of her head.

"You ready?" he asked Keely, who was doing her best to pretend that looking at Jack with Candy, how good and natural he was with Candy, wasn't enough to make her want to weep.

"Ready," she said, then cleared her tight throat.

"Okay, let's get moving, the car's already outside, waiting. Bye, sweetheart. I'm going to miss you so much," he said, kissing Candy again, then handing her to Petra.

Keely headed for the door, then stopped, walked over to the table, picked up the sleeping, napping, eating schedule, and ripped it into two neat pieces. "Just go with the flow, Petra, and try not to lose her anywhere. Okay, Jack, I'm ready. Let's go."

She didn't hear Petra tell Candy, "What we have seen here today, honey, is one small step for you and one giant leap for your Aunt Keely. Now come on, let's go find Uncle Sweetness and let him drive us to the park to feed the ducks."

# Chapter Twelve

*It ain't the heat,*
*it's the humility.*

—Yogi Berra

THEY WERE BARELY BUCKLED INTO THEIR SEATS, THE small jet taxing out to the runway, when Keely started in on him. She thought she'd shown remarkable restraint until then, but now she needed to know everything.

"What did Jimmy say? Did he get the order keeping Candy in Pennsylvania? How about a restraining order on Joey? I know that would be pushing it, considering the fact that you've actually *invited* the man to stay at the house, but did Jimmy even think of it? And what about—"

"I think I liked the silent ride to the airport better," Jack told her, bracing his hands on the armrests as the jet lifted off the tarmac. "Oh, damn. I hate small planes. Damn Mort. He knows I hate small planes."

"Really? I think this is great. Flying coach, now that I hate." Keely looked out the window as the ground fell away beneath them, then grinned at Jack. "You're white as a ghost. I don't believe it. You flew all over the country when you were with the Yankees."

"Yeah, in *real* planes, not tin cans. Jim Croce, Richie Valens, the Big Bopper. The list goes on and on. Celebrity, small plane, small plane crash. You'd think people would have learned by now." Then he yawned. "But I'll be okay. I downed air-sickness pills right before we left. They make me sleepy enough that I

202

probably won't start screaming and kicking, demanding they land the plane."

"Oh. Good," Keely said, trying not to laugh. She looked over at him. Back stiff, head pressed against the headrest, hands, white-knuckled, gripping the armrests. "I can see how well the pill's working so far. Should we join our hands in prayer, or do you think we can talk about Candy?"

He turned his head toward her. "Not funny. Everybody's got a phobia of some sort. I'll bet you can't stand mice."

"Actually, I had one as a pet when I was a kid," Keely told him, accepting a glass of orange juice from the steward. "Aunt Mary didn't want the responsibility of a cat or a dog. He was white, with the cutest little pink nose. I called him Mr. Squiggles. I really loved that mouse."

"I'm happy for you," Jack told her, tight-lipped. "Now, do you want to hear what Jimmy had to say, or can I just move to another seat before I choke you?"

"Sorry," Keely apologized, not sorry at all. At least the man was no longer holding on to the armrests as if, if he let go, the whole plane would fall from the sky. "Please tell me what he said."

Jack shifted in his seat. "Not much, unfortunately. What he did say is that he has no choice now but to make this all official. Inform the local child welfare authorities, stuff like that. We'll be assigned a case worker, probably as early as Monday."

"And that's not good news?" Keely was pretty sure of his answer but had to ask.

"Not really. This is no longer Cecily dropping Candy off for me to baby-sit her for a few days. Now it's official, like she is guilty of abandonment. After all, if Candy wasn't abandoned, if I *were* just baby-sitting, then I wouldn't be going for custody, right? Bottom line, the case worker might decide to place Candy in some foster home while Joey and I fight this whole thing out in court."

"No!" Keely sat up straight, her heart pounding. "They can't *do* that. Candy belongs with us—you. Jack?"

He reached over, took her hand. "Relax. Jimmy says it's only one possibility. If we can show the child welfare people that Candy's in a good, safe environment, well taken care of, then we've got a pretty good shot at retaining physical custody, at least for now. Damn, I wish Joey were dead broke instead of sitting on that cushy trust fund, because then he'd jump at my offer if I tried to pay him to make him go away. Because he doesn't want Candy. He just doesn't want me to have Candy."

Keely blinked back tears, tears born of fear and her frustration at not being able to do anything to help. "You are going to keep fighting, though, aren't you?"

Jack nodded, even as he yawned again. "I never give up without a fight, Keely."

She knew what he meant. "Baseball. You didn't give that up without a fight."

He smiled, a sad smile, and rubbed at his forehead. "Baseball. God, that seems like two lifetimes ago. And not very important, to tell you the truth. But Candy?" He shook his head. "This is different. If anyone had told me, even a couple of weeks ago, that I'd care this little about baseball, or this much about one small, goofy little kid . . ."

"You love her, don't you?" Keely asked quietly. "This isn't just because Cecily asked you to take care of her, or to make Joey mad, or even because you've got nothing better to do and need something to take your mind off having to retire. You really love her. You'd do anything and everything it took to keep her."

Jack's eyelids looked heavy, and he was already near sleep. "Yes, I would. Anything," he said around another yawn. "Damn, maybe I should have followed the directions and only taken one pill. Keely, would you mind if we didn't talk for a while? I'm really tired."

Anything? He'd do anything? Is that what she was to him, a convenient *anything?* Is that why she was on this plane? How far would he go? Would he even make love to her, pretend to want her, even love her, in order to present that solid home life that would gain him custody of Candy?

"Sure, Jack," Keely said, blinking back tears, watching as the steward handed Jack a pillow and a blanket. "You just sleep," she said, turning to look out the window, "while I try to figure out why I shouldn't be screaming for a parachute."

Jack only woke up as the plane was setting down at an unbelievably small airport somewhere in Arizona. He probably should have found out just where he had been heading before he got there, but at the time it hadn't seemed important. The commercial was just something he'd agreed to do, something to help prolong the career he no longer missed.

"Where's Phoenix, or Tucson, or something like that? We're in the middle of nowhere," he said as he and Keely deplaned and he looked around. Flat . . . more flat . . . mountains in the distance. And heat. Arizona must have cornered the market on heat.

"Oh, how lovely," Keely exclaimed, squinting into the sun. "I'll want to take lots of pictures. Excuse me while I go fish my camera out of my suitcase."

Keely walked over to the small pile of luggage as Jack turned in time to see his agent striding toward him, his five-foot, nine-inch, heavily packed frame decked out in a colorful Hawaiian shirt and a pair of khaki shorts that clipped the top of his pudgy knees.

"Jack! Right on time! And smart, bringing your own entertainment. Now kiss the lady good-bye and let's get moving. Brad—he's the director—he says we can maybe get this done today, but we're losing light in a couple of hours."

Jack took his agent by the arm and steered him away from the plane before Keely could hear the man. "Where the hell are we?" he asked as his agent pulled out a huge white handkerchief and began patting at the perspiration dotting his forehead.

"In the great Southwest, if anyone should ask, Jack, in the great Southwest, and you just love it here, may even buy some land, put up a hacienda. It's hot, sure, but it's a dry heat, and it doesn't bother you at all." Mort looked back over his shoulder. "Why's that girl following you? I'll have someone drive her to the motel. Oh, and great taste there, Jack; she's a real looker."

"She's stays with me. And no more cracks, Mort, I'm warning you."

"Serious?" Then Mort looked at Jack. "My God, serious. I never thought I'd see the day. Who is she? Is she anyone important? Do I leak this to the press or make a formal announcement?"

"Mort, the last thing I want or need right now is the press. I just want to do this commercial, get back on that plane, and go home. Make this easy for me, Mort, and you'll have my eternal gratitude."

"Thanks, but I'm happy enough with my ten percent. So, who is she?"

Jack sighed. "I'll introduce you, but you have to behave yourself."

"And when don't I behave myself?"

"I don't know, Mort. Maybe it's the dozen phone calls I've had about rumors the White Sox are looking at me. Of course, you wouldn't know anything about that, right?"

Mort crunched up his mobile face as he looked off into the bright sun. "Jack, Jack, Jack. It's necessary to keep your name out there, at least while I'm trying to line up some more endorsements. Right now I'm working a real sweetheart deal with a glove manufacturer that will remain nameless for the moment. You know how I hate speaking too soon; it could queer the deal."

"Jack?"

He turned around to see Keely standing ten feet away from him, pointing at a limousine that stood with its back doors open. Grabbing Mort by the arm once more, he took him over, made the introductions, then helped Keely into the backseat, following right after her, to act as a buffer between her and his agent.

"Keely, huh?" Mort said, leaning across Jack. "Only other Keely I ever heard of was Keely Smith, the singer. You know, Jack—Louis Prima and Keely Smith?"

"No, I don't," Jack told him, pushing Mort back into his seat. "And Keely doesn't, either, because both of us were born after the Ice Age. Now, tell me where we're going."

"Not very far," Mort assured him. "You've only got one thing to do, and that's to walk up to the car with this female model, put her in it, put yourself in it, and drive off down this long road. That's it."

"That's it? That's all? I don't have any lines?"

"Nope. Somebody does the voice-over back in the studio. All you do is walk up, put the girl in the car, put—"

"Okay, okay, I think I've got it," Jack said, holding up his hands. "Then it's back to the hotel, and back to Whitehall in the morning, right?" He looked at Keely. "This is even better than I'd hoped."

"Some things are," Keely told him flatly.

Jack immediately got the feeling he was missing something. "Hey, are you okay? I'm sorry I fell asleep on you."

"Yes, you did. Literally. And yes, I'm fine. Let's just get this over with. Trust me, Jack, I want to go home even more than you do. This trip was a bad idea. A bad, bad idea."

Yes, he'd definitely missed something. There was enough of a chill in the air that the car's air-conditioning probably wasn't necessary. What had happened between the time they'd gotten on the plane and the moment they'd touched down in the Arizona version of the Outback?

Jack wanted her to explain herself, but the look she gave him warned him off. They rode in silence—well, Jack and Keely did; Mort kept up a running monologue that touched on everything from his latest deal to the great fajitas he'd had for lunch—until they got to the site, where two red Corvette convertibles, three vans, about twenty people, and a mess of lights and other equipment all stood, waiting. All to film one lousy thirty-second commercial meant to air during the World Series.

The limousine had barely come to a halt when one of the men broke away from a small group and came trotting up to talk to Mort while Jack was still trying to extricate his long legs from the backseat and Keely had already gotten out on the other side of the vehicle. "Problem. Julie's plane was grounded in Vegas. Something with the engine, and she won't be here until late tonight. We have to shut down, do it all again tomorrow. It's a bitch and going to cost a fortune, but I don't see any other way to—who's that?"

Jack watched as the man pointed to Keely, and Mort's gears began to turn inside his avaricious brain. He could almost hear the whirl and whiz, the *ca-ching* of his agent's internal cash register. "Who? Oh, you mean Keely Sm—McBride? She's mine, of course. A new face. The face of the new millennium, as a matter of fact. I suppose we could . . . but I don't know, Brad. Revlon's looking long and hard at her . . ."

Jack rolled his eyes. Mort was definitely a piece of work.

Still, Brad seemed ready to deal. "I understand your problem, Mort. And I'd still have to pay Julie; she's union. But that wouldn't make a dent in the cost overrun if I have to have an entire crew here for another day and night. I wouldn't do any real close-ups of her, just your boy here, so she wouldn't be overexposed for Revlon. I really want to bring this in under budget, now that I've decided I could. Let's talk." The director took Mort's arm, walked him over to the shade beside one of the vans.

"There's a problem?" Keely asked, walking around the limo to join Jack. "Is there a problem? Jack, are you going to tell me what's going on?" she asked him as he leaned back into the limousine, grabbing two bottles of iced water out of the built-in cooler. "Not that I have any right to know. I'm just along for the ride, right?"

He offered her one of the bottles, which she declined. "We're both just along for the ride, Keely. This is

Mort's show. I just want it over with so we can go to the motel, maybe take a swim, and put our heads together about Candy without Petra or Sadie or the Beast and Worst of Bayonne under our feet."

Keely shook her head. "I don't get it. Mort's your agent, your manager. That's fine. But don't you take *any* interest in what goes on around you?"

Jack looked at her, his thoughts still more on the motel and the coming night than on anything else. He just wanted the two of them to be alone together. Was that too much to ask? Apparently it was. "I pay Mort to do that. I play ball, he works the money. What's wrong with that?"

"Well," Keely said, rolling her eyes, "if you don't know, I'm certainly not going to tell you." Then she told him: "First, you don't play ball anymore. Second, it's one thing to be trusting, but it's downright stupid not to take more of an interest in your own life. Third—"

"Okay, okay, I get the point," Jack said quickly, to shut her up. He didn't bring her here so that they could fight. Fighting they could do at home.

"You're right, I should pay more attention."

"Do you even have a ballpark figure of how much you're worth?" Keely persisted.

"Ballpark," Jack admitted, looking down at the ground. "Big ballpark. That is, I know within a couple of million. I take an allowance and Mort handles everything else."

"Ohmigod," Keely breathed, looking at him as if he were a helpless incompetent. Actually, she might have been looking at him as if he was the stupidest thing in nature, but he'd rather she saw him more as incompetent than just plain stupid. As long as she thought he might be lovable.

"I don't get it, Jack," Keely pressed him. "You've already let me know you're careful about spending, never wanting to be extravagant like some athletes. But now you're telling me you don't even know how much money you *have?*"

"Look, Keely," Jack tried to explain, "Tim and I signed with Mort straight out of college, with Dad's blessing. Dad trusted him, and now that he's gone, Tim and I still trust him. There's never been a reason not to trust him."

"Oh, really? Tell me, Jack, how would you know?" Keely asked, sniffing. "I'm not saying your agent is a thief. I'm sure he's not. But isn't it time you started paying some *real* attention to your own life?"

"I've been busy."

"Yes, playing ball. I know. Now you've got a house, you've got Candy, you've got the rest of your life in front of you. Honestly, Jack, you need a keeper."

He glared at her. Okay, so they'd fight. What was so unusual about that? "I'm not looking for volunteers."

"Good, because I'm not volunteering." She took the bottle of water from him, then turned and walked away.

"It's so nice to know you *don't* care," he called after her, then turned around angrily when Mort poked him in the arm. "What?"

"We need Keely."

Jack shook his head. Mort needed Keely? Hell, he'd thought *he* needed Keely, except that the Keely he thought he needed was a whole hell of a lot nicer than the Keely who'd flown to Dipstick, Arizona, with him. "What are you talking about, Mort? Say that again."

"I said, we need Keely. Well, Brad does. The actress they hired can't get here until late tonight or tomorrow. So it's either call it quits for today and start over tomorrow or try to at least rehearse today and shoot tomorrow. Who knows? If they're really lucky, and the little lady doesn't freeze with stage fright, everything can get wrapped up today."

"So they want Keely to . . . she'd never do it."

"Ten grand, less my fifteen percent, of course. If she works out, I sign her permanently, get her all hooked up with the right promo, and, bam—whole new career for the little lady."

Jack narrowed his eyes as he looked at his agent. "I only pay you ten percent."

Mort shrugged. "Time marches on. Yours is an old contract. I now charge fifteen percent. Everybody does, except the few who charge twenty. But, hey, I'm not greedy. You want ten, I'll go with ten, but just for this one shot. Let me go talk to her."

Jack looked to where Keely was bending over, examining the interior of one of the Corvettes. Even after a long plane ride, even in this God-awful heat, she looked cool, collected, and classily, classically beautiful in a soft yellow silk blouse and a pair of slim, palest yellow slacks. Her hair, which had started the day in a neat twist, must have gotten mussed on the plane, so now she only had it pulled away from her face and clipped against the back of her head, her heavy mane of curls tumbling onto her shoulders.

"Sort of Grace Kelly-ish, don't you think?" Mort commented, also looking at Keely. "Just please tell me she's an amateur and doesn't have her own agent. I mean, I might stick with athletes, but that doesn't mean I can't branch out, get into agenting models."

"She's an interior decorator," Jack said, still looking at Keely, seeing her now as Mort saw her, and deciding he'd rather see her the way he'd been seeing her: in his

212

house, playing with Candy, sitting across the dinner table from him, slowly taking over his world. "I don't think she'll do it, Mort."

"Why? She's independently wealthy? She doesn't need a windfall like this? Imagine the loss to the world if Marilyn Monroe had said that," Mort said, resorting once more to his oversized handkerchief. "Come on, Jack. Just let me ask. We're all going to melt out here."

That was it, Jack realized. The money. Keely needed money in order to go back to New York. An unexpected windfall like this would help her a lot. Did he have any right to keep her from earning that money? No, he didn't. He didn't have the right to ask Keely to do or not to do *anything*.

"Oh, hell. Go ahead, Mort. Ask her," Jack said, then walked toward the guy his agent had called Brad, who was frantically motioning to him.

Four hours later, with the hotter than hot sun still hanging above the mountains, Jack wanted Brad dead, Mort dead, and Keely dead most of all. Oh, yeah, and the makeup girl, who kept telling him not to sweat. She could join that list, too.

Jack would rather have blisters on every finger of his pitching hand than hear Brad yell, "Cut! Let's do it again!" one more time.

It had all sounded so simple. Not as simple as Mort had told him, but not brain surgery either. Stand next to the car with Keely, facing each other, holding both her hands. Step away, open the car door, help her inside. Walk around the front of the car, lightly trailing his fingers over the hood as he tossed the keys in the air a couple of times, get in the car, start the car, and drive away.

How hard could that be?

213

Hard enough.

Take one, he'd been unable to fish the car keys out of his pocket.

Take two, he'd gotten them out of his pocket, but then dropped them.

That had started it. His confidence deserted him, and he began trying so hard not to make any more mistakes that mistakes seemed to be all he *could* make.

Take six, he closed the door on the long, trailing scarf some idiot believed should be tied around Keely's throat so it would blow in the wind as they drove away.

Take fourteen, he'd . . . oh, hell, he'd forgotten what he'd done wrong that time.

And all while Keely performed beautifully. She'd hold his hands, gaze up at him adoringly, then gracefully slip onto the front seat. Perfect. Every time.

He was the one who couldn't seem to get it right. And every time he got it wrong, everything stopped. Some guy had to come wipe off the hood of the car. Someone else had to move a light (why did they need all these hot lights, if the sun was still out?), or suggest another camera angle. The makeup girl would have to come running over to comb his hair, dab junk on his face, and tell him not to sweat.

"Okay, kids, listen up," Brad called out as the makeup girl was blotting Jack's forehead after take twenty-two had gone sour when Jack tripped over the Corvette's front bumper. "We get one more shot at this tonight or else we're back here tomorrow, doing it all over again. Jack? You ready? Bottom of the ninth, with the bases loaded and two out. Let's go for the gold, all right!"

"Yeah, sure. Go for the gold? In baseball? What the hell was that idiot talking about?" Jack grumbled, and

214

walked over to Keely the Perfect. She didn't even sweat!

"Jack? Are you all right?" she asked him as he looked everywhere but at her.

"No, damn it, I'm not. I can't believe I can't do this. A monkey with a tambourine could do this."

"So it isn't that you're upset because they asked me to be in the commercial? Because Mort said you weren't too happy, and—"

"Happy? I'm happy. Why wouldn't I be happy? Hell, I'm delirious, I'm that happy. It means less of my money will go in your pocket for your big move back to Manhattan, and that means you won't have to worry that Mort might be robbing me blind, or that Candy will ever have to go without new shoes. Damn. You make money, you get to go back to New York, and I don't have to listen to you ask me if I'm all right or tell me I'm all wrong, because you'll be gone, out of my life. How could I possibly be anything *but* happy?"

Keely pressed the back of her hand against his cheek. "Have you been drinking enough water, Jack? You have to drink a lot of water in this heat or you could get heatstroke, become disoriented, maybe even delirious."

Jack glared at her. Was she insinuating that he was making mistakes on purpose so that they'd have to go back at it tomorrow, with the model, and Keely wouldn't get paid the whole ten thousand? And was she right? God, please, he thought, don't let me be that petty. "I'm *fine.*"

"Could have fooled me," Keely mumbled, then took her spot when Brad started yelling instructions yet again. "Look, Jack," she said, holding his hands, "just relax, okay? There aren't any lights, any cameras. No Mort, no Brad, no nobody. Just the two of us, going for a ride."

215

She squeezed his hands, and Jack took a deep breath, looked into her face. She smiled back at him. "Just you and me, Jack. Just you and me."

"I like the sound of that." He took a deep breath, let it out slowly. "Keely? I know there's still a lot for us to talk about, a lot of problems, big problems. I know there are times I want to tell you to mind your own damn business, and times you want to belt me with one of those frying pans you've got hanging in the kitchen, but, just for now, are you about as ready to get out of here as I am? Because I really want to be alone with you. Now."

Her brown eyes went all sort of soft and liquid. "Oh, Jack, you make me so mad . . . and then you say something like that and . . ."

"I can't help it, Keely. I like the sound of it—'Just you and me,' " he said quietly, repeating her words, slowly pulling her closer, bending his head to kiss her inviting mouth. They stood there, hand in hand, sharing a moment, and then Jack helped her into the car, walked around it, patted the hood of the convertible twice, deftly flipped the keys in his hand, hopped into the front seat without opening the door. He looked at Keely, leaned over, kissed her again, started the car, and drove off down the road, Keely's scarf trailing in the breeze.

"And *cut* and *print!*" Brad yelled out as Jack drove past him.

Jack kept driving.

"Jack?" Keely asked, looking back over her shoulder as the vans and people were left in the dust. "Brad's waving to us. Do you think we should turn around now."

"Do you?" he asked her. "Because Mort said the motel is only about five miles down this road." He looked over at her, took her hand in his. "Or am I way off base, and misreading the signals?"

"Um . . . what do you mean, Jack? Are you asking me if I'll go to . . . I mean, are you thinking . . . oh, the hell with it." Keely wet her lips, faced forward. "How fast does this thing really go?"

They pretty much fell through the doorway to the motel room together, hand in hand, two escapees making good on their getaway. Breathless. Giggling like fools about the way the desk clerk had goggled at Jack, asking for his autograph. All but abandoning the Corvette in the parking lot in their rush to get to their room.

Jack kicked the door shut, tossed the key on its heavy metal ring in the direction of the king size bed. It hit the clock radio on the nightstand, and suddenly a voice was saying, ". . . your number one station. Next up, a newcomer and her sizzling, sexy hit, *Every Night, Every Delight.*"

Jack stepped closer, his blue eyes dark, intense.

*"Aaaah, baby, every nigh t. . ."*

Keely tried to breathe, couldn't. Their laughter died, because, suddenly, there was nothing to laugh about anymore. There was nothing but Jack, and her. The four walls surrounding them, the bed behind them. And a growing tension, a growing need, that was almost suffocating.

She put her hands on Jack's shoulders, looked into his eyes. He looked hungry, almost as hungry as she felt.

Her for him.

Him for her.

*"Aaaah . . . every delight . . ."*

Keely gasped as his mouth took hers, hard, and fast, just as hard and fast as she returned his kiss.

He buried his mouth against the side of her neck, and she pushed herself closer. Melted. Burned.

Madness. Lovely madness.

His hands were on her, roughly pulling her blouse free from her slacks as she buried her face against his chest. He smelled of sun and heat and man, and she tried to swallow, couldn't.

"... *no place but you for me*..."

Keely tugged Jack's golf shirt loose from his slacks, moaning in frustration because it had no buttons to open, the way he had already opened the buttons of her blouse.

"... *when you're here, it's destiny*..."

"Off," she managed to whisper, hoarsely, her breath gone. "Take it off."

Jack stepped back, ripped the shirt over his head, flung it toward the bed, then pushed Keely's blouse down over her shoulders.

"Oh, God," he said, breathing heavily, looking at her, seeing the ivory lace underwire bra she'd put on earlier, with such low expectations. "You're unbelievable."

"... *Aaaah*... *aaaah*... *every night, every delight*..."

He seized her mouth again, even as his hands fumbled at the front closing of her bra until, just as impatient as he, she unhooked it herself.

His hands touched her and Keely's knees went weak, her body turned to liquid heat. She moaned into his mouth, moaned again as he pressed his lower body against hers, let her feel his hardness.

"... *aaaah*... *baby you're my delight*..."

Together, they fell onto the bed, hands moving, zippers opening, clothing disappearing, not without a struggle.

Again and again Jack's mouth ground onto hers, his

218

tongue probing, hers dueling in response. She held him, dug her nails into him, couldn't get enough of him . . . never enough of him.

"*. . . do it, do it, do it, baby . . .*"

Her body was fire and ice, melting and shivering, responding wildly to his every touch. Her back arched as his mouth closed over her nipple, as he suckled her, as his hands cupped her hips, slid between her thighs.

Not enough, not enough. She dragged at him, pulling him back up her body, just as much the aggressor as he, biting his bottom lip, nipping at his earlobe. Raining kisses all over his face, his neck. Stabbing her fingers into his hair, pulling him closer. Closer.

Sweet madness.

"*Oh, oh, baby, yessssssss . . .*"

Jack's aggression matched her own. He wouldn't stop. His mouth on hers, his hands on her, all over her, inside her, stroking her most intimate parts, seeking . . . finding. Feeding her, thrilling her, tightening the already tightly coiled sensations in her belly . . . until it became too much . . . too much . . . and she flowed beneath him, flowered beneath him. Bloomed.

"*. . . yes, every night . . . yes, delight . . . oh, oh, oh!*"

She half-raised herself as he left her, rummaged madly in his slacks pocket. He threw his slacks, and they hit the clock radio, knocking it to the floor, silencing it.

And then he was with her again, just as fierce and frantic as before, so that she quickly regained her own hunger that had been not quite sated.

"Do you need more . . . ?"

"No . . . God, no . . ." Keely told him, reaching for him, opening herself to him.

"Good, because I . . . I can't . . . oh, God," he moaned, sinking into her, filling her.

She raised her legs, wrapped them around him, wrapped her arms around him, threw back her head as he began to move inside her. Slowly, but not for long. Nothing was happening slowly. He moved faster, and she lifted herself to meet thrust after thrust, feeling the pressure within her build, the need grow, and grow.

His arms were around her, and he lifted his head slightly, then brought his lips to hers, moist, open, his tongue mimicking the movements of his body.

"*. . . Ooooh . . . ooooh . . .*"

The sounds were Keely's, ripped from her throat as her body convulsed, as the muscles in Jack's back tensed beneath her hands and he joined her in a release so intense Keely thought she just might lose consciousness.

Then it was quiet in the room. Perhaps too quiet, as Jack held her close for a few more moments, the only sounds that of their ragged breaths, their pounding hearts. Then, pressing a last kiss against her hair, he stood up, gathered his slacks and underwear, and headed for the bathroom, leaving Keely alone on the bed.

Keely realized with a quick, embarrassed start, that she was glad he'd gone, glad he hadn't talked to her, said something that he might not mean . . . or worse, something he did mean, like, "Sorry, we shouldn't have done that. It won't happen again."

She dressed quickly, her fingers fumbling with the buttons of her blouse. She extracted a comb from her purse, fixed her tangled hair, drew it back into the clip again. Did her best to ignore the sensations still tingling between her legs, the heavy fullness in her lower abdomen.

Then, as the shower ran in the bathroom, she sat in the single chair in the room, her hands folded in her lap, wondering what would happen next.

They could laugh at the same absurdities, argue with each other over any stupidity. They could have great sex together.

But, obviously, they still couldn't talk to each other. Not about anything important.

There was a knock at the door and Keely, after quickly checking her reflection in the mirror, opened it, to see Mort Moore standing there.

"Everything all right in here?" he asked. "I've got your luggage."

Keely stepped outside, her purse in her hand, and closed the door behind her. Without preamble, she asked, "How do I get a plane back to Pennsylvania? Allentown, Philadelphia, anywhere even close to Whitehall?"

Mort screwed up his face, scratched a spot above his left ear. "Good question. Only private planes fly in and out of the airport here. I guess you'd have to get to Phoenix."

"Fine," Keely told him, taking his arm and walking him toward the limousine parked beside the Corvette. "Tell this guy to take me to Phoenix. And I need an advance on my pay for today. In cash. I have to buy a ticket, and maybe a hotel room for the night. Scratch that: definitely a hotel room for the night. I want to stand in the shower for about three hours."

Mort looked back over his shoulder. "But—"

"Two choices, Mort," Keely told him, her heart pounding. She had to get away and she had to get away *now*, before Jack came looking for her. "Either lend me the money and the limo or become an accessory to murder. Because if I have to stay here another minute, Mort, you're going to have one damned hysterical female on your hands. It could get ugly, Mort, really ugly. Your choice."

221

Mort looked at her, and Keely returned his look with an unblinking stare. "Well, that was very clear, wasn't it? Do you mind if it's big bills?"

# Chapter Thirteen

*There are only two places in the league—first place and no place.*

—Tom Seaver, pitcher

Jack could have kicked himself back to Whitehall, but once he had kicked himself around the motel room, he decided it would be faster if he took the plane. Which he did, taking off at midnight once Mort had found, awakened, and bribed the pilot.

Having lost his small package of airsick pills, Jack was forced to anesthetize himself with several small bottles from the plane's minibar. His first drink was to calm his nerves as the plane raced down the runway. The second was to hopefully blot out the raw hell he'd felt on discovering that Keely had bolted, run away. The third got him through some turbulence over Oklahoma and the fourth—well, after the third, everything became pretty much of a blur.

Jack, his luggage, and his hangover arrived back at the house around eight fifteen in the morning, at which time he decided to shower, nap, and make out his will, probably not in that order. Then, before Keely could arrive, he would come up with a plan to make her love him, forgive him, and not kill him—again, probably not in that order.

The cab he'd grabbed at the airport rolled up to the front door, stopping behind a gray compact sedan Jack didn't recognize. He overtipped the driver, grabbed a canvas bag, his single piece of luggage, and headed for the steps. He'd made it to the second step before two huge arms wrapped around him from behind, lifted him clear off the ground, and carried him to the side of the house, his bag still hanging from his shoulder.

Only his hangover, and the resultant loss of brain function and reflexes, kept him from struggling until he was rather gently set back down on his feet in front of Petra Polinski.

"Thank you, Sweetness, that was perfect," Petra said as the grinning, bald mountain patted Jack's shirt, as if smoothing away any injuries, and then joined Petra, the two of them now facing Jack.

"Yes, thank you, Sweetness," Jack said, wondering if either of them had noticed that the top of his head had just cracked open. Then he looked at Petra, blinked, and looked at her again.

The girl was dressed in sharply creased navy slacks, shoes *and* socks, and a crisply starched white blouse. She had her hair, all the same color, tied back at her nape, she was wearing horn-rimmed glasses, and she was carrying a book . . . Poems *of Elizabeth Barrett Browning.*

"What the hell . . ." Jack asked, making a sweeping motion toward Petra. "And why the hell . . . ?" he continued, pointing at Sweetness.

"She's here," Petra said, whispering, almost hissing the words.

"She? Who she?" Then Jack's blood ran cold. "Cecily? Cecily's here?"

"You wish," Petra said, rolling her eyes. "Her we could deal with, according to Aunt Sadie. No, Jack, your cousin isn't here. The county social worker is here.

She showed up about twenty minutes ago, but Jimmy had already tipped us off, so I had a chance to change, try to make a good impression."

Oh, God, but his head hurt. And his stomach was doing somersaults. "Why would you have to make a good impression, Petra? You're not going for custody."

"No, but I am the caretaker you hired, and I therefore reflect your judgment, your concern for Candy. Honestly, Jack, try to keep up, okay?"

"She put Ms. Peters in the kitchen with Aunt Sadie," Sweetness said helpfully. "Aunt Sadie found out from your agent that you were going to be home soon, so she's stalling, but Ms. Peters wants to see Candy, and you and Keely."

"Oh, God," Jack groaned, pressing both hands against his head, trying to think. "Oh God, oh God, oh God. Look—you go keep Aunt Sadie company and I'll go shower and change."

"Yes, and brush your teeth," Petra told him. "You smell like my dad after one of his lodge meetings. Been knocking them back, haven't you, Jack? I guess it's just a blessing you didn't come home wearing a moose head. Must have been one bummer of a trip, if Keely's coming home on a different plane. Now go on—chop-chop. Sadie's good, but she can't hold this woman off forever."

Jack nodded, then wished he hadn't, because his head fell off, rolled off over the grass—or at least it felt like that. He took two steps, then turned around, asked, "Joey? Where's Two Eyes? Please tell me he's locked in the cellar."

Petra shook her head as she rolled her eyes. "Men. You don't understand a thing, do you? Joey's in the kitchen with Aunt Sadie and Ms. Peters, of course.

Where else would you want a jerk like that except front and center, proving he's a jerk?"

"Oh, okay. Right," Jack said, nodding. "And Candy? She's with them, too?"

"No. *Her* we locked in the cellar. Of course she's with them," Petra told him. "Where else would she be if she's not with us?"

"Damn," Jack swore under his breath. He'd wanted to see Candy, hold Candy—grab her up, find Keely, and move all three of them out of the reach of the social worker. But he couldn't do any of that, not before he'd showered and changed. "Give me ten minutes, Sweetness, then bring me a fistful of aspirin and some orange juice, okay? Oh, and thanks. Both of you."

Then he was off once more, heading for the front door, the staircase, and the coldest shower he could manage.

He was still towel-drying his hair when Sweetness walked into the room, carrying the orange juice, a small white bottle of pills, and the cordless phone. "Your lawyer," he said, handing the phone to Jack.

"Jimmy? She's here, the social worker is here," Jack said without preamble. "What do I do? Do I say anything? Do I tell her anything?" Then he listened, and paced, and listened and paced some more before pushing the OFF button and throwing the phone on the bed. "Damn."

"Trouble, Mr. T?" Sweetness asked, wringing his hamlike hands.

"Not yet, Sweetness," Jack assured him, then sighed. "Not yet, but it's coming. My lawyer thinks the private investigators he hired may already have located Cecily, and he's only half sure that's a good thing."

"Uh-huh," Sweetness said, tapping three aspirin into

225

his palm, then handing them, and the orange juice, to Jack. "What's the half sure it's a bad thing?"

Jack looked at Sweetness with new respect. "You're right on top of this, aren't you, Sweetness? The bad thing is that Cecily, if we tell her what's going on, might just fly back here and try to take Candy. Then we'd have a three-way battle for custody, and it would get even uglier. Joey, I figure I can handle, but Cecily is Candy's biological mother, and if she does her crying, hiccuping, poor-little-me thing, some judge might just believe she really cares about the baby. Which is bull, because she left her, didn't she? Hasn't even called to see how she is, nothing. Typical irresponsible Cecily. So Jimmy says I'm to just play nice until he can contact Cecily himself, feel her out about handing over custody."

Sweetness nodded his large head. "So you still need Keely. Petra said you'd still need Keely. Petra said you screwed up somehow, but Keely will still probably bail you out, because she loves Candy, even if you made her mad. Oh, and Ms. Peters wants to meet her, anyway, because she's taking care of Candy. Mr. T? You're still looking a little funny. Maybe you should have a bologna sandwich or something? I always feel better when I have a bologna sandwich."

Mention of Keely had brought back all the rest of Jack's problems, the most major being that he didn't know where Keely was, if she'd even come back, and how he could ever explain to her that he didn't normally all but attack women in a sexual frenzy. He'd wanted her so badly, and she was sending him signals, wasn't she, and maybe it was a little crazy the way they couldn't keep their hands off each other, and how quickly they'd fallen into bed together. But then he'd

226

tried to put some space between them so that she could collect herself, so he could collect himself, and he'd come back out of the bathroom to an empty room. When he'd thought of space, he'd thought from the motel bedroom to the bathroom. Keely, obviously, thought it better to put several *states* between them.

"Mr. T? A bologna sandwich?" Sweetness offered once more.

"Thanks, but I'll pass. Has Keely called?" he asked, facing the mirror, drawing a comb through his still-damp hair.

"No, sir, she hasn't, but Mr. Moore did, and he said he's right on top of things, and that her plane should be landing at the airport here at nine this morning. Petra and me, we're gonna go meet her there, explain everything so that she knows what's up. We were going to leave just as you showed up, so I have to go now or we'll be late."

Jack glanced at the clock radio on the table beside his bed. Twenty till nine. "You're cutting it close, Sweetness. Get moving. We can't have Keely just walk into this cold."

"Yes, sir," Sweetness agreed, already heading for the door. "Whoops, almost forgot. Aunt Sadie says you should have that box, so you and Keely look like you're not lying."

Jack waited until Sweetness had gone, then picked up the small blue velvet box on the dresser, opening it to see his mother's engagement ring tucked inside.

Would Keely wear it? Would she go along with the fraud in order to save Candy from Cecily and Joey? Would she go so far as to marry Jack in order to keep Candy safe? Would she agree to marry him, not loving him, not even hearing from him that he loved her?

He really had to talk to her.

"Sure, that's what I'll do. I'll grab her before she can say anything, tell her the social worker is here and we have to save Candy, slip a diamond on her hand and, real quick, I tell her, oh yeah, and I love you—desperately—and that makes everything all right and you can just forget going back to New York and all that career stuff, right? Why wouldn't she go for that, believe that?" Jack muttered, taking the diamond ring from the case and stuffing it in his pocket. "God, I'm a dead man."

He sat down on the edge of the bed, put his head in his hands, and decided his Aunt Sadie couldn't do too much damage if he delayed his entrance just another ten minutes.

Keely left her suitcase on the front step and walked around to the kitchen entrance, hoping to be able to sneak up the back stairs without anyone seeing her.

The red-eye flight from Arizona had gone by too fast, thanks to a stiff tail wind that had gotten them into Philadelphia almost an hour ahead of schedule, so that she could catch an earlier shuttle to Allentown.

She hadn't slept on the plane, had only used the hotel room to shower and change before heading to the airport in the hope of getting out of town before Jack could find her.

If he'd even looked for her.

Maybe she should have called ahead, used the telephone on the seat back in front of her, asked Petra or Sweetness to meet her at the airport. But she hadn't, and she had arrived early anyway, and a taxi was more anonymous, which suited her; she still had this stupid tendency to start crying for no reason, no reason at all.

228

Just because she'd made a total fool of herself, attacking Jack like some love-starved idiot, then running away because he'd taken what she'd offered.

Of course, she could sit him down, talk to him.

Ask him what those minutes in the motel room had meant to him, told him what they'd meant to her. Sure. She could do that. Right after she stuck a sharp stick in her eye. What in this world could be worse than saying, "Hey, I think I love you," and then waiting for the words, "Hey, thanks, but I was only out for a good time, weren't you?"

Blinking back tears, she turned the knob on the back door and stepped into the kitchen, then stopped dead. Aunt Sadie was there, sitting at the kitchen table with a middle-aged woman in a dark blue suit. The woman had her gray streaked hair pulled back in a tight bun. Two spots of artificial red stained her cheeks and wire-rimmed glasses sat low on her incongruously pert, turned-up nose.

The social worker. Had to be the social worker. Who else could it be but the social worker?

Except that Sadie—clad in a bright pink sundress and wearing red high-top sneakers—was holding the woman's hand, obviously reading her palm.

". . . a strong heart line, Edith. That means—oh, hullo, Keely," she said, letting go of the woman's hand, then sitting back comfortably on her chair. "Were you out looking at the pool already? I told you we'd have the man in to fix it, didn't I? We just needed a new part for the pump. And just look at your eyes. What a shame. We hoped the change in climate might get rid of those pesky allergies. Jack's taken the luggage upstairs, I imagine, since he isn't with you and we all know he's home. Did you two have a nice flight back from visiting your Aunt Mary in Arizona?"

Keely had never heard so much information, and so many blatant lies, in her life—at least not at one go. She bit her bottom lip, trying very hard not to say, "Huh?" and then just smiled at the lady in the blue suit. "Where . . . where's Candy?" she asked at last, looking down at the empty jump seat.

"Petra and Bruno took her for a walk because she likes to look up, see the planes go by overhead," Sadie said. "Not to worry, they'll be back soon. And before you, ask about Joey, I'll tell you that he's hot foot on his way to Bayonne, to confer with his mouthpiece. He raced out of here about five minutes ago."

Okay. Keely knew it was translation time.

Jack was home and stashed away upstairs, obviously not yet introduced to the social worker because, as far as that lady was to know, they had flown back from Arizona together.

Petra and Sweetness and Candy were at the airport, most probably because they had checked on her flight and had gone to pick her up.

Joey was still going to try for custody and had hired a lawyer, which meant that This Was War.

She had allergies, which explained her red-rimmed eyes, they'd been to Arizona to see Aunt Mary, not shack up in some love nest, and, within minutes, anything that had not yet hit the fan was going to hit it unless Keely played along.

All things considered, Sadie was actually pretty easy to understand.

"That . . . that's good," Keely remarked, desperately trying to regain some of her brain, at least the small part that living among the Trehan clan had left her. "And you would be . . . ?" she asked, looking at the lady who was *staring* at her in the oddest way.

"Oh, oh yes," Sadie soldiered on. "I should be introducing you two, shouldn't I? Silly me. Keely, this is Edith Peters, from the social welfare something-or-other, come to see Candy. Edith, my nephew's fiancée, Keely McBride."

Edith Peters stood up, pulled at the bottom of her suit jacket, then extended a hand to Keely. "I'm sorry to have arrived unannounced, but that is the way we often do things."

Keely kept smiling, even as she gritted her teeth. So Sadie's lies had extended to include an engagement? Probably nobody had told her about the orange jumpsuits that would come with Hers as well as His monograms. "I'm just glad we could all be here to meet with you, Ms. Peters," she said, wishing the woman would stop looking at her as if she were a bug under a microscope. "But . . . um . . . if you'll just excuse me for a moment? I'll go see what's keeping Jack."

"Yes, do that, dear, and don't forget to put on your ring. I found it on the sink after you'd left yesterday and put it in Jack's room," Sadie said, going for the world's record in Whopping Great Fibs. "Not that she sleeps with Jack, you understand," she added quickly, turning to Ms. Peters. "My good heavens, no. Even if that is a hickey on her neck."

Keely's eyes went so wide she was astonished they didn't drop right out of their sockets. She looked at Ms. Peters, who was still looking at her, then raised her hand to her throat, realizing that her scarf had slipped, exposing the small red mark on her skin. "Oh, no, no," she said hastily. "I . . . I . . . um . . . I scratched at a bug bite, that's all."

"Of course you did, dear," Sadie told her soothingly. "Now why don't you go find Jack?"

"Bug bite? Is that what they call them now?" Edith asked Sadie as Keely all but ran for the back staircase. "I'm only a few years younger than you, Sadie, but in my day, too, they called them hickeys, trophies from make-out sessions in the backseats of Fifty-five Fords. I had a few in my day."

Somehow, Keely made it to the top of the stairs, then all but bounced, wall to wall, down the hallway, heading for Jack's bedroom. *Please let him be there . . . please don't let him be there . . .*

"Jack?" she asked even as she opened the door, then stepped inside to see him sitting on the edge of the bed, looking like a man with the world hanging on his shoulders. She wanted to kill him, she wanted to hug him and tell him everything was going to be all right. Then she wanted to kill him again.

He looked up, glancing first at the clock radio. "Keely? You weren't supposed to land until nine. What are you doing here?"

"Never mind that," she told him, heading for the bureau and the small jeweler's box she saw sitting there. She had to keep moving, keep talking, and not look at him. Not throw herself into his arms. "Your aunt is downstairs lying her head off and we've got to go help her, and the worst is still happening because Joey just bolted for Bayonne and his attorney. There's nothing else for it, Jack; we have to lie right along with Aunt Sadie. I figure we'll each only get five years, with time off for good behavior. Where's the ring?" she asked, turning back to him, holding the open, empty box, aware that her hand was shaking. "Come on, Jack, I need the ring."

232

"Sorry. I have a hangover, and everything you said sort of hit me in a time delay before it sank in." Jack stood up, fished in both pockets until he came up with the ring. The band was gold and quite wide, the large marquis-cut center stone flanked by three rows of baguettes. They both looked at it for a moment, then he held it out to her.

"It was my mother's. Dad bought it for her on their twenty-fifth anniversary, and she didn't speak to him for a week for being so extravagant. Then she wore it every day, never took it off. Sadie was supposed to save it, give it to the bride of the first twin to marry."

Keely took the ring, slipped it onto her third finger, left hand, trying not to see it, trying not to love the way it looked, the way it felt, the story behind the gift. "I'll give it back when this is over," she promised quietly.

"Yeah, you do that," Jack said tightly. "Did you have a good flight?"

Keely nodded, so completely nervous that she found it difficult to believe that just yesterday the two of them had . . . the two of them had . . . maybe it was better to just forget that. "You?"

"I don't remember. I drank my way through it," Jack told her, heading for the hallway, both his words and his tone telling her that the reason for their separate flights back from Arizona was a closed book, not to be opened again right now, maybe never. He stopped just outside the doorway, turned to her. "Are you sure you want to go through with this? They could withhold custody until we actually get married, you know, and put us in jail if we don't."

"Do I have a choice?"

Jack swore under his breath. "Yes, Keely, you have a choice. And I know it's going to be hard for you to play the loving fiancée, considering that you hate my guts."

"I have a hickey on my neck, Jack," Keely told him, readjusting her scarf, the one from the commercial shoot. "Both Aunt Sadie and Ms. Peters remarked on it, damned near waxed poetic over it. So I don't think I'll have to play the loving fiancée all that much, do you?"

Jack's cheeks went pale under his tan and he reached toward the scarf. Keely backed away from him. "I . . . I don't remember doing that," he said quietly.

"I don't think either of us remembers much of anything," Keely told him. "It's probably better that way."

He looked at her, nodded. "Probably. May have had something to do with all that sun and heat."

"Yes," Keely agreed, avoiding his eyes. "That was probably it. And proximity. There's a lot to be said for proximity."

"Proximity. Right."

Keely wanted to die. She wanted to just lie down, right here in the hallway, and die. "Can we get on with this?" she asked, her eyes beginning to sting again, her voice, quavering slightly.

Jack stepped closer to her, held her arm as he reached out, pushed down the scarf. "I'd never hurt you, Keely. I . . . I care for you a lot. This isn't just about Candy."

Keely wiped a tear from her cheek. "Thank you, Jack," she said. "I care about you, too. But . . ." Her voice trailed off and she shrugged yet again.

"Proximity," Jack repeated yet again. "I know. You and me, you Candy and me, you Candy and me against the world. It's difficult to know just *what* any of us is really feeling, isn't it? Everything's happening pretty fast."

"Too fast," Keely said, twisting the ring on her finger.

234

"But we can't leave Aunt Sadie down there alone with Ms. Peters too much longer. When I came in, she was reading the woman's palm, and Ms. Peters seemed to be liking it."

Jack's smile was small, rueful. "That's my aunt. She's probably telling her that she's about to be rewarded for doing a good and generous deed. I only hope she stops short of offering her money outright to throw the case. Come on, we'd better get down there."

"Funny, I think I just said that. About five times."

Keely followed him as he headed for the back staircase, then nearly bumped into him when he abruptly stopped at the head of the stairs. "Thank you," he said, holding her upper arms as he looked down into her face. "I mean it, Keely. Thank you."

Oh, how she loved this man. "You're welcome," she said, because she couldn't say, "Oh, how I love you."

"When this is over," he went on, "you just go to New York and pick any building you want for your shop, and it's yours. No strings, Keely, it's yours. I promise."

Oh, how she hated this man. "Thanks," she said, because she couldn't say, "Oh, how I want to push you down these steps, you blind idiot!"

". . . So then Joey says to Edith, 'I'm gonna go to Bayonne right now, ya know, get my mouthpiece, see, and then, ba-da-bing ba-da boom, da kid's mine.' I think that's when Edith and I decided to be friends. I mean, when you spend five straight minutes laughing together, it's rather difficult *not* to be friends."

Jack stood in front of the wide-screen TV, holding a glass of ice water (his beverage of choice for the next twenty years, at least), and looked at his aunt. She was reclining on the base of her spine on his couch, her red high-top sneakers planted firmly on the coffee table. He actually said that, Sadie? Ba-da bing ba-da boom?"

"Oh, my, yes, he said it. Ba-da-bing ba-da boom! And he did this rather elaborate sort of snapping of his fingers and banging of his fists on top of each other while he said it. I was very impressed. After all, this is a boy who couldn't seem to learn the words and motions to 'Ring Around the Rosie' when he'd visit here as a child."

"Can we get on with this?" Keely asked from her seat, also on the couch. Hell, everyone was on the couch: Sadie, Keely, Petra. All but Sweetness, who was in the matching chair, quality-testing it for its weight bearing properties.

"There isn't much more to tell, Keely," Sadie said kindly. "We were tipped off by Jack's lawyer, we were ready and waiting, and we handled everything beautifully. Edith's a lovely woman, and smart, too. She saw through Joey instantly."

"She was nice, wasn't she?" Keely said, looking at Jack. "I mean, I thought we'd get the stereotypical social worker. No humor, no insights, no bending of stupid rules. She didn't even take notes or have us fill out a single form."

"And I was brilliant, of course," Petra put in with her usual lack of shyness or inhibitions of any sort. "Although next time maybe I'll carry a Bible instead of a book of poems. That ought to impress the hell out of her."

Jack looked up at the ceiling. "Nope. No lightning strikes heading for you, Petra. Amazing. Still, Keely, I wouldn't sit too close to her if I were you."

Keely didn't smile, but only looked at him, her head tipped to one side. "I think Jack is our weak link," she

236

said, turning to Sadie. "He just doesn't know when to shut up, does he? I had to kick him when Edith wasn't looking."

"What? And yeah, why *did* you kick me? I was only showing her all that great stuff we bought for Candy. All those safety things for the electrical outlets, the cabinet doors, the table edges. And the knee pads. I thought she was very impressed with the knee pads."

"Pathetic," Petra declared, rolling her eyes.

"Pathetic how?" Jack asked, truly not understanding. He thought he'd done a good job, impressing Ms. Peters with how well he was providing for Candy.

Keely got up from the couch, walked over to him. "What Petra is trying to say, Jack, is that Ms. Peters is glad to know about the safety plugs and the knee pads, but what she's assigned to do is check out how we *feel* about Candy, if we're going to provide her with a loving home life, not just *things*. Joey can afford to buy her *things*."

Jack rubbed at his forehead, still holding on to the remnants of his hangover headache. "So I goofed?"

"Not really, Jack," Keely assured him. "She probably did need to see where Candy sleeps, how well you're providing for her. But she'll be coming back, unannounced, to see how we interact with Candy. So you can't be so stiff, so formal. You've told me to relax around Candy, and now you're doing your own stiff-as-a-statue impression. You have to just sort of pretend Ms. Peters isn't here, just be yourself."

"Yeah? Well *myself* was under a little strain here," he responded testily. "Jimmy's people may have found Cecily, we're lying to a very nice woman who could put all of us in jail, and I'm trying to hang on to Candy while Joey is ba-da-bing-ba-da booming all over

Bayonne, hunting up his own lawyer. And that's only the beginning of what's on my mind right now. There's just a little bit of stress here, folks."

He felt Keely's hand on his arm and damn near flinched. Pity? She was going to offer him pity again? Oh, no, not in this lifetime.

"Jack," she said quietly, "we probably need to talk. Privately."

"Well, I can take a hint," Petra said, popping up from the couch. She reached out a hand to assist Sadie to her feet. "Come on, Aunt Sadie, Sweetness. I think they're going to talk about the separate planes. Do you think if we were to put our ears to the vent on the floor upstairs, we'd be able to hear them? Because I think I'd like to take notes for this thesis I'm considering."

"Pet-ra," Jack and Keely said at the same time, so that the girl grinned at them, then led her two cohorts out of the room.

Jack stood very still for a few moments, then motioned for Keely to sit down once more. She returned to the couch, and he sat in the chair, a small corner of his mind happy to learn that Keely had chosen well and the springs had survived Sweetness.

"Well?" Keely said, breaking an uncomfortable silence. "Talk."

He sat forward, poked himself in the chest. "Me? You're the one who said we had to talk. Privately."

"Oh, so you've got nothing to say? Okay, Jack, that suits me. That suits me just fine." Keely went to stand up, leave the room.

"Sit," Jack said, sighing. "I'll talk."

"Well, good," Aunt Sadie said from the kitchen, her hand in the cookie jar. "I thought we'd have to bring out the thumbscrews." As Jack and Keely glared at her, she

238

raised both hands, began backing toward the door. "I'm going, I'm going . . ."

Jack waited until the kitchen door had closed, then looked at Keely. She looked wonderful. She always looked wonderful. "I screwed up," he said at last. "Out there, in Arizona. I screwed up."

"Really? How so?"

He grinned ruefully. "You're not going to make this easy on me, are you?"

"No. I don't think so, Jack. How did you screw up?"

Jack was a jock, a man of action. He wasn't the most articulate man in creation, but he wasn't incapable of expressing himself, either, damn it. Except for when he was looking at Keely, and she was sitting there, so cool, so collected, looking back at him just as if she hadn't, just a day earlier, had her bare legs wrapped around his hips; a wild woman in his arms, a woman he'd made wild, gone wild with. The woman had an ON/OFF switch, and he'd found the on switch only to have her shut it OFF again. How did she do that?

He cleared his throat, ordered his mind to stop thinking about the wild Keely, the Keely he'd held in his arms. "I . . . I took advantage of a . . . of a situation."

Jack could have carved an ice statue out of the chill from her breath. "Really?"

He pressed on, knowing he was committing suicide yet unable to stop himself. "Yes. I . . . I invited you to go with me, and then I took . . . advantage."

"Gee, I'm impressed. You did this all by yourself? You didn't have any help?"

Jack bit the inside of his cheek, narrowed his eyes at her. She was giving him a way out? "Well, I guess I didn't hear you saying no, did I?"

Wrong. She'd led him into a trap, and now she

slammed the cage door. "So I'm to blame? Is that it, Jack? You were weak, but I took advantage of that weakness? My goodness, I should probably change my name to Delilah or Jezebel. Or Madonna."

Jack pushed his fingers into his hair, mentally looking for a way out of the cage she'd put him in, he'd helped her put him in. "That's not what I mean and you know it, so don't twist my words, Keely. We're under a lot of stress here. We got pushed into pretending to be engaged because I opened my big mouth in desperation. We both love Candy and want what's best for her. We've been stuck together in this house—that proximity thing—and then I invited you along to Arizona. How much of what happened, happened because of the stress, the playacting, the hoping to get Candy? Can either of us know?"

She didn't answer him. He didn't know which was worse: her short, cryptic answers or no answers at all.

"Keely? Do you understand what I'm trying to say here? Because I don't want you thinking you want something just because we . . . we maybe got a little carried away by circumstances. You have your career, remember? When I met you, you told me right up front. You want nothing more than to get back to Manhattan, back to the life you love, the career you love. And I can understand that. Hell, I made a jackass out of myself, trying to get back to the career I loved."

At last she talked to him.

"If—and this is just a hypothetical, Jack—if there had been no Candy, no . . . no *me* . . . would you still be trying to get back into the majors? Would you have taken that job in Japan?"

Now he knew which was worse, and he wished she would have continued her silent treatment. "I don't know," he said honestly. "I honest to God don't know."

She closed her eyes for a moment, then stood up. He stood with her. "Wait. Let me explain. I didn't have a choice, Keely. I know that; you know that. The arm is shot, period. So even if I don't know what I would have done, I don't *have* to know. But it's different for you. You do have another shot at your dream. You love Candy, I know you do. But are you trying to tell yourself you love me, too, in order to help Candy? And—and this is a biggie, Keely—will you resent Candy, resent me, if you one day decide that you let yourself be talked into staying here while your heart really wants to be back in Manhattan? You have to know that before any of this goes on for another minute."

She looked at him levelly. Looked at him for a long, long time, then said, "You know your problem, Jack Trehan? You think too damn much."

And then she was gone, heading for the back door and probably Sadie's apartment, leaving him to figure out just what the hell had just happened.

That took about two minutes.

He'd said—well, at least alluded to—the two of them maybe getting married, raising Candy.

He'd said—he was sure he'd said—something about Keely maybe thinking she loved him.

But he'd never said a word about him loving her *back*.

He should have kicked himself all the way back here from Arizona. Then he wouldn't have been here now, to bury both his big, dumb jock feet in his big, dumb jock mouth.

241

# Chapter Fourteen

*If anyone wants me*
*tell them I'm being embalmed.*

—Casey Stengel

"I'M . . . GONNA-GET-CHA," KEELY SAID, GENTLY "walking" her fingers up Candy's bare belly, then lightly tickling the baby's neck. Candy held her breath in expectation, then giggled, kicked her legs as she lay on the padded dressing table. "I'm . . ." Keely repeated as Candy held her breath again, ". . . gonna-get-cha." The baby giggled, squealed in delight.

Still playing with her, Keely quickly, confidently dressed Candy in diaper, sleeveless undershirt, and a soft pink cotton dress with a white collar and a parade of yellow ducklings embroidered on the bodice.

At first, after Jack's warning about her stiffness, Keely'd had to work at relaxing around Candy. But Candy was such an easy baby, a happy baby, that Keely had begun to find it equally easy to drop her fears, her stiffness, and just enjoy her. Now she could flip Candy onto her hip with the best of them and just go with the flow. The difference in Keely, she knew, had made a difference in Candy, who cuddled with her more, giggled more, and held her arms up to her more.

It was nice. Really nice. Even great, and Keely fell more in love with Candy by the minute.

Once Candy was sitting on the changing table, Keely poured a few small drops of baby oil into her own palms, then stroked her hands through the baby's two-inch-long, wispy blond curls. With a soft brush, she fluffed out the sides and back of Candy's hair, ending by putting a finger-roll fat sausage curl smack in the middle of her head.

"There," Keely said, pulling back slightly to inspect her handiwork. "Every child should want to grow up hating Mommy just a little bit for taking a picture of a curl like that. And you'll have to admit, sweetheart, that I'm being kind here. I could have taken a picture of you lying naked on the changing table, that cute rump of yours stuck in the air. Then I could blackmail you into coming home early from your first date—or else I'd show the boy what a cute baby you were."

Candy looked up at Keely as if she knew exactly what was being said, then grabbed hold of the hem of her dress and tried to stuff it into her mouth.

"Oh, no, you don't," Keely said, quickly freeing the material from Candy's grip. "We're going to take pictures and we're going to look beautiful for those pictures. We are *not* going to have a wrinkled wet spot in the middle of our skirt because we want to gnaw on something."

Candy's bottom lip pushed forward and she batted her long, dark eyelashes, clearly deciding whether she wanted to cry or she wanted to . . . she grinned, reached out, and grabbed onto Keely's nose.

"Hey, not my nose, either," Keely protested, reaching for the pacifier that sat on the back shelf of the changing table. "Here," she said, holding it in front of Candy. "We'll make a trade. My nose for your pluggie, okay?"

The exchange made, Keely quickly located Candy's socks—so cute; small and white, the cuffs tipped with pink lace. She hadn't yet bought shoes for the baby, but that was all right. She'd be walking soon enough.

Would she still be here when Candy took her first steps? Who would hold out their hands to her? Who would she walk to, to be swept up in a congratulatory hug, be smothered with kisses?

"Stop it," Keely warned herself out loud, picking up Candy and carrying her over to the rocking chair. "We're not going to think about that now, are we, sweetheart? We're just going to take a bunch of pictures of my pretty little girl."

She sat Candy down on the padded chair, right beside her stuffed bear, then stepped back, fished the one-time-use camera from her skirt pocket in time to catch Candy trying to aim her mouth at the bear's big black nose.

She snapped photographs of Candy looking into the camera, smiling straight into the camera.

She got three shots of Candy resting her head against the huge bear, playing her new game of "I-I." All Keely would have to do is say, "I-I, Candy. Play I-I with the teddy," and Candy would tip her head and press it against the bear, loving it.

The child was brilliant, simply the smartest baby in the entire world. There just wasn't any question about it. Da-da, I-I. Tomorrow, nuclear physics!

"Whoa," Keely said, rethinking that as she scooped Candy into her arms once more. "I'm not so sure the world is ready for another Petra Polinski. Now come on, we'll go find Aunt Sadie and take some pictures with her, okay? And Dada. We'll take pictures with Da-da. Lots of pictures, Candy. Lots and lots of pictures."

*So I will have something to take with me when this is all over and I have the rest of my life to get through without you or that stupid man.*

Keely carried the baby downstairs, then walked through the still mostly unfurnished rooms, looking for somebody, anybody. But nobody else appeared to be in the house. Well, fine. It was a beautiful day, so maybe

244

everyone was outside. Outdoor pictures would be good, right?

Besides, it was probably time Keely faced the family again, after pretty much locking herself and Candy away during two days of damp and rain, two days of her and Jack trying to avoid each other. They did meet at meals, but having Sweetness and Joey sharing the table had protected her, kept her from having to speak to him, him having to speak to her.

She never thought she'd be grateful for Joey Two Eyes, but the man certainly knew how to talk and eat at the same time, not that he said anything anyone would want to remember or comment on. Except that one time, of course, when Joey had told them, on his first night back, that his mouthpiece had told him to get himself back to Whitehall, plant himself, and not move until he heard from him.

Keely had looked across the table at Jack then, wordlessly asking him if he thought Joey had a snowball's chance in hell of gaining custody of Candy. He'd just rolled his eyes, shook his head, and grabbed another warm roll from the basket, while Joey took off on another subject—something about making a real killing selling baseballs he wanted Jack to autograph for him.

The odd thing was that Jack had agreed, and there were now three cartons of baseballs stacked in the den, ready for his signature. Keely had decided that Jack was going to be as nice as he could be to his cousin, then toss him out on his ear as soon as Jimmy the lawyer said he could do it.

She spared a look at the cartons as she passed the otherwise unoccupied den and headed for the kitchen door—then stopped dead in her tracks. Three cartons. There had been *three* cartons.

So how come there were now about ten cartons, ten *huge* cartons?

Retracing her steps, Keely approached the cartons, to see that they were marked as stereo equipment. There was a shipping order lying on top of one of the boxes, and she picked it up and read it, her eyes widening as she realized just how extensive a collection of equipment was sitting in Jack's den. Woofers, tweeters, surround-sound speakers, equalizer—what was that, a great big gun to shoot it all with? Who the hell was appearing here tonight—Aerosmith? What did one man need with so much equipment?

Worse, where the hell was she going to put it? And in what? Wasn't that monster of a television set enough for the man? Did anyone except women ever even *think* about the problems inherent in trying to decorate around a bunch of big, ugly black boxes?

"Ah, you've seen my stuff," Jack said, startling Keely so that she turned around and shook the papers at him, forgetting that, basically, she wasn't speaking to him.

"Why didn't you consult me, Jack?" she asked, adjusting Candy more firmly on her hip. "This is . . . this is a decorating nightmare!"

His smile stopped her, because he looked so entirely pleased with himself. "Really? Gonna take you some time to figure out how to make it all look right and still keep the speakers in the right places? That's okay. Take all the time you need."

"Da! Da-da-da!" Candy called out, reaching her arms toward Jack, who quickly scooped her up, planted a kiss on her cheek as he told her that she looked like a blond hot dog had landed on her head.

"It's a curl, Jack. I have pictures of me with that same curl on my head. It's a tradition."

"If you say so," he responded, kissing Candy again. "Personally, I'd hunt down and burn any picture that had me looking like a hot dog just landed on my head."

"It does *not*—oh, the hell with it. What am I going to do with all this . . . all this *stuff?*"

He smiled again, looking a little like Jim Carrey at his most adorably evil. "Not my problem," he said. "But since you're asking, I was sort of thinking of shelves. Built in shelves. Lots of them. I could show you how it's all supposed to be arranged and, together, we can figure out just what we need."

"Together," Keely repeated hollowly.

"Yeah, together," Jack went on, grabbing Candy's hand as she tried to shove it into his mouth. "You know, that thing we haven't been for a couple of days. Together."

Keely narrowed her eyes, lifted one hand, and sort of slowly twirled it in front of her. "Kind of like a truce, huh? You wanted to ease the tension around here, right? And this is what you thought of? Some men send flowers, Jack. Some men even *talk*. You buy stereo equipment?"

He shrugged. "We're talking again, aren't we? See how that worked out?"

Keely opened her mouth to answer him, then realized she had absolutely nothing to say. The man was a nutcase. And she adored him.

"Hey," Jack went on as Keely realized that it could take days—weeks—to have shelving custom-made for the den, "I was coming to get you anyway, you know. You've got to see this, Keely. Petra's giving Sweetness boxing lessons."

Keely snapped out of her half-frightened, half-hopeful reverie. "She's giving him—you're kidding."

247

"Would I kid about something like that?" Jack asked, turning for the kitchen, Keely close at his heels. "They've got this sort of ring set up over on the side of the house, where the land is flat. Joey's acting as timekeeper, and Sadie keeps telling everyone she should be wearing a swimsuit, then parading around the ring, holding up numbers between rounds. I wish I had a camera."

"I have a camera," Keely told him, skipping to keep up with him. "I was taking pictures of Candy with that special throwaway camera we bought, remember? But there are already some sort of built-in borders for every picture that will show up on the finished photograph. You know, baby blocks, little baby-type toys and stuff?"

"Perfect," Jack said, grinning at her. "Sweetness surrounded by a pink and blue border of teddy bears. Please be sure you get a couple of Joey, too. I may want to send them out to our mutual relatives at Christmas."

Keely smiled, shook her head. Jack certainly seemed to be in a good mood today. "Why are you so happy? Nothing's changed, has it? Or have you heard something you haven't told me?"

He stopped, looked at her. "Nothing much. Jimmy's got an official copy of Candy's birth certificate now, and it matches the one Cecily included with her note. Mother, Cecily Morretti, father unknown. He's got a letter from the pediatrician, saying that Candy's in great health but didn't have any of her baby shots, which looks bad for Cecily when it comes to the 'competent mother' portion of our program. And"—he took a deep breath, grinned—"five minutes ago Jimmy phoned to say he's talked to Cecily and she says she thinks Wyatt Earp would make a great daddy."

Keely had been smiling as she listened to Jack, but

now she frowned. "Wyatt Earp? Wyatt Earp is dead."

"Wrong. Wyatt Earp is alive and living in Whitehall. You're looking at him. But don't worry; Jimmy didn't understand, either. He just thought Cecily was nuts."

"That makes two of us," Keely admitted. "But wait a minute. Are you saying that *you're* Wyatt Earp?"

"Bingo! So now, if the court will buy the idea that Cecily's got her head strapped on tight enough to be able to make an informed, rational choice, Candy could be mine."

"Oh . . . Jack . . ." Keely said, opening her arms as she walked toward him, hugging both him and Candy. "Who would have thought it could be this easy?"

He brought his free hand around her back, rubbed it up and down her spine. "Probably because it isn't. Joey swears he's still going ahead with his lawyer, and Cecily changes her mind about as often as she changes lovers, which is about once every three weeks. But I can't help it, Keely. I'm feeling pretty optimistic. Even if . . ."

His hand stilled on her back, and Keely suddenly realized where she was standing, *how* she was standing. She let go of him, backed up three paces. "Even if what, Jack?"

"Even if Jimmy says we can't call off the engagement lie yet or else it would look too much like the lie it is." He cupped his free hand around Candy, pulled her close as the baby said "I—I," then laid her head against his shoulder. "Do you mind?"

"Mind?" Keely said, fishing in her pocket for the throwaway camera, hiding her stinging eyes behind it as she snapped three quick photographs. "No, of course not. I don't mind. Okay, I've got it. Little devil; I swear she knows she's posing for the camera. Now come on, I want to see this boxing ring."

She started forward, but Jack grabbed hold of her arm at the elbow. "Keely, I—"

"Yes, Jack?" she asked, not looking at him, not allowing him to see the tears brimming in her eyes.

"Never mind. We'll talk later. Let's go see Sweetness in action."

Moments later, her tears nearly forgotten, Keely thanked her lucky stars that Sadie Trehan, Petra Polinski, Bruno Armano, and even Joey "Two Eyes" Morretti had come into her life—because she would have had to be dead and already growing cold not to be cheered by the sight that met her as she turned the corner of the house.

Jack hadn't been kidding; there *was* a ring of sorts set up on the grass—four metal garden umbrella poles with two badminton nets strung around them to form a square, she found out later. Very inventive.

Joey and his stopwatch were on a folding chair on one side of the ring. He held his finger on the button of the stopwatch, while in his other hand he held a white ceramic figure of Miss Piggy in a Southern belle gown, a little china clapper under her skirts serving as the bell that was rung between rounds.

Aunt Sadie, clad in paisley shorts and a fairly normal light pink blouse, and wearing a hot pink sweatband low on her forehead, stood beside one of the poles, a metal bucket at her feet, a dripping sponge in her hand.

"She's the corner guy," Jack told her as Keely stared at Sadie. "She cools Sweetness off between rounds."

"Of course she does," Keely said, biting back a giggle. "Where did Petra get the trampoline? I mean, I'm assuming it *is* hers."

"Just so you didn't think it was mine," Jack said, walking with her, moving closer to the ring.

Inside the ring, Petra was standing on a small, one-person trampoline. Bouncing on it, actually, dancing about in baggy blue nylon shorts and a T-shirt stamped EVERLAST. She wore bright red boxing gloves and her mouth looked all puffy—thanks to the mouthpiece protecting her teeth.

The trampoline put the slightly built teenager more on a level with Sweetness, who stood, gloves up, facing her, his muscles bulging, his black satin trunks edged with three-inch-long fringe, the words BEAST OF BAYONNE tattooed on their back side.

Keely lifted the camera, snapped a few quick pictures.

Petra raised a glove to her mouth, struggled to remove the mouthpiece, then turned to grin at Candy. "Hiya, sweetie. Come to watch Petra show Sweetness how to throw a right cross?"

"I know how to throw a right cross, Petra," Sweetness told her. "I'm just being nice to you."

"Of course you are," Petra countered, winking at Keely. "That's why you're oh-and-twelve, right?"

"But Joey says—"

"I know, I know. Joey says kiss the canvas. Well, not anymore, Sweetness. Not now that I'm here."

Joey stood up, holding Miss Piggy by the head as he shook the little bell furiously. "Enough of dat, big mouth. Round three, comin' up."

Keely frowned at Jack. "Am I missing something here?"

"Only that ol' Two Eyes—not Blue Eyes, Two Eyes—gets a better paycheck when Sweetness goes down. He even gets to pick the round."

"Oh," Keely said, watching as Petra replaced her mouthpiece, then began dancing on the trampoline once more, her gloved fists flashing out, drawing back, making absolutely no contact. "I think I vaguely remember something about that. I think it's not illegal in Bayonne."

Jack snorted. "Yeah. Right. And maybe you want Two Eyes to sell you the Bayonne Bridge while he's at it."

Keely glared at him, opened her mouth to say something, then just snapped, "Never mind. I get the picture."

Once again, Petra had taken the mouthpiece out, this time spitting it onto the grass. "Oh, come on, Sweetness. Hit me. You've been dancing around ever since we started, not throwing a single punch."

"I can't hit you, Petra," Sweetness said, remarkably very able to talk around his own mouthpiece. "I'd break you in half."

"Oh, yeah?" Petra countered, bouncing up and down on the trampoline, her right hand protecting her face, her left arm sort of cocked, ready to jab, to punch. "You and whose army, buster? Come on. Make a move."

Sweetness looked at Jack. "Mr. T?" he asked piteously. "What do I do?"

"You bust her one in da chops, dat's what you do! Stupid dames! She's beggin' fer it," Joey called out from the other side of the ring, earning himself a swipe in his own chops with a wet sponge. He sat back down, clutching his stopwatch and Miss Piggy, pouting as if he might just cry.

"Mr. T?" Sweetness persisted, looking lost.

"Let her hit him," Keely suggested, speaking softly, out of the corner of her mouth.

"What?" Jack asked.

"I said . . . let *her* hit *him*," Keely repeated. "That's all she wants, really. Not that Petra is thinking about becoming a boxer or anything like that. But there isn't a woman alive who hasn't wanted to legally throw at least one good punch at somebody. Besides, she says boxing is a science. Let's see some science."

Jack looked at her owlishly for a moment, then sighed and motioned for Sweetness to approach the ropes. "Let her hit you," he said quietly, as Petra kept bouncing on the trampoline, throwing out punches at the air.

Sweetness turned his head, looked at Petra. "Ya think?" he said to Jack, who looked at Keely, who nodded at him, so that he nodded to Sweetness.

Jack said, "She can't hurt you, right?"

Sweetness's eyes sort of clouded. "Uh—I guess not."

"What do you mean, you *guess* not?" Jack asked, but then Joey started ringing the Miss Piggy bell again and Sweetness turned away, approached Petra once more.

"You ready now?" Petra asked, swiping at her nose with the thumb of her glove. "Now watch me, Sweetness, because the right cross is a real thing of beauty. Keep your hands up, protect yourself in the clinches, and all that good stuff, because I'm coming for you, baby."

"Oh, good grief," Keely said, sighing. "She'll probably break her hand on him."

"Go get him, Petra!" Aunt Sadie called out, then frowned. "Go get her, Sweetness!" she added, then smiled, happy with her compromise.

Joey consulted his stopwatch, then shook Miss Piggy one more time, signaling the beginning of another round.

Sweetness raised his hands, balanced himself on the balls of his feet.

Petra raised her own hands, bounced her weight from side to side on the trampoline, bobbed and weaved with her head, made herself a moving target.

She threw out her left arm with a snap as she turned her gloved hand so that it was knuckles-up. Jab-jab-jab.

"She's good," Jack told Keely, who was watching with one eye closed. "I mean it. Most women would just slap at an opponent, but she's got it down."

"Remind me to ask her for a few lessons," Keely grumbled. "What do you mean, *most women?* Would that be the same as *women drivers?* Because if it is, I think I'm insulted."

Jack shot her a quick look. "Sorry. But she must have been studying, unless she's a fight fan, and I sort of doubt that. See how she's got her legs? Perfect position. And she's keeping the right up, jabbing with the left. Drops her shoulder a little, but a lot of beginners do."

Keely looked at him, watched him watching Petra. "I don't get it. You boxed?"

Jack smiled. "No, I fought. Tim and I. Fought with each other. A lot. So Dad bought us gloves, taught us the basics. We thought it was pretty neat, until we figured out that the gloves were so big and so padded, we couldn't hurt each other. We'd each throw about fifty punches, then fall to the floor in the living room, exhausted from trying to lift those big gloves. Smart man, my dad. Look—she thinks she's setting him up. But Sweetness has to be too smart to fall for that. God, you'd think he'd throw at least one punch and not just use his arms to block hers."

Keely watched the ring as Petra continued to jab, to move . . . and to drop her shoulder before she threw the right, just as Jack had pointed out to her. "Is that a feint?" she asked, whispering her question.

Jack took his eyes off the pair in the ring to look at Keely. "A feint? Where did you hear that one? But no. A feint is where she'd, say, pretend to throw a left, then catch him with her right when he goes to defend against the left. Got it?"

Oh, yes, Keely got that. Not immediately, but very soon, because only about ten seconds later Petra, still trying to goad Sweetness into throwing a punch, finally threw one of her own with her left, aiming it at his gut.

Sweetness moved to cover up, block the left, and Petra—packing all her might and the helpful bounce of the trampoline into her punch—delivered a roundhouse right to Sweetness's jaw, just in front of his ear.

He went down like a stone.

It all happened so quickly. One moment Sweetness was standing there, outweighing Petra by at least one hundred and fifty pounds, towering over her by at least a foot and a half in height (minus the trampoline, of course) . . . and the next moment his knees had turned to rubber and he was flat on his face in the grass.

"Oh, well, that *is* depressing, isn't it?" Petra said, looking down at Sweetness, who just lay there.

If Sweetness was a cartoon, Keely thought wildly, there'd be a string of stars turning in a circle over his head. Because he was *down*; he was *out*.

Petra, jumping down from the trampoline, was the first to reach Sweetness, who, thank goodness, had begun to move, even groan. She helped him to a sitting position as Jack stood on the badminton net so that Keely could step over it, get into the ring.

Sadie, without Jack to help her, merely crawled under the other side of the net on her hands and knees. She knelt beside Sweetness, squeezed the sopping sponge over his head.

"Is he all right?" Keely asked Petra, who was in the process of holding up two of Sadie's pudgy fingers in front of Sweetness's face, asking him to count them for her.

"Yeah, yeah, he's fine," Joey said, slipping the stopwatch back in his pocket. "It's his jaw. Solid glass. And he's a wimp, a wuss. Don't want to hit nobody. That's how come nobody knows fer sure he's taking a dive. Hell, *he* don't know he's taking a dive; he just thinks maybe he is, ya know. Everybody knows he gonna lose. I just knows what round to pick, then tell him to drop his hands, do dat Muhammed Ali rope-a-dope as he dances around the ring. Some dope. He drops his hands and *blam!* One good poke in dat jaw of his and out he goes. That's da beauty of it."

Keely watched as Petra's eyes narrowed, as a deep pink flush rose in her cheeks.

"Now, Petra . . ." she said, grabbing at the girl's arm, but Petra was too quick for her and was already on her feet, heading for Joey.

"You no good, lousy, rotten—"

Petra had been right, Keely thought later, looking at Joey Two Eyes—for the moment, pretty much Joey One Eye—sitting across from her at the dinner table, his left eye swollen shut. Boxing *was* a science, and the girl had very scientifically cleaned Joey's clock for him with a single punch.

Jack was unpacking his new stereo equipment after dinner. Keely had run to the store to pick up more formula and diapers—and two more ice bags—and Petra was watching Candy, pretending to play patty-cake with her on the floor in the den.

"She wouldn't come to me for a while," she told Jack

as he slit open yet another box. "I think she was afraid of me after what I did to Sweetness. I just can't believe I did that to Sweetness. I didn't know it, but I think I'm a pacifist. You know, anti-violence?"

"As the man letting you baby-sit for his cousin, I thank you," Jack said, then sat back on his heels, looking at the teen. "Hey, you're really upset, aren't you?"

"Wouldn't you be?" she asked, gathering Candy into her arms, letting the baby practice her standing in her lap. "I hit a man and I knocked him out. I'm not proud of that."

"Oh, I don't know, Petra. I think you're pretty proud of what you did to Joey."

"No!" She shook her head. "I'm even less proud of that. Sweetness and I were boxing; I hit Joey because I hated his guts. I probably would have hit him again if he hadn't run away, squealing like a pig."

"Squealing like a Miss Piggy," Jack corrected, smiling, and Petra finally relaxed her shoulders, smiled back at him.

"Did you see his eye?" she asked him. "How's he going to explain that one to Ms. Peters?"

"Hmmm, I hadn't thought about that," Jack admitted, pulling a large speaker up and out of its box. "I'll bet Joey hasn't, either. But that's okay, because I think I'll mention it to him tomorrow morning, hint that it might be better if he went back to Bayonne, stayed out of Ms. Peters's way until the swelling goes down."

Petra brightened even more. "In that case, do you want me to hit him again, go for both of his two eyes? Still, do you think he'll buy it?"

"He might. Especially when I point out that Ms. Peters is going to ask how he got that shiner, and how

I'm going to have to tell her that my babysitter beat him up. Joey's way too macho-man to want anyone to hear the truth. By the time he gets back to Bayonne, he'll have gotten his black eye taking on three goons from a rival family—that's Mafia family, of course—and beating the snot out of all of them."

"That's pitiful," Petra told him. "Don't you think maybe he's sick? That he might need some psychiatric help? Not that I like him, or even feel sorry for him, because I don't. But . . . well, you have to admit it; your family is a little . . . out there."

Jack pulled out yet another speaker and set it on the floor. "Tell me about it. Mom always said Dad was the only normal member of the Trehan family. Not that Aunt Sadie isn't normal. I'd rather have a happy old maid like Sadie than some dry stick who only talks about her arthritis. She's just . . . well, she's just her own person, that's all, a woman on a mission of self-discovery, I think she calls it."

"And her sister Florence was like her?"

"Aunt Flo? Nah, she was pretty normal, too, I think, except that she fell for Uncle Guido. That wasn't normal; at least most people wouldn't think so. Uncle Guido was . . ." He searched for the right word. "Uncle Guido could talk martinizing for hours, without taking a breath. Show up in a new suit and he'd tell you how to clean it. He once made my dad take off his shirt so he could press the collar again, because he said it had a crease in it. That wouldn't have been so bad, I guess, except that it was in the middle of Christmas dinner at my grandmother's house. He probably whispered dry cleaning formulas into Aunt Flo's ear as he"—Jack smiled. "Never mind."

Petra held Candy's hands as the baby bounced up and

258

down in her lap. "So how did Candy's mother and Joey get to be so weird? And don't tell me *they're* normal, because I've heard about Cecily and met Joey."

Jack shrugged. "Money?" he suggested. At Petra's quizzical look he continued, "No, really. Money. They were eighteen and seventeen when Aunt Flo and Uncle Guido died, leaving them tons of money. There were trust funds set up, but even the income was enough to allow both of them to go wild. And then, when they turned twenty-one, they each got checks for three million bucks. We're not talking Rhodes scholars here, Petra. They went nuts, both of them. Cecily with men, drugs for a while, and now her endless search to find herself. Joey? He just wanted people to be afraid of him, so he decided to join the Mafia. He didn't make the cut."

"And your brother? Tim? Is he another nutty Trehan, or did both of you escape it? I mean, you both have lots of money, too, right?"

Jack sat down on the edge of the couch, thought about Petra's question. "Right. But we had Mom and Dad, at least at the beginning, and we had all those years of being raised right to help keep us sane. Cecily and Joey were allowed to run wild from the time they were kids. Which is why," he said, slapping his hands on his knees as he stood up again, "Candy stays with me."

"Da. Da-da-da."

Jack smiled, looked down at Candy, but the baby hadn't been looking at him. She was talking to Petra, calling Petra dada.

"She called you da-da," he said, not feeling stupid until the words were out of his mouth. "She calls *me* da-da."

"Sure she does," Petra answered, kissing Candy's

little nose. "She calls you da-da, she calls me da-da, she calls her teddy and her bottle and her pacifier da-da." She looked up at Jack, who was feeling a little hollow inside. "Da-da is the easiest sound for a baby to make. All she has to do is sort of slap her tongue against the roof of her mouth, like this—da. Da-da-da."

"Da-da-da," Candy repeated, snuggling against Petra's chest.

"Now, ma-ma—that's hard," Petra continued reasonably. "With ma-ma, she has to be able to make her lips press together while she sort of keeps her tongue still. Ma. See? Ma. Ma. Ma. Very difficult. That's why kids always say da-da first. But mama's shouldn't get upset about it, because once a kid learns how to say ma-ma, she never stops saying it—when she's hungry, tired, bored, you name it." Petra kissed Candy's fingers. "At least that's what it says in the books."

Jack was listening, if only with one ear. "So she really hasn't been calling me da-da?" he asked quietly.

"Nope," Petra said brightly, then seemed to realize her mistake. "Hooboy, you're all broken up about this, aren't you?"

"No. No, I'm not," Jack said quickly, walking back over to the boxes still to be unpacked. "Not at all. So, Petra, tell me, does your genius include hooking up speakers? Because I don't have the smallest damn idea how to organize this stuff."

"Ah, electronics," Petra said, standing up, handing Candy to Jack. "How lucky you are. Another area of Petra Polinski, proficiency and expertise. Let me find the instruction book, okay? Not that I need it, of course, although I could impress you by reading the French or the Japanese versions. And, hey—thanks. I feel better about hitting Joey, now that I know he really is a jerk and deserved it.

"You're welcome." Jack held Candy as Petra got to work, feeling good about the way the child's small arm draped on his shoulder as she leaned her head against him. "I—I, Candy," he whispered, turning away from Petra. "I—I. Daddy loves Candy."

"Da. Da-da-da," Candy said.

She knows, Jack told himself, his heart swelling. He didn't care what it said in those stupid damn books. She knew her daddy.

# Chapter Fifteen

*We made too many wrong mistakes.*

—Yogi Berra.

"DAMN IT!" KEELY LOOKED AT THE PLATE, NOW IN three pieces, as it lay on the kitchen floor. Yesterday a glass, this morning the lid of the sugar bowl, and now one of the dinner plates. She was a menace. She shouldn't be allowed near breakable objects.

"Well, that's three, dear," Aunt Sadie said commiseratingly as she sat at the kitchen table, dunking dry wheat toast in hot tea as Keely picked up the pieces and dumped them in the trash can under the sink. "Bad luck always comes in threes, so you're done now. Unless you go to four, in which case you'll go to five, and to six." She frowned. "Maybe you'd better sit down, not touch anything else?"

"Maybe I should," Keely agreed, using her foot to kick the dishwasher door shut. She grabbed a can of soda from the refrigerator, not trusting herself to use a glass, and sat down across from Sadie. "It's just so nerve-racking, Aunt Sadie. Will she show up today? When will she show up? Will she check to see if Candy's hamper is too full, or make me recite her schedule . . . or just take Candy away from us because she knows"—she leaned forward, whispering the rest, as if someone might overhear—"we're lying to her?"

"We're talking about Edith Peters, aren't we?" Aunt Sadie asked, nodding her head. "Edith, and your sham engagement to my nephew, the idiot."

Keely sat back in her chair, looked at Sadie owlishly. "The idiot? Two Eyes is the idiot, Aunt Sadie, remember?"

The older woman shrugged. "Yes, well, that's a given. We've always known about Joey. But I must say, I never thought I'd see the day when Jack began to exhibit signs of idiocy."

"By taking in Candy?"

"No, dear," Aunt Sadie said, reaching over to pat Keely's hand. "By not telling you he loves you and stopping off in Las Vegas or somewhere for a quickie wedding before you two ever came back here from Arizona. Of course, with the two of you coming home on separate planes, I imagine that might have been difficult. And you never said—what happened out there in Arizona? Oh, I know it was all Jack's fault, it always is the man's fault, but exactly what did happen?"

"Too much," Keely said, avoiding Sadie's eyes. After all, the woman had seen the hickey. She'd probably already drawn her own conclusions. "And you're wrong about the rest of it. Jack doesn't love me. He loves Candy, and he should. I drive him nuts. Just ask him; he'll tell you. I'm bossy, I'm too neat, and I'm spending all his money."

Sadie held a piece of toast suspended over her teacup. "My dear girl, you couldn't possibly spend all his money. He had a six-million-dollar signing bonus, straight out of college, and the contract he signed five years ago was positively *obscene*, made his first signing bonus look like pocket change. He has his condo in New York, this house, drives a nice car, but that's about it. He has always lived within his allowance. Mort and I take care of everything else."

Keely's eyes widened. The woman who loved pink—elephants, pumpkins, wallpaper, you name it—had control of Jack's money? The woman who wore outlandish clothing, liked to pal around with Petra Polinski, had pretty much gotten the role of "dotty old aunt" down to a science? *She* handled Jack's money? "What? *You?* You and Mort? You're kidding. Please tell me you're kidding."

Sadie patted at her silver curls and lifted her chin—both her chins. "Jack didn't tell you? Oh, yes, I'm in charge, with Mort pretty much under my thumb, bless him. I handle Jack's money, and Timothy's, too. Always have. Jack didn't tell you that I put in thirty years as a trust officer at one of the local banks? Not that we have very many local banks anymore. My goodness, in the last ten years I worked there, I believe we were bought out three times. I took to just answering the phone with my name and department, because I couldn't remember who I worked for anymore. Anyway, I wasn't always the free spirit I'm enjoying being now. Goodness, no. I wore navy suits and white blouses and sensible shoes and rose to vice president before I looked around, saw my life passing me by, and retired and bought my little convertible. It took a while, sixty-five years as a matter of fact," she said, grinning, "but I finally let the crazy Trehan out, and I've never been happier. You probably don't know this, but life without a girdle is a marvelous thing."

Keely had begun shaking her head slowly halfway through Sadie's monologue and finally said, "I don't believe it. Oh, oh—not that I don't think you're *competent*, Aunt Sadie," she added quickly, because she really hadn't thought the woman was all that competent. "But Jack has already told me that Mort handles his money."

"Mort handles the *acquisition* of money, and quite well," Aunt Sadie corrected. "*I* handle the distribution. Stocks, bonds, some lovely property. This land, this house? I bought the land for Jack four years ago—this plot, and another five hundred acres. Paid mere pennies per acre, and then this area became *the* place to be."

She smiled, shook her head. "You wouldn't *believe* the money his neighbors were willing to plunk down for three-acre lots these past couple of years. That doughnut shop down at the corner, at the end of the lane? Jack's land. The entire strip mall Jack's. Now Timothy, he's more into businesses he can play with, like the bowling alley, the golf course, the—oh, you get the idea, don't you, dear? Right now I'm negotiating to put the two of them into a multifranchise car dealership."

Keely swallowed, tried to collect herself. "*You* handle their money," she repeated yet again. "Why couldn't he tell me that? He let me think, let me believe . . . oh! There are times I could just *murder* that man!"

"Yes," Aunt Sadie agreed, dunking another piece of toast. "It's why I never married. I would have killed the poor guy, probably within a week, even if he looked like Tom Cruise. Well, maybe not if he looked like him. I'm not a fool."

Keely smiled wanly. "Well, I am. I feel like such an idiot," she said, turning the soda can around in her hands. She looked at Aunt Sadie. "Why does Jack go out of his way to act as if he doesn't have a serious brain cell in his head? He let me think he doesn't even know how much money he has."

Aunt Sadie dabbed at some tea she'd dribbled onto her chin. "Well, dear, I don't think he does know. Not to the penny, probably not to the nearest half-million, when you consider that his investments are so diverse, and I only give him reports twice a year. But it's not to worry. Jack's undergraduate degree was in business, you know, with a minor in communications. Magna cum laude. He just likes his dear old aunt to feel useful."

Keely dropped her elbow onto the table and propped her chin in her hand. "I could just choke him. Magna cum laude? Jack the jock—magna cum laude?"

"Summa cum laude for Timothy," Aunt Sadie said, visibly preening. "And Timothy can act dumber than spit when he wants to. We're a strange family."

Keely was intrigued. Angry, but intrigued. Confused, but intrigued. "And Joey and Cecily? Do they just act dumb, too?"

Aunt Sadie had been sipping tea and choked, had to cough into her napkin. "Joey and Cecily? God bless them, no. There was potential there, and we had some hopes for Cecily until she ran away at fifteen, with some felon and his motorcycle, quit school at sixteen, and had to be detoxed. Grand theft auto at seventeen. Prescription drugs later that same year. I think her brains are permanently scrambled, poor thing."

She shook her head. "And Joey? Well, you've seen Joey. As a child, he thought he was that cartoon character—Speed Racer, I believe—which was cute. He'd spend hours running in circles around the dining room table, holding a paper dinner plate in front of him, pretending it was a steering wheel. Then he was Luke Skywalker—that one lasted for quite a while and wasn't quite so cute. Now he's a mobster, or at least dresses the part. I blame Flo, rest her soul. She gave them everything on a platter—clothes, cars, money—and asked nothing in return. And, sadly, that's just what she got."

"Jack's adamant that Cecily can't have Candy," Keely said. "I imagine Jimmy—the lawyer—will bring up her run-ins with the law?"

"I don't know, Keely. Cecily was a juvenile, remember, so perhaps those records are sealed. She's cleaned up her act, as much as Cecily can, and is into health food and gurus right now, won't even eat red meat, let alone snort anything. I'm just hoping she'll realize on her own that she can't be a fit mother. I only wish my sister had figured out that she wasn't, either. I think that's why I never had children, worried that, as Flo's twin, I might be the same failure she was. No marriages, no children. And I probably would have been a bad mother, too. Flo saw nothing but Guido, and I saw nothing but the bank. At least I lived long enough to realize my mistake while I still had time to experience a little of the rest of the world."

Keely reached out, squeezed Aunt Sadie's hand. "Jack adores you, you know," she said, blinking back tears. "And so do I."

Sadie covered Keely's hand with her own. "Thank you, dear. Now, I hope you've learned something."

Keely looked at her quizzically.

"Grab at life, Keely. Grab at it with both hands. Don't

266

limit yourself to one dream, one possibility. Jack had one dream, had it for a long time. Now he's finding other dreams. But what about you? Are you still hanging on to the same dream? Do you still think that only that one dream will make you happy?"

Keely sat back in her chair. "Going back to Manhattan, opening another shop," she said, sighing. "Is that what you mean, Aunt Sadie?"

"Jack believes that's all you want in life—other than driving him crazy, that is," Aunt Sadie said with a small smile.

"He offered to finance my shop if I go along with the pretend engagement until he gets custody," Keely said quietly.

"Yes, I can imagine he did. And I can imagine that it killed him to say that. But he took a second shot at his dream before he realized that there was more to life than baseball. He turned down that offer from the Japanese team because he finally realized that. Now you've been offered a second chance at your career. Jack offered it to you. You have figured out that he's done that, done it very much on purpose, whether he's even aware of what he's doing. So, what are *you* going to do about it, Keely?

"I don't know," Keely answered honestly. "I don't know."

"Yes, that's also obvious," Aunt Sadie said, picking up her plate and cup and carrying them over to the sink. "And in the meantime, with all that's going on around here, I think I'll take over loading the dishwasher, all right? You might want to go find Jack, maybe even *talk* to him."

"But I've stripped all the beds and haven't gotten clean sheets on them yet," Keely protested, a now familiar panic setting in again. "The cleaning service isn't due for another two days, and I've got the vacuum cleaner sitting in the living room. Candy's diaper pail is almost overflowing. Joey spilled orange juice all over the floor earlier and it's still sticky, has to be washed. What if Ms. Peters shows up?"

"I'll hand her a mop," Aunt Sadie said, shrugging. "Edith wants to see how you are as a family, not whether or not you pass some sort of white glove test. Jack's in the pool, Keely. Get your suit on and join him. Talk to him, honestly. Get to know each other better. Solve at least one of your problems."

Keely looked toward the backyard and the pool, then at the few dirty dishes still stacked on the countertop. Then she smiled, felt this warm, wonderful sort of *swelling* in her chest. She went over to the older woman, kissed her cheek. "You were wrong, Aunt Sadie," she told her. "You would have made one hell of a great mother."

Jack wondered how many laps he'd have to swim before his mind shut down and he didn't have to think about Keely. Didn't see her every time he shut his eyes, didn't long to hold her, kiss her, make long, lazy love to her.

He pushed off from the edge, began another lap, his arms and legs moving mechanically, his brain whirling, whirling.

What had happened in that motel room in Arizona—plus what had come before it, and after it—would always remain one of his best, and worst, memories. If only he *could* remember all of it.

For hours, the director had him looking at Keely, supposedly gazing into her eyes in a romantic haze, holding her hands, then driving away with her. For hours, Keely had obediently followed Brad's directions and gazed adoringly back attack, waiting for him to help her into the car, drive away with her.

The more Jack had thought about driving away with Keely, the more clumsy he'd become. Dropping the keys, tripping over the fender, fumbling with the door handle.

He reached the end of the pool, did a kick flip, and struck out once more.

Drive away . . . drive away . . . drive away . . . get away. Take her away. Take her places the two of them had never gone.

Just the two of them. No Candy, much as he loved her. No Sadie, no Joey, no Petra. No nobody. No baseball, no Manhattan business, no custody battles.

Just Keely, only Keely.

By the time he had gotten her alone, he'd been half out of his mind from wanting her. Couldn't keep his hands off her, couldn't slow down, couldn't woo her, soothe her. Just take, take, take. Like a randy teenager. Like a man who hadn't been with a woman for a dozen long, lonely years.

Like a man who couldn't believe she'd stay, if only he offered to let her go.

It was the pressure, that's what it was. They'd both felt it, been under the gun. A custody battle, a mock engagement, a baby they both adored.

And proximity.

That's what Keely had called it. Proximity.

Bullshit. That's what he called it.

She drove him nuts. She was a worrywort, a perfectionist. Nosy. Bossy. A know-it-all, yet desperately afraid of making a mistake. Prickly. Driven to succeed. And she had a *mouth* on her . . .

One more lap. Maybe one more lap would shut down his brain.

He was crazy about her. Nuts about her.

The way she looked at Candy, the way she cared for her. The way she was making his empty house a home, a house that would be empty again if she ever left, no matter how much furniture, drapes, and what the hell else she left behind. The way she had taken over his life, sticking her nose into every last part of it, because she *cared*. She wasn't just nosy or bossy. She cared.

And she knew. She knew what it was like to fail, to lose. They shared that. Except that he had finally accepted that his baseball career was over, finished, kaput. She hadn't accepted that about her business in Manhattan. She wanted, needed, to try again.

Just as he had needed to try again.

So he'd send her away once this was over. Suck it up, keep his mouth shut, and let her go. Buy her way back to Manhattan if he had to, so she could rub that Gregory character's nose in her success. Would that make her happy?

He didn't know. Getting the offer from the Japanese team hadn't made him happy. He'd thought he'd known what he wanted, up until the minute he was offered it. So now he'd offered that second chance to Keely. Would she take it?

What would he do if she took it?

Out of breath, he surfaced at the far end of the pool, holding on to the edge, feeling a shadow move over him. Keely? Could it be Keely? He looked up, shielding his eyes with his hand, a smile already on his face, and saw: "Joey? When did you get back?"

"What's it to ya?" Joey asked, stepping back a pace.

"Ya keepin' tabs on me now, Jack? Maybe got my room bugged? You'd like dat, wouldn't ya?"

"Ah, we're being paranoid today. Always something new with you, Joey," Jack said, hauling himself out of the pool, looking at his cousin. "Nice look. It works for you."

Joey was dressed in a black Speedo that was definitely a one of a kind, because it bulged *nowhere.* He had huge black-rimmed sunglasses covering what was left of his shiner. And his skinny legs were hidden to the calf beneath black Banlon socks and heavy-soled, lace-up black Florsheims. Bayonne's in-your-face rebuttal to *GQ.*

Joey grabbed hold of the ends of the towel slung around his nearly nonexistent shoulders and glared at Jack. "You'll be laughin' outta da other side of yer mouth when I show that Peters lady what I've got. Papers, Jack-o, I've got *papers.* That's docu . . . f-ing . . . *tation!*"

Jack glanced at the crotch of the Speedo. "You're showing everybody what you've got, Joey. I don't want to burst any bubbles for you, but it's not all that impressive."

"Why, you—"

But Jack wasn't listening, because he'd spied Keely walking toward the gate of the fence surrounding the pool. She was dressed in that same mind-blowing bathing suit and nothing else. Imagination had guided him the first time he'd seen her that way, but now he knew. Perfection lay beneath that suit, and he had touched, tasted, loved that perfection.

No wonder he was going crazy.

"Later, Joey," he said, brushing past his cousin to meet up with Keely as she neared the pool. "Hi. Gonna take a swim?"

271

"No, actually I'm waiting for a bus," she told him, and she didn't smile. "Can we talk?"

"Here?" Jack turned, looked at Joey, who was approaching them, holding out a tape recorder no larger than his palm. "Joey? What the hell?"

"My mouthpiece says to get everything on tape," Joey told him. "I told him how rotten you are, and he wants everyone to know. So come on, Jack, talk. Tell the little lady how you're tryin' ta steal my beloved niece from me."

"Jack?"

He slid his arm around Keely, gave her a quick squeeze. "It's all right, Keely. Joey has just entered the paranoid portion of our program. Take a hike, Joey, before I twist you into a pretzel and then drown you."

Joey began to dance around like a little kid, holding up the tape recorder. "Ha! Got it! Got that on tape! Violent tendencies. We're gonna *bury* ya, Jack. Bury ya!"

Jack stepped up, put a hand on his cousin's chest, and backed him up, pushed him into the pool. He watched as Joey sank in the middle of a large splash, waited until he'd surfaced and grabbed onto the side of the pool, minus his tape recorder, his sunglasses sitting cockeyed on his head. "Ba-da-bing-ba-da-boom, Two Eyes," he said, then took Keely's arm and walked her away from the pool.

"That wasn't nice," Keely said, but she was laughing as she said it. "Do you think the water ruined his little minitapee thing?"

"And his shoes, too, if we're lucky," Jack told her, scooping up a towel as they headed for the gate. "I don't mean to take you away if you really want to go for a swim, but I'm thinking I should have the pool drained, cleaned, and refilled before anybody else uses it."

"Now that really isn't nice," Keely told him. "When did he get back?"

"Just now," he said. "With documentation, whatever that means. I just know he was too happy to make *me* happy." He continued walking, then stopped dead. "You don't think he somehow contacted Cecily, got her to fax him a letter giving him custody?"

"Oh, God," Keely said, grabbing Jack's forearm. "I don't know. What do you think?"

Jack pressed thumb and forefinger against the bridge of his nose, trying not to panic. "I don't know either. Jimmy's people found her. Maybe Joey's people found her, too. Damn Cecily! She probably said yes to both of us. She hates scenes."

"Jack, stop it. You're overreacting. This is Joey, remember? Aunt Sadie says he doesn't play at being dumb—he *is* dumb. Would a dumb man hire a smart lawyer?"

Jack glanced back at the pool, to where Joey was sitting on the cement pool surround, pouring out his Florsheims. "Good point," he said, trying to control his pounding heart, his leaping conclusions. "Come on, come with me. I'm not going to let this drag out, drive myself nuts."

He grabbed her hand and walked back to the pool. "Joey? What kind of docu-f-ing-tation do you have?"

"Hah!" he exclaimed, desperately trying to pull off one of his thigh-high socks with little success. "That's for me to know and youse ta find out."

Jack squatted in front of his cousin, looking him straight in his two eyes. "Wanna go for another swim? It can be arranged. Only this time, I might just tie a rock around your neck first. Right after I make you eat your minirecorder."

"Papers, okay!" Joey exclaimed, backing up on all fours, rather like a black-socked crab. "I've got papers."

"What kind of papers?" Jack asked, still glowering at his cousin.

"Papers! You deaf? Papers!"

"Excuse me," Keely said, tapping Jack on the shoulder, motioning for him to rise. "You're not doing this right."

Jack bristled. He loved Keely. Really, he did. But, man, she was bossy, a real know-it-all. "Oh? And I suppose you think you could do it better?"

Joey looked at Jack, shivered. Looked at Keely, sighed.

"Yes, I could," she told Jack smugly, "and without threatening him. You two aren't kids anymore, you know, even if you both act it." Then she sat down cross-legged on the grass edging the cement surround, and helped Joey remove his socks. "There. That's better. Now, what are the papers, Joey? Can you tell me? Do you have papers from Cecily?"

Joey looked up at Jack once more, shook his head. "Cecily? No. Nobody even knows where she's at, right? I got other papers, stuff dat shows what an upstandin' citizen I am, ya know?"

Jack sort of laughed, sort of coughed, and Keely gave him a punch in the shin. "That's interesting, Joey," she pressed on. "So you're talking about character letters, aren't you? Letters from friends, maybe the mayor of Bayonne? The local priest? People who can vouch for you?"

"Naw," he said, shaking his head. "I tried to get Monsignor Rafelli to write one of them character letters, but he says I gotta come to church again before he'll help me out."

274

"Monsignor Rafelli?" Jack broke in, chuckling again. "I've got a memory coming here—a real Joey moment. Back from when you were an altar boy, right? Wasn't it Monsignor Rafelli who chased you all the way home after you drank the holy water?"

"So it was July, and hot, and I was thirsty," Joey said challengingly. "Anybody woulda done dat. Besides, I didn't know he'd blessed it already."

"Aunt Flo called my mom, as I remember it, crying her eyes out, sure you were going to hell," Jack said, still waxing nostalgic over days gone by. The good old days, when Joey was just funny, not pathetic.

"Can . . . can we get back to the papers?" Keely asked, her voice sounding just a little choked. "Joey?"

"I don't know that I wants to tell youse now," he said, visibly pouting as he squeezed water from his socks.

"Please?" Keely said, leaning forward, putting a hand on Joey's arm, and if she was giving him as good a look at her cleavage as Jack was getting from where he was standing, he might just have to kill his cousin. Unless she got him to talk.

"Well, okay," Joey said, shrugging his thin white shoulders. "I've got my birth certificate, of course. To prove I'm in the country legally, ya know. Lots of people think I'm Sicilian, ya know."

"Of course," Keely agreed, and Jack could actually see her shoulders beginning to shake as she tried to hold on to her composure. "What else?"

"Well, da mouthpiece, he said I was to get anything that showed me—how'd he say it?—in a good light. So I got Uncle Sal to write a letter sayin' I'm his favorite nephew. He's about the richest guy in Bayonne, so that's big, really big. I got other letters, from Marco, the grocer on the corner, because I didn't shoplift nothin' after that last time he caught me, and dat was years ago. One from my shrink. A couple of boccie ball trophies, to show I'm an all-round sorta guy. Oh, and my perfect attendance plaque from when I won it in the third grade."

Jack had, halfway through Joey's recitation, pushed both palms against his head, to keep it from exploding. Keely lasted longer, not falling over onto her side, beating one fist against the grass, howling with laughter, until Joey got to the bit about his perfect attendance plaque.

Jack collapsed beside her, relief making him weak, hilarity replacing the fear that Cecily had given Joey custody. Keely grabbed at him, laughing, gasping for breath, and he held her, and the two of them rolled onto the grassy slope, arms and legs tangling, ignoring Joey, who was threatening both of them with cement shoes or taking them both for a ride or whatever the idiot was trying to say.

And then Joey was saying something else. He was saying, "Gotcha! Here comes Ms. Peters, and the two of ya are gropin' each other, right out here where anybody can see ya. I'm gonna go tell her ya tried to drown me."

"Oh, God," Keely said, pushing herself away from Jack, trying to stand up while simultaneously pulling up her swimsuit with one hand and tugging it down with the other. "Ms. Peters!" she exclaimed, taking off toward the house as Jack, who'd also hopped to his feet, blocked Joey's progress. "How good to see you again."

Jack joined the two women just as they reached the house, the towel he'd wrapped around his waist hopefully making him seem more presentable.

"Oh, yes," Keely was saying even as she tried to smooth down her hair, which bounced around her head because she'd somehow lost her clip as they'd flailed about on the lawn—while Jack restrained himself from pulling several blades of grass from her curls. "We have several baby monitors. We started out with just one, the one in the den, that actually has a television screen, so that we can see Candy as she sleeps. But I went back to the store—that is, *we* went back to the store and bought more. We've got the base set in Candy's room and the receiver is cordless, so that we can take it out to the pool or anywhere in the house, monitor Candy from anywhere while she sleeps."

"So the monitor is back at the pool?" Ms. Peters asked Jack, her pen poised over the top sheet of a thick stack of papers on her clipboard. Obviously today's surprise visit was going to be more in-depth than the first one.

"Er . . . um . . . Keely?"

"Hmmm? Um . . . no," Keely said, still trying to pretend her bathing suit was really a kimono that covered her from neck to ankles. "There . . . there was no need, because Petra is watching her right now. She and Sweet—she and Bruno, an employee of Mr. Trehan's cousin. They're playing with her up in her room, actually. I . . . I checked on them just before changing to come outside for a swim."

"Bug bite scratches, out for a swim," Ms. Peters said, scribbling on the clipboard. "Sometimes, Ms. McBride, it's as if I lived my youth on a whole other planet. Very well, let's go upstairs then, and see Candy."

"She's not being as nice as she was the first time," Keely whispered out of the corner of her mouth as Ms. Peters preceded them up the back stairs. More loudly, she said, "We'll be with you in a moment, Ms. Peters. I just have something I need to ask Mr. Trehan. Jack," she added, wincing.

"Yeah, Jack. Don't be too formal. And don't worry about anything," Jack whispered back bracingly as they walked a few feet away from the stairs. "Now that we know that Joey's shooting blanks, all we need is that document from Cecily and we're home free."

"Not if she thinks we're two sex starved maniacs who barely pay any attention to Candy," Keely countered. "What must she think of me?"

"That you can't keep your hands off me?" Jack asked, then ducked when it looked as if Keely might be wanting to take a swing at him.

But she was distracted, suddenly looking around the kitchen, into the den. "Where's Aunt Sadie? The dishes are gone, so she finished those before she left. But I didn't see her outside, heading back to her apartment. Do you think she's upstairs, putting clean sheets on the beds? I want her to stick close to us while Ms. Peters is here. The woman likes her."

Keely was speaking quickly, her words all but tumbling over each other, so Jack took hold of her shoulders and gave her a small shake. "Would you calm down, please?" he asked, pulling her into his arms. "Relax, just relax."

"I can't. This is too important."

Jack kissed the top of her head. "Thank you, Keely. Thank you for thinking this is important. Thank you for caring."

Her body was warm, sun-kissed, and fairly naked. He felt her legs against his own bare legs, could press his hands on her bare back. "Keely?" he said, pushing her slightly away from him, but not too far, definitely not too far. "Ah, hell, Keely . . ." he said, drawing her close once more, his mouth descending to capture hers.

And he almost got there.

"Jack! Jack—Keely! Get up here this minute!" his Aunt Sadie was yelling. "Edith just fainted!"

# Chapter Sixteen

*You can learn a little from*
*victory. You can learn*
*everything from defeat.*

—Christy Mathewson, pitcher

KEELY KNEW SHE AND JACK RESEMBLED NOTHING more than a slapstick scene from an old Keystone Kops routine as they battled each other to get to the stairs, be first up the stairs.

By the time they made it down the hallway to Candy's bedroom, they were in a dead heat, and both slid to a stop, Keely having to grab onto the doorjamb because she was sliding on the polished hardwood in her bare feet.

Keely looked at Jack.

He looked at her.

"You go first," they said in unison.

Aunt Sadie made their decision for them, sticking her head out of the room, looking flustered. "I don't know why she got so upset. It's only temporary."

"What's only temporary?" Jack asked as Keely brushed past the older woman and entered the room.

The first thing she saw was the rocking chair . . . and Edith Peters sitting sort of slumped in that rocking chair, her support-hose-stockinged legs spread rather inelegantly, her eyes closed, and her mouth open.

The second thing she saw was Candy.

And she nearly joined Edith Peters in a swoon. Except she was too angry to faint.

"I know what that is," she said, advancing toward Petra and Sweetness, who were sitting with Candy, all of them on a bed sheet—hopefully one from the hamper—spread on the floor. "You found the box, didn't you?"

"This box?" Petra asked brightly, lifting the Baby Memories box Keely had bought just to tick off Jack, then stuffed into the closet, forgotten.

"Yes, that box," Keely said as Jack joined her.

"What the—?"

"They're taking impressions of Candy's feet," Keely told him as Candy, seemingly no worse for her experience, giggled and gurgled and held up her arms to Jack.

"That's why they're that sort of pea green?" Jack asked. "Does that come off?"

"If it doesn't, I know two pea-brained people who are going to have pea-green heads," Keely informed him through gritted teeth as she looked at Candy. The baby's little feet and ankles were covered in ugly green goo that appeared to be hardening quite quickly.

"Oh, would you two just relax?" Petra said, rolling her eyes. "This stuff sets into a sort of soft rubber in just a couple of minutes. Then we peel it off, pour some plaster of Paris stuff in the molds, and bingo—Candy's little tootsies, preserved for posterity. Sweetness, show them your hands."

The big guy ducked his head. "Nah, that's okay."

"Oh, go on," Petra persisted. "He's a little worried because we did it sort of wrong when we tested this stuff on him. Didn't put it on thick enough, I guess, and then tried to take it off too soon. But he'll get it all peeled off, right, Sweetness? Go on, show them."

Sweetness sighed, then reluctantly pulled his hands from behind his back, holding them up, fingers spread, to show Keely and Jack.

His huge hands looked like they were molting. At least a few of his fingers were; some of them were still solidly encased in rather lumpy pea-green rubber. The rest of the coating, the molting part, hung from his hands in strips. There were even, Keely belatedly noticed, some pea-green strips stuck to his face. All in all, he wasn't a pretty sight.

"That's what Ms. Peters saw when she came in here," Petra informed them. "Sweetness was kind of walking around, muttering and moaning as he and Aunt Sadie tried to rip off the rest of that gunk sticking to him. Sweetness was getting a little upset, and Aunt Sadie was yelling at him to stop—stop ripping at his hands, that is, although Ms. Peters probably thought he was attacking her or something. I think she's maybe seen *Young Frankenstein* too many times, you know? She took one look at Aunt Sadie, yelled out 'Run for your life!' and then passed out. Sweetness caught her and put her in the rocker. She'll be fine."

Keely looked at Ms. Peters, who was showing some signs of returning consciousness now that Aunt Sadie had reappeared to press a cold wet rag against the woman's brow. Then, hearing a muffled sort of *snort* behind her, she whirled to face Jack. "This is funny? You think this is *funny?*"

"No," Jack said, obviously doing his best to be sober. "No, of course I don't think this is funny." Then he grinned. "Okay, so yes, I do. Cripes, Keely, look at him. Big, bald, green? Growling, shaking his hands? All he needs is a couple of bolts in his neck and he'd be perfect."

Keely blinked furiously, close to tears. She turned back to Petra and glowered at her—which made Candy pout, then begin to cry. "Give me that poor child," she declared coldly, grabbing up the baby and

281

stomping out of the room, Petra close on her heels.

"Hey, wait! It's time to take the rubber stuff off her," Petra said as Keely held Candy tightly, carrying her into her own bedroom and sitting her down on the bed. "Look, I'll do it. Just stop crying."

"She isn't crying," Keely told her.

"No, but you are," Petra said, shaking her head. "Go get dressed or something. I'll take the molds off. Besides, you're scaring the bejesus out of the kid."

Keely stood very still, watching as Petra sat on the bed with Candy, talking to her, teasing her, and at the same time peeling off the pea-green rubber. Petra could handle Candy, could handle a crisis.

Why couldn't she?

Why was she crying—and she *was* crying. Why had she seen only the disaster facing them instead of the humor that Jack saw, that everyone else—except Ms. Peters, probably—saw in what had just happened. She really had to get hold of herself, get a grip, stop panicking as if she'd built a house of cards that kept tumbling down on her.

"I . . . I'm going to go get dressed," she said quietly.

"Yeah, do that," Petra said, then grinned as she held up the two molds, which looked like a pair of pea-green snow boots—with toes molded into them. "Aren't they adorable?"

"Oh, God," Keely said, taking the molds. "They are, aren't they?" And then she ran into the bathroom, where she'd left her clothing, turned on the shower so Petra couldn't hear her, and burst into tears again.

Edith Peters was sitting at the kitchen table, sipping iced tea, when Keely got up the courage to come downstairs about a half hour later.

282

Edith sat in one chair, Sadie in another, the two of them flanked by Jack and Joey. Ms. Peters was scribbling on a paper on her clipboard.

"So, Mr. Morretti, what you're saying is that you feel that, as the closest blood relative, you should be given custody of your niece?"

"Well, yeah," Joey said, sitting back, looping an arm over the back of the chair. "Ain't it obvious?"

"Mr. Morretti, I'm learning that nothing is obvious, especially around here. But I would like some information from you, if I might, as Ms. Morretti is your sister."

"Yeah, go ahead—shoot," Joey told her, sniffing. He rubbed a forefinger under his nose, adjusted his dark glasses. "What does ya wants to know?"

Keely walked over to the counter, took down a glass, then filled it with ice water from the refrigerator-door dispenser. She shook her head at Jack as he half rose from his seat and hoisted herself into one of the tall chairs that lined the breakfast bar.

"Well, Mr. Morretti, if you don't mind," Ms. Peters continued, "I believe I'd like to know, for starters, if you're aware of the identity of Candy's father."

Joey's grin was positively evil as he leaned forward, propped his elbows on the table. "First, Sis would hafta know, and she don't," he said with some glee. "Sis gets around, if youse all take my meanin'."

"Down boy," Jack said tightly, looking disgusted. "Ms. Peters, I understand it was donor sperm."

"Yeah," Joey sniffed. "Some bozo named Rain Dance, or somethin' like dat. So if any of youse is thinkin', ya know, dat there's some daddy gonna show up, he ain't. Yer're lookin' at the *responsible* person here. I've got papers."

283

"Yeah, that's true enough, he does have papers," Jack said, looking at Ms. Peters. "And with a little luck, we'll have him fully trained in a couple of weeks."

Keely pressed a hand over her mouth, her earlier tears obviously having given way to a tendency toward hysterics, because Jack's words—and the memory of Joey's perfect attendance plaque—struck her as unbelievably funny. She was probably losing her mind, she decided.

Ms. Peters unclipped the thick packet of papers and thumped them against the edge of the table. "I can see that this was a mistake," she said, looking at Aunt Sadie. "I believe I need to interview each of you separately, as I feel more than a hint of animosity in this room. Mr. Trehan? If you and Ms. McBride and Ms. Trehan would step outside, please? I'd like to complete my interview with Mr. Morretti. I'll be back tomorrow to complete my interviews with the rest of you, then make my preliminary recommendations to the court. This is one case I definitely don't want to have drag out too long."

Keely's stomach did a small flip as Jack's cheeks went pale, as he rose slowly, obviously reluctant to leave his cousin and Ms. Peters together. "All right, tomorrow then. But we'll . . . we'll be available at any time, if you need us any more today," he said, then held out his hand to Keely, who took it. "Aunt Sadie? Are you coming?"

"No, dear, not just yet," she told him. "I want to go check on Sweetness. The boy's still terribly upset."

"That's my fault, Sadie," Edith Peters told her. "I overreacted, definitely. It's just that the last time I saw a jolly green giant, he was on a bag of frozen peas."

"I know, dear," Aunt Sadie assured her, patting her

284

shoulder. "You're a good sport, Edith, a really good sport."

"In this job, Sadie, you have to be. Either that or go heavily into self-medication."

Keely, amazed, smiled her best smile at Edith Peters as Jack all but dragged her out the back door.

Jack didn't stop until they'd reached the garages; then he fished his car keys from his pocket and opened the door of the bright red Corvette. "Come on, let's go for a ride. I can't stay around here, thinking about Joey up there, talking to Ms. Peters."

"Isn't this . . . ?" Keely asked him as he loaded her into the convertible.

"Yeah, it arrived this morning. Part of my payment for the commercial. Bring back any memories?"

"I don't know," Keely said, looking up at him. "Let's see if you can make it to your side of the car without tripping over something."

"Very funny," Jack snapped, heading around the front of the car, not daring to try patting the hood or flipping the keys. He'd done that enough, unsuccessfully enough, to not want to try it again. "Where are we going?" he asked, once he was in the driver's seat, his hands on the wheel.

"What do you mean, where are we going? You're the one who put me in this car, remember?"

"True enough. Do you have the keys to your aunt's apartment? We could go there. It seems more logical than just driving around, going nowhere. I'm going nowhere enough now as it is."

"Well, I should probably pick up the mail, check for phone messages. And I think I'll go crazy, too, if I have to stay here, knowing Ms. Peters is talking to Joey.

Candy's napping, and Petra's here. All right. The key is on the ring with the van keys, and that's probably still in the ignition," Keely told him, and Jack was out of the car, heading for the van before she could finish.

He wanted out, he wanted out now. He couldn't stick around here, knowing Joey was talking to Edith Peters, saying God only knew what. Besides, a million years ago, when Keely had come out to the pool, she'd said they had to talk. This place was about as private as Yankee Stadium on opening day. If they wanted to talk, they'd have to go somewhere else.

"Got 'em," he said, closing the car door and putting the gear shift into reverse. "Let's enjoy the ride, okay, and wait until we get to the shop. Then we'll talk. You did say you wanted to talk, right?"

"Whatever," Keely said, shrugging, and sat back, folded her arms over her chest, and was quiet as the proverbial tomb until they'd parked the car behind the shop and were heading up the stairs to the apartment.

Once inside, Jack headed for the couch and sat down, then buried his head in his hands. "God. This has got to be over soon. I can't take much more of this, Keely, I really can't. Edith Peters putting us all under a microscope, green feet, Joey's stupid mouth, waiting for Cecily's fax . . ."

Keely sat down beside him, put an arm around his shoulder. God, it felt good to have her sitting beside him.

"I know, Jack. We're under a lot of pressure. I fell apart today, and I'm sorry. I shouldn't have deserted you all like that—but when I saw Candy with those green feet . . . I wanted to murder Petra, which was stupid, because she's marvelous with Candy."

Jack lifted his head, turned to her. "No, *you're*

286

marvelous with Candy. Petra plays with her. You make sure she's fed and changed and bathed. You sing to her, pat her to sleep, make sure she gets to the doctor. You do that, you cook, you take care of the house, you're still *decorating* the house, and you make it all look easy. I don't know how you do it."

"Smoke and mirrors," Keely told him with a wry smile. "I'm really scared out of my mind half the time. The other half I *know* I'm out of my mind."

"You're doing much better with Candy," he told her, taking her hand. "You should see her little head pick up every time she hears your voice. She's crazy about you."

Keely looked at him, blinked, and then turned her head away.

"Hey, what did I say?" he asked, grabbing her shoulders, turning her back so he could see her face. See the tears in her eyes. "Keely, what's wrong?"

"I love her so much," she said, then pressed a hand to her mouth, obviously trying to compose herself. "How can I . . . what will I do when . . . oh, *hell!*" She jumped up from the couch and ran into the other room. Jack heard a door slam and figured it was probably the one to the bathroom. She'd be bound to choose a door with a lock on it.

He could follow her, stand outside the bathroom door. Listen to her cry. Call through the door that he loved her, wanted her with him for the rest of their lives, wanted them to raise Candy together, raise a whole bunch of kids together.

That would be cool. Not.

So he'd wait. Give her some time to collect herself, try to put some of this seesaw day behind her, all the up and down seesaw days they'd had since she'd first

287

shown up on his doorstep looking like the salvation he'd prayed for as he'd tried to figure out what to do with Candy.

Because she did want to talk to him. She'd said so. Was it the cowardly way out to want to wait, listen to what she had to say, before he opened his big mouth and maybe made a fool out of himself?

And what was so bad about making a fool of himself? Asking her to make their fake engagement real? Taking that great big leap, asking her to give up her career in New York, stay with him, be a mother to Candy? Asking her to be his wife? His love?

Was he that unsure of himself? That unsure that Keely knew her own feelings, could separate her love for Candy from her love—please let it be love—for him?

Yup. He sure was, because he admittedly had some trouble separating his love for Candy from his love for Keely. They were a set, arriving in his life at the same time, taking over his house, taking over his heart. How could he separate one from the other? It would be like asking himself which of the two of them he loved more.

While he mentally beat himself up, Jack walked around the small, well-furnished living room, not really paying attention to what he was looking at, but only moving, because sitting still was impossible.

And then he saw the blinking light on the answering machine.

He looked toward the open doorway leading down the hallway. Looked at the blinking red light. Looked down the hallway once more.

Gregory?

Jack's fingers touched the edge of the desk; then he slowly walked his hand toward the answering machine, tapped its plastic surface, dangled a finger over the PLAY button . . . took one last look down the hallway.

He hit PLAY.

"Hello, darling," a woman's voice chirped, and Jack fumbled with the slide on the side of the machine, lowering the volume. "I wish you'd picked up. I hate talking to machines. But this can't wait. You'd better sit down, Keely, because I've got a surprise for you. I'm retiring. Yes," the woman's voice went on, now with a bit of girlish giggle in it, "it's true. We've decided to move to Florida once we get home. Sand, sun, the ocean. It won't be Greece, or even Paris, but oh, Keely, just the thought of dealing with one more housewife with all her taste in her mouth is just *so* defeating. And now the best surprise. I'm going to give you the shop. All yours, no strings. Oh, not that you'll want it. You'll want to sell it all, go back to Manhattan.

I know you, I know how badly you want that. So, fine. Do it, with my blessing. Now, aren't you glad I told you to sit down? Ah, Keely, I'm *so* happy. I only wish you could be this happy. Bye, darling"—another girlish giggle—"someone seems to want me. Darling, stop that! I was talking to—" *Click.* "End of messages."

Jack hit the REWIND button, his mind whirling. Did he save the message? Erase it? Kill himself?

The message rewound, and the red light began blinking again, the message sitting there, ready for Keely to play it.

"Jack?"

He turned around, using his body to block the sight of the blinking message light. "You okay?" he asked as she slowly walked into the room, sat down on a small chair that looked too fragile to hold Candy.

"Yes, I'm all right. And I'm sorry," she told him,

289

folding her hands in her lap. "There's just been so much . . . so much . . . well, there's just been so much, you know? My business failing, coming back here, wanting the job furnishing your house so badly. Candy, you . . . Arizona."

Jack winced. "Yeah. Arizona. That's what you want to talk about, isn't it? I thought so."

"No, that's not really—"

"Yes, it is, Keely," he interrupted her, going over to her, taking her hands, pulling her to her feet. "You're dying to talk about it. And what you want to say is that I disappointed the hell out of you."

She had kept her head down, avoiding looking at him, but now she raised her head, looked at him with astonishment written all over her beautiful, expressive face. "What?"

"Don't be kind, Keely," he said, still holding on to her hands. "Bears have attacked with more grace. I can apologize, and I do, but I'll never be able to tell you exactly what the hell happened out there."

"We did get a little carried away," Keely told him, her voice low, so that he had to bend his head to hear her. "But it was mutual. You didn't do anything I . . . anything I didn't want you to do."

"You said it was proximity," he reminded her quietly.

"Yes, I did, didn't I?"

"We're pretty . . . approximate now, aren't we?" he asked her, stepping slightly closer to her, letting go of her hands, using one of his hands to tip up her chin.

Her smile was tremulous. "I don't think that's a proper use of the word."

"Maybe not, but it's close enough. We're close enough. Can we try again? I really do want to try again, Keely."

She pressed her lips together, wet them with the tip of her tongue.

But he held on, didn't give in, even though that unconscious wetting of her lips had tipped his libido switch to ON with a vengeance. "Keely?"

"Shouldn't . . . shouldn't we be talking about Ms. Peters, and Joey, and . . . and strategy?"

"Should we?" he asked her, lightly rubbing her bare arms, watching the way her powder-blue sleeveless cotton sweater breathed with her, her chest rising and falling, rising and falling, driving him crazy.

"We . . . we should probably be talking about a lot of things," she told him, even as her arms made their way around his neck.

"We only get into trouble that way, Keely," he reminded her. "Maybe, just for now, it's better this way."

She closed her eyes, nodded.

He bent his head closer, kissed her. Softly. Gently. One kiss. Two kisses. Advance and retreat.

"I'm not made of crystal, Jack," she said, tightening her arms around him.

"I know," he breathed against her ear, sliding his hands low on her back. "You're much too soft . . . and warm. You don't have any edges when I hold you, Keely. No brittle pieces."

"No defenses," Keely said, sighing as he kissed her throat, as she melted into his arms. "You leave me with no defenses."

"Good," he told her, bending his legs, slipping one arm beneath her knees as he lifted her. "Am I safe in asking you to tell me where to go?"

She buried her head against his chest. "Down the hallway, then to your right," she said, already pushing off her sandals, so that they dropped, one after the other, to the floor.

He stepped into her bedroom, vaguely registered pieces of dark furniture before his attention was caught by a huge four-poster bed covered with a blue-and-green-flowered quilt. "Fantasyland," he muttered, waiting as Keely leaned half out of his arms to pull down the quilt. Several decorative pillows pulled down with it.

The bed was almost waist high, making it easy for him to transfer her from arms to bed, even easier for him to follow after her, his loafers left behind on the floor.

Sunlight dappled the bed, shot golden highlights into Keely's hair as she lay there on the blue-and-green-flowered sheets, a perfect Sleeping Beauty he was about to awaken with his kiss. "God, Keely, you're beautiful."

He watched as a faint flush of color rose into her cheeks. "I . . . I thought we weren't going to talk. You're making me nervous, looking at me like that."

"Like what?" he asked, pushing his hand under the hem of her sweater, pressing his palm against her flat midriff. "How am I looking at you, Keely?"

"I . . . I don't know," she answered, fresh tears glistening in her eyes. "Nobody's ever looked at me like this before."

"Nobody's ever wanted you like this before," he whispered, bending low, easing his side against hers, moving his lips over her cheeks, her throat. "Nobody in the world has ever wanted anyone the way I want you."

"Oh, Jack . . ."

*Oh, Jack.* He loved the way she said his name. Loved the way she looked at him. Loved the way she felt as he moved his hand higher, cupped her left breast. Loved the way she closed her eyes, sighed.

292

He'd missed all of this, they'd both missed all of this, in their mad rush to put out the fire between them that had burned so hot in Arizona.

The fire was still there, but now there was more. He didn't know what that *more* was, but there was something . . . something swelling deep inside him, washing over him in wave after wave, each higher, deeper, stronger than the last. More than lust, more than hunger, more than wanting, even more than needing.

His hand left her breast, slid around to her back, lifting her slightly as he brought his mouth to hers, as he slanted his lips against hers, as she opened to him, as he slid his tongue inside her. Exploring. Learning. Glorying in the way her arms came up and around his neck, how she melded against him, how the want and the need took second place to the cherish and the hold and the please God *forever* that he felt.

Clothing disappeared as the world disappeared, as everything except Keely disappeared. He kissed her breasts, captured her nipple in his mouth, cupped her, molded her.

Worshipped her.

Touching. Caressing. Learning.

She moaned softly when his hand slipped between her thighs, when he found her moist and ready for him. She pressed kisses against his chest, her head half lifted, as he probed her, let her move against his hand, felt her go very still when he found her point of greatest pleasure.

Slowly. He'd take this slowly. Bring her pleasure, bring her to pleasure, watch her eyes go dark as the pleasure built, as she went liquid in his arms.

But now she was touching him, gripping him intimately. Stroking him. Her touch light yet firm, her quick, nibbling kisses on his neck, the lobe of his ear, tightening a coil inside him, sending electric tingles through him, building his passion, building his need.

He moved his fingers. Keely went very still in his arms, her hips rising, her thighs spread wide, inviting him to every intimacy. She was his, open and giving, and he felt her body contract, heard the soft whimper that barely escaped her throat. She trusted. She allowed. She let him give.

He let her take . . . and take . . . and take.

And then she was moving again, rather desperately clasping at him, entwining her legs with his, pulling him closer to her, her rounded nails dragging across his back, not hard enough to hurt but with just enough pressure to guide him to her, cover her body with his own.

"I . . . I've never . . ." she breathed into his ear as he held her, let her hold him, as she slowly relaxed even as her breathing remained quick, shallow.

Neither had he. He'd never wanted to give like that, taken such pleasure in the giving. It was almost enough.

Almost, but not quite.

Keely seemed to sense that and began touching him again, moving provocatively beneath him, sliding one hand between their bodies . . . finding him, guiding him . . .

"Wait," he whispered, using the single part of his mind that retained even a hint of sanity. He groped on the bed with one hand, found his slacks, found the packet he'd carried with him since Arizona. In his heart of hearts, he must always have been an optimist, always believed he'd hold Keely again, please God be allowed to love her again.

And then he was with her again, in her again, deep inside her, moving inside her, moving with her, building toward a climax that terrified him with its promised intensity.

He held her, as she had held him, his face buried in her neck. Trying to regain control of his breathing. Trying to locate the strength that had seeped out of his every muscle during their mutual release. Trying to tell himself that, no, he wasn't going to cry.

But he could . . .

Keely stood under the shower, her head thrown back, allowing the water to cascade over her face, her breasts, her belly. Her skin was supersensitive, still remembering Jack's touch, her response to that touch.

He hadn't left her this time. She'd left him, but not before they'd lain together, quietly, cuddled together. That was nice. That had been much more than nice. It was a memory she'd have forever, no matter what happened next.

They still hadn't talked. They might never talk. Hell, they might marry, have six kids, live together for the next fifty years, and never really talk.

Probably because some things didn't have to be said. Some things were just known. And sometimes it was better not knowing, not digging too deeply, investigating too thoroughly.

Which had come first, her love for Candy or her love for Jack? And did it matter? She couldn't think about Candy without thinking about Jack, and vice versa. She loved them both. Was that a crime?

Keely tensed as slightly cooler air slid across her back, then turned to see Jack entering the glassed-in shower.

"I thought we'd get done quicker this way, so we can head back to the house. And it conserves water," he added, resting his hands on her shoulders.

Keely fought the urge to cover her nakedness, then realized how ridiculous that was. There wasn't a part of her Jack hadn't seen, touched, kissed. "You're crazy," she said, pressing her palms against his bare chest, stealing a look at him, then grinning at his arousal. "And you think this is going to be *faster*?"

"Probably not." He reached for the soap, moved it between his hands, then began soaping her breasts. "I've been wrong before."

Jack was whistling as he reentered the living room of the apartment, happier than he'd been since his shoulder had begun hurting again last August and he'd known, just known, that this time surgery wasn't going to fix him.

". . . you could be this happy. Bye, darling"—a girlish giggle—"someone seems to want me. Darling, stop that! I was talking to—" *Click.* "End of messages."

Keely stood at the desk, her back to him.

"Keely? Was that your aunt?" he asked, wondering if he could pull this off, wondering if she now trusted him enough to tell him the truth. Tell him what her aunt had said in her telephone message.

"Hmmm?" she asked, slowly turning around, but not before he could see her finger find and press the ERASE MESSAGES button. "Oh . . . oh, yes, that was Aunt Mary. She's obviously enjoying her honeymoon, because she didn't even mention when she might be home."

"No?" he asked, raising his eyebrows. "So, what did she have to say?"

Keely shrugged. "Nothing important. She's happy." She looked around the living room, spread her arms. "I don't need to do anything else. I already checked the messages on the machine in the shop, and nothing's urgent. So . . . I guess we ought to head back home . . . back to the house. I was planning on tuna fish salad for dinner and want to hard-boil some eggs."

Jack tipped his head to one side, looked at her. "That's it? We go back to the house, boil eggs?"

She frowned at him, gave a nervous laugh. "Well, of course that's it. Why? I don't understand."

"Never mind," Jack said, taking her hand as he walked past, heading for the door. "Like you said, it's time to get back to the house. I want to call Jimmy anyway, and find out if that fax arrived from Cecily."

Keely stopped, tugged on his hand. "Wait. Something's wrong, isn't it? What's wrong?"

"Nothing," Jack said, his cheeks feeling tight. "Not one damn thing."

# Chapter Seventeen

*The game isn't over until it's over.*

—Yogi Berra

THEY MADE IT HALFWAY HOME BEFORE KEELY FIGURED it out, but she waited until he'd parked the Corvette and they were heading up to the house before she confronted him. "You listened to the message from Aunt Mary, didn't you?"

"That's my brother's car back there, at the garages," Jack answered shortly. "Maybe we can postpone World War Three until he's gone, okay?"

"Then you *did*," she exclaimed, chasing after him after having stopped dead for a moment, until her mind engaged, sorted through Jack's response. "You didn't deny it, Jack, so you did. You listened to my *private* phone message! When, Jack? Before . . . or after?"

"Does it matter?" he asked, skirting the fence around the pool as he aimed himself at the back door.

"Does it—oh, for crying out loud, Jack! Of *course* it matters. It changes everything. Did you make love to me because you wanted to, or because it was the best way you could think of to keep me here so you can get custody of Candy?"

He turned on her, lifted a finger to her face. "I would *not* do that," he said slowly, precisely.

"Sure, you would. That's *exactly* what you would do," Keely persisted, chasing after him again, catching the door as he let it go behind him, entering the kitchen.

"Hi, Jack—Keely."

Keely looked at Tim Trehan, sitting at his ease in the den, munching popcorn out of a big blue bowl. Petra and Sweetness sat there with him, and one of the *Godfather* movies was playing on the DVD.

"Hello," Keely bit out, turning her back on him.

"What are you doing here?" Jack asked testily.

"I don't know. If I'd known the welcome I'd get, I suppose maybe I wouldn't have come here at all. But, bighearted brother that I am, I thought I'd personally deliver tickets to tomorrow night's game. I'm nice that way. Besides, Mort's coming here any minute now and wanted me here when he arrived. I think I'm supposed to convince you something's the right thing to do. I just don't know what it is yet."

Keely stood, her back still to Tim, her arms folded across her belly, one foot tap-tap-tapping on the tile kitchen floor. "Get rid of him," she said through gritted teeth, not caring if she was being as bossy as her aunt often accused her of being. "I need to kill you."

"Hey, they're fighting," Petra said, and Keely turned

298

around, glaring at the teenager. "Oh, yeah," Petra gloated. "They're fighting. This could be good. Tim, pass me the popcorn."

"Jack . . ." Keely ground out.

"No," he said firmly. "No, I'm not going to throw my brother out because you've got some stick up your—" He shut up abruptly, pulled open the refrigerator door, yanked out a can of soda, popped the top. Soda fizz ran over his fingers, dripped onto the floor.

"*Now* look what you've done!" Keely said accusingly, going over to the sink to rip off a length of paper towels, wet them under the tap. "I just washed this floor."

"And it's a beautiful day for baseball. This is Tim Trehan, who will be bringing you your play by play," Tim said, holding up the TV controller as if it were a microphone. He, Petra, and Sweetness had moved from the couch to the low bar that separated the two rooms, the popcorn bowl balanced between them as they watched from the bleacher seats.

"Not funny. Go away, Tim," Jack said, contradicting his previous statement. "Keely and I have something to discuss."

"No, we don't," Keely said from the floor, where she was wiping up the spill. "I changed my mind. I have nothing to say to you. Nothing."

"Nothing?"

"Nothing."

"Okay, folks, they're feeling each other out," Tim spoke into the controller.

Keely lost it. She just lost it. She didn't care if the entire mad Trehan gang were here, making comments, taking notes. "You did, Jack. You listened to my private phone message. You heard Aunt Mary say she's giving me the shop. Admit it."

"Okay, so maybe I did listen," Jack shot back at her. "What's the big deal? It's no big deal. I was going to tell you . . . sometime."

"He's trying to pitch out of a jam, folks," Tim said, as Petra giggled.

"No big deal? Aunt Mary gave me the shop, Jack, so I can sell it, go back to New York. You hear that, and then you *lure* me into bed. And you don't see that as a big deal?"

"I shouldn't be hearing this," Sweetness said, taking hold of Petra's elbow. "You either. Come on, let's go for a walk or something."

"Take him, too," Jack ordered, pointing at his brother.

"Nice try, Jack, but I'm staying. But, hey, don't let me interrupt."

Jack growled low in his throat, and Keely grabbed his arm. "Just forget about him," she ordered. "Besides, I don't care if the whole world hears this. You're a rat, Jack. A great big *rat*!"

Jack gave his brother one last look, then turned to Keely, slapping a hand to his chest. "Me? *I'm* the rat? Hey, I gave you an opening. I *asked* what the message was about, and you said it was nothing. Big nothing, Keely. Just your ticket out of here, back to the big time."

"Somebody check the radar gun," Tim commented from the box seats. "He's really throwing some heat now."

"I already *have* my ticket back to the big time, Jack," Keely yelled at him. "You offered it to me, remember? Anything I want, that's what you said. Anything to get rid of me after you get custody, right, Jack? Taking me to bed was just a little added insurance."

"It's a nail biter now, fans," Tim said into the sudden silence. "And here comes the payoff pitch . . ."

300

Jack stabbed his fingers into his hair. "What in *hell* are you talking about? I don't want to get rid of you, Keely. I thought you wanted to go. I thought . . . I thought you *needed* to go. Give it another shot."

Keely pulled out one of the tall chairs at the breakfast bar, sat down before she fell down, as she felt suddenly deflated. "Well, I did. I thought I did."

Jack walked over to the breakfast bar, put both palms on the countertop. "You want to talk, Keely, we'll talk. Tim," he said, looking over his shoulder, "get out of here."

"Well," Tim said, putting down the remote controller. "That took the crowd out of the game."

"Tim!"

"I'm going, I'm going."

Keely kept her head down, waited until Tim walked past them, closed the kitchen door behind himself.

"Keely," Jack said, taking one of her hands in his, "you've always been very upfront about what you wanted. You wanted to go back to Manhattan, give this interior decorating thing another shot. If you don't remember how badly you wanted that, I do."

"You wanted another shot at baseball," Keely said, wishing he'd stop rubbing his thumb over the back of her hand. She couldn't think when he was touching her. Didn't want to think.

"And I took it, and I learned that I was wrong, I didn't really want it anymore. There wasn't any burning in my gut anymore. But you haven't had that opportunity, Keely. Do you want to spend the rest of your life wondering if you could have made it, made it to the big dance, the big time?"

"As opposed to staying here with you and Candy," Keely said, unable to be anything other than direct, now

301

that they finally were talking, really talking, to each other.

"We could be a way of not having to try, risk another failure."

She lifted her head, looked at him. "Is that how you see it, Jack? How you see Candy, and me? As an excuse not to risk failure again?"

His smile was slow and very real, and she felt tears stinging her eyes. "I worried about that, I admit it," he said, lifting her hand to his lips. "About rebounds, and proximity, and confusing gratefulness for your help for something bigger, deeper. But then, I'm a jerk. Luckily, not that much of a jerk, because I figured it out, Keely. I love you. *You*. But loving you, I need *you* to be sure, too."

"Oh, Jack," Keely said, sighing as she reached across the breakfast bar, cupping a hand behind his head. "I'm sure. I've never been more sure of anything in my entire life."

"And you love me?" he asked, disengaging her clinging arms long enough to walk around the bar, gather her close.

"I love you," Keely told him. "You big jerk, how could I do anything but love you?"

He kissed her, and Keely swore she could hear bells, just as she could have sworn she'd heard music that first time, in Arizona. But then she heard more. She heard knocking.

Jack must have heard it, too, because he broke their kiss, looked toward the hallway. "What is it, Sweetness?"

"You've got company, Mr. T."

"Mort?" he asked as Keely reluctantly slid her arms away from him, took hold of his hand. There was so much more they needed to say to each other, but it could wait. She'd probably spend half her life waiting for chances to talk to Jack, waiting for some moment of peace and quiet to talk to Jack. And yet one of the things she loved best about him was that excitement seemed to follow him.

"No, sir," Sweetness said, shaking his head. "It's some lady and her friend. Moon Flower?"

Keely winced as Jack's grip on her hand nearly crushed her fingers. "Cecily?" he asked.

"That's what Mr. Morretti called her, but she told me Moon Flower. I'm sure of it. There's somebody else, too, but I didn't catch his name."

"Oh, God, Jack, your cousin's here?" Keely asked, suddenly terrified. Where was Candy? She looked up at the clock—nap time. Candy was upstairs, sleeping. She had to go to Candy.

As if reading her thoughts, Jack asked Sweetness, "Where's Candy? Does Petra have her?"

Sweetness nodded vigorously. "She woke up kind of early, so we took her down to Aunt Sadie's place for a visit. That's where we went, too, when you two started . . . when we thought we should leave. Ms. Peters is still there, having tea with Aunt Sadie and playing with Candy. And your brother's there, with some guy named Mort. Whole bunch of us there. I came back up here to get Candy's pacifier and heard the doorbell. Should I go get everybody, bring them all up here?"

"No!" Keely and Jack said in unison.

"But, I thought—I'll just ask Petra, I think she'll know."

"Don't think, Sweetness," Jack warned. "Just keep everybody away until I can talk to my cousin. Are you telling me Joey's with her?"

"Yes, sir," Sweetness said, already heading for the back door, a wise man who knows when he's been dismissed. "Is that all right? I could get him out of there, if you want."

"I'll just bet you could, Sweetness, but no thanks," Jack said, and Sweetness shrugged, left the kitchen. "Come on, Keely," Jack said to her, squeezing her hand. "The timing sucks, but then, what else is new? Let's go talk to Cecily."

Keely hung back, more frightened than she wanted to admit. "Shouldn't we call Jimmy? Call your lawyer?"

"Not yet," he told her. "First we see what planet Cecily's on today, and then go from there."

Cecily hadn't changed much since the last time Jack had seen her, which was, he thought, Christmas, two years ago. She was still blond, although she did have a red streak in her hair now. She was still small, prettily petite. And she was still wearing those long, flowing dresses that made her look like a great-grandmother in training.

She saw him as he and Keely entered the large, nearly empty living room, and half ran, half hobbled toward him, her heavy brown clogs scraping the hardwood floor. "Jack! Oh, Jack, don't you look wonderful! And such a pretty house, except you really ought to think about maybe getting some more furniture," she exclaimed, then launched herself into his arms.

"Hello, Cecily," Jack said, looking past her to a rather tall, thin, ponytailed man of about thirty-five dressed in, it appeared to Jack, a potato sack and wrinkled slacks. "Who's your friend?"

"Oh, yes, yes, of course," Cecily trilled, taking Jack's hand—ignoring Keely completely—and pulling him across the room. "This is Blue Rainbow, my guru, my mentor."

"Hadley Hecuba, actually," Blue Rainbow said when Cecily skipped away, to go hug Joey, who told her to "Knock it off, you did that already!"

Hecuba extended a hand so that Jack had to shake it. Well, he didn't have to, but if he didn't, Cecily would probably notice, cause a scene, and it just wasn't worth the hassle.

"No," Jack said quietly, dredging his memory for the facts Jimmy's investigators had dug up in the past few days as his grip tightened on the man's hand. "It's Lester James Schmidt, age thirty-seven, born in Milwaukee, arrested twice for embezzlement, once for credit-card fraud, still officially married to Olivia Bertrice Schmidt, who'd love to know where you are because you're a little tardy with the child-support checks. About five years tardy. How am I doing so far, Lester, old sport?"

Jack felt Keely squeezing his hand as she half-leaned against him and looked at her, smiled. "Those *D&S* guys were worth every penny, weren't they?"

"I had no idea you knew this much," Keely told him, obviously impressed. And, unfortunately, Jack decided, still as direct and honest as all hell. "Now tell me what good it does."

"None, little lady," Blue Rainbow said, leering at her. "I saw that fax from your lawyer, Trehan, and we decided to rip it up. She's the kid's mother and we're keeping her. Unless maybe you can *persuade* us that the kid's better off with you?" As he said this, he lifted his left hand, rubbed his thumb and two fingers together.

"Money," Keely said as Jack all but dragged her away from Cecily's guru. "Jack, he wants money. It's so *simple*. We pay them, and they go away. Oh, thank God, I've been so worried."

"Keep worrying," Jack told her as they stood near the hallway, Jack watching Cecily and Joey as his cousins fell into what looked like a whispered argument. "One, if we give them money to go away, they'll just come back for more money. Not that Cecily needs any, but obviously Lester doesn't know when he's got it good—or maybe he's on his way out and he knows it. Cecily isn't known for her constant heart. Two, we've already got Ms. Peters and the whole child-welfare thing involved here. Maybe I can buy Cecily and Lester off, but that still leaves Joey."

Keely sighed. "I want to just go grab Candy and run away with her."

"Can I go along?"

She smiled, laid her head against his chest. "I wouldn't take so much as a single step without you."

"Yes, you would. You'd take lots of steps, actually. All the way to Sadie's house, which is what I want you to do now. Gather up Ms. Peters, Keely, and bring her back here. Sneak her into the sunroom through the outside door, and then join me again here. I'll make sure I have the doors to the sunroom open by then, so she gets to hear everything."

"What everything?"

"I don't have a clue," Jack admitted, trying not to show his own nervousness. "Just be ready to go wherever Cecily and Joey and Lester take us, okay?"

"Okay." Keely turned to head down the hallway, then stopped, turned back. "I love you."

"I love you, too. Tell Petra and Sweetness to take Candy for a walk or something. I don't want her anywhere near here. Cecily hasn't asked to see her, and

306

if she does, I want to be able to say she isn't here right now."

Keely nodded, then left the room, and Jack followed her, grabbed another soda from the refrigerator. He watched the clock for five minutes to give Keely time to get Ms. Peters into position, then returned to the living room, opened the doors to the sunroom, and walked over to his cousins. "So, Cecily, how was Tibet?"

"Tibet? Oh, Jack, we didn't go to Tibet, you silly. We would have, but Blue Rainbow wanted to see the sun rise over Monaco. Told me it was mystical, and it was, it was. I felt such *energy* there. And Princess Grace was there, you know. I saw her. Oh, she's dead, but I saw her. Did you know I can do that now? Conjure spirits? I may write a book. I've got just the title—*Seeing Grace*. You get it? Not *saying* grace, but *seeing* her. Isn't that wonderful?"

Cecily was being Cecily—physically here, but her brain floating somewhere in the stratosphere. Just like always. It was as if she worked at it, practiced being flaky. "Monaco, huh?" Jack said once she'd sighed, giggled, and finally shut up. "The place with the casino? I hadn't heard that, Cecily. I just knew you were somewhere in Europe when my lawyer located you."

"Oh, yes. The casino. Blue Rainbow has a system. I was his banker." Cecily frowned, looked confused. "What's wrong, Jack? You look all tense. Is something wrong? Blue Rainbow said you'd be so happy to see me, but you don't look happy at all. And Joey's being so *mean* to me . . ." Her voice faded away and she hiccuped, then went over to the couch and picked up a rather large canvas bag and began fishing in it until her hand emerged, clasping a blue plastic bottle of Fun Bubbles and a plastic stick with a circle at one end of it.

307

"What did you say to her, Joey?" Jack asked his cousin, who was in the midst of popping a small square of gum into his mouth.

"Nuthin'," he said, sniffing. "I just told her da truth. She's a flake. Batty. Nutso. So dat means I get the kid, and that means I get alla Uncle Sal's money from his share of da dry-cleaning business when he croaks. He told me, told me plenty, first one to settle down, get a kid, gets the dough."

Cecily, who'd overheard, stepped up to Joey, her angelic face screwed up not all that prettily. "Oh, yeah? Wel—*hic*—that's what you know, Joey. Uncle Sal said the first one who gets mar—*hic*—ied and settles down, has a kid, gets his—*hic*—his money, you big stupid, you. Nobody'd marry you, Joey, you big stupid. I'm the one who's going to get Uncle Sal's money."

*Please God, let Ms. Peters have heard that*, Jack prayed silently, then relaxed as Keely reentered the room, nodding toward the open doors to the sunroom.

The only problem was, Keely wasn't alone. Tim was with her, and Aunt Sadie and Mort. They had enough for two tables of pinochle, if he had card tables, which he didn't think he did. And he wasn't in the mood to play games.

As Cecily did a mercurial turn from whining to giggling and repeated her launch-herself-into-his-arms greeting to Tim, and Joey went to sit on the couch, obviously to sulk, Jack whispered to Keely, "What, no brass band? Mort would probably be great with any wind instrument."

"I couldn't stop them, Jack," she told him. "And Mort has an idea."

"Oh, no," Jack said, shaking his head. "God save us

from Mort and his ideas." Then he realized that *he* didn't have any ideas. "What is it?"

"You'll see," Keely said, looking at Lester, or Hadley, or Blue Rainbow, or Prisoner Number 55589, or whatever name the guy answered to—and he'd probably answer to Dog Dirt if there was a buck in it for him. "Why don't you go introduce everyone while I save Aunt Sadie from Cecily, then see how close you can get them to the door."

"You don't want to be introduced to Cecily?"

Keely's face went rather stiff. "No, I don't think so. You'd have to bail me out of jail."

"She is Cecily's mother, Keely," Jack reminded her.

"She gave birth to her, Jack. I'm grateful for that, but that's as far as it goes. Look at her over there, blowing bubbles, for crying out loud. What a twit! Has she even asked to see Candy yet?"

He shook his head. "No, she hasn't."

Keely's spine went very straight and she lifted her chin imperiously. "Then I definitely don't want to talk to her."

"You're tough," Jack said appreciatively.

"I'm scared half out of my mind, but don't tell anybody," she said, then called to Aunt Sadie to help her in the kitchen, lay out some drinks and snacks for their "company."

Tim approached, twirling some sort of beads around his hand.

"What's that?" Jack asked, glad to have his brother here, glad to know he'd back him up, no matter what happened.

"Worry beads," Tim told him. "Cecily gave them to me. She's the same old Cecily, isn't she? Always a few bricks shy of a load. What's she doing with those

309

bubbles? Are we about to have a love-in or something? Unless she's doing some weird Lawrence Welk impression, and I kind of doubt that. Oh, and did Keely tell you what Mort's up to?"

"She told me to watch and see."

"Sounds like a plan. So, are you two getting married? And can I be best man, or referee?"

"We don't always fight," Jack told his brother. "You just caught us at a bad time."

"I know. I'm not to blame, am I? I mean, putting that rebound idea into your head?"

Jack smiled. "No, I got dumb all by myself, actually. What was that quote from Dizzy Dean? Oh yeah, 'The doctors X-rayed my head and found nothing.' "

"I've got a better one. Tug McGraw: 'I have no trouble with the twelve inches between my elbow and my palm. It's the seven inches between my ears that's bent.' "

"Bent, scrambled, you name it. But I'm smarter now, and damn lucky. You like her, right?"

"Hey, bro, you like her; that's good enough for me. Just don't think I'm going to follow you down the aisle. This twin stuff goes only so far. Uh-oh, there goes Mort. Come on, this ought to be good."

Jack and Tim followed as Mort left Blue Rainbow—and Lord only knew what those two had to talk about—and walked over to Cecily, pulling one of his business cards from his pocket. "Ms. Morretti?" he said, holding out his card. "You don't know me, but I represent your cousins, Jack and Tim. I'm primarily a sports agent, but I'm branching out, taking on other clients, other venues. I just cast a rather large commercial in Arizona, as a matter of fact. And I have to tell you, you have the most *original* face and persona I've ever seen. I could make

310

you the face of the new millennium. You're free to travel, aren't you? Because I have this account in Europe . . ."

Cecily blew one more round of bubbles, then leaned forward, squinted at the card, looked up at the agent. "Mortimer Moore?" she said, looking adorably vague. "That's a funny name."

"Says Moon Flower Morretti," Jack whispered in an aside to his brother, quickly coming up to speed with just what Mort had in mind. He was offering Cecily money, just to see how fast she jumped on it. Money, and a reason to make sure she wasn't encumbered, like with a baby. Now to hope Cecily said all the right things, with Ms. Peters listening. "Ah, look, here comes the guru. Is his nose twitching? Maybe he'll be able to explain all of this to Cecily."

"Yes, here he comes, and with his tail pointing in the air, like a hound catching a scent," Tim said, chuckling. "Keely told us, when she came running into Aunt Sadie's, that she was pretty sure Cecily and her guru were after money, not custody. That's when Mort had this light bulb sort of go off over his head. Pretty good so far, huh?"

Mort took Cecily's arm, deftly steering her toward the open doors of the sunroom, Lester making a U-turn to follow after them.

"Now, Ms. Morretti," Mort continued, smooth as butter. "What I'm going to propose is that you sign with me, exclusively, and together we will take the world by storm. I can see your face, that lovely face, thirty feet high, fifty feet wide, on every billboard in New York. Yes, New York, not just Europe. Revlon's looking for a new face, you know. I had somebody else in mind, but she pales—*pales*—next to you."

311

"There goes Keely's other chance at a career," Jack said quietly as Cecily looked confused, then happy, and then confused again.

"Oh," she said, "but I can't. I'm sorry, but I just can't."

Jack's heart hit his toes. Cecily was going to turn Mort down because she wanted Candy. Was here to take back Candy. There was going to be a long, ugly custody battle—the very last thing he wanted for Candy, for Keely.

"I'm getting married, Mr. Mortimer," Cecily said then, looking toward Lester. "We're flying to Vegas tonight, with little Magenta Moon. We're going to be a family. It's all settled."

Jack, suddenly optimistic once more, cocked an eyebrow at Lester Schmidt. Mort might not have been going here, but they'd arrived at a very hopeful place anyway. "Nice work if you can get it, Blue Rainbow," Jack said quickly, and rather loudly. "Don't you think you might need a *divorce* first?"

Cecily's blue eyes went very wide. "A div . . . a div—*hic*—vorce?"

"Here we go," Tim said, backing up a step. "Open the floodgates."

"Now, Cecily," Lester said quickly as Cecily's face crumpled up like a paper bag. "I was going to tell you . . ."

"Get out!" Cecily shrieked, pointing toward the door. "Get out, get out, get out! First you want me to make Jack pay—*hic*—pay for Magenta Moon . . . and then you *lie* to me? You're *married?* You said you loved me. Go away! I never wa—*hic*—ant to see you again. Ever!"

"Uh-oh, Tim. I thought we were home free for a minute there, but I don't like where this is going all of a sudden. Is she really going to dump him, try to keep Candy?" Jack asked his brother as Keely came back into the room, carrying a tray filled with a plate of cookies and some cups, and a pitcher of iced tea.

"Oh, knock it off, Cecily," Lester shot back at her, clearly a man who knows he's lost but isn't about to go down on his own. "Just cut the bull, because it's making me sick. You know I'm still married, so don't use that to try to cut me out of the deal. You know a whole lot more than that dippy-little-me crap you try out on everyone. These stupid clothes, these stupid names you gave us. Blowing bubbles. Do you really think these people are dumb enough to *buy* any of this crap? Why don't you blow those bubbles out your—"

"Zipper it, Lester, you jackass!" Cecily snapped, and Jack looked at Keely, stunned. This was his cousin? No crying? No hiccups? No Betty Boop voice rising in hysterics? Who stole his cousin when he wasn't looking and replaced her with this steely-eyed, rough-voiced stranger? And what the hell was Lester talking about? Cecily wasn't putting on an act. Unless she'd *always* been putting on an act.

"Well, I'll be damned," Jack said quietly.

"Okay, it's family now, and I'm getting uncomfortable. I'll see you later, everybody. I'll be at Sadie's until the smoke clears." Mort, his job done—or half done, before Lester and Cecily began ignoring him—then left the room, snatching up a cookie as he went.

"He hates scenes," Tim said, jerking a thumb at Mort's departing back. "That's why he invited me here today. As backup, if you go nuts over his latest idea for you."

"Shut up, Tim," Jack said, barely hearing him,

because he was fascinated with Cecily, still working out the details of the revelation that had hit him. This *look* had come over Cecily's face. Wise. Crafty. Still petite and blond and beautiful, but now more closely resembling Joey, who always looked like he had a plan—never a good one, but a plan.

"It was all her idea," Lester was all but whining, appealing to Jack. "She dumped the kid on you because she doesn't want it, never did, and said you were such a sap, you'd just take her, get her out of her hair. The kid cramped her style. But you didn't know that, and she saw her chance when that lawyer contacted her about giving up the kid. First we were going to make you pay so she'd sign away custody, but then she decided she'd probably get more money from her Uncle Sal when he kicks off if she could show up with a kid and a husband in tow. I said take the money and run, that this Sal guy could live another twenty years, but she wouldn't listen. She doesn't want the kid. She wants the money. She went through about a million bucks in Monaco."

"I said, *zipper it!*" Cecily screeched, racing at Lester, beating her small fists against his chest.

Keely sat on the floor of Candy's room, watching as the baby, lying on her belly, tried her best to lift her rear end in the air and move forward toward her favorite rattle.

Candy tried, she really did, but then she got frustrated as her nose hit the carpet one time too many, and she began to cry. Keely scooped her up, held her close. "It's all right, sweetheart," she said, giving her the rattle, "you'll grow up soon enough, and be crawling, and walking, and running . . ."

"And driving a car," Jack said as he leaned against

the doorjamb. "And if that isn't enough to turn both our heads gray, I don't know what is. Let's just keep her little forever, okay?"

Keely smiled up at him, looking closely to see if he was all right, if he had survived the afternoon without harm. "Are they gone now? All of them? I'm sorry I bailed on you, but when Lester ran out and Cecily started screaming at Joey, and Joey started screaming back at her—well, I had to get out of there."

"You aren't used to family fights, are you?" Jack asked, sitting down cross-legged beside her. "We had some doozies over the years. I'd sort of forgotten Uncle Guido's temper but sure remembered it today when Joey and Cecily started going at it. I'm just sorry you had to see all of that."

"She wasn't anything like I'd imagined."

"She wasn't like anything *I'd* imagined. Silly, dizzy, airheaded Cecily. I think I liked her better that way. But it was all an act, all of it. All those years. It probably explains why Aunt Flo was always making excuses for her. Cecily, the poor little girl without a brain in her head. We all were always making allowances for her, giving her anything she wanted. Kind of blows your mind, doesn't it?"

"Kind of makes me like Joey better. I guess he had to get a little nuts himself, just to get your aunt's attention," Keely said, shrugging. "But they're both gone now?"

Jack nodded his head. "But not before both of them gave up custody. Joey's custody of Sweetness—his contract, you know—and Cecily's custody of Candy. Ms. Peters had all the papers for Cecily to sign, and then doctored one of them for Sweetness. Great lady, Ms. Peters. Petra says she'd get it framed for him, but

315

Sweetness headed back to Bayonne with Joey. Petra thinks she's talked him into going to trade school. Seems Sweetness wants to be a chef."

"That's nice," Keely said, wiping at her moist eyes, for she'd noticed that Jack might be talking to her, but he was looking at Candy. Staring at Candy. "I can't believe it's over. Did you talk to Jimmy?"

"I did. We have to apply for permanent custody, still jump through a bunch of legal hoops, but both Jimmy and Ms. Peters say we're in good shape. With any luck, we can officially adopt Candy in about six months. Have her name changed to Mary Margaret Trehan, the whole nine yards."

He lay back on the floor, his knees bent, put his hands on his head. "God. It's over. What a day. Was there ever another one like it? We had it all—the good, the bad, the really ugly. I can't believe it's over."

"Da! Da-da-da!" Candy chirped, and Keely lifted her onto Jack's stomach, so that the baby could lean forward and play I-I by pressing her head against his chest.

"Oh, God," Jack said, wrapping his arms around Candy's chubby little body. His eyes closed as his bottom lip trembled, and he suddenly jackknifed to a sitting position and buried his face against Candy's curls.

Keely put her arms around both of them and began to rock, crying with Jack, then laughing with him as Candy squirmed and squealed, trying to break free of these two blubbering fools who were holding her too tight.

Jack leaned over, kissed Keely, then helped her to her feet. "You know, I can remember crying four times in my life. When my parents died, the day I announced my retirement from the Yankees, and now today. Except,

316

today, I'm feeling wonderful. I've got you, we've got Candy, and we have a whole long, wonderful life in front of us. Two months ago, I thought my life was as good as over."

With Jack holding Candy high against his chest, they walked toward the back stairs and went down to the kitchen, where Aunt Sadie, Petra, and Tim were sitting at the table, munching on take-out pizza.

"Let me rephrase what I said upstairs," Jack said, shaking his head. "I've got you, Candy, Sadie, Tim, and one wise-mouthed teenager. My world is complete."

"Except for Mort," Tim said around a mouthful of pizza. "He left right after you gave your conditional okay to the deal. I think he's going to be able to fly back to New York without a plane, he's that jazzed."

"Deal?" Keely asked. "What deal? Why's Mort jazzed? Do we like it when Mort's jazzed? Talk to me, Jack. Jack—you really have to learn to *talk* to me."

"Here, I've got to go talk to the woman. I'm not making *that* mistake anymore." Jack handed Candy to Petra, then took Keely's hand and led her toward the back door. "I'm not giving a final yes to anything until I talk to you, but, well, darling, just like I said upstairs, all in all, it's been a rather full day around here . . .

# Epilogue

*Ya gotta believe.*

—Tug McGraw

KEELY WAS STANDING AT THE LIVING-ROOM WINDOW, watching for Jack's Corvette to pull into the drive in front of the house.

She would have gone to New York with him, as she'd done ever since their marriage, but Candy'd had another baby shot that afternoon and Keely wanted to stay home with her. The baby had been fussy for a little while, but she'd been asleep now for hours, and Keely had gotten to watch all of the game on television.

She pulled back the floor-length white sheers as headlights flashed in the darkness, breathed a sigh of relief because she was still the worrywart Jack called her, then walked into the foyer to meet the conquering hero as he came in the door.

"You were wonderful," she told Jack, slipping her arms aroud his neck, lifting her face for his kiss.

Jack grinned at her, put his arm around her waist as, together, they walked into the kitchen. "I was good, wasn't I? And they liked the baseball quote I used tonight. You heard it? The Drysdale quote? They want me to use as many of them as I want. Tim and I have been collecting them for years."

"That's what the color man does, isn't it?" Keely asked, taking two cans of soda from the refrigerator and putting them on the table. "Chris does the play-by-play and you add the color—the human interest, the explanations of how it feels to be staring down the

318

league's leading hitter in the top of the ninth, the count three and two, the tying run on third with two out."

Jack grinned at her. "That's exactly what I do," he agreed, hooking his foot under the chair leg, pulling it out so that she sat down at the table with him. "Three months of this, and I still can't believe it. Me, Jack Trehan, television color man for the Yankees. You know," he said, propping his chin on his hand as he leaned his elbow on the table, "I think Mort was right— I *was* born to do this. I really was. What bugged me about retiring was being away from the game, not knowing what to do with the rest of my life. Except that we go out to the coast next week. I'm going to miss you and Candy. Are you sure you can't come along? I know you're busy with the shop, but maybe Jean can cover for you? You said she's a great assistant."

"Well . . ." Keely said, tracing a small pattern with her fingertips on Jack's forearm. "I did ask the pediatrician today about the idea of taking Candy on such a long flight, and he said it would be fine. Although I guess we couldn't travel on the team plane."

Jack stood up, took her hands as he pulled her to her feet. "We'll travel in a commercial jet. Hell, we'll take one of those small jets if we have to, if you promise to hold my hand and keep telling me air flight in small planes *is* possible."

"Ah-ah, don't say hell, Jack. You know how Candy's beginning to pick up new words."

"And you think saying *heck* is better? My wife, the new queen of *darn* and *heck* and *gee-whiz*. Motherhood has changed you, Keely. And I like it."

"You *love* it," Keely all but purred, going up on her tiptoes to kiss him on the cheek. "Come on, let's get you

319

to bed. It's been a long day, driving back and forth from New York."

"If you're trying to find out just how sleepy I am, sweetheart, all you've got to do is ask," Jack told her as he followed her up the stairs.

She stopped on the top step, turned, put her hands on his shoulders. How she loved this man. "Okay. How tired are you, Mr. Sportscaster?"

And then she buried her face against his chest, hoping her delighted squeals wouldn't wake their daughter, as Jack gathered her in his arms and headed toward their bedroom.

Dear Reader:

I hope you enjoyed reading this Large Print book. If you are interested in reading other Beeler Large Print titles, ask your librarian or write to me at

>   Thomas T. Beeler, *Publisher*
>   Post Office Box 659
>   Hampton Falls, New Hampshire 03844

You can also call me at 1-800-818-7574 and I will send you my latest catalogue.

Audrey Lesko and I choose the titles I publish in Large Print. Our aim is to provide good books by outstanding authors—books we both enjoyed reading and liked well enough to want to share. We warmly welcome any suggestions for new titles and authors.

Sincerely,